Important question: To research the book, did Amanda herself travel
with the circus? She did.

✴✴✴✴✴

This memorial award is intended to aid a young woman writer of 32
years or younger who both embodies Amanda's personal strengths—
warmth, generosity, a passion for community—and who needs some
time to finish a book in progress. The book in progress needn't be the-
matically or stylistically close to Amanda's work, but we would be
lying if we said we weren't looking to support another writer of
Amanda's outrageous lyricism and heart. Cold-blooded minimalists
(not to say all minimalists are that) might have a more difficult time.

✴✴✴✴✴

REQUIREMENTS AND GUIDELINES:
Applicants should send a work in progress, between 5,000 and 40,000
words, and a statement of their financial situation. You may list any
and all ridiculous jobs performed to facilitate your writing, and you
may include two other short pieces, published or otherwise, which will
be read if you feel they would help in the understanding of your work
generally. The reading group will consist of McSweeney's editors and a
handful of writers and readers close to Amanda.

✴✴✴✴✴

The award will be given in one lump-sum grant, with no strings
attached. Deadline is October 15, 2003. Winners will be notified
November 30, 2003. Send materials in paper form
(please don't send discs or url addresses) to:

The Amanda Davis Highwire Fiction Award
826 Valencia Street
San Francisco, CA
94110

For more or updated information:
www.mcsweeneys.net

The photographs of the antennae within are by Ian McDonnell. They are selections from a larger project, titled "I like aerials," which is a collection of images taken over time at various locations, presenting a new look at the televison antennae which form an integral part of our modern landscape.

DEAR MCSWEENEY'S:

Do you know what a twitcher is? Apparently, in bird-watching circles, the term is used to refer to people so beguiled by the spectacle of rare birds that they will actually twitch and tic in rapture. At first I thought this too rare a condition to deserve a name, but then I remembered my friend Rabs. I suspect that he's a twitcher and doesn't even know it.

I was twelve years old walking across Anderson's field toward K-Mart when I first heard Rabs express an interest in birds. Of course, he wasn't Rabs back then. Then he was Mark Jacobson. It would be another year until he renamed himself to match the white embroidery of a second-hand jacket his mom gave him for Christmas—I doubt Mark ever knew the real "Rabs."

Anyway, that day we were walking to K-Mart to steal basketball cards because Rabs collected them. I remember thinking how warm and blue the air was. I also remember looking down at my feet. That's how I saw the bunny. It was tucked away in some thick grass, all curled up in itself. I called Rabs over and he picked it up. The bunny unfolded in his palm like wet origami. It had holes where its eyes used to be, and looking at it lying there so dead on such a perfect day made me sure that everything in life was hopeless. I looked over at Rabs to tell him so, but before I could explain, he hurled that bunny at Mr. Anderson's house. It fell twenty feet short. We kept walking.

"Aren't birds amazing?" Rabs announced near K-Mart's entrance. "I mean, we live on Earth and all over there are these things that just hang in the air, and we call them birds. It's so beautiful."

I didn't know this was the start of something, McSweeney's, so I just nodded, unzipped the back pocket on Rabs's backpack, and walked inside.
Sincerely,
TREVOR KOSKI
CHICAGO, ILLINOIS

DEAR EDITOR,

I'm drawing a picture of the last time I saw you. Notice the heavy line. That's from the fat charcoal pencil I used. I managed to render the dizzy anger on your face with only two or three strokes. In the background you can see the margarita volcano, erupting into those big green tumblers. Moments later the volcano was dormant. Then it would erupt again and everybody would scream. The place was packed.

The room was strung with those oppressive yellow streamers—remember? Here in the picture they look like an overcast sky, like a low cloud ceiling, because the charcoal smudged. You can even see out that one mural window onto the cobblestone pedestrian mall where that guy was playing the steel drum. You said you hated Gordon Lightfoot, and I said, no, it's Jimmy Buffet. Well, you just hit the roof. That's what I'm trying to capture here.

You probably wanted to leave me before we went on vacation, but you knew how I'd react. And it was probably better to be at the beach. Plus the nachos and all made it seem okay. But when I got back, that's when it really hit me. I had to draw this picture so I'd remember in detail everything that happened. You had a pomegranate daiquiri, which was pretty good. And

I'd just finished my third Tecate in a can. Typical. I think you made that Lightfoot comment just when the nachos arrived. They were chicken mole, and it seemed like we got kind of ripped off considering how much they cost. Just before that, you told me how you thought I was going to be the father of your child, back when we met, but now you knew that wasn't possible.

The service was lousy, but what do you expect at one of these theme restaurants. You'd get the same thing at the ESPN Café. But at least there they have the rock-climbing wall. I said I'd always wanted to talk about having a baby, but I was too scared you'd get into one of your moods that lasts all year. I tried to draw the nachos, but they ended up just looking like a wig or a pineapple. You can see how surprised I was—my jaw about landed in the guacamole. We'd been together for three years, and you never complained about anything. I didn't even know you wanted to get more serious. You said I should have known. I said I couldn't read your mind. You said something else in response to that.

That's when that local kid came in with those sugarcane sticks. I bought two of them, and you said it was insensitive and that I always interrupted you. You were really surprised at me, Jim, you said, and disappointed. After all the time you'd put in to making the relationship work. You tried to throw pomegranate daiquiri all over my blazer. That's what the gray blob is, floating above the table. It probably looks more like one of those Rastafarian hats with the dreads sewn in. I can't draw.

Anyway, you missed me and the daiquiri landed on that huge guy's chinos. He came over and said what the

fuck?! And you just pointed at me, so he asked me if I was funny, queer, or something else I didn't understand. I think he was Irish. You said I might as well be, which really stung, under the circumstances. He picked me up by the neck and dropped me on the steam table. I ended up with Sterno burns on suit pants and a bump on my head where I hit the chili-pepper wall sconce.

When I came to, you were long gone. But the waitress brought out some new nachos and said the Irish guy paid for them. I should draw a picture of that, too.

Sincerely,
JEFFREY ROTTER
NEW YORK, NEW YORK

DEAR MCSWEENEY'S:
I'll give you this: sunny as it was, that day in Anderson's field may have been just a day. But there were more like it. A lot more.

When Rabs and me were fifteen, my little brother Jonathan got a green and yellow parakeet. I wanted to name it Motorbike, but since it was Jonathan's bird, and since he was only four, we ended up calling it Pedro the Parrot.

Rabs was furious. He came straight over, walked up to Jonathan, and demanded an audience. They met in Jonathan's room.

Since I wasn't invited, and since they closed the door, I can't tell you exactly what was said. Still, with an ear pressed to the thin bathroom wall, I can give you the gist of it. There are over three hundred types of parrots.

"If Pedro should have a last name at all, it should be Parakeet." I heard Rabs yell. "Or better yet, Budgerigar."

Rabs had a point. It turns out that

"Pedro the Parrot" was even more than a parakeet, he was a particular kind of parakeet. Pedro was a budgerigar.

It's too bad this bit of ornithology didn't impress Jonathan, because Rabs didn't give up. He started coming over every night after dinner just to lecture Jonathan. It got to the point where if you wanted to find Rabs, you'd look in Jonathan's room first. More often than not he'd be there, pointing at some picture, book, or bar graph while little Jonathan sat, legs dangling from the edge of his bed.

They'd be at it for hours. Sometimes mom had to kick Rabs out so Jonathan could get some sleep. Before he would leave though, Rabs always extended his hand to Jonathan and asked for Pedro to be renamed. Jonathan would shake that hand and his own head simultaneously.

A year passed before this stalemate was finally broken. On Pedro's birthday, we liberated him from his cage and he flew straight for the bay window in my family room. Before Rabs showed up for cake, Jonathan had me cross out "REEBOK" and write "Pedro the Parrot" on the coffin.

Rabs took it hard. He told me he never wanted to hear the name Pedro the Parrot again. If I thought he'd listen, I'd have told him what my mom let me in on earlier that day. Apparently, Jonathan knew all along that Pedro was more than a parrot. He just couldn't pronounce *parakeet*, let alone *budgerigar*. He was only four.

Sincerely,
TREVOR KOSKI
CHICAGO, ILLINOIS

DEAR MR. MCSWEENEY,
It has come to my attention that you have been sending me a great deal of e-mail from various e-mail accounts. I must beg you to stop.

I do not want any more herbal viagra, I do not want to make $5000 a week at home in my spare time, and I certainly do not want to see what your uncle has got up to with his prize Texas Longhorns. I feel that my anatomy is fine in its current state, without adjustment. Nor am I interested in having my bank account used to launder the money of General Abacha, whatever the monetary incentive therein.

Mr. McSweeney, allow me to speak frankly: this behavior is beneath you. You have so much to offer the world, without resorting to these cheap attention-getting ploys. I appeal to you, as a man of letters, to desist.

It has occurred to me that perhaps this strange campaign on your part conceals a hunger for some kind of dialogue or contact between us two. This, I can certainly understand. As a peace offering—and in an attempt to set our relationship on a new course—I here enclose some notes on a story that I have been developing. It goes something like this:

Crack!

The detective takes a blow; the butt of a pistol against the back of his skull.

Perhaps the detective wakes up tied to a chair, is interrogated, outwits his captors, and escapes to solve the case.

Perhaps he dies. That was a mean blow. Look, he's fallen to the ground. He's still. There's blood. There's blood inside his skull.

Perhaps he's crippled by the blow. Paralyzed on one side. His speech will be fuzzy and inarticulate. He will sit in the chair by the window at the managed care facility. They will keep him well-shaven. He will wear a bib and shudder.

The femmes fatales will not visit. The hard-eyed policemen who respected and resented him will come once a month to sit in dull, dutiful silence. His pretty, sad assistant will come every Sunday and read him the paper. Or Dickens, his favorite.

The villain comes to gloat but stays to mull it over, awed: what a little thing can bring us down so low. There but for the grace of God go I.

The case is not clear in the detective's mind. Not quite yet. There are a few outstanding details. He counts his peas. Forty-five peas. The caliber of the murder weapon. It may be a clue. He makes a note on the napkin.

It becomes a comfortable routine over the years. At Christmas the villain has the detective wheeled up to his mansion. The pretty, sad assistant comes as well. She has succeeded the detective; she and the villain are enemies. Sometimes she foils his plots; sometimes he goes to jail. But not for long. He has good lawyers.

But on Christmas they put all that aside. The detective eats his sweet potatoes with molasses and hums. The assistant strokes his hair. After a few witty barbs between the villain and the assistant, a bit of bravado, they eat, and then they sit in silence and listen to the carolers. It feels like family.

They put the gramophone on and the villain and the pretty, sad assistant waltz. The detective looks on with shining eyes.

Please let me know if you would like to see more.

Expectantly,
BENJAMIN ROSENBAUM
BASEL, SWITZERLAND

DEAR MCSWEENEY'S:
Something as small as a four-year-old's speech impediment couldn't have tripped up Rabs. Not even Tammy could.

Tammy was our friend and we loved her. The whole town did. Growing up, you could go into almost any public bathroom, and scratched in some pocked wood, between a bunch of dick-suckers and sluts, you'd see how we all thought: "Tammy is the sweetest."

It's funny, McSweeney's, but even as an avid reader of bathroom walls, this never struck me as strange. Whenever I read something about how smart or funny Tammy was, I'd think of college applications, not obituaries.

We found out about Tammy over the school's PA system. Until then, the biggest thing that ever happened in our town was Friday night. So when we first heard, all we knew to do was get in our cars and drive Main Street. All we knew to say was beep our horns.

Later that night, we met up in my basement. There must have been twenty of us. We were all drinking and crying, and then we started taking turns saying something nice about Tammy. It was just like TV. Our friend Brad, his giant shoulders shaking with grief, told how Tammy would buy him a Big Mac when he was broke. And Lisa, one of those bathroom-wall sluts, said that Tammy always helped her when she got behind in Algebra II. Even I talked about how Tammy was my only friend in fourth grade, the year I wouldn't go outside at recess. Then Rabs spoke, two people ahead of his turn.

"I bet when birds kill themselves, they fall up," he said. "I bet they keep going up and up into the cold sky until their heart beats so fast it shatters inside their tiny bird chest. Their suicides are rare but spectacular."

By then, everyone was pretty much used to Rabs, so they ignored him and went on with their show. But McSweeney's, looking over at him, sitting on the floor with eyes closed and half a smile, I had to think about Tammy to keep from crying. Rabs was that beautiful.

Sincerely,
TREVOR KOSKI
CHICAGO, ILLINOIS

ABOUT THE NEXT LETTER
[*In 1972, Dow Mossman published his first novel,* The Stones of Summer, *which* The New York Times *called "a marvelous achievement." Mossman gave up writing shortly afterwards and has not written another book since; a new documentary,* Stone Reader, *directed by Mark Moskowitz, follows the filmmaker's search for Mossman's current whereabouts. The following letter, from Mossman to a college student who had recently reviewed the book for a campus newspaper, was written in May 1973.*]

DEAR SCOTT,
Good of you to write. I appreciated the news of your friend's reading of my novel, that's the best sort of encouragement there is, and I found Newman's piece a fair statement of the economic gloom surrounding my predicament. He makes the classic liberal mistake of thinking Idealism and Reason exist, and can be made tools in the explanation and solution of the world, but I thought it valuable and lucid, if academic finally by profoundly underestimating the lousy nature of man. It's of course no accident we wound up where we are—it's our most intricate plot, fulfills our innermost needs, and we call it history. I was especially fond of Literary Law #6, however—"It doesn't matter what you say, or how you say it, but where. A classical totalitarian society censors at the production point. An oligopolistic democracy censors at the distribution point"—and found it worthy of Marx.

There were many other fine things in the piece, which I wouldn't be able to discuss in monologue, but for myself I can only say the worst is that it is very hard to mature as a voice (indeed even have the presumption to speak), year after year, when you are treated forever, financially/socially/psychologically, as an idiot and child. This I resent most, much more than the idea of being screwed, as it interferes with your natural song. Once you've been dumb enough to play their game once, they've got you no matter which way you jump.

I like to think, at least, poets can afford to drift, but narrative writers need their chance. It seems to me most novelists who have gone on in this country to build up a body of work have had enough early success to proceed. This wouldn't matter to a European or Russian, perhaps, with a culture and intellectual tradition to fall back on, but in America (even yet) no one tells you anything without it and, year to year, you develop the notion there must be vastly obvious things you don't know about, besides. Makes it hard to have the nerve to proceed. Gorky aside, the lower depths remain too narrow for me. I've had my share, and while I never expected to go first-class (nor did I ever even believe in it), not going at all remains the mystery and disappointment. The star system aside (you get it all, kid, or you get nothing) a workmen's wages would have been nice. For myself—since I'm not getting very straight looks from The Academic Placement Office here—I am enrolling in a truck driving course in July. I'd go back to welding but factories, in my experience, have such limited geography. Anyway, all of this just about should take care of my thirties (the years that I need) or, at least, my concentration. I'd get busy and write my way out of all of this, but that only brings us back to where we have begun.

Most basically, I think the problem lies in the "serious writer's" imagination, his conception of himself in the "real" world; in the fact that, almost by definition, he holds himself so cheaply (I don't know how good I was, but I was definitely serious). I also have the suspicion that if a writer could keep scribbling every day he could just manage to keep his head above water (that's just at the level, coincidentally, where the western world thinks his dignity belongs, and his honesty flourishes), but that's not really the issue. The real issue is: Do writers get to travel and breed and do the other things other people do, and, more importantly, do they get to make enough from one book to try another (at their own pace of imagination)? Since they perform a real, utilitarian role in the psycho-drama of society— that of the romantic down-and-outs; the merely honest—the answer is: Hell No and Probably Not. The only blessing in all of this, of course, remains that there is absolutely no reason for doing a book unless you have to. This has the advantage of allowing the imagination to proceed at its own pace and would, if the information were far enough abroad in the land, solve the glut of books overnight. Finally, the most sobering, maturing lesson in the publication of fiction is that it is, without doubt, the slowest and most dreary racket around. Once, in this connection, literature seeped from the control of the aristocrat, who used it truly for leisure and fucking, the decline of major writers (i.e. ones who went on, and on, to do bodies of work) into pessimism became inevitable. What they reflected of the commerce of the world, generally, metaphysically was the commerce they knew—publishing—and that commerce was the slowest and most nihilistic around. A thin thesis but partially skateable... its larger moral being: narrative writers must be taken into the world—even if they have to be dragged.

The only other thing I would want to ask Newman would be: How much does the *TriQuarterly* pay?—And: Do you think there might be a career in preaching Trade Unionism to the overly washed?

At any rate, pardon this letter. I'm sending you a copy of the paperback, and glad to be able to do it. I wanted to send you a couple of them—you'll probably do more with them than any-one else I know, including my agent or editor—but they only sent me six of them and I'm not up just now to buy-ing a gross. The rights were sold with-out my permission (or even my knowl-edge) at auction for $4,000—half of it payable to me at the hardback publish-er's leisure and discretion—so none of this alters any of the foregoing in the least. The figures on the cover ignored, it's 'fun' to see it in paper (what other word could I choose in terms of sanity and appropriateness considering—at two fell swoops—I was whittled down to 3% of the deal without even try-ing)... but then this ability to be thrilled at merely seeing oneself in print, you see, I take to be the very flaw in the first place.

Incidentally, you're certainly right about Pynchon's novel. I've just begun it but, so far, it seems he has managed nothing less than synthesizing Anglo-American fiction with the Russian novel. It seems he has also accom-plished present-future by means of the past. It looks to be a true masterpiece but everyone has recognized it so immediately there must be something amiss.

Also drop me a letter in the near or dim future, whenever you're in the damn mood.

Best regards,
DOW MOSSMAN
IOWA CITY, IOWA

DEAR SIRS:
When Edison invented the incandes-cent light bulb, he had his people send out a press release. It said, "A Bright Idea Has Been Born." When Watson and Crick discovered the double-heli-cal structure of the DNA molecule,

they had their people send out a press release. It said, "DNA is Tangled Up In YOU." It is this spirit of entrepre-neurial invention that has guided the drafting of this letter, which will serve as an official announcement of the cre-ation of the world's first and only Conceptual Art Registry.

The Conceptual Art Registry shares traits with both the double helix and the light bulb. On the one hand, it is complex and self-referential; on the other hand, it has the power to illumi-nate. It can best be explained as a kind of catalog that collects hundreds, and possibly thousands, of brief descrip-tions of ideas for conceptual art shows, ideas which will be organized by type and published to the World Wide Web. Artists of all types, working in all media, from all regions of the world, will then be invited to browse the catalog. Should an artist find an idea that appeals to him, he can license it for his own use. The licensing fee will be determined by a simple formu-la that takes into account the size of an artist's project, the duration the show is designed to run, the independence of an idea (in other words, whether it is to be used on its own or in combina-tion with other ideas), and an artist's previous reputation. One-time licens-ing is expected to run between $100 and $500.

This document is the wrong place to describe the contents of the Registry in detail, but the right place to furnish an overview. The Registry will deal with all varieties of artwork, including gallery shows, performance pieces, video installations, sound sculptures, and new media artwork. Each category will be denoted with a three-letter abbreviation (GAL for gallery shows,

PER for performance pieces, VID for video installations, and so on), and each work assigned a three-digit number, thus limiting the number of conceptual pieces in each category to one thousand, which should be sufficient. The only unifying principle behind the works described in the catalog is that they are conceptual: to wit, that they contain some recursive feature, whether self-referential, self-aggrandizing, or self-annihilating, that renders them both superior and inferior to more conventional fine art. Take, for example, GAL387, a variation on an ordinary gallery show that reverses the size relationship between the title cards (those anonymous white labels that contain information about the works displayed in the show) and the works themselves. In any show that uses GAL387 as a conceptual foundation, the labels must be at least five feet square, and the works themselves can be no larger than six inches square. The result is both a comic visual shock and a canny commentary on the ways in which attempts to define works of art can be a form of subversion. Alternatively, there is GAL499, in which all paintings are turned to face the wall. In this case, the paintings can be landscapes, abstracts, portraits of historical figures, hyperrealistic scenes of battle, or any other image, The Registry is only responsible for the idea of turning the images toward the wall.

GAL387 and GAL499 are only two of many gallery-themed conceptual art pieces that will soon be available for licensing in the Registry. One more example will clarify the matter for those who are still hazy: VID089, which is a video installation that consists of twelve monitors set into gallery walls like paintings, complete with frames. Over each monitor, there is a camera, recessed into the wall and placed behind plate glass but not hidden. The cameras run throughout active gallery hours—in fact, they run only during the active gallery hours. More to the point, the monitor beneath each camera displays precisely what the camera witnessed the previous day, in real time. In other words, the show consists entirely of a record of the previous day's audience's reaction to the show, which itself consisted entirely of a reaction to the previous day's audience's reaction, and so forth. The footage displayed on the monitor the first day of the show can be of two varieties: either video of an empty room (that would be VID089a) or video created by gallery employees that mimics the reactions of average gallery patrons (VID089b). Again, the Registry does not stipulate—indeed, it does not care about--the exact size of the monitors, the nature of the frames, or whether or not the images are accompanied by sound. These are questions that can be answered by individual artists after they have licensed the idea. The Registry cares only about furnishing inspiration to artists, and being compensated appropriately.

The Conceptual Art Registry, privately owned and produced, will be administered by a small staff of accountants and auditors. The terms of usage will be governed by a Standard Licensing Agreement, which will also reside on the site and include such essential sections as "Definition," "Usage," and "Payment and Delivery." Finally, it is worth noting that the Conceptual Art Registry is also its first customer: just this morning, the

Registry paid itself a generous fee of $500 for the rights to license NEW065, which is a new-media art project described as a "a kind of catalog that collects hundreds, and possibly thousands, of brief descriptions of ideas for conceptual art shows."

Yours,

BEN GREENMAN
FOUNDER AND SOLE PROPRIETOR
CONCEPTUAL ART REGISTRY
WWW.BENGREENMAN.COM

BROTHER,

I know we have had our bad days, and far too many of late, driving you from my life. My earliest memories were without you, as I fought and scrapped to liberate a Peach from the barbarous tyranny of a big ape. How I made it through so many adventures without ever realizing you had your own dreams is testament to my failure as your flesh and your blood. I had barely realized you were of age when we were working side by side to unclog the plumbing of our friends and neighbors. Remember our initial days, when I first tumbled in to that big, dark pipe, and you, my loving brother, pursued, without a second's thought of your own safety. You followed me, and we unclogged that pipe from which no water poured. Damn those congestive turtles! Damn them to hell!

Later, we explored further into the exciting new realm of the Mushroom Kingdom (which was serendipitously well-suited to our own vocational dexterity). We learned of the plight of a people not our own, and of their beautiful Peach, captive again, this time in a tiny, brick castle. I never though to ask why you were so adamant about helping; I presumed you were merely aiding in righting a wrong, but it was

I who was wrong. Your thoughts were consumed by a lust that raged within your green overall'd loins, and your every breath was motivated by a desire to plumb my Peach. If I had only looked, I would have seen steam pouring out your ears as that diminutive, green flag went up in that flurry of mushroom powered fireworks. So while we would rescue again and again, it was I who each night would enjoy those spoils, while you and Toad fell asleep on the couch. If only you had told me, and thwarted my egocentric propensity towards exclusion. But you did not, and a seed that was planted silently germinated and blackened your once beautiful heart.

Please, brother, I beseech you. See these words as my battle hardened plunger, and this letter as my attempt to extract the kernel that has corrupted your thoughts and tainted your feelings towards me. I have discussed it with Peach, and we are willing to let you into our home, and more importantly, into our bed. We will live again as we once did, clearing pipes and getting the job done. I only ask that I go first.

Fraternally,

M
BROOKLYN, NEW YORK

DEAR MCSWEENEY'S:
Even grown-up, even now, Rabs still is.

I wish I got to see him more. After high school, I left for the city and stayed. Rabs stayed home. I did get back a few years ago though. I brought my wife Courtney.

Courtney's from the city, so I was excited to show her where I grew up. I wanted her to like it, but she said Anderson's field looked more like a back yard and that my basement smelled like mildew. And then there was Rabs.

The last day we were there, I had him meet us for breakfast at this little diner where we used to smoke cigarettes. Rabs looked a little more crazed than I remembered, but pretty soon me and him were telling jokes and laughing. It was like old times.

Except for Courtney. I could tell she made Rabs uneasy with her complicated smiles. It wasn't either's fault. They both tried. Especially Rabs. He's not the questioning type, but after breakfast, he asked Courtney about me, the new baby, and the city. Then he asked her how she liked it up here.

"It's certainly different." She said slowly. "But I really appreciate the chance to see where my husband used to live... and to meet the people who used to be his friends."

"Yeah," Rabs replied, nodding. "I really appreciate that birds don't have testicles on the outsides of their bodies. Could you imagine having to see testicles every time you looked up in the air? It'd be disgusting."

This made me think about how, with time, love's intensity gives way to relief, about how the glorious can later be loved all the same for inconspicuous testicles. But Courtney didn't know Rabs like I did—it just made her mad.

The car ride home that day was terrible. Courtney stared straight ahead through her big black sunglasses. Her posture was Emily Post perfect. I knew what she was thinking, but I asked anyway.

"I'm happy we're going home," she snapped. "I hate that place."

I told her that place is my home, but she just shook her head, and with a cruelty I'd never heard in her, mut-

tered, "And that Rabs... words can't describe... words just can't describe."

I figured she was right, plus the skyline was looming on the horizon, so I kept quiet.

McSweeney's, I guess my point is this: Do you know that game where you pretend you can go back in time to relive a moment in your life, and you have to choose which one? If you and me were playing that game right now, I bet you'd choose something sweet— something like flying cross country toward your steady, listening to love songs. I wouldn't. I'd choose to be back in the car that day. Only this time, I wouldn't just sit there dumb.

"Technically, Courtney, you're wrong," I'd explain. "Rabs is a twitcher."
Sincerely,
TREVOR KOSKI
CHICAGO, ILLINOIS

DEAR MCSWEENEY'S,
Every time I see another cell fall off my retina, I can picture myself riding it like a slow-motion Slim Pickens, ruddy-cheeked and cowboy-hatted, the lethal plunge stretching an exclamatory tail on what would otherwise be a harmless periodic polyp—the atomic unstopping of uncountable mutated punctuations. And on the periphery, two windows into the windowless basement of follicular suffering. How many sorrows per cilium? My eyes and ears are ganging up on me. This is some kamikaze shit, slowly degenerating, physically disappearing, and for what? To make me sad? Yes.
Thanks,
EMILIO OLIVEIRA
NORTH OLMSTEAD, OHIO

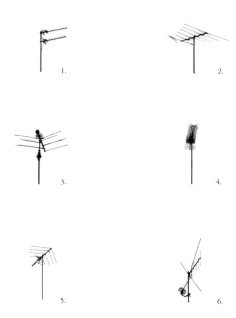

1.

2.

3.

4.

5.

6.

1) Park Road, London

2) Langham Street, London

3) Belmont Avenue, London

4) Carlisle Street, Newcastle

5) Bairo Court, London

6) Kincraig Street, Cardiff

GOD LIVES IN ST. PETERSBURG

by TOM BISSELL

GOD, IN TIME, takes everything from everyone. Timothy Silverstone believed that those whose love for God was a vast, borderless frontier were expected to surrender everything to Him, gladly and without question, and that those who did so would live to see everything and more returned to them. After college he had shed America like a husk and journeyed to the far side of the planet, all to spread God's word. Now he was coming apart. Anyone with love for God knows that when you give up everything for Him, He has no choice but to destroy you. God destroyed Moses; destroyed the heart of Abraham by revealing the deep, lunatic fathom at which his faith ran; took everything from Job, saw it did not destroy him, then returned it, which did. Timothy reconciled God's need to destroy with God's opulent love by deciding that, when He destroyed you, it was done out of the truest love, the deepest, most divine respect. God could not allow perfection—it was simply too close to Him. His love for the sad, the fallen, and the sinful was an easy, uncomplicated love, but those who lived along the argent brink of perfection had to be watched and tested and tried.

Timothy Silverstone was a missionary, though on the orders of his organization, the Central Asian Relief Agency, he was not allowed to admit this. Instead, when asked (which he was, often and by everyone), he was to say he was an English teacher. This was to be the pry he would use to widen the sorrowful, light-starved breach that, according to CARA, lay flush across the heart of every last person in the world, especially those Central Asians who had been cocooned within the suffocating atheism of Soviet theology. "The gears of history have turned," the opening pages of Timothy's CARA handbook read, "and the hearts of 120 million people have been pushed from night into day, and all of them are calling out for the love of Jesus Christ."

As his students cheated on their exams, Timothy drifted through the empty canals between their desks. His classroom was as plain as a monk's sleeping quarters; its wood floors groaned with each of his steps. Since he had begun to come apart, he stopped caring whether his students cheated. He had accepted that they did not understand what cheating was and never would, for just as there is no Russian word which connotes the full meaning of *privacy*, there is no unambiguously pejorative word for *cheat*. Timothy had also stopped trying to teach them about Jesus because, to his shock, they already knew of a thoroughly discredited man who in Russian was called *Hristos*.

Timothy's attempts to create in their minds the person he knew as Jesus did nothing but trigger nervous, uncomfortable laughter Timothy simply could not bear to hear. Timothy could teach them about Jesus and His works and His love, but *Hristos* grayed and tired his heart. He felt nothing for this impostor, not even outrage. Lately, in order to keep from coming apart, he had decided to try to teach his students English instead.

"Meester Timothy," cried Rustam, an Uzbek boy with a long, thin face. His trembling arm was held up, his mouth a lipless dash.

"Yes, Rustam, what is it?" he answered in Russian. Skull-clutching hours of memorizing rows of vocabulary words was another broadsword Timothy used to beat back coming apart. He was proud of his progress with the language because it was so difficult. This was counterbalanced by his Russian acquaintances, who asked him why his Russian was not better, seeing that it was so simple.

After Timothy spoke, Rustam went slack with disappointment. Nine months ago, moments after Timothy had first stepped into this classroom, Rustam had approached him and demanded (actually using the verb demand) that Timothy address him in nothing but English. Since then his memorized command of English had deepened, and he had become by spans and cubits Timothy's best student. Timothy complied, asking Rustam "What is it?" again, in English.

"It is Susanna," Rustam said, jerking his head toward the small blond girl who shared his desk. Most of Timothy's students were black-haired, sloe-eyed Uzbeks like Rustam—the ethnic Russians able to do so had fled Central Asia as the first statues of Lenin toppled—and Susanna's blond, round-eyed presence in the room was both a vague ethnic reassurance and, somehow, deeply startling. Rustam looked back at Timothy. "She is looking at my test and bringing me distraction. Meester Timothy, this girl cheats on me." Rustam, Timothy knew, had branded onto his brain this concept of cheating, and viewed his classmates with an ire typical of the freshly enlightened.

Susanna's glossy eyes were fixed upon the scarred wooden slab of her desktop. Timothy stared at this girl he did not know what to do with, who had become all the children he did not know what to do with. She was thirteen, fourteen, and sat there, pink and startled, while Rustam spoke his determined English. Susanna's hair held a buttery yellow glow in the long plinths of sunlight shining in through the windows; her small smooth hands grabbed at each other in her lap. All around her, little heads bowed above the clean white rectangles on their desks, the classroom filled with the soft scratching of pencils. Timothy took a breath, looking back to Rustam, unable to concentrate on what he was saying because Timothy could not keep from looking up at the row of pictures along the back wall of his classroom, where Ernest Hemingway, John Reed, Paul Robeson, and Jack London stared out at him from plain wooden frames. An identical suite of portraits—the Soviet ideal of good Americans—was found in every English classroom from here to Tbilisi. Timothy knew that none of these men had found peace with God. He had wanted to give that peace to these children. When he came to Central Asia he felt that peace as a great glowing cylinder inside of him, but the cylinder had grown dim. He could barely even feel God anymore, though he could still hear Him, floating and distant, broadcasting a surflike static. There was a message woven into this dense noise, Timothy was sure, but no matter how hard he tried he couldn't decipher it. He looked again at Rustam. He had stopped talking now and was waiting for Timothy's answer. Every student in the classroom had looked up from their tests, pinioning Timothy with their small impassive eyes.

"Susanna's fine, Rustam," Timothy said finally, turning to erase the nothing on his blackboard. "She's okay. It's okay."

Rustam's forehead creased darkly but he nodded and returned to his test. Timothy knew that, to Rustam, the world and his place in it would not properly compute if Americans were not always right, always good, always funny and smart and rich and beautiful. Never mind that Timothy had the mashed nose of a Roman pugilist and a pimply face; never mind that Timothy's baggy, runneled clothing had not been washed for months; never mind that once, after Rustam had asked about the precise function of "do" in the sentence "I do not like to swim," Timothy stood at the head of the class for close to two minutes and silently fingered his chalk. Meester Timothy was right, even when he was wrong, because he came from America. The other students went back to their exams. Timothy imagined he could hear the wet click of their eyes moving from test to test, neighbor to neighbor, soaking up one another's answers.

Susanna, though, did not stir. Timothy walked over to her and placed his hand on her back. She was as warm to his touch as a radiator through a blanket, and she looked up at him with starved and searching panic in her eyes. Timothy smiled at her, uselessly. She swallowed, picked up her pencil and, as if helpless not to, looked over at Rustam's test, a fierce indentation between her yellow eyebrows. Rustam sat there, writing, pushing out through his nose hot gusts of air, until finally he whirled around in his seat and hissed something at Susanna in his native language, which he knew she did not understand. Again, Susanna froze. Rustam pulled her pencil from her hands—she did not resist—snapped it in half, and threw the pieces in her face. From somewhere in Susanna's throat came a half-swallowed sound of grief, and she burst into tears.

Suddenly Timothy was standing there, dazed, rubbing his hand. He recalled something mentally blindsiding him, some sort of brainflash, and thus could not yet understand why his palm was buzzing. Nor did he understand why every student had heads bowed even lower to their tests, why the sound of scratching pencils seemed suddenly, horribly frenzied and loud. But when Rustam—who merely sat in his chair, looking up at Timothy, his long face devoid of expression—lifted his hand to his left cheek, Timothy noticed it reddening, tightening, his eye squashing shut, his skin lashing itself to his cheekbone. And Timothy Silverstone heard the sound of God recede even more, retreat back even farther, while Susanna, between sobs, gulped for breath.

Naturally, Sasha was waiting for Timothy in the doorway of the teahouse across the street from the Registan, a suite of three madrasas whose sparkling minarets rose up into a haze of metallic, blue-gray smog. Today was especially bad, a poison petroleum mist lurking along the streets and sidewalks and curbs. And then there was the heat—a belligerent heat; to move through it felt like breathing hot tea.

Timothy walked past the tall, bullet-shaped teahouse doorway, Sasha falling in alongside him. They did not talk—they rarely talked—even though the walk to Timothy's apartment in the Third Microregion took longer than twenty minutes. Sasha was Russian, tall and slender with hair the color of new mud. Each of Sasha's ears was as large and ornate as a tankard handle, and his eyes were as blue as the dark margin of atmosphere where the sky became outer space. He walked next to Timothy with a lanky, boneless grace, and wore blue jeans and imitation-leather cowboy boots that clomped emptily on the sidewalk. Sasha's mother was a history teacher from Timothy's school.

When his drab building came into sight Timothy felt the headachy swell of God's static rushing into his head. It was pure sound, shapeless and impalpable, and as always he sensed some egg of sense or insight held deep within it. Then it was gone, silent, and in that moment Timothy could feel his spirit split from his flesh. *For I know*, Timothy thought, these words of Paul's to the Romans so bright in the glare of his memory they seemed almost indistinct from his own thoughts, *that nothing good dwells within me, that is, in my flesh. I can will what is right, but I cannot do it.*

As they climbed the stairs to Timothy's fifth-floor apartment, Sasha reached underneath Timothy's crotch and cupped him. He squeezed and laughed, and Timothy felt a wet heat spread through him, animate him, flow to the hard, stony lump growing in his pants. Sasha squeezed again, absurdly tender. As Timothy fished for the keys to his apartment door Sasha walked up close behind him, breathing on Timothy's neck, his clothes smelling—-as everyone's clothes here did—as though they had been cured in sweat.

They stumbled inside. Sasha closed the door as Timothy's hands shot to his belt, which he tore off like a rip-cord. He'd lost so much weight his pants dropped with a sad puff around his feet. Sasha shook his head at this—he complained, sometimes, that Timothy was getting too skinny— and he stepped out of his own pants. Into his palm Sasha spit a foamy coin of drool, stepped toward Timothy and with the hand he spit into grabbed his penis. He pulled it toward him sexlessly, as if it were a grapple he was making sure was secure. Sasha laughed again and he threw himself over the arm of Timothy's plush red sofa. Sasha reached back and with medical indelicacy pulled himself apart. He looked over his shoulder at Timothy, waiting.

The actual penetration was always beyond the bend of Timothy's recollection. As if some part of himself refused to acknowledge it. One moment Sasha was hurling himself over the couch's arm, the next Timothy was inside him. *I can will what is right, but I cannot do it.* It began slowly, Sasha breathing through his mouth, Timothy pushing further into him, eyes smashed shut. What he felt was not desire, not lust; it was worse than lust. It was worse than what drove a soulless animal. It was some hot tongue of fire inside Timothy that he could not douse—not by satisfying it, not by ignoring it. Sometimes it was barely more than a flicker, and then Timothy could live with it, nullify it as his weakness, as his flaw. But without warning, in whatever dark, smoldering interior shrine, the flame would grow and flash outward, melting whatever core of Timothy he believed good and steadfast into soft, pliable sin.

Timothy's body shook as if withstanding invisible blows, and Sasha began to moan with a carefree sinless joy Timothy could only despise, pity, and envy. It was always, oddly, this time, when perched on the edge of exploding into Sasha, that Timothy's mind turned, again, with noble and dislocated grace, to Paul. *Do not be deceived!* he wrote. *Fornicators, idolaters, adulterers, male prostitutes, sodomites—none of these will inherit the kingdom of God. And this is what some of you used to be. But you were washed, you were sanctified, you were justified in the name of Lord Jesus Christ and in the Spirit of our God.* It was a passage Timothy could only read and reflect upon and pray to give him the strength he knew he did not have. He prayed to be washed, to be sanctified in the name of Jesus, but now he had come apart and God was so far from him. His light had been eclipsed, and in the cold darkness that followed, he wondered if his greatest sin was not that he was pushing himself into non-vaginal warmth but that his worship was now for man and not man's maker. But such taxonomies were of little value. God's world was one of cruel mathematics, of right and wrong. It was a world that those who had let God fall from their hearts condemned as repressive and awash in dogma—an accurate but vacant condemnation, Timothy knew, since God did not anywhere claim that His world was otherwise.

A roiling spasm began in Timothy's groin and burst throughout the rest of his body, and in that ecstatic flooded moment nothing was wrong, nothing, with anyone, and he emptied himself into Sasha without guilt, only with appreciation and happiness and bliss. But then it was over, and he had to pull himself from the boy and wonder, once again, if what he had done had ruined him forever, if he had driven himself so deeply into darkness that the darkness had become both affliction and reward. Quickly Timothy wiped himself with one of the throw pillows from his couch and sat on the floor, sick and dizzy with shame. Sasha, still bent over the couch, looked back at Timothy, smirking, a cloudy satiation frosting his eyes. *"Shto?"* he asked Timothy. *What?*

Timothy could not—could never—answer him.

* * *

The next morning Timothy entered his classroom to find Susanna seated at her desk. Class was not for another twenty minutes, and Susanna was a student whose arrival, on most days, could be counted on to explore the temporal condition between late and absent. Timothy was about to wish her a surprised "Good morning" when he realized that she was not alone.

A woman sat perched on the edge of his chair, wagging her finger and admonishing Susanna in juicy, top-heavy Russian. Her accent was unknown to Timothy, filled with dropped Gs and a strange, diphthongal imprecision. Whole sentence fragments arced past him like softballs. Susanna merely sat there, her hands on her desktop in a small bundle. Timothy turned to leave but the woman looked over to see him caught in mid-pirouette in the doorjamb. She leapt up from his chair, a startled gasp rushing out of her.

They looked at each other, the woman breathing, her meaty shoulders bobbing up and down, her mouth pulled into a rictal grin. "*Zdravstvuite,*" she said stiffly.

"*Zdravstvuite,*" Timothy said, stepping back into the room. He tried to smile and the woman returned the attempt with a melancholy but respectful nod. She was like a lot of women Timothy saw here—bull-necked, jowled, of indeterminate age, as sexless as an oval. Atop her head was a lumpen yellow-white mass of hairspray and bobby pins, and her lips looked as sticky and red as the picnic tables Timothy remembered painting, with his Christian youth group, in the parks of Green Bay, Wisconsin.

"Timothy Silverstone," she said. *Teemosee Seelverstun.* Her hands met below her breasts and locked.

"Yes," Timothy said, glancing at Susanna. She wore a bright, bubble-gum-colored dress he had not seen before, some frilly, ribboned thing. As if aware of Timothy's eyes on her, Susanna bowed over in her chair even more, a path of spinal knobs surfacing along her back.

"I am Irina Dupkova," the woman said. "Susanna told me what happened yesterday—how you reacted to her... problem." Her joined hands lifted to her chin in gentle imploration. "I have come to ask you, this is true, yes?"

Her accent delayed the words from falling into their proper translated slots. When they did, a mental deadbolt unlocked, opening a door somewhere inside Timothy and allowing the memory of Rustam's eye swelling shut to come tumbling out. A fist of guilt clenched in his belly. *He had struck a child.* He had hit a boy as hard as he could, and there was no place he could hide this from himself, as he hid what he did with Sasha. Timothy felt faint and humidified, his face pinkening. "Yes, Irina Dupkova," he said, "it is. And I want to tell you I'm sorry. I, I—" He searched for words, some delicate, spiraled idiom to communicate his remorse. He could think of nothing, entire vocabularies lifting away from him like startled birds. "I'm sorry. What happened made me... very unhappy."

She shot Timothy a strange look, eyes squinched, her red lips kissed out in perplexion. "You do not understand me," she said. This was not a question. Timothy glanced over at Susanna, who had not moved, perhaps not even breathed. When he looked back to Irina Dupkova she was smiling at him, her mouthful of gold teeth holding no gleam, no sparkle, only the metallic dullness of a handful of old pennies. She shook her head, clapping once in delight. "Oh, your Russian, Mister Timothy, I think it is not so good. You do not *vladeyete* Russian very well, yes?"

"Vladeyete," Timothy said. It was a word he was sure he knew. "Vladeyete," he said again, casting mental nets. The word lay beyond his reach somewhere, veiled.

Irina Dupkova exhaled in mystification, then looked around the room. "You do not know this word," she said in a hard tone, one that nudged the question mark off the end of the sentence.

"Possess," Susanna said, before Timothy could lie. Both Timothy and Irina Dupkova looked over at her. Her back was still to them, but Timothy could see that she was consulting her CARA-supplied Russian-English dictionary. "*Vladeyete*," she said again, her finger thrust onto the page. "Possess."

Timothy blinked. "Da," he said. "*Vladeyete*. Possess." For the benefit of Irina Dupkova he smacked himself on the forehead with the butt of his palm.

"Possess," Irina Dupkova said, as if it had been equally obvious to her. She paused, her face regaining its bluntness. "Well, nevertheless, I have come here this morning to thank you."

Timothy made a vague sound of dissent. "There is no need to thank me, Irina Dupkova."

"You have made my daughter feel very good, Timothy. Protected. Special. You understand, yes?"

"Your daughter is a fine girl," Timothy said. "A fine student."

With that Irina Dupkova's face palled, and she stepped closer to him, putting her square back to the doorway. "These filthy people think they can spit on Russians now, you know. They think independence has made them a nation. They are animals, barbarians." Her eyes were small and bright with anger.

Timothy Silverstone looked at his scuffed classroom floor. There was activity in the hallway—shuffling feet, children's voices—and Timothy looked at his watch. His first class, Susanna's class, began in ten minutes. He moved to the door and closed it.

Irina Dupkova responded to this by intensifying her tone, her hands moving in little emphatic circles. "You understand, Timothy, that Russians did not come here willingly, yes? I am here because my father was exiled after the Great Patriotic War Against Fascism. Like Solzhenitsyn, and his careless letters. A dark time, but this is where my family has made its home. You understand. We have no other place but this, but things are very bad for us now." She flung her arm toward the windows and looked outside, her jaw set. "There is no future for Russians here, I think. No future. None."

"I understand, Irina Dupkova," Timothy said, "and I am sorry, but you must excuse me, I have my morning lessons now and I—"

She seized Timothy's wrist, the ball of her thumb pressing harshly between his radius and ulna. "And this little hooligan Uzbek thinks he can touch my Susanna. You understand that they are animals, Timothy, yes? *Animals*. Susanna," Irina Dupkova said, her dark eyes not leaving Timothy's, "come here now, please. Come let Mister Timothy see you."

In one smooth movement Susanna rose from her desk and turned to them. Her hair was pulled back into a taut blond ponytail and lay tightly against her skull, as fine and grained as sandalwood. She walked over to them in small, noiseless steps, and Timothy, because of his shame for striking Rustam before her eyes, could not bear to look at her face. Instead he studied her shoes—black and shiny, like little hoofs—and the thin legs that lay beneath the wonder of her white leggings. Irina Dupkova hooked Susanna close to her and kissed the top of her yellow head. Susanna looked up at Timothy, but he could not hold the girl's gaze. He went back to the huge face of her mother, a battlefield of a face, white as paraffin.

"My daughter," Irina Dupkova said, nose tilting downward into the loose wires of Susanna's hair.

"Yes," Timothy said.

Irina Dupkova looked over at him, smiling, eyebrows aloft. "She is very beautiful, yes?"

"She is a very pretty girl," Timothy agreed.

Irina Dupkova bowed in what Timothy took to be grateful acknowledgment. "My daughter likes you very much," she said, looking down. "You understand this. You are her favorite teacher. My daughter loves English."

"Yes," Timothy said. At some point Irina Dupkova had, unnervingly, begun to address him in the second-person familiar. Timothy flinched as a knock on the door sounded throughout the classroom, followed by a peal of girlish giggling.

"My daughter loves America," Irina Dupkova said, ignoring the knock, her voice soft and insistent.

"Yes," Timothy said, looking back at her.

"I have no husband."

Timothy willed the response from his face. "I'm very sorry to hear that."

"He was killed in Afghanistan."

"I'm very sorry to hear that."

"I live alone with my daughter, Timothy, in this nation in which Russians have no future."

Lord, please, Timothy thought, make her stop. "Irina Dupkova," Timothy said softly, "there is nothing I can do about any of this. I am going home in three months. I cannot—I am not able to help you in that way."

"I have not come here for that," she said. "Not for me. Again you do not understand me." Irina Dupkova's eyes closed with the faint, amused resignation of one who had been failed her whole life. "I have come here for Susanna. I want you to have her. I want you to take her back to America."

Struck dumb had always been a homely, opaque expression to Timothy, but he understood, at that moment, the deepest implications of its meaning. He had nothing to say, *nothing*, and the silence seemed hysterical.

She stepped closer. "I want you to take my daughter, Timothy. To America. As your wife. I will give her to you."

Timothy stared her in the face, still too surprised for emotion. "Your daughter, Irina Dupkova," he said, "is too young for such a thing. *Much* too young." He made the mistake of looking down at Susanna. There was something in the girl Timothy had always mistaken for a cowlike dullness, but he could see now, in her pale eyes, savage determination. The sudden understanding that Susanna's instigation lay behind Irina Dupkova's broke through Timothy's sternum.

"She is fourteen," Irina Dupkova said, moving her hand, over and over again, along the polished sheen of Susanna's hair. "She will be fifteen in four months. This is not so young, I think."

"*She is too young*," Timothy said with a fresh anger. Again he looked down at Susanna. She had not removed her eyes from his.

"She will do for you whatever you ask, Timothy," Irina Dupkova was saying. "Whatever you ask. You understand."

Timothy nodded distantly, a nod that both understood but did not understand. In Susanna's expression of inert and perpetual unfeeling, he could see that what Irina Dupkova said was right—she would do whatever he asked of her. And Timothy Silverstone felt the glisten of desire at this thought, felt the bright glint of a lechery buried deep in the shale of his mind. *My God*, he thought. *I will not do this.* He was startled to realize he had no idea how old Sasha was. Could that be? He was tall, and his scrotum dangled between his legs with the heft of post-adolescence, but he was also lightly and delicately haired, and had never, as far as Timothy could tell, shaved or needed to shave. Sasha could have been twenty-two, two years younger than Timothy; he could have been sixteen. Timothy shook the idea from his head.

"I have a brother," Irina Dupkova was saying, "who can arrange for papers that will make Susanna older. Old enough for you, in your nation. It has already been discussed. Do you understand?"

"Irina Dupkova," Timothy said, stepping backward, both hands thrust up, palms on display, "I cannot marry your daughter."

Irina Dupkova nearly smiled. "You say you cannot. You do not say you do not want to."

"Irina Dupkova, *I cannot do this for you.*"

Irina Dupkova sighed, chin lifting, head tilting backward. "I know why you are here. You understand. I know why you have come. You have come to give us your Christ. But he is useless." Something flexed behind her Slavic faceplate, her features suddenly sharpening. "*This* would help us. *This* would save."

Timothy spun around, swung open his classroom door, poked his head into the hallway and scattered the knot of chattering children there with a hiss. He turned back toward Irina Dupkova, pulling the door shut behind him with a bang. They both stared at him, Irina Dupkova's arm holding Susanna close to her thick and formless body. "You understand, Timothy," she began, "how difficult it is for us to leave this nation. They do not allow it. And so you can escape, or you can marry." She looked down at herself. "Look at me. This is what Susanna will become if she remains here. Old and ugly, a ruin." In Irina Dupkova's face was a desperation so needy and exposed Timothy could find quick solace only in God, a mental oxbow that took him to imagining the soul within Susanna, the soul being held out for him to take away from here, to sanctify and to save. That was God's law, His imperative: *Go therefore and make disciples of all nations.* Then God's distant broadcast filled his mind, and with two fingers placed stethescopically to his forehead Timothy turned away from Irina Dupkova and Susanna and listened so hard a dull red ache spread behind his eyes. The sound disappeared.

"Well," Irina Dupkova said with a sigh, after it had become clear that Timothy was not going to speak, "you must begin your lesson now." Susanna stepped away from her mother and like a ghost drifted over to her desk. Irina Dupkova walked past Timothy and stopped at his classroom door. "You will think about it," she said, turning to him, her face in profile, her enormous back draped with a tattered white shawl, "you will consider it." Timothy said nothing and she nodded, turned back to the door, and opened it.

Students streamed into the room on both sides of Irina Dupkova like water coming to a delta. Their flow hemmed her in, and Irina Dupkova's angry hands fluttered and slapped at the black-haired heads rushing past her. Only Rustam stepped aside to let her out, which was why he was the last student into the room. As Rustam closed the door after Irina Dupkova, Timothy quickly spun to his blackboard and stared at the piece of chalk in his hand. He thought of what to write. He thought of writing something from Paul, something sagacious and unproblematic like *We who are strong ought to put up with the failings of the weak.* He felt Rustam standing behind him, but Timothy could not turn around. He wrote the date on the board, then watched chalkdust drift down into the long and sulcated tray at the board's base.

"Meester Timothy?" Rustam said finally, his artificial American accent tuned to a tone of high contrition.

Timothy turned. A bruise like a red-brown crescent lay along the ridge of Rustam's cheekbone, the skin there taut and shiny. It was barely noticeable, really. It was nothing. It looked like the kind of thing any child was liable to get, anywhere, doing anything. Rustam was smiling at him, a bead of wet light fixed in each eye. "Good morning, Rustam," Timothy said.

Rustam reached into his book bag, then deposited into Timothy's hand something Timothy remembered telling his class about months and months ago, back before he had come apart; something that, in America, he had said, students brought their favorite teachers. It got quite a laugh from these students, who knew of a different standard of extravagance needed to sway one's teachers. Timothy stared at the object in his hand. An apple. Rustam had given him an apple. "For you," Rustam said softly, turned and sat down.

Timothy looked up at his classroom to see five rows of smiles. Meester Timothy will be wonderful and American again, these smiles said. Meester

Timothy will not hit us, not like our teachers hit us. Meester Timothy will always be good.

Woolen gray clouds floated above the Registan's minarets, the backlight of a high, hidden sun outlining them gold. Some glow leaked through, filling the sky with hazy beams of diffracted light.

Timothy walked home, head down, into the small breeze coming out of the Himalayan foothills to the east. It was the first day in weeks that the temperature had dipped below 38 C., the first day in which walking two blocks did not soak his body in sweat.

Sasha stood in the tall doorway of the teahouse, holding a bottle of orange Fanta in one hand and a cigarette in the other. Around his waist Sasha had knotted the arms of Timothy's gray-and-red St. Thomas Seminary sweatshirt (Timothy didn't recall allowing Sasha to borrow it), the rest trailing down behind him in a square maroon cape. He slouched in the doorway, one shoulder up against the frame, his eyes filled with an alert, dancing slyness. Sasha let the half-smoked cigarette drop from his fingers and it hit the teahouse floor in a burst of sparks and gray ash. He was grinding it out with his cowboy-boot-tip when Timothy's eyes pounced upon his. "*Nyet*," Timothy said, still walking, feeling on his face the light spume of rain. "*Ne sevodnya, Sasha.*" *Not today, Sasha.* Timothy eddied through the molded white plastic chairs and tables of an empty outdoor café, reached the end of the block and glanced behind him.

Sasha stood there, his arms laced tight across his chest, his face a twist of sour incomprehension. Behind him a herd of Pakistani tourists was rushing toward the Registan to snap pictures before the rain began.

Timothy turned at the block's corner even though he did not need to. In the sky a murmur of thunder heralded the arrival of a darker bank of clouds. Timothy looked up. A raindrop exploded on his eye.

Timothy sat behind his workdesk in his bedroom, a room so small and diorama-like it seemed frustrated with itself, before the single window that looked out on the over-planned Soviet chaos of the Third Microregion: flat roofs, gouged roads that wended industriously but went nowhere, the domino of faceless apartment buildings just like his own. The night was impenetrable with thick curtains of rain, and lightning split the sky with electrified blue fissures. It was the first time in months it had rained long enough to create the conditions Timothy associated with rain: puddles on the streets, overflowing gutters, mist-cooled air. The letter he had started had sputtered out halfway into its first sentence, though a wet de facto period had formed after the last word he had written ("here") from having left his felt-tip pen pressed against the paper too long. He had been trying to write about Susanna, about what had happened today. The letter was not intended for anyone in particular, and a broken chain of words lay scattered throughout his mind and Timothy knew that if only he could pick them up and put them in their proper order, God's message might at last become clear to him. Perhaps, he thought, his letter was to God.

Knuckles against his door. He turned away from his notebook and wrenched around in his chair, knowing it was Sasha from the lightness of his three knocks, illicit knocks that seemed composed equally of warning and temptation. Timothy snapped shut his notebook, pinning his letter between its flimsy boards, and winged it onto his bed. As he walked across his living room, desire came charging up in him like a stampede of fet-locked horses, and just before Timothy's hand gripped the doorknob he felt himself through his Green Bay Packers sweatpants. A sleepy, squishy hard-ness there. He opened the door. Standing in the mildewy darkness of his hallway was not Sasha but Susanna, her small nose wrinkled and her soaked hair a tangle of spirals molded to her head. "I have come," she said, "to ask if you have had enough time to consider."

Timothy could only stare down at her. It occurred that he managed to let another day go by without eating. He closed his eyes. "Susanna, you must go home. Right now."

She nodded, then stepped past him into his open, empty living room. Surprise rooted Timothy to the floorboards. "Susanna—" he said, half reach-ing for her.

After slipping by she twirled once in the room's center, her eyes hard and appraising. This was a living room that seemed to invite a museum's velvet rope and small engraved plaque: Soviet Life, Circa 1955. There was nothing but the red sofa, a tall black lamp which stood beside nothing, and a worn red rug that did not occupy half the floor. Susanna seemed satisfied, though, and with both hands she grabbed a thick bundle of her hair and twisted it, water pattering onto the floor. "We can fuck," she said in Eng-lish, not looking at him, still twisting the water from her hair. She pro-nounced it *Ve con foke*. She took off her jacket and draped it over the couch. It was a cheap white plastic jacket, something Timothy saw hanging in the bazaars by the thousand. Beneath it she was still wearing the bubble-gum dress, aflutter with useless ribbonry. Her face was wet and cold, her skin bloodless in the relentless wattage the lightbulb glowing naked above her. She was shivering.

Timothy heard no divine static to assist him with Susanna's words, only the awful silent vacuum in which the laws of the world were cast and acted upon.

"We can fuck," Susanna said again.

"Stop it," Timothy said.

"We can," she said in Russian. "I will do this for you and we will go to America."

"No," Timothy said, closing his eyes.

She took a small step back and looked at the floor. "You do not want to do this with me?"

Timothy opened his eyes and stared at the lamp that stood next to nothing. He thought that if he stared at it long enough, Susanna might disappear.

"I have done this before with men."

"You have," Timothy said—it was a statement—his throat feeling dry and paved.

She shrugged. "Sometimes." She looked away. "I know what you think. You think I am bad."

"I am very sad for you, Susanna, but I don't think that."

"You will tell me this is wrong."

Now both of Timothy's hands were on his face, and he pushed them against his cheeks and eyes as if he were applying a compress. "All of us do wrong, Susanna. All of us are bad. In the eyes of God," he said with listless conviction, "we are all sinners."

A knowing sound tumbled out of Susanna. "My mother told me you would tell me these things, because you believe in *Hristos*." She said nothing for a moment. "Will you tell me about this man?"

Timothy split two of his fingers apart and peered at her. "Would you like me to?" he asked.

She nodded, scratching at the back of her hand, her fingernails leaving a crosshatching of chalky white lines. "It is very interesting to me," Susanna said, "this story. That one man can die and save the whole world. My mother told me not to believe it. She told me this was something only an American would believe."

"That's not true, Susanna. Many Russians also believe."

"God lives for Russians only in St. Petersburg. God does not live here. He has abandoned us."

"God lives everywhere. God never abandons you."

"My mother told me you would say that, too." From her tone, he knew, she had no allegiance to her mother. She could leave this place so easily. If not with him, she would wait for someone else. She shook her head at him. "You have not thought about marrying me at all."

"Susanna, it would be impossible. I have a family in America, friends, my church… they would see you, and they would know. You are not old enough to trick anyone with papers."

"Then we will live somewhere else until I do." She looked around, her wet hair whipping back and forth. "Where is your bed? We will fuck there."

"*Susanna—*"

"Let me show you what a good wife I can be." With a shoddy fabric hiss her dress lifted over her head and she was naked. For all her fearlessness, Susanna could not anymore meet Timothy's eye, her xylophonic ribcage heaving, the concave swoop of her stomach breathing in and out like that of a panicked, wounded animal. She hugged herself, each hand gripping an elbow. She was smooth and hairless but for the blond puff at the junction of her tiny legs. She was a thin, shivering fourteen-year-old girl standing naked in the middle of Timothy's living room. Lightning flashed outside—a stroboscope of white light—the room's single bright light bulb buzzing briefly, going dark, and glowing back to strength.

His bedroom was not dark enough to keep him from seeing, with awful clarity, Susanna's face tighten with pain as he floated above her. Nothing could ease the mistaken feeling of the small tight shape of her body against his. After it was over, he knew the part of himself he had lost with Sasha was not salvaged, and never would be. *I can will what is right, but I cannot do it.* He was longing for God to return to him when His faraway stirrings opened Timothy's eyes. Susanna lay beside him, in fragile, uneasy sleep. He was drawn from bed, pulled toward the window. The beaded glass was cool against his palms. While Timothy waited—God felt very close now—he imagined himself with Susanna, freed from the world and the tragedy of its limitations, stepping with her soul into the house of the True and Everlasting God, a mansion filled with rooms and rooms of a great and motionless light. Even when Susanna began to cry, Timothy could not turn around, afraid of missing what God would unveil for him, while outside, beyond the window, it began to rain again.

WHY NOT
A SPIDER MONKEY JESUS?

[SELECTED SCENES FROM THE NOVEL]

by A.G. PASQUELLA

#1

TERROR ENTERS IN the form of a drum-beating teddy bear. Baby Cyrus blinks, doubletakes & rubs his eyes with long chimp fingers. Screeching, The Baby Chimp hotfoots it across the cage. Above Cyrus the cage door opens & gloved scientist hands toss in a sock puppet monkey. The Baby Chimp leaps onto the sock puppet & there he clings, fur bristling, burying his face into the soft chest of his artificial mother.

"Perfect. Time?"

"Six-point-six-five seconds."

"Mark it down."

"Doctor—I, ah, I'm not sure I understand the point of these tests."

Dr. Bob frowns at his young labcoated assistant. "It's like this, Janet. We're Scientists, see? We have Scientifically Proven that A Terrified Infant Wants Its Mother. Any more questions? No? Good. Now get out the electrodes."

Janet The Lab Assistant carries a Sedated Cyrus back from the testing room, past the other chimps & monkeys stacked in single cages from floor to ceiling, urine & feces dripping down onto the unlucky ones below. The monkeys run in circles & vomit & bang their heads against the bars. One

Spider Monkey lies dead on his back, hairy limbs splayed, one hand reaching through the bars.

Groggy Cyrus spots The Spider Monkey lying caged & dead. Baby Cyrus trembles terrified as Janet carries him past the dead monkey's outstretched hand.

Into The Refrigerator Room: Stainless Steel Isolation Chambers Line Every Wall. Each isolation chamber has a plexiglass window & through every window is a Baby Chimpanzee. Janet (Green Eyes, Brown Hair, Flapping Lab Coat) unlatches an isolation box: WHOOSH of escaping air followed by the humming of an industrial fan. Inside the isolation box is another barred cage. Janet unlocks the cage and tenderly places Cyrus inside. Janet pauses before closing the cage door & stares at the baby chimp. The baby's head is shaved & a blood-spotted bandage is wrapped around his throat. Janet slides socks onto the baby's hands to prevent him from digging into his wounds.

"I—I'm sorry, Baby."

Janet slides the cage door closed.

#3

Bob The Scientist kicks back, feet propped up, threadbare socks on beautiful teak desk. Bob sips Scotch & flips through his folded, crinkled & chocolate-stained copy of *Curious George Gets a Medal*.

Janet The Lab Assistant stands shivering in the doorway of Bob's icy office.

"Excuse me, Doctor—"

"Ah, Janet! Come on in! Ever read this book?"

"Yes, I—"

"It's about a Little Chimp Rocket Pilot named Curious George who flies the first rocket into space. Curious George parachutes back to Earth & gets a Hero's Welcome & also a medal inscribed 'To George, The First Space Monkey.' You know what really gets me about this book?"

"You mentioned—"

"This book was written by H.A. Rey & published in 1957. That's a full four years before NASA started using Astrochimps. Janet, have I ever told you my H.A. Rey Theory?"

"Yes, Sir. Many—"

"H.A. Rey was a Time-Traveling Spy."

DATELINE: NASA, 1961. H.A. Rey in Trenchcoat & Fedora lurks in the alley outside NASA waiting for the scientists to toss out the trash. H.A. Rey rips into the trash bags like a starving raccoon. His feverish eyes scan the debris: Chimponauts! Space Monkeys! Just The Thing for The Latest Book!

"There's another Space Monkey Scenario, Doctor."
"Oh So?"

A NASA SCIENTIST, STUCK WITHOUT A BABY SITTER,
TAKES HIS LITTLE DAUGHTER SUSIE TO WORK:
    "Hmm... we need to test our new Capsule—but how?"
    Little Susie kicks her heels & flips her picture book.
    "Well, uh—we could send a dog."
    "No, no. We have to measure Mental Ability. We've got to be sure as shooting that firing our boys into space won't fry their brains."
    Little Horrified Susie drops her book & begins to cry.
    Jenkins picks up the book & spots the little chimp on the cover. "Say, Boss—take a gander at this book your kid's reading."
    "Not now, Jenkins. We've got a lot of work to do and I—Good Lord! Monkeys! Of Course!"
    "I'm pretty sure it's an ape, sir."
    "Six of one, half a dozen of the other."
    "Well, they're pretty different, sir."
    "No, no, Jenkins. That's how many we'll need. Six chimps, half a dozen monkeys—no, wait. Scrap the monkeys. When I come in tomorrow, Jenkins, I want to see Sixty-Five Chimps suited up & whipping around that Zero Gravity Machine."
    Jenkins Snaps A Salute.
    "Yes, Sir!"

JANUARY 31, 1961: Rocket Fuel & Fire, blasting past the atmosphere at five thousand miles an hour & then faster, too fast, Eighteen Thousand Miles An Hour—The Mercury Capsule plummets back through the atmosphere, capsule charred & burning while A Nation Holds Its Breath. SPLASH DOWN: Ham The Astrochimp pops from the capsule unharmed. Applause thunders from coast to coast. Ten days later Ham (Short for "Hollman Aeromedical"— The Scientists, no doubt, chose the name from a Baby Book: "How about Henry?" "Nope." "Herman?" "Nope." "Hollman Aeromedical?" "THAT'S IT!") is flashing a grin at The World from the cover of *Life* Magazine.

*   *   *

November 29, 1961: A Mercury Capsule Piloted by Enos The Astrochimp Orbits Perfectly Around The Earth. During The Second Revolution, Everything Falls Apart: A Gas Jet Sticks & Spurts Fuel & The Crippled Capsule Wobbles Around The World. The Banana Pellet Machine Breaks Down: Enos Pulls The Right Levers, but instead of Tasty Treats, Electric Shocks Shiver Through His Spine.

On The Ground, Carl The NASA Scientist throws his clipboard to the floor.

"Well, that's it. This mission's kaput."

Philip The NASA Scientist stares at his monitor.

"Wait a sec, Carl. Take a gander at this."

Rocketing Through Space, Electricity Crackling Through His Hairy Frame, Enos The Astrochimp Overrides NASA's Spluttering Command System. He Shrugs Off The Shocks & Performs The Tasks He Knows Are Right. The Astrochimp splashes down in The Bahamas, alive & well.

Back in his office, Bob The Scientist pours himself another Scotch.

"'Enos' is Hebrew for 'Man.' Did you know that?"

Janet shuffles her feet & coughs.

Bob kicks back in his chair.

"Yes, Sir—my heart soared when I saw those Astrochimps. Right then & there I knew I was destined to become A Scientist."

Janet with Flashing Eyes & Determined Jaw stands in front of Bob The Scientist's Desk. Bob peers up over his glasses. Janet splashes her ID badge into Bob's freshly-poured Scotch.

"Hey Bob—I quit."

#4

Lance The Lab Director barges into Dr. Bob's office.

"Knock, knock—how goes it, Bob?"

"Well, Janet just quit. But this morning we—"

"Great, great. Hey, that's great. Guess what? We're pulling the plug on The Chimp Project."

"What? But—"

"Sorry, Bobby. We need the space for The Frog Array."

"The what?"

"Exactly. Remember Galvani's Electroconductivity Experiment? Ran Electric Current Through Disembodied Frogs Legs & Made Them Kick?"

"You Bet. It's An All-Time Classic."

"Got That Right. Anyway, The Boys & I got to thinking about Galvani's experiment over poker Thursday Night, so we took a few sacks, went out to the swamp and rounded up Ten Thousand Frogs. What we're going to do, see, is create a Gigantic Bank Of Twenty Thousand Electrified Frogs' Legs, Row After Row Of Shiny Green Glistening Legs All Ready To Kick At The Press Of A Button. The Frogs' Legs Kick, Frog Feet Hit A Flywheel—Flywheel Spins Out Electricity. We Feed That Electricity Back Into The Machine, Generating a Constant Pulse to Power The Legs. Legs Keep Kicking, Electricity Keeps Flowing. You see? Perpetual Energy!"

Lance The Lab Director beams in triumph. Dr. Bob scratches his balding head. Flakes of dandruff float onto the shoulders of his brown corduroy blazer.

"Well, uh—Lance—there's a problem with that theory. Basic Thermodynamics says some of that energy is bound to be lost, so The Frog-Generated Energy Pulse will eventually taper off to nothing. Creating a Race Of Super Chimpanzees, on the other hand—see, now that just makes sense."

Lance The Lab Director Scowls. "Perpetual Frog-Generated Electricity Equals Big Consumer Savings."

"But a race of Super Chimpanzees—"

"Jesus, Bob, don't you read The Papers? A race of Super Chimpanzees would take over The Planet & Enslave Us All. But with Frog-Generated Electricity, folks could cut their power bills in half. Really, Bob, Frog-Generated Electricity is for The Good of Humanity."

Lance straightens up, smiling. "Well, time to get crackin', Bob. Tonight we start bringin' in the frogs."

"Tonight? But—I'll need a few days to relocate all the chimps—and the monkeys—a few days, at least!"

Lance The Lab Director sighs. "This part is never easy. The Board thinks it would be too much trouble to relocate the chimps, & I tend to agree—after all, they pay my salary! Ha Ha! Anyway, tell Sally in Supply you need some Cyanide. That oughta do it. When you're done just pile 'em onto a gurney & I'll have Raoul wheel 'em out to The Incinerator."

"But—"

"And oh yeah, whip up a Final Report on these chimps, okay? Make sure it has a lot of Positive Results. You know how much The Board loves those Positive Results. Well, duty calls!"

Lance The Lab Director walks off whistling.

* * *

#5

Which blanket for The Superchimp? Bob opts for soft blue cotton with that fresh lilac smell. Bob The Scientist walks from his bedroom closet to the garage where he rummages through oil-stained boxes of burnt-out robot parts & broken circuit boards before he finds his trusty crow bar. Bob The Scientist takes a deep breath—Ah, That Musty Old Garage Air—and tugs on a pair of black leather gloves. A Freshly-built Chimp Cage is in the back of Bob's van, waiting to be filled.

Stomach churning, bubbling bile rising, tangy taste of tin on his tongue—oily fear-sweat oozing through his pores, soaking his black woolen burglar hat & his black leather burglar gloves purchased earlier today from a Downtown Department Store: "Yes, and, um... these gloves won't leave fingerprints, will they?" "Oh, No, Sir. All our gloves are Guaranteed Fingerprint Proof." The Salesman Wraps It Up.

Fusebox Disabled, Fence De-Electrified: Clippers Snip & The Fence Is Peeled Back. Beyond, bathed in roaming flood lights, is the laboratory yard, crisscrossed with sidewalks & helpful friendly signs: This Way! To Evisceration Room!

Black-Clothed Figure Slips Between The Flood Lights & Makes Tracks Toward Chimpanzee Quarantine Zone Six.

Hydraulic WHOOSH of steel door opening & Baby Chimp Cyrus blinks against the sudden rush of fluorescent light falling across his cage. Leather-gloved hands reach in & yank Cyrus up & away.

Bob The Scientist Talks Softly To The Baby In His Arms.

"Don't worry, #1138. I'm busting you out of this Steel Refrigerator, see?"

Bob injects Cyrus with a calmative, wraps the baby chimp tenderly in the pale blue blanket and hastens for the exits.

Halfway down the hallway (fluorescent lights, speckled ceiling tile, faint whiff of Experimental Grade Industrial Cleanser hanging in the air) alarm sirens start blaring, bells start clanging & the hallway light turns red. Bob The Scientist jumps & slides on the slick white floor & almost loses his grip on the baby chimp but he hangs on, oh he hangs on tight to that warm little bundle that is The Future & Bob slides around the corner bumping SMACK into another Black-Clad Burglar: down they go in a tangled mass of legs & arms & hats & gloves.

Eye to Eye on the floor, wide-eyed shock of Mutual Recognition: Bob The Scientist & Janet The Lab Assistant face each other on their hands & knees in black burglar garb. Baby Cyrus lies bundled on the floor, sedated & sleeping through the clanging & whooping of the alarms compounded by the shrieking of Five Hundred Terrified Monkeys & Five Hundred Terrified Apes.

Without a word Bob stretches his hands through the red light (senses panic-heightened: hands & arms move slow, as if through Cherry Jello), gathers up Cyrus & almost falls like a sucker but then regains his balance & hauls ass to the window with Janet close behind—like acrobats they flip over & out onto the lawn.

On the lawn Bob & Janet are instantly pinpointed by five spotlights at once. Security Guard Chuck Norris (No Relation) leans his left arm out of the guard tower window & raises his megaphone.

"All Right, Bonnie & Clyde—You're Flat Busted. Drop The Blanket, Jack, & Put Your Hands On Your Head."

Bob clutches Cyrus like a Football, Tucks His Head Down & Makes Tracks for The Fence. In Fast Motion Bob Heaves Cyrus Over The Fence Scampers Under A Peeled-Back Portion Of The Fence Catches Cyrus In Midair Foots It Across The Highway & Dives Into His Waiting Van. A Hand Extended & Bob Pulls Janet Inside & Slams The Door Closed. Tires Spin Out & Screech Off Into The Night.

Chuck The Security Guard shrugs, lowers his megaphone & goes back to popping paperclips at The World's Best Employee poster taped to the guardtower's gray cinderblock walls.

#6

Inside Bob's Van: "We were both at the lab to rescue #1138—I mean, Cyrus. Right? So I Propose An Alliance. You & I, Janet—we take Cyrus & we hole up at my beach house & we continue the experiment."

"You mean—"

"That's right." Bob The Scientist Grins. "We're Going To Teach Cyrus The Chimpanzee How To Speak."

"All right—I'm In, if you Treat Him Humanely. And Bob—No Hanky Panky. There's Nothing Between Us. It's a Baby Chimp Thing, that's all."

#8

Fourth of July BBQ Slide Show For The Neighbors: bored, sleeping—checking watch—looking wistfully toward the open window. Finally Mr. Barbarini has had enough. With a roar Mr. Barbarini leaps through the window & catapults into the rose bushes.

The other neighbors shift & yawn, balancing precarious paper plates of food. Sauce & Potato Salad slop onto the couch & the living room carpet.

"Bob—I just had that carpet cleaned."

"It'll be all right, Janet. Show's almost over. Just twelve more trays!"

Janet groans. Bob grins & clicks on the next slide.

Slide of Cyrus The Chimp with this throat sliced open, bloody & raw. Nauseated Audience groans & pushes away their plates of shredded pork.

"Oh, this is a good one. What we did, see, is we cut through the throat & whittled down the larynx, remodeled the whole throat & mouth to facilitate the formation of Human Speech. We're talking some Serious Surgery here, folks. This one time, we—Ha! Ha!—we just couldn't get the bleeding to stop. This Big Chimp Vein was jumping & spurting like A Runaway Firehose—"

"Next slide, Bob."

"Right." Cute shot of Baby Cyrus with baby blue blanket over his head, face cocked toward the camera, ignoring Bob & his flash cards crouching in the background.

"AWWWW!" The Neighbors go misty-eyed & clutch their hearts.

"That's right. Here's Cyrus learning Sign Language. He's a fast learner. If we don't give him pie when he asks for it, he gives us the finger."

Neighbor Sally-Ann leans forward, frowning. "Wait a sec, Bob—this Chimp can actually talk?"

"At this stage Cyrus is learning Sign Language at an amazingly rapid rate. And, thanks to my surgeries, he should be physically capable of forming Human Vocal Speech."

Old Mr. Cornelius Harrumphs. "Well? Can He Talk Or Not?"

Janet leaps into the breech. "Well—uh—results have been Erratic. At best."

Hooting from the hallway & all heads turn: Cyrus scampers in twirling his diaper lasso-style over his head. Shit flies everywhere. Shit on the carpet, shit streaked across the walls, shit splattering the drapes, shit dripping from the ceiling. Shit-spotted family photographs illuminated by shit-covered lamps. Shit-drenched party guests sitting on a shit-splattered sofa.

Old Mr. Cornelius The War Veteran splutters & clutches his chest.

Cyrus hoots & slops the diaper atop his head & runs from the room, Angry Bob in close pursuit: shit-speckled loafers sliding across the shit-covered carpet.

A Happy Fly tracks shit-colored footprints across the Red White & Blue bunting pinned shit-covered to the walls. The fly surveys the shit-laden banquet laid out before him, winks at Cyrus & rubs his hands in glee.

"Atta Boy, Kid! Keep Up The Good Work!"

#12

"He can't talk. The Project is a failure."

"Bob—you can't quit now."

"You're Right! Strap him down, Janet—I'll start sterilizing the knives."

Janet, Fearful of Bob's Machinations Against Young Cyrus, places a bindle of clothes into the chimp's hands and pushes him toward the open door.

"We have to get out of here. I'll go create a distraction & you wait for me outside."

Outside by the driveway Neighbor Dave is trimming a topiary-style hedge, a Giant Leafy Rabbit. With one gloved thumb Neighbor Dave pushes his Gardening Hat farther up his sweaty forehead, better to peer from beneath the brim & eyeball Cyrus The Chimp with bindle on his shoulder come loping out the door & down the driveway.

"Howdy, Cyrus. Doin' some traveling?" Dave chuckles & snips his clippers at the hedge.

Cyrus nods. "Sure Am, Dave. Tell Bob & Janet I Said Goodbye."

Neighbor Dave stares goggle-eyed as Cyrus lopes down the driveway. Dave reaches into his back pocket & pulls out the gasoline-soaked rag he's been huffing on all day. He solemnly shakes his head & tosses the gas rag over his shoulder. The Giant Leafy Hedge Rabbit pats Neighbor Dave on the shoulder.

"You did The Right Thing, Dave."

Neighbor Dave grins & nods, then grabs his shears & resumes his clipping.

At the end of the driveway Cyrus sticks out his hairy thumb. A Red & Yellow Mobile Home Covered With Illustrations of Sword Swallowers & Fat Women Screeches to a halt. On the side of the Mobile Home, painted in Red & Gold letters, is a Sign: THE COLONEL'S TRAVELING CURIOSITY EMPORIUM.

Behind The Wheel of The Emporium The Colonel Grins & Tips His Hat: White Stetson over Silver Hair, White Goatee & A Silver CattleSkull Bolo Tie. Cyrus scrambles up the side of The Emporium & dives through the passenger window. The Traveling Emporium lurches into gear & speeds off, chimp feet kicking in the air.

#14

Bob The Scientist is on hold, drumming his fingers against Janet's kitchen table. "Yes, hello. I'd like to file a Missing Persons Report. His name is

Cyrus. He's, uh, about three foot four and covered with hair. What? No, he's a Chimpanzee."

Constable Bernard sighs.

"Look, buddy, we don't do Missing Persons Reports on pets. That's why we call them Missing PERSONS."

"But he's not a pet."

Constable Bernard is horrified.

"You weren't going to EAT him?"

#15

The Colonel, At The Wheel Of The Emporium: "Yessir, noticed you scamperin' around on the beach a few days ago. Made some inquires as to your Buyability. Thought to myself, Colonel, That Monkey's Got Spirit. Speaking of which—" The Colonel tilts back his head & sips bourbon from a silver flask. The Emporium veers across the highway & Cyrus tumbles from the passenger seat & rolls to the back, coming up THUMP against the cold steel bars of a Monkey Cage.

"Meet Floyd The Spider Monkey. Found him in a dumpster behind a laboratory during one of my, ahem, routine searches for Curiosities To Amaze The Eyes & Astound The Soul." Floyd stares at Cyrus through the bars. The Spider Monkey blankly chews on the tip of his tail.

The Mobile Home veers again & Cyrus tumbles forward into a shelf of dusty jars. Up top, a jar of Pickled Siamese Twins totters & falls. Cyrus dives, catching the jar with both hands & both feet.

#19

"Rejoice & Sound The Trumpets! The Colonel's Traveling Curiosity Emporium Has Arrived! Carlsbad Community Seniors Center, Here We Come!

"These Old Folks are chompin' at the bit to see some Honest-To-God Curiosities & By God We Won't Shirk. We'll set up a little stage in front of The Emporium & give 'em One Hell Of A Show."

Cyrus tugs on The Colonel's Trousers. "What's The Program?"

"Hm? Oh, well, I figure you'll march in there & do a little dance, you know, a little soft shoe—"

The Colonel Stops Dead In His Tracks.

"Boy, did you just say—I mean, did I hear you say—"

Cyrus frowns down at his bare feet.

"Soft Shoe?"

"A Talking Monkey!" The Colonel fans himself with his hat. "Well,

This Changes Everything. Okay—you'll march out there & recite some famous speeches, Four Score & Seven, I Had A Dream, stuff like that. Then you toss up The Jazz Hands & that's that."

Cyrus flexes his hairy fingers.

"Jazz Hands?"

#20

The Colonel shakes pulped tomatoes from his hat.

"Well, that didn't go well. Don't worry, son. Opening Night Jitters. Happens To Everyone."

Television static & crackle: slumped in the shadows in the back of the mobile home, Cyrus fiddles with the rabbit ears & the picture comes in clear.

"Hello, my Beautiful Friends! I'm so glad you could join us on this Beautiful God-Given Morning for Another Episode of Tim & Sally's Good-Times Gospel Variety Hour! Can I Get An Amen? Amen! Hallelujah! Praise The Lord!"

On the shelf above Cyrus, shrunken heads bobble in their dusty jars.

The Audience sways & claps. Cyrus claps along, staring slack-mouthed at the screen.

The Colonel snorts from The Driver's Seat.

"For a Talking Chimp you sure got some Strange Tastes."

Cyrus ignores The Colonel & keeps watching television. His Mind Absorbs The Screen.

"Are you ready for The Second Coming? Are you prepared for The Return of Christ Our Lord? Well, start thawin' out the turkey because It Won't Be Long Now!"

"That's right, Brothers & Sisters. You gotta be Vigilant. You gotta be On Your Toes. You must be prepared to Shake Hands With Christ , Every— Single—Day Of Your Life! He's Going to Be Here, Brothers & Sisters. He's Going to Be Here Soon. You Never Know, Do You? He might be driving next to you on the freeway in that lime green El Dorado! Why, He might— He just might—He Might Be Sitting Next To You Right Now."

Next to Cyrus, Floyd The Caged Spider Monkey scratches his ass & burps. Cyrus's eyes go wide.

#23

FLAT TIRE—The Drunken Colonel tumbles from the driver's seat & The Chimp grabs the wheel. The Colonel's Traveling Emporium skids off the highway into the gravel parking lot of the Ardmore, Oklahoma Bible

Outlet Store.

Inside The Outlet Store, disgruntled customers rummage through the racks.

"Hey, there ain't no Apostle named Julia!"

"And here in Revelation it says The Lamb has six & one-half horns instead of seven!"

Ned The Proprietor puffs his pipe.

"What can I say, folks. Those are the 'As Is' Bibles. Slightly Irregular. 99 cents a pound."

The Door Bells Jingle-Jangle & In Strides Cyrus, Chest Puffed-Out Confident:

"Brothers! Sisters! Let Us Open Our Hearts & Receive The Ever-Lovin' Blessings Of Our Lord JESUS!"

Charlie The Cub Reporter (Green Eyes, Rusty Hair, Smattering Of Freckles Across His Nose & Cheeks, Fedora with PRESS pass stuck in the band) drops to his knee & adjusts his camera.

"A Preaching Chimp! What A Scoop!"

#25

An Aging Gangster In An Ill-Fitting Suit (JACKIE BOB) sits at his desk in the offices of The Happy Hallelujah Party, A Division of TransChristian Broadcast Industries Ltd. A Short Stocky Man (BOBBY JACK) Approaches, Stepping Cautiously Across The Carpet.

"Jackie Bob, we got trouble."

Behind his desk Jackie Bob's mouth drops open & his cigar falls onto the carpet. Jackie Bob leaps up & runs to his filing cabinet & starts dumping whole armloads of files into the big green Industrial-Sized Shredder that takes up the whole back half of his office.

Jackie Bob huffs for breath & wipes his brow. "Call Rodreguez. Tell him to gas up the Hydrofoil. I've got the Fake Passports & Twenty Thousand Dollars Cash strapped to my ass. We'll be in Brazil by Noon."

Bobby Jack wrinkles his nose.

"Naw, Jackie—nothing like that. It's The Ratings. Tim & Sally's Good-Times Gospel Hour is Eating us Alive."

"Goddamn Them! Maybe it's time we paid them a little visit."

Jackie Bob reaches into his desk drawer & pulls out an aluminium base-ball bat.

"Boss, wait! You seen today's papers?" Bobby Jack tosses the newspaper onto Jackie's desk. Jackie scans the photograph. His eyes go wide.

Jackie Bob jabs at the intercom.

"Roxy! Get Me The Preaching Chimp!"

#27

"Thanks for coming down, Colonel. Let's cut straight to the chase. We like the cut of your monkey's jib. "

"We admire his Verve."

"He's got Verve To Spare."

"We'd Like To Take His Act Nationwide, Colonel. Straight Out Over The Airwaves, Right Into One Million Homes."

Bobby Jack heaves a canvas money sack against The Colonel's chest.

The Colonel stands Speechless. Dollar Signs Blossom In The Colonel's Eyes.

Jackie Bob grins & slides A Contract across the desk. Bobby Jack hands The Colonel a fountain pen.

"There you go, Colonel. Don't press too hard—you'll chip the veneer."

#28

In The Penthouse Suite Of Little Rock, Arkansas's Swankest Hotel sits Corpulent Cyrus, fingers covered in Ruby Rings, Black Suit with A Red Tie & A Diamond Stickpin Shaped Like A Dollar Sign. Hair slicked back with The Colonel's Own Pomade. Sunglasses to block out the Red Light filtering through the drapes.

Bobby Jack, nostrils powdered with cocaine, approaches the corpulent chimp.

"Brother Cy—"

"Shh!" Cyrus holds out a finger. On the TeeVee is a repeat of The Happy Hallelujah Party Hour. Brother Cyrus The Preaching Chimp rides a tricycle up a ramp & through a hoop labeled 'Heaven.'

"That's An All-Time Classic."

At Cyrus's Side Jackie Bob Chuckles. "You Got That Right. Whatchoo Want, Bobby Jack?"

"Tim & Sally are At It Again, Boss. They're building an Amusement Park."

"They're building a WHAT? Goddamn Them!"

Jackie Bob lurches to his feet & stumbles over to the Hotel Intercom.

"Roxy, Get Me A Construction Crew. Tell 'em to Get Crackin'! What? An Amusement Park, Goddamn It! Twenty Times Bigger & Forty Times Shinier Than That Half-Assed Pile Of Sticks They're Putting Together Uptown!"

#31

The Night Before The Grand Opening Of TransChristian Broadcast Industries Ltd.'s New Theme Park JESUS WORLD, Cyrus The Chimp hosts a wild blow-out in his suite.

Drunken Cyrus weaves happily toward Bobby Jack & Jackie Bob.

"Hey! You havin' a Good Time? Anybody see The Colonel?"

Jackie Bob & Bobby Jack Shoot Each Other A Look.

"He's, uh, he's all wrapped up at the moment. Listen, take it easy on that stuff, Cy. You got A Big Day Tomorrow."

"Nuts To That." The Chimpanzee Scowls & Clutches His Bourbon.

The Penthouse blurs, shakes & shimmers as The Last Guests Leave. On all fours Cyrus stumbles over Empty Bourbon Bottles, feeling for his fallen cigar.

"Ow! Cyrus sucks burned fingers & puts the cigar back into his mouth—Burning End First.

"YAARGH!" Cyrus falls backward, pulling on a tablecloth. Empty cheesetray tumbles & gongs him on the skull.

A Knock At The Door. Cyrus crawls over, whimpering.

Neil The Bellboy With The Faraway Eyes stands there smiling.

"Bottle of Bourbon you ordered, sir."

"Swell. Put it on my tab, & send up some more of those Sexy Dames."

"I'll call The Chimp Farm, sir. "

Neil The Bellboy frowns.

"Cy—you all right?"

"Never—" Cyrus hiccups. "Never Better."

"You sure?"

"Yeah, yeah. Go on, Kid—Beat It."

Cyrus opens the Bourbon Bottle with his teeth & takes a swig. His Bladder Shrieks. Cyrus stumbles toward The John.

Q: How Much Bourbon Could A Chimp Throw Up If A Chimp Could Throw up Bourbon?

A: A Lot.

Cyrus wipes his mouth with the back of his hairy hand & splashes cold water on his face. Cyrus stares up at The Mirror & screams.

Cyrus's flesh melts & shifts like wax. The Mirror Shimmers: bright reds & blues & fierce fangs of the Mandrill Baboon, tiny delicate orangeness of the Golden Lion Tamarin, long swooping arms of the Gibbon, black & white leaf-eating Colobus, massive chest & shoulders of the Mountain Gorilla, long serious face of the Barbary Macaque, huge whiskers of the Gelada, wide eyes & ringed tail of the Ring Tail Lemur, red-faced Japanese

Macaques rising through thermal steam, wise ancient eyes of the Orang-utan, flat face of the Howler Monkey, Squirrel Monkey, Spider Monkey…

#33

On The Road Again: Dr. Bob Drives & Sulky Janet Mans The Chimp Detector.

"Janet—is that a walking carpet?"

"Gosh, I don't know, Professor. Why don't you rip apart my house & make a Walking Carpet Detector & find out?"

Dr. Bob pulls to the side of the road & rolls down the window. The Walking Carpet Bends In Close. From The Rolled-Up Carpet Peeks The Colonel's Muddy Face.

"Howdy, Folks. Apologies for The Mussed-Up Duds but some Sneaky Pete snuck a Mickey Finn into my Kickapoo Joy Juice & chucked me into this here ravine. Ever been wrapped up in a carpet & had to crawl up a ravine? WHOO-EE! Use muscles you didn't even know you had. Point bein', folks, I'd be Eternally Grateful if you would unroll me from this dang fool thing."

#42

Deep-Voiced Announcer of a Radio Talk Show: "Last Night During The Opening Of The Jesus World Christian Amusement Fun Center Cyrus The Preaching Chimp Went Live On International Television & Claimed That The Second Coming Of Christ Had Happened. Jesus Is Back, In Spider Monkey Form. Do You Still Believe? We Want To Hear From You."

#44

In His Secret Underground Headquarters, The General Munches Toast.

"Disgusting. You see The Daily Commie Times? Filthy Pack Of Filthy Lies."

"Sir?"

"Imagine printing Filth like this:

SAVIOR IS A SPIDER MONKEY, CLAIMS TALKING CHIMP
Vatican, Pope 'Confused'

"The Savior a Spider Monkey! My Grandmother was a Die-Hard Catholic, Jenkins, & She Sure As Hell wasn't squandering her Sundays mumbling to a Goddamn Spider Monkey!"

"It's Reynolds, sir."

"What Did You Say?"

"My name, sir. It's, uh—" Reynolds stares at the massive vein throbbing in The General's forehead. "Jenkins, sir."

"Damn Straight! Assemble A Crack Force, Jenkins. This Spider Monkey Jesus Nonsense Stops Here & Now!" The General hurls his breakfast tray to the floor & pouts. "And I want fried eggs, not scrambled! And Jenkins, when I tell you to scrape out the cat's litter box I want that box scraped!"

"Jenkins" snaps to attention. "Sir Yes Sir!"

#46

Inside The Freshly-Vacuumed Conference Room of The Swankmore Hotel: fresh pitchers of ice water on the table. The Media file in. The Colonel kicks back, Cigar in Mouth, Boots on The Table.

On The Dais, In Front Of The Lights & Cameras, Jackie Bob Clears His Throat.

"Thank You For Coming, Ladies & Gentlemen. Brother Cyrus Would Like To Issue A Retraction Of Last Night's, Uh, Erratic Outburst. Brother Cyrus?"

Jackie Bob shoves the microphone toward Cyrus, Zooked Out Of His Skull on Jesus & Drugs.

"Whaaaooooaaa—" A Thin Tendril of Drool Dangles From Cyrus's Chin.

Jackie Bob yanks away the microphone & smiles out into the sea of cameras.

"There you have it, folks. A Complete Retraction. Has Nothing To Do With Jesus World, Which Is Open Six Days A Week, Eleven A.M. to One A.M.

"Jackie Bob! Josh Squires, American Globe. Is it safe to say that last night Cyrus was being coerced by Communist Agents intent on bringing down The Christian Religion from within?"

Jackie Bob nods. "Communists, yeah. And Also, Terrorists."

The Colonel jumps up. "Now, Hold Your Horses, Folks. There were no Communists or Terrorists. Ol' Cyrus was just a mite confused, that's all. & With Good Cause. Floyd here is the only Spider Monkey I know of who Came Back From The Dead."

Gasps of Shock & Screams. One woman faints & falls into the aisle.

The screams snap Cyrus back into The Here & Now.

"Hey, somebody bring that lady some water! Lady, you all right? It's all right, folks. Don't you worry. Ol' Floyd isn't some kinda Zombie Spider

Monkey that's gonna swing through your house on your chandeliers waiting for you to walk past so he can POUNCE & start devouring your still-warm living brain—each Tooth-Crunch Dislodging Such Succulent Brain Juice, In Each Drop A Memory, Licked Clean & Digested & Later Shat Out—& Say You Don't Got Chandeliers! Then It's Even Worse!"

The Colonel leans down toward Cyrus & stage whispers from the side of his mouth. "Boy, you better let me do the talkin'.

"I believe what Cyrus here is drivin' at is that Floyd is a Salvaged Lab Monkey, left for dead in a laboratory dumpster but behold! Torn from his Science-Crypt Floyd sits caged before you, Reborn!"

Next to Snuffling Floyd & His Filthy Cage Sits Cyrus, His Head Lolling Backward. The Super Ape's Amplified Snoring bounces off the walls.

Charlie The Cub Reporter stands up. "Colonel—Hey, Colonel! Are You Saying Floyd The Spider Monkey Actually Came Back From The Dead?"

"He surely did, Charlie. He surely did. Saw it happen with my own two eyes."

"Colonel, folks come back from the dead every day. That doesn't make them Jesus."

"It's Pretty Damn Miraculous though, ain't it?"

"I—" Charlie scratches his head with his pencil & smiles a freckle-cheeked smile. "I suppose it is, Colonel. I suppose it is."

Whacked-Out Cyrus Raises His Drug-Filled Head.

"Colonel! I Hear Everything Twice!"

"Calm It Down, Boy. Anyone Got Any Other Questions?"

"Vicki Tobey, The Daily Vaticanian. This Question's for Cyrus. So you no longer believe that A Spider Monkey could be Jesus?"

Defiant Cyrus snaps awake. "The Spider Monkey IS Jesus!"

Gasps from The Assembled Crowd. Reporters tip over chairs & crawl over each other in a mad scramble for the phones.

Cyrus The Preachin' Chimp Jumps Onto The Table & Commences To Strut.

"Ladies & Gentlemen, Children Of All Ages, I Give You The Second Coming Of Jesus Christ, Spider Monkey! See It Daily At Spider Monkey Jesus World! The Amusement Park That Will Thrill Your Soul—& Save It, Too! Ride The Spider Monkey Jesus, Tallest Tubular Steel Roller Coaster Built On God's Green Earth! Thrill To The Proverbs Acted Out Daily By Floyd The Spider Monkey Jesus At Eleven & Then Again At Eleven Fifteen! We've Got Spider Monkey Jesus Burgers, We've Got The Spider Monkey Jesus Operating System for Windows—Watch for Spider Monkey Jesus 2.0

Coming Soon! "

"Delia is Classic in her Spider Monkey Jesus Wear!"

The Spider Monkey Jesus Baby Monitor, Spider Monkey Jesus Flavored Jello—You've Got A Spider Monkey in my Jesus! You've Got Jesus in my Spider Monkey! Ride That Spider Monkey Express down to Spider Monkey Jesus World in Beautiful Spider Monkey Jesus, U.S.A.! We've Got The Spider Monkey Jesus Quit-Smoking Patch, The Spider Monkey Jesus Mayan-Style Hammock, Spider Monkey Jesus Brand Nail Polish Remover, Spider Monkey Jesus In Space, Spider Monkey Jesus Adult Disposable Undergarments, Spin The Spider Monkey Jesus, Spanking The Spider Monkey Jesus, Terror In Spider Monkey Jesus Land, Spider Monkey Jesus Brand Genetically Altered Wheat—now with 50% More Spider Monkey Flavor! Spider Monkey Jesus Meals With Your Free Glow-In-The-Dark Spider Monkey Jesus Right In The Box, The Spider Monkey Jesus Family of Mutual Funds—we teach you to Invest Like A Spider Monkey Jesus!

A Spider Monkey Jesus On Rye, A Spider Monkey Jesus On The Rocks:

    1 tumbler

    3 ice cubes

    2 ounces of Scotch

    2 ounces of Tequila

"When I'm Enjoying A Nice Cool Spider Monkey Jesus, I Like To Use My Spider Monkey Jesus Graphic Interface! Everything Looks 'Extra Fine' Through My Spider Monkey Jesus Goggles!"

"Hey, Spider—can you Monkey Me Up A Jesus until Payday?"

Porn Star: "Fill Me With Your Hot Throbbing Spider Monkey Jesus Of Love, Baby!"

Throw Your Spider Monkey Jesus In The Air!

And Wave Him Like You Just Don't Care!

"Mmm! Why, Dolores! This Laundry is Spider Monkey Jesus Fresh!"

Black & White TV Crackle: Smiling Announcer With Thick Black Spectacles.

"These Days Everything's Coming Up Spider Monkey Jesus!"

"DAMN! She Got Her Spider Monkey Jesus On!"

New Marvel Comic: Spider Monkey Jesus Man.

Hit Parade: She Blinded Me With Spider Monkey Jesus; Stop The Spider Monkey Jesus, I Want To Get Off!; Like A Bridge Over Spider Monkey Jesus, Spider Monkey Jesus Gals Won't You Come Out Tonight.

"This Year's Model Comes With A Fully Loaded Spider Monkey Jesus!"

"Say there—puttin' up some fiberglass?"

"No, this stuff is better than your crummy old fiberglass! It's New Spider Monkey Jesus Board!"

Available At A Spider Monkey Jesus Depot Near You.

#50

"Well, that's it for us. We're Ruined."

Jackie Bob loots the office while Bobby Jack pours the gasoline.

"It's the only way, Colonel. A Good Ol' Fashioned 'Texas Bankruptcy.' With the Insurance Money We'll Rise Again."

Jackie Bob slides on his sunglasses. Jackie Bob, Sunglasses, Narrow Tie, Heads Into The Hallway. In Slow Motion He Strikes A Match & Tosses It Over His Shoulder.

The Colonel Grins. "Aw Well. Easy Come, Easy Go. C'mon, Cyrus. Let's Hit That Open Road."

The Colonel opens the door & fills his lungs with sweet fresh air.

"Yessir—it's A Brand New Day." The Colonel picks up Floyd's cage &, Cyrus by his side, Steps Into The Sunshine.

At That Exact Same Moment, a man wearing camouflage pants, a camouflage shirt, camouflage jacket, camouflage makeup & little bush branches strapped to his head pops up from the manhole in the middle of the street.

A Single Shot Rings Out.

Cyrus hangs like a dust mote in the doorway, Suspended In Light.

7.

8.

9.

10.

11.

12.

7) Rosemary Avenue, Cardiff

8) Fordham Road, London

9) 9th Avenue, New York

10) Cumbria Avenue, Newcastle

11) 64th Street, New York

12) Stanley Road, London

BLINDED BY THE LIGHT

by T. CORAGHESSAN BOYLE

SO THE SKY is falling. Or, to be more precise, the sky is emitting poisonous rays, rays that have sprinkled the stigmata of skin cancer across both of Manuel Banquedano's cheeks and the tip of his nose and sprouted the cataracts in Slobodan Abarca's rheumy old eyes. That is what the tireless Mr. John Longworth, of Long Beach, California, U.S.A., would have us believe. I have been to Long Beach, California, on two occasions, and I give no credence whatever to a man who would consciously assent to live in a place like that. He is, in fact, just what my neighbors say he is—an alarmist, like the chicken in the children's tale who thinks the sky is falling just because something hit him on the head. On his head. On his individual and prejudicial head. And so the barnyard goes into a panic—and to what end? Nothing. A big fat zero.

But let me tell you about him, about Mr. John Longworth, Ph.D., and how he came to us with his theories, and you can judge for yourself. First, though, introductions are in order. I am Bob Fernando Castillo and I own an *estancia* of 50,000 acres to the south of Punta Arenas, on which I graze some 9,000 sheep, for wool and mutton both. My father, God rest his soul, owned *Estancia* Castillo before me and his father before him, all the way back to the time Punta Arenas was a penal colony and then one of the great trading towns of the world—that is, until the Americans of the North broke through the Isthmus of Panama and the ships stopped rounding Cape Horn. In any case, that is a long and venerable ownership in anybody's book. I am fifty-three years old and in good health and vigor and I am married to the former Isabela Mackenzie, who has given me seven fine children, the eldest of whom, Bob Fernando Jr., is now twenty-two years old.

It was September last, when Don Pablo Antofagasta gave his annual three-day *fiesta primavera* to welcome in the spring, that Mr. John Longworth first appeared among us. We don't have much society out here, unless we take the long and killing drive into Punta Arenas, a city of 110,000 souls, and we look forward with keen anticipation to such entertainments— and not only the adults, but the children too. The landowners from several of the *estancia*s, even the most far-flung, gather annually for Don Pablo's extravaganza and they bring their children and some of the house servants as well (and even, as in the case of Don Benedicto Braun, their dogs and horses). None of this presents a problem for Don Pablo, one of the wealthiest and most generous among us. As we say, the size of his purse is exceeded only by the size of his heart.

I arrived on the Thursday preceding the big weekend, flying over the *pampas* in the Piper Super Cub with my daughter, Paloma, to get a jump on the others and have a quiet night sitting by the fire with Don Pablo and his eighty-year-old Iberian *jerez*. Isabela, Bob Fernando Jr. and the rest of the family would be making the twelve-hour drive over washboard roads and tortured gullies the following morning, and frankly, my kidneys can no longer stand that sort of pounding. I still ride—horseback, that is—but I leave the Suburban and the Range Rover to Isabela and to Bob Fernando Jr. At any rate, the flight was a joy, soaring on the back of the implacable wind that rakes our country day and night, and I taxied right up to the big house on the airstrip Don Pablo scrupulously maintains.

Don Pablo emerged from the house to greet us even before the prop had stopped spinning, as eager for our company as we were for his. (Paloma has always been his favorite, and she's grown into a tall, straight-backed girl of eighteen with intelligent eyes and a mane of hair so thick and luxuriant it almost seems unnatural, and I don't mind saying how proud I am of her.) My old friend strode across the struggling lawn in boots and puttees and one of those plaid flannel shirts he mail-orders from Boston, Teresa and two of the children in tow. It took me half a moment to shut down the engine and stow away my aeronautical sunglasses for the return flight, and when I looked up again, a fourth figure had appeared at Don Pablo's side, matching him stride for stride.

"Cómo estás, mi amigo estimado?" Don Pablo cried, taking my hand and embracing me, and then he turned to Paloma to kiss her cheek and exclaim on her beauty and how she'd grown. Then it was my turn to embrace Teresa and the children and press some sweets into the little ones' hands. Finally, I looked up into an untethered North American face, red hair and a red mustache and six feet six inches of raw bone and sinew ending in a little bony afterthought of a head no bigger than a tropical coconut and weighted down by a nose to end all noses. This nose was an affliction and nothing less, a tool for probing and rooting, and I instinctively looked away from it as I took the man's knotty gangling hand in my own and heard Don Pablo pronounce, "Mr. John Longworth, a scientist from North America who has come to us to study our exemplary skies."

"Mucho gusto en conocerle," he said, and his Spanish was very good indeed, but for the North American twang and his maddening tendency to over-pronounce the consonants till you felt as if he were battering both sides of your head with a wet root. He was dressed in a fashion I can only call bizarre, all cultural differences aside, his hands gloved, his frame draped in an ankle-length London Fog trenchcoat and his disproportionately small head dwarfed by a pair of wrap-around sunglasses and a deerstalker cap. His nose, cheeks and hard horny chin were nearly fluorescent with what I later learned was sunblock, applied in layers.

"A pleasure," I assured him, stretching the truth for the sake of politesse, after which he made his introductions to my daughter with a sort of slobbering formality, and we all went in to dinner.

There was, as I soon discovered, to be one topic of conversation and one topic only throughout the meal—indeed, throughout the entire three days of the *fiesta*, whenever and wherever Mr. John Longworth was able to insinuate himself, and he seemed to have an almost supernatural ability to appear everywhere at once, as ubiquitous as a cockroach. And what was this penetrating and all-devouring topic? The sky. Or rather the hole he perceived in the sky over Magallanes, Tierra del Fuego and the Antarctic, a hole that would admit all the poisons of the universe and ultimately lead to the destruction of man and nature. He talked of algae and krill, of acid rain and carbon dioxide and storms that would sweep the earth with a fury unknown since creation. I took him for an enthusiast at best, but deep down I wondered what asylum he'd escaped from and when they'd be coming to reclaim him.

He began over the soup course, addressing the table at large as if he were standing at a podium and interrupting Don Pablo and me in a reminiscence of a salmon-fishing excursion to the Penitente River undertaken in our youth. "None of you," he said, battering us with those consonants, "especially someone with such fair skin as Paloma here or Señora Antofagasta, should leave the house this time of year without the maximum of protection. We're talking ultraviolet-B, radiation that increases by as much as one thousand percent over Punta Arenas in the spring because of the hole in the ozone layer."

Paloma, a perspicacious girl educated by the nuns in Santiago and on her way to the university in the fall, gave him a deadpan look. "But Mr. Longworth," she said, her voice as clear as a bell and without a trace of intimidation or awe, "if what you say is true we'll have to give up our string bikinis."

I couldn't help myself—I laughed aloud and Don Pablo joined me. Tierra del Fuego is hardly the place for sunbathers—or bikinis either. But John Longworth didn't seem to appreciate my daughter's satiric intent, nor was he to be deterred. "If you were to go out there now, right outside this window, for one hour unprotected under the sun, that is, without clothing—or, er, in a bikini, I mean—I can guarantee you that your skin would blister and that those blisters could and would constitute the incipient stages of melanoma, not to mention the damage to your eyes and immune system."

"Such beautiful eyes," Don Pablo observed with his customary gallantry. "And is Paloma to incarcerate them behind dark glasses, and my wife too?"

"If you don't want to see them go blind," he retorted without pausing to drawn breath.

The thought, as we say, brought my kettle to a boil: Who was this insufferable person with his stabbing nose and deformed head to lecture us? And on what authority? "I'm sorry, señor," I said, "but I've heard some far-fetched pronouncements of doom in my time, and this one takes the cake. Millenarian hysteria is what I say it is. Proof, sir. What proof do you offer?"

I realized immediately that I'd made a serious miscalculation. I could see it in the man's pale leaping eyes, in the way his brow contracted and that ponderous instrument of his nose began to sniff at the air as if he were a bloodhound off after a scent. For the next hour and a half, or until I retreated to my room, begging indigestion, I was carpet-bombed with statistics, chemical analyses, papers, studies, obscure terms and obscurer texts, until all I could think was that the end of the planet would be a relief if only because it would put an end to the incessant, nagging, pontificating, consonant-battering voice of the first-class bore across the table from me.

*   *   *

At the time, I couldn't foresee what was coming, though if I'd had my wits about me it would have been a different story. Then I could have made plans, could have arranged to be in Paris, Rio or Long Beach, could have been in the hospital, for that matter, having my trick knee repaired after all these years. Anything, even dental work, would have been preferable to what fell out. But before I go any further I should tell you that there are no hotels in the Magallanes region, once you leave the city, and that we have consequently developed among us a strong and enduring tradition of hospitality—no stranger, no matter how personally obnoxious or undeserving, is turned away from the door. This is open range, overflown by caracara and condor and haunted by *ñandú*, guanaco and puma, a waste of dwarf trees and merciless winds where the unfamiliar and the unfortunate collide in the face of the wanderer. This is to say that three weeks to the day from the conclusion of Don Pablo's *fiesta*, Mr. John Longworth arrived at the *Estancia* Castillo in all his long-nosed splendor, and he arrived to stay.

We were all just sitting down to a supper of mutton chops and new potatoes with a relish of chiles and onions in a white sauce I myself had instructed the cook to prepare, when Slobodan Abarca, my foreman and one of the most respected *huasos* in the province, came to the door with the news that he'd heard a plane approaching from the east and that it sounded like Don Pablo's Cessna. We hurried outside, all of us, even the servants, and scanned the iron slab of the sky. Don Pablo's plane appeared as a speck on the horizon, and I was astonished at the acuity of Slobodan Abarca's hearing, a sense he's developed since his eyes began to go bad on him, and before we knew it the plane was passing over the house and banking for the runway. We watched the little craft fight the winds that threatened to flip it over on its back at every maneuver, and suddenly it was on the ground, leaping and ratcheting over the greening turf. Don Pablo emerged from the cockpit, the lank raw form of John Longworth uncoiling itself behind him.

I was stunned. So stunned I was barely able to croak out a greeting as the wind beat the hair about my ears and the food went cold on the table, but Bob Fernando Jr., who'd apparently struck up a friendship with the North American during the *fiesta*, rushed to welcome him. I embraced Don Pablo and numbly took John Longworth's hand in my own as Isabela looked on with a serene smile and Paloma gave our guest a look that would have frozen my blood had I only suspected its meaning. "Welcome," I said, the words rattling in my throat.

Don Pablo, my old friend, wasn't himself, I could see that at a glance. He had the shamed and defeated look of Señora Whiskers, our black Labrador, when she does her business in the corner behind the stove instead of outside in the infinite grass. I asked him what was wrong, but he didn't answer—or perhaps he didn't hear, what with the wind. A few of the men helped unload Mr. John Longworth's baggage, which was wound so tightly inside the aircraft I was amazed it had been able to get off the ground, and I took Don Pablo by the arm to escort him into the house, but he shook me off. "I can't stay," he said, staring at his shoes.

"Can't stay?"

"Don Bob," he said, and still he wouldn't look me in the eye, "I hate to do this to you, but Teresa's expecting me and I can't—" He glanced up then at John Longworth, towering and skeletal in his huge flapping trenchcoat, and he repeated "I can't" once more, and turned his back on me.

Half an hour later I sat glumly at the head of the table, the departing whine of Don Pablo's engine humming in my ears, the desiccated remains of my reheated chops and reconstituted white sauce laid out like burnt offerings on my plate, while John Longworth addressed himself to the meal before him as if he'd spent the past three weeks lashed to a pole on the *pampas*. He had, I noticed, the rare ability to eat and talk at the same time, as if he were a ventriloquist, and with every bite of lamb and potatoes he tied off the strings of one breathless sentence and unleashed the next. The children were all ears as he and Bob Fernando Jr. spoke mysteriously of the sport of basketball, which my son had come to appreciate during his junior year abroad at the University of Akron, in Ohio, and even Isabela and Paloma leaned imperceptibly toward him as if to catch every precious twist and turn of his speech. This depressed me, not that I felt left out or that I wasn't pleased on their account to have the rare guest among us as a sort of linguistic treat, but I knew that it was only a matter of time before he switched from the esoterica of an obscure and I'm sure tedious game to his one and true subject—after all, what sense was there in discussing a mere sport when the sky itself was corrupted?

I didn't have long to wait. There was a pause just after my son had expressed his exact agreement with something John Longworth had said regarding the "three-point shot," whatever that might be, and John Longworth took advantage of the caesura to abruptly change the subject. "I found an entire population of blind rabbits on Don Pablo's ranch," he said, apropos of nothing and without visibly pausing to chew or swallow.

I shifted uneasily in my chair. Serafina crept noiselessly into the room to clear away the plates and serve dessert, port wine and brandy. I could hear the wind at the panes. Paloma was the first to respond, and at the time I thought she was goading him on, but as I was to discover it was another thing altogether. "Inheritance?" she asked. "Or mutation?"

That was all the encouragement he needed, this windbag, this doomsayer, this howling bore with the pointed nosed and coconut head, and the lecture it precipitated was to last through dessert, cocoa and *maté* in front of the fire and the first, second and third strokes of the *niñitos'* bedtime. "Neither," he said, "though if they were to survive blind through countless generations—not very likely, I'm afraid—they might well develop a genetic protection of some sort, just as the Sub-Saharan Africans developed an increase of melanin in their skin to combat the sun. But, of course, we've so radically altered these creatures' environment that it's too late for that." He paused over an enormous forkful of cheesecake. "Don Bob," he said, looking me squarely in the eye over the clutter of the table and the dimpled faces of my little ones, "those rabbits were blinded by the sun's radiation, though you refuse to see it, and I could just stroll up to them and pluck them up by the ears, as many as you could count in a day, and they had no more defense than a stone."

The challenge was mine to accept, and though I'd heard rumors of blind salmon in the upper reaches of the rivers and birds blinded and game too, I wasn't about to let him have his way at my own table in my own house. "Yes," I observed drily, "and I suppose you'll be prescribing smoked lenses for all the creatures of the *pampas* now, am I right?"

He made no answer, which surprised me. Had he finally been stumped, bested, caught in his web of intrigue and hyperbole? But no: I'd been too sanguine. Calamities never end—they just go on spinning out disaster from their own imperturbable centers. "Maybe not for the rabbits," he said finally, "but certainly this creature here could do with a pair..."

I leaned out from my chair and looked down the length of the table to where Señora Whiskers, that apostate, sat with her head in the madman's lap. "What do you mean?" I demanded.

Paloma was watching, Isabela too; Bob Fernando Jr. and the little ones sat rigid in their chairs. "Call her to you," he said.

I called. And the dog, reluctant at first, came down the length of the table to her master. "Yes?" I said.

"Do you see the way she walks, head down, sniffing her way? Haven't you noticed her butting into the furniture, scraping the doorframes? Look into her eyes, Don Bob: She's going blind."

*   *   *

The next morning I awoke to a sound I'd never before heard, a ceaseless rapid thumping, as of a huge penitential heart caught up in the rhythm of its sorrows. Isabela awoke beside me and I peered through the blinds into the courtyard that was still heavy with shadow under a rare crystalline sky. Figures moved there in the courtyard as if in a dream—my children, all of them, even Paloma—and they fought over the swollen globe of a thumping orange ball and flung it high against an orange hoop shrouded in mesh. They were shouting, crying out in a kind of naked joy that approached the ecstatic, and the trenchcoat and the nose and the shrunken bulb of the bobbing head presided over all: *basketball*.

Was I disturbed? Yes. Happy for them, happy for their fluid grace and their joy, but struck deep in my bowels with the insidiousness of it: first basketball and then the scripture of doom. Indeed, they were already dressed like the man's disciples, in hats with earmuffs and the swirling greatcoats we'd long since put away for winter, and the exposed flesh of their hands and faces glistened with his sunblock. Worse: their eyes were visored behind pairs of identical black sunglasses, Mr. John Longworth's gift to them, along with the gift of hopelessness and terror. The sky was falling, and now they knew it too.

I stood there dumbfounded at the window. I didn't have the heart to break up their game or to forbid the practice of it—that would have played into his hands, that would have made me the voice of sanity and restraint (and clearly, with this basketball, sanity and restraint were about as welcome as an explosion at *siesta* time). Nor could I, as *dueño* of one of the most venerable *estancia*s in the country, attempt to interdict my guest from speaking of certain worrisome and fantastical subjects, no matter how distasteful I found them personally. But what could I do? He was clearly deluded, if not downright dangerous, but he had the ready weight of his texts and studies to counterbalance any arguments I might make.

The dog wasn't blind, any fool could see that. Perhaps her eyes were a bit cloudy, but that was to be expected in a dog of her age, and what if she was losing her sight, what did that prove? I'd had any number of dogs go blind, deaf, lame and senile over the years. That was the way of dogs, and of men too. It was sad, it was regrettable, but it was part of the grand design and no sense in running round the barnyard crowing your head off about it. I decided in that moment to go away for a few days, to let the basketball and the novelty of Mr. John Longworth dissipate like the atmospheric gases of which he spoke so endlessly.

"Isabela," I said, still standing at the window, still recoiling from that subversive thump, thump, thump, "I'm thinking of going out to the upper range for a few days to look into the health of Manuel Banquedano's flock—pack up my things for me, will you?"

This was lambing season, and most of the *huasos* were in the fields with the flocks to discourage eagle and puma alike. It is a time that never fails to move me, to strengthen my ties to the earth and its rejuvenant cycles, as it must have strengthened those ties for my father and his father before him. There were the lambs, appeared from nowhere on tottering legs, suckling and frolicking in the waste, and they were money in my pocket and the pockets of my children, they were provender and clothing, riches on the hoof. I camped with the men, roasted a haunch of lamb over the open fire, passed the bottle of *aguardiente*. But this time was different, this time I found myself studying the pattern of moles, pimples, warts and freckles spread across Manuel Banquedano's face and thinking the worst, this time I gazed out over the craggy *cerros* and open plains and saw the gaunt flapping figure of Mr. John Longworth like some apparition out of Apocalypse. I lasted four days only, and then, like Christ trudging up the hill to the place of skulls, I came back home to my fate.

Our guest had been busy in my absence. I'd asked Slobodan Abarca to keep an eye on him, and the first thing I did after greeting Isabela and the children was to amble out to the bunkhouse and have a private conference with the old *huaso*. The day was gloomy and cold, the wind in an uproar over something. I stepped in the door of the long low frame building, the very floorboards of which gave off a complicated essence of tobacco, sweat and boot leather, and found it deserted but for the figure of Slobodan Abarca, bent over a chessboard by the window in the rear. I recognized the familiar sun-bleached *poncho* and *manta*, the spade-like wedge of the back of his head with its patches of parti-colored hair and oversized ears, and then he turned to me and I saw with a shock that he was wearing dark glasses. Inside. Over a chessboard. I was speechless.

"Don Bob," Slobodan Abaraca said then in his creaking, unoiled tones, "I want to go back out on the range with the others and I don't care how old and feeble you think I am, anything is better than this. One more day with that devil from hell and I swear I slit my throat."

It seemed that when John Longworth wasn't out "taking measurements" or inspecting the teeth, eyes, pelt and tongue of every creature he could trap, coerce or pin down, he was lecturing the ranch hands, the smith and the household help on the grisly fate that awaited them. They were doomed, he told them—all of mankind was doomed and the drop of that doom was imminent—and if they valued the little time left to them they would pack up and move north, north to Puerto Montt or Concepción, anywhere away from the poisonous hole in the sky. And those spots on their hands, their throats, between their shoulderblades and caught fast in the cleavage of their breasts, those spots were cancerous or at the very least pre-cancerous. They needed a doctor, a dermatologist, an oncologist. They needed to stay out of the sun. They needed laser surgery. Sunblock. Dark glasses. (The latter he provided, out of a seemingly endless supply, and the credulous fools, believers in the voodoo of science, dutifully clamped them to their faces.) The kitchen staff was threatening a strike and Crispín Mansilla, who looks after the automobiles, had been so terrified of an open sore on his nose that he'd taken his bicycle and set out on the road for Punta Arenas two days previous and no one had heard from him since.

But worse, far worse. Slobodan Abarca confided something to me that made the blood boil in my veins, made me think of the braided bullhide whip hanging over the fireplace and the pearl-handled duelling pistols my grandfather had once used to settle a dispute over waterfowl rights on the south shore of Lake Castillo: Mr. John Longworth had been paying his special attentions to my daughter. Whisperings were overheard, *têtes-à-têtes* observed, banter and tomfoolery taken note of. They were discovered walking along the lakeshore with their shoulders touching and perhaps even their hands intertwined (Slobodan Abarca couldn't be sure, what with his failing eyes), they sought each other out at meals, solemnly bounced the basketball in the courtyard and then passed it between them as if it were some rare prize. He was thirty if he was a day, this usurper, this snout, this Mr. John Longworth, and my Paloma was just out of the care of the nuns, an infant still and with her whole life ahead of her. I was incensed. Killing off the natural world was one thing, terrifying honest people, gibbering like a lunatic day and night till the whole *estancia* was in revolt, but insinuating himself in my daughter's affections—well, this was, quite simply, the end.

I stalked up the hill and across the yard, blind to everything, such a storm raging inside me I thought I would explode. The wind howled. It shrieked blood and vengeance and flung black grains of dirt in my face, grains of the unforgiving *pampas* on which I was nurtured and hardened, and I ground them between my teeth. I raged through the house and the servants quailed and the children cried, but Mr. John Longworth was nowhere to be found. Pausing only to snatch up one of my grandfather's pistols from its velvet cradle in the great hall, I flung myself out the back door and searched the stables, the smokehouse, the generator room. And then, rounding the corner by the hogpen, I detected a movement out of the corner of my eye, and there he was.

Ungainly as a carrion bird, the coatends tenting round him in the wind, he was bent over one of the hogs, peering into the cramped universe of its malicious little eyes as if he could see all the evil of the world at work there. I confronted him with a shout and he looked up from beneath the brim of his hat and the fastness of his wrap-around glasses, but he didn't flinch, even as I closed the ground between us with the pistol held out before me like a homing device. "I hate to be the bringer of bad news all the time," he called out, already lecturing as I approached, "but this pig is in need of veterinary care. It's not just the eyes, I'm afraid, but the skin too—you see here?" I'd stopped ten paces from him, the pistol trained on the nugget of his head. The pig looked up at me hopefully. Its companions grunted, rolled in the dust, united their backsides against the wind.

"Melanoma," he said sadly, shaking his visored head. "Most of the others have got it too."

"We're going for a ride," I said.

His jaw dropped beneath the screen of the glasses and I could see the intricate work of his front teeth. He tried for a smile. "A ride?"

"Your time is up here, señor," I said, and the wind peeled back the sleeve of my jacket against the naked thrust of the gun. "I'm delivering you to *Estancia* Braun. Now. Without your things, without even so much as a bag, and without any goodbyes either. You'll have to live without your basketball hoop and sunblock for a few days, I'm afraid—at least until I have your baggage delivered. Now get to your feet—the plane is fueled and ready."

He gathered himself up then and rose from the ground, the wind beating at his garments and lifting the hair round his glistening ears. "It'll do no good to deny it, Don Bob," he said, talking over his shoulder as he moved off toward the shed where the Super Cub stood out of the wind. "It's criminal to keep animals out in the open in conditions like these, it's irresponsible, mad—think of your children, your wife. The land is no good anymore—it's dead, or it will be. And it's we who've killed it, the so-called civilized nations, with our air conditioners and underarm deodorant. It'll be decades before the CFCs are eliminated from the atmosphere, if ever, and by then there will be nothing left here but blind rabbits and birds that fly into the sides of rotting buildings. It's over, Don Bob—your life here is finished."

I didn't believe a word of it—naysaying and bitterness, that's all it was. I wanted to shoot him right then and there, on the spot, and have done with it—how could I in good conscience deliver him to Don Benedicto Braun, or to anyone, for that matter? He was the poison, he was the plague, he was the ecological disaster. We walked grimly into the wind and he never stopped talking. Snatches of the litany came back to me—ultraviolet, ozone, a hole in the sky bigger than the U.S.—but I only snarled out directions in reply: "To the left, over there, take hold of the doors and push them inward."

In the end, he didn't fight me. He folded up his limbs and squeezed into the passenger seat and I set aside the pistol and started up the engine. The familiar throb and roar calmed me somewhat, and it had the added virtue of rendering Mr. John Longworth's jeremiad inaudible. The wind assailed us as we taxied out to the grassy runway—I shouldn't have been flying that afternoon at all, but as you can no doubt appreciate, I was a desperate man. After a rocky takeoff we climbed into a sky that opened above us in all its infinite glory but which must have seemed woefully sad and depleted to my passenger's degraded eyes. We coasted high over the wind-whipped trees, the naked rock, the flocks whitening the pastures like distant snow, and he never shut up, not for a second. I tuned him out, let my mind go blank, and watched the horizon for the first weathered outbuildings of *Estancia* Braun.

They say that courtesy is merely the veneer of civilization, the first thing sacrificed in a crisis, and I don't doubt the truth of it. I wonder what became of my manners on that punishing wind-torn afternoon—you would have thought I'd been raised among the Indians, so eager was I to dump my unholy cargo and flee. Like Don Pablo, I didn't linger, and I could read the surprise and disappointment and perhaps even hurt in Don Benedicto's face when I pressed his hand and climbed back into the plane. "Weather!" I shouted, and pointed to the sky, where a wall of cloud was already sealing us in. I looked back as he receded on the ground beneath me, the inhuman form of Mr. John Longworth at his side, long arms gesticulating, the lecture already begun. It wasn't until I reached the verges of my own property, *Estancia* Castillo stretched out beneath me like a worn carpet and the dead black clouds moving in to strangle the sky, that I had my moment of doubt. What if he was right? I thought. What if Manuel Banquedano truly was riddled with cancer, what if the dog had been blinded by the light, what if my children were at risk? What then?

The limitless turf unraveled beneath me and I reached up a hand to rub at my eyes, weary suddenly, a man wearing the crown of defeat. A hellish vision came to me then, a vision of 9,000 sheep bleating on the range, their fleece stained and blackened, and every one of them, every one of those inestimable and beloved animals, my inheritance, my life, imprisoned behind a glistening new pair of wrap-around sunglasses. So powerful was the vision I could almost hear them bleating out their distress. My heart seized. Tears started up in my eyes. Why go on? I was thinking. What hope is there?

But then the sun broke through the gloom in two pillars of fire, the visible world come to life with a suddenness that took away my breath, color bursting out everywhere, the range green all the way to the horizon, trees nodding in the wind, the very rock faces of the *cerros* set aflame, and the vision was gone. I listened to the drone of the engine, tipped the wings toward home, and never gave it another thought.

13.

14.

15.

16.

17.

18.

13) Essex Road, London

14) Larch Road, London

15) Avenue A, New York

16) Carlisle Street, Newcastle

17) 106th Street, New York

18) Green Lanes, London

THE SPECIALIST

by ALISON SMITH

THE FIRST ONE said it was incurable. The next agreed. "Incurable," he sighed. The third one looked and looked and found nothing. He tapped her temple. "It's all in your head," he said. The fourth one put his hand in and cried, "Mother! Mother!" The fifth never saw anything like it. "I never saw anything like it," he gasped as he draped his fingers over his stethoscope. The sixth agreed with the first and the seventh agreed with the third. He parted her legs and said, "There's nothing wrong with you."

Alice sat up. The paper gown crinkled. Her feet gripped the metal stirrups. "But it hurts," she said and she pointed.

"Maybe it's a rash," Number Seven said and he gave her some small white pills. They did not help. "Maybe it's spores," he said and he gave her a tube of gel. This

made it worse. "Maybe it's a virus." He gave her a bottle of yellow pills. When Alice returned for the fourth time and told Number Seven it was not better, he slumped against the examining table, his white coat trailing. "There's nothing left," he said.

"Nothing?" Alice asked. "What am I going to do?"

He put his finger to her lips and shook his head. "Not here," he said.

That evening, Number Seven took Alice out to dinner. He leaned in over the herb-encrusted salmon croquettes. "Do you mind if I call you Alice?" he asked.

Alice frowned. "What's wrong with me?"

Number Seven pushed the fish around his plate. "I don't know," he said and then he started to cry.

"It's okay," Alice murmured. "At least you tried."

He touched her hand. She held her napkin. She could not eat. Everything tasted incurable. The rice, the saffron asparagus soufflé, the flaming liquor in the dessert—all of it, incurable.

The eighth told her it was the feminine bleeding wound. "All women have it," he said. The ninth told her she didn't use it enough. "It's atrophied," he said as he peeled off his latex gloves with a little shiver.

"But," said Alice as she sat up on her elbows, "it hurts."

The tenth said, "Call me Bob, why don't you?" He looked inside and shook his head. He sat next to her. Alice held on to the edge of the metal table. "I've been thinking," he whispered. She could smell the Scope on his breath. "I've got something that could fix this."

"Oh?" said Alice and she brightened. She felt the hair on his arm brush against her thigh.

"Yes," said Bob. He nodded his head up and down. It was then that she caught sight of the bulge inside Number Ten's slacks.

Alice decided to try a new town, a larger one. Back east, she thought, where the civilized people live. This town had underground tunnels with trains inside. On her first day, Alice descended the cement stairs, walked onto a waiting car and sat down. The orange plastic seat cupped her thighs. The doors sighed shut. The rails rushed along beneath her. She liked the dark, jerking movement of it, the idea of the ground flying by, right beside her. When the car stopped and the doors flew open, Alice emerged. She walked up another cement staircase and found herself in an entirely different part of the city.

"Brilliant," Alice thought.

She road the underground trains for days.

Then Alice discovered take-out. As she did not have a phone in her one-room walk-up, she had to call from the payphone on the corner when she wanted to place an order. But she did not mind. Alice liked everything about take-out. She liked the warm white boxes with their fold-away lids, the plastic utensils, the stiff paper bags that held in the gooey warmth. She believed that a city which could deliver such delicacies right to your door was a city of great promise. Alice stayed up late, ate Indian lentil soup from a box and said, out loud, "This is it. This is where I'll find it."

She found a job stocking shelves in a book store.

The eleventh told her try something different.

"I've seen this before. There's nothing for it," he said and he gave her a card with a number on it. "Try this anyway." Under the number were printed the words, "Psychic Healer."

This card led Alice to Number Twelve. She was alternative. "Find a piece of gold," Number Twelve said, "real gold. Boil it for three days and keep the water. Store it in a cool place. Drink this water every day for a month."

Number Twelve nodded. Alice nodded. "It aches," she said.

A pinched smile lighted across Number Twelve's face. She clasped her hands together. Gold bangles tripped down her arms and she nodded some more.

Alice did not have any gold. No ring, no broach, not even a pendant. So she bought a set of gold-rimmed plates at the Salvation Army and boiled them for three days. The painted flowers dissolved into the water, turning it pink, then green and then, finally, the color of mud. Alice slurped at her box of green lentil soup and stared into the murky liquid.

The thirteenth was also alternative. He said, "Imagine a white light entering your body. Its energy fills you. Imagine this white light healing your internal wound."

"A wound?" Alice thought. "Is that what I have?"

Alice ordered more take-out.

The fourteenth was recommended by the thirteenth. This one did not even have a card. Instead, he had fountains, dozens of them. In the waiting room tiny gurgling pumps sprouted out of copper bowls. Held in place with river stones, they bubbled and chattered all around her.

Number Fourteen was a mumbler. He swallowed his words, half-spoken. He talked into the collar of his shirt. Alice leaned in. She could not hear him over the sound of running water. "I beg your pardon?" she asked.

"Become one with the water," Number Fourteen mumbled, "and you will find your cure."

"How?" asked Alice.

Number Fourteen spread his arms. He smiled. He closed his eyes. Alice leaned in and waited. He said nothing. She thought perhaps he had fallen asleep. "Sir," she whispered. "Sir?"

But Number Fourteen did not answer.

Alice found an indoor lap pool. After her morning shift at the bookstore, she swam up and down between the ropes. The water soothed her—

the buoyancy of it, the soft fingers of cold. That winter, Alice swam and swam. She swam so many laps that her fingers pruned and her shoulders grew broad and taut. Every day, when she had completed her laps, Alice would linger in the pool. She held on to the side, gasping for breath, and floated. She spread her arms, tilted her head back and let the water surround her like a shapeless, soft eraser. But every time she stepped out of the pool, the ache returned.

Alice waited. She thought perhaps what she needed was rest. Perhaps what the ache wanted was to be left alone. So for an entire year she tried to ignore it. She did not see a single doctor. She swam up and down between the ropes. She shelved books. She rode the subway. Closing her eyes, she leaned her head against the plastic seat and waited for her life to change. Every night, she called for take-out from the pay phone on the corner. Every day, she gazed down at the neat lines of bills in the bookstore cash register.

Through it all, the ache zinged and popped. It burned and festered. And the pain of it began to eat away at her. At times, Alice felt certain there must be little left inside her. And that year, the-year-of-not-trying, something cold and hard slipped inside Alice and her heart became like a knife drawer. Sharp and shining, she kept it closed.

Then Alice met the Specialist.

"The best in the city," her coworker whispered handing her a card as she adjusted the sale sign by the overstock books. "He's a specialist."

Alice shook her head. "I'm done with doctors," she whispered back.

"Just try," her coworker said. "Try this one."

Alice had to wait a month for an appointment and when she did finally see him, when at last she climbed up onto his metal table and leaned back, the Specialist said she was empty.

"Empty!" he shrieked, his head popping up from behind the paper sheet. "There's nothing there!" He probed deeper. "It's cold," he cried. "It's so cold!" And then something strange happened, something entirely new. Alice heard a muffled shrieking and a great sucking sound. The room filled with a gust of cold air and then—silence. The Specialist was gone.

Alice sat up on her elbows and looked around her. "Where is he?" she asked the nurse.

"In there!" the nurse cried as she pointed between Alice's legs. "And he's caught!"

Alice plucked at the sheet, looking beneath it. Nothing. She leaned over and peered under the table. Still nothing. The Specialist was nowhere. Alice sat back on the metal table, her feet suspended in the stirrups. She lay very still and listened. She could hear a distant sound. The Specialist's voice, frantic and screaming, echoed somewhere below her. Alice looked over at the nurse. The nurse shook her head. Alice crossed her arms and waited.

After twenty minutes Alice shifted her weight and moved to rise. As she did, the distant echo grew louder. Then, with a terrible rush of cold air, The Specialist reemerged. His head rising above the paper sheet, his teeth chattering, a single icicle hung from the end of his nose.

"This is unbelievable," cried the Specialist. He pressed a red button. "Code Blue," he screamed into a mesh speaker in the wall. "I need a second opinion!" He paced. The icicle at the end of his nose began to melt. "I've got to get documentation," he said. "I need pictures. I need verification." He pressed the red button again and called into the mesh speaker. "Please, can I get some help in here!" His icicle dripped on the paper sheet.

"I'll help," the nurse said. She set down her clipboard.

"No," said the Specialist. "I need a doctor. This is, is…" he looked down at Alice and shook his head, "unprecedented."

"I don't know about that," said the nurse and she ducked her head below the paper sheet. "How deep did you get?" she asked.

"Deep enough," the Specialist said.

"Hmm," said the nurse.

"Oh!" said the Specialist, "If you don't believe me, I'll prove it."

The Specialist rushed out of the room. He returned moments later with a snowsuit, a pith helmet, and a flashlight. He suited up. "I'm going in," he said. "Do you need anything?" he asked Alice.

Alice shrugged.

"Why don't you order Chinese," he said. "I may be a while."

"Take-out," thought Alice, and she warmed to the Specialist. "Even if he did say I was empty and cold inside."

The Specialist put his hand inside Alice, then his arm. Before he could say another word, there was a great sucking sound, the room filled with a gust of cold air and, for the second time that day, the Specialist fell inside Alice.

The hours passed. The take-out arrive. Alice slurped her noodles. She asked for a pillow, but the Nurse was busy peering into the pages of an enormous black book. She wondered where the Specialist had gone. She stretched her arms up over her head, sat back, and picked up her box of noodles.

An hour later, the Specialist emerged. When she saw him rise up from between her legs, covered in icicles and shivering, Alice set down her chopsticks.

"My God, there's nothing in there!" the Specialist cried, his face shining with cold. "Nothing! Miles of it! I could not even find the edges of her."

Alice gazed at the Specialist's chapped hands. She had to admit that they did look quite frostbitten. Alice reached for her sweater. The Specialist set down his flashlight and rushed away to record his findings. The nurse followed, waving a clipboard. Alice was alone.

One at a time, she removed her feet from the stirrups. She stretched out. She pulled the paper gown tight against herself. She looked around the room. On one wall hung a print of a field of poppies, red and bursting. On the other, a picture of a snowy tundra. After waiting on the table for quite a while, Alice sighed. "They must have forgotten about me," she thought. She looked at her watch. If she didn't leave now, she would be late for her shift at the bookstore. She stood up, found her slacks and blouse, and began to dress.

Just as she was stepping into the second pant leg, the Specialist burst into the room holding a camera. "I must have you for my new research project," he cried. "You must stay with me and work." He grasped her shoulders. Alice held on to the waist of her slacks. "A woman with nothing inside but a cold, hard breeze!" he gazed out beyond her, at the field of poppies. Then he looked down at Alice, as if he were seeing her for the first time. "I've never found anything like you," he smiled. "Come with me! We'll travel the world. We'll meet all the great doctors. We'll stay in the best hotels. Separate rooms, of course."

Alice thought for a moment. She knew it could not be true. She knew that there was something inside her, something more than a cold, hard breeze. But no one had made this much of a fuss over her before. No one had ever seemed to care like he did. This Specialist may not have understood her, but something about her thrilled him.

"Maybe that's more important than understanding," Alice thought. She looked into the Specialist's eyes. They were green, the color of shallow ocean water. She felt a little pull in her chest, a soft tug, as if the drawer of her heart were opening. She saw the roped lane at the swimming pool and the beige mouth of the bookstore cash register, gaping and she realized that she was lonely.

"Will you help me, then?" she asked. "If I go with you, will we find a cure for the constant ache? The pain of it, it tires me so."

"Pain?" The Specialist tilted his head to one side. No one had told him this. "You have pain?" He paused a moment, then he shrugged and embraced Alice. He picked her up and swung her around twice.

The rush of air past her face, the whirl of the white, sanitary room as it flew by, it startled Alice. A new feeling, a feeling she could not quite describe, flooded her veins. It was not happiness, but it was close. The closest she had been in a long time.

In Atlantic City they praised her, treated her like royalty. "The Queen of Emptiness!" they said. In Hershey they offered her a complimentary sunsuit with a picture of the arctic printed on it, and a sash that read: "Miss Iceberg," its pink letters marching across the white satin.

The Specialist developed a slide show to accompany his demonstration. "Dim the lights," he said. Alice liked this part best. She hated it when he called her up on stage, when he poked and prodded with his cold, clammy hands. Alice sunk back in her seat and watched the photographs glow and shimmer against the white screen. She never tired of looking at them. "A distant landscape," the Specialist barked, his hand on the remote. "Cold, empty, devoid of life as we know it." Alice watched as the mysterious vistas appeared before her: a blue wash of glaciers, a white seamless line of snow. "The Interior of Alice N. is like a frozen tundra. Nothing can live there!" the Specialist bellowed across the darkened room.

This is where Alice always lost track. It never failed. Every time the Specialist started in on the part about the cold and the snow stuck up inside her, Alice felt the room begin to spin. Her vision tunneled. She watched the Specialist's mouth move and she knew that he was talking, that he was explaining to the crowd of doctors behind her what it was like to be her, what it was like to be inside of her. But she could not make out what he said.

In Gainesville she could smell the ocean, but it was too far to reach. She wanted to swim. The Specialist said, "We have no time for recreation." And so she lay on the bed while he rifled through his papers. She imagined herself in the water, the salt shine rising up, coating her white arms.

In Louisville they laughed her off stage and the Specialist after her. "There's no such thing," the doctors said. "No such thing as a woman with nothing inside but a cold, hard breeze!"

"You don't believe me?" the Specialist said. He pointed at Alice, "Then why don't you look for yourself?"

The room fell silent. The doctors blanched. They stepped away from the stage. Someone dropped a clipboard. It skittered across the concrete floor.

The Specialist nodded. He stepped up to the podium once again. "I thought so," he said. "I thought that would stop you." He put his arm around Alice. "When you're ready to do some real research, you'll know where to find us." He guided her off.

They headed west. Later, years later, long after the National Guard had captured him, the Specialist would say that it was Los Angeles where it all started to go wrong. For it was there, swept along by the bright lights and the promise of fame, that he decided to put Alice in the talk show circuit. "To broaden your audience," the Specialist said and he spread his arms wide to make his point.

The Specialist bought her a new suit. He said it was a present for their success. "Now we've hit the big time!" he beamed at her.

Alice met the talk show host in the dressing room moments before she was to go on air.

"It is a pleasure to meet you, Miss Empty," he said and he kissed her cheek.

His mustache made her sneeze. Alice wiped her nose and asked for a glass of water. The host smiled at Alice. His white teeth shimmered under the green room lights. He leaned in close to Alice and looked at her, into her face, closely. It had been so long since someone had looked at her like that. Alice tipped her head down. She blushed. She placed the rim of the glass against her lips and sipped.

"She's going to need make-up!" the Host bellowed.

After her make-up session, the host guided her on stage. Under the bright lights, the makeup felt like a thick, gooey mask.

"Here's the little lady with the big empty!" the Host said.

An applause sign popped up. The Host turned toward the Specialist. He wanted to see all the comparative charts. He wanted the entire history of his research. "Start from the beginning," the host said, leaning forward in his over-stuffed chair, "and don't leave out a thing."

The Specialist was happy to oblige. He pulled out statistics on the discrepancy between the size of Alice's outside and her inside. "The circumference of her torso," he said and he pointed at one chart, "as opposed to the circumference of her interior." He pointed to a second chart. "Alice defies logic!" This is where he always got excited. "She's an impossibility!" he cried. "And here she sits before you."

The Host smiled. "A woman who laughs in the face of science!"

The camera cut to a psychiatrist who spoke about the physical-manifestation-of-a-mental-state-brought-on-by-extreme-stress. He ended with, "It's remarkable. Quite remarkable."

The Host opened the discussion up to the audience. Alice was asked questions about her personal life that puzzled her. "How much do you eat?" "Do you like cold weather?" "Do you have a boyfriend?" Alice squirmed in her seat. The Host broke in. "Don't worry," he patted Alice's hand. "We'll find you a boyfriend," he said. "No doubt about that!" The audience cheered. Then a woman from the back row stood up, tapped the mike, and asked, "Does it ever hurt? I mean, does it ache?"

Alice felt her face flush and tingle. Finally, a question that she wanted to answer. She cleared her throat. "As a matter of fact," Alice began and then she lost the thread of her thought. She faltered.

The Host tapped his fingers together and waited. The Specialist shifted in his seat. "Go on," he nodded.

"As a matter of fact," she tried again, but the words would not come.

The Host put his hand on Alice's shoulder. "Hold that thought," he smiled. He turned and spoke to the camera lens. "We'll be right back."

"We're going back to Gainesville," the Specialist said the following morning while they were in a cab on the way to the airport. "You're not ready for the big time. We need to rehearse."

As they handed in their boarding passes and headed for the gate, they were intercepted by a man in a black suit with an ear prompt. "Excuse me," he said. "I've been sent by the talk show. They want you back."

The Specialist blinked. "Really? They want us?"

The man held his ear prompt and nodded. It turned out that Alice was a hit. Alice and her frozen tundra were the topic-of-the-day on every major morning newscast.

So Alice and the Specialist returned to the studio. Alice submitted to the creams and cover-up, the blush and shadow of the make-up artist. Once again, Alice and the Specialist found themselves under the hot studio lights, awaiting further instruction. The host beamed at them. The second interview went better than the first. The Specialist showed more slides.

Alice was relieved when they dimmed the lights. The monitor flooded with the bright grays and whites of the frozen tundra. A distant sun bounced off all that glacial terrain. Before she knew it, the show was over and Alice found herself in her new suit in the green room once again, scraping make-up off her face.

By the end of the week Alice and the Specialist were regulars on the talk show. "It seems like everybody wants a piece of the little girl with the big empty," the host smiled. He winked at Alice.

Reporters hounded them. Hotel staff hovered. Crowds formed around them wherever they went. And then, one day, the tide turned. The skeptics arrived—researchers and doctors, lab technicians and the geologists—all of whom did not believe in the cold-and-empty theory. They sat in the studio audience, crossed their arms and waited. "For some solid evidence," they whispered. "For one verifiable fact," they sneered.

The skeptics stared dubiously at the Specialist's charts. They recalculated his measurements. They scratched their heads. They lifted their chins. "Impossible," they said. "There's no such thing."

The Specialist was right there, his hand on Alice's shoulder, starting in with his challenge. "If you don't believe me," he began, "then why don't you see for yourself?"

Again, the room fell silent. Someone dropped a pen. They all stepped back.

"I thought so," the Specialist said.

But he spoke too soon. From the back, a white-coated lab technician with a shock of bright red hair, stepped out of the crowds and raised his hand. "I'll go," he said. "I'd like to see."

And then another stepped forward. And another. And another. They all wanted to see this empty landscape, firsthand. Soon there was a line forming at the edge of the stage.

"We'll go," they cried. "We want to see this cold hard breeze for ourselves."

"But," the Specialist stammered, waving his arms above his head, "it's too dangerous! It's not for the faint of heart!"

They would not listen to reason.

In the end, four men suited up and approached Alice. Each one ducked below the paper sheet. Each one slipped in, slowly at first, and then, with a rush of cold air, they disappeared.

Only three came back. Snow-crusted and shivering, one by one they climbed out of her, a gust of wind sweeping through the studio as they stepped onto solid ground. They brushed the snow off their shoulders. They straightened their wool caps. They rubbed their chapped hands together. They clapped each other on the back and nodded.

"It's true," they said. "It's huge and empty."

They nodded. They smiled. They looked around and counted. One. Two. Three. Their smiles faded. The fourth man was not among them. The three men turned around and stared at Alice. They gazed at the modesty sheet draped over her knees. They peeked under it. Nothing. So they sat down and waited.

"I'm sure he's just late," said the first man. "He stopped to take some photos," said the second. The third shifted in his seat, brushed the snow off his mittens and said nothing.

And so they waited, all of them, the three men, the Specialist and the studio audience. The Host paced. "This is highly irregular," he muttered. Then the network offered him round-the-clock coverage till the fourth man returned and the Host brightened.

The hours turned into days and still they waited. A vigil formed around the examination table. Doctors trickled in throughout the day, journalists clamored at the studio doors. The three men sat up front, right next to Alice. They called for him, the lost man, alone and wandering up inside Alice.

"I told you," the Specialist cried. "I warned you all!"

But no one was listening to him. The three men talked of extreme temperatures, the endless landscape, and lost provisions.

"Did he bring any food?" an audience member asked. "Did he pack his canteen?" asked another. "Did he wear his long johns?" his mother cried over the television satellite. Then someone suggested forming a search party. The three men who had survived to tell the story of Alice's insides shook their heads. "Why?" the people asked.

"Because it's cold in there," the three who came back said. "It's damn cold." They held their arms and shivered.

The Specialist nodded. "That's true," he mumbled as he sidled toward the door.

Someone grabbed his arm. "Where are you going?"

"I forgot my lunch," he said. "I'll be right back."

The doctors all shook their heads. "You'll stay right here," they said, "until you return the Fourth Man."

The Specialist threw up his hands. "Don't look at me! I didn't take him." He pointed at Alice. "She did."

Alice lay on the studio's examination table. By the third day, her back was in knots. Bed soars formed on Alice's skin. They grew weepy with infection. She asked if she could get up and try shaking him out. The doctors huddled in the corner and discussed the possibility. They nodded at each other. One of them stepped forward. "It might work."

Slowly, very slowly, Alice removed her feet from the stirrups, first the right and then the left. She slid her body to the edge of the examination table and placed one foot on the ground.

Alice shook and shook. She stomped her feet. She jumped up and down. She walked up the center aisle of the auditorium. She walked down the side aisle. She held on to the edge of the stage and stomped until her feet burned and her breath came hard. But it did not work. The fourth man did not emerge.

The three men who made it back alive helped her up onto the examination table. They tried calling his name. They tried playing his favorite music, pressing the speaker against Alice's exposed abdomen. They tried baking his favorite foods. They called in a diviner with his forked stick. They called in a meteorologist. He lined his instruments up and down her body, and shook his head. "Storm's coming," he said.

The doctors leaned in. "Storm's coming?" they asked. "Where?"

The meteorologist pointed at Alice. "In there."

They called in an Eskimo. "There are 437 words for snow," he whispered.

"But how do we get him out?" the doctors asked.

The Eskimo nodded, his fur cap shining under the examination lamp. "437 words," he said.

By then, it was day six. The doctors shook their heads. "There's no way," they whispered, "what with the exposure and the lack of food, there's no way he's still alive."

On the seventh day of the vigil, they sent for the lost man's wife. She spread Alice's legs, bent down and shivered. "What do I do?" she trembled. "What do I do down here?"

"Call to him," the doctors urged. "Call his name."

She called. "Honey?" she crooned. "Come out, come home!"

There was no answer. The wife began to sob. She clung to Alice. Her arms wrapped around Alice's bent legs, "Give him back," she pleaded. "Give him back!"

For a while, the story of the girl with nothing but a cold, hard breeze inside her swept through all the news stations. When the drama heightened with the missing fourth man, the networks' ratings went through the roof. It was all anybody could talk about: "What does it mean that she is cold and empty inside," they asked. "Where did the fourth man go?" When Alice and the Specialist disappeared, the story made international news.

They had slipped out one night, three weeks into the vigil for the fourth man. It was not a well-planned escape, but somehow it worked. They tiptoed right past the studio security guards, cut the wire that led to the exit alarm and crawled out onto the highway. They flagged down a passing car. The driver took them all the way to the Nevada border. Desert rain washed across the stranger's windshield as Alice huddled close to the Specialist. They were on the lam together. For once, they were running in the same direction, with the same goal in mind—to get away from the doctors. A week later, he left her.

It was an eerily still day. They were holed up in an Econo Lodge outside Las Vegas. "We're going to split up," he had whispered, his hands grasping her shoulders as they had on their first meeting. "I'll go north. You go west."

"Why?" she asked.

He let go of her, walked over to the motel window. Parting the curtain an inch with his index finger, he stared out at the parking lot. "If you don't know that by now, I'm not going to be the one to tell you."

Alice gazed at him. There he stood in his rumpled seersucker suit, pigeon-toed and balding, a slice of desert sunlight cutting across his stricken face. Despite his odd theories, Alice had grown fond of the Specialist. She stood up, smoothed her skirt, and crossed to him. He held a photo in his hand. In it, the Specialist stands in full gear, his bright blue parka shining in the winter sunlight, surrounded by vast fields of snow, miles of it mounding up, soft and seamless and white. He smiles into the camera. Alice took his shaking hand in hers. "That's not really me," she said. She looked into his eyes—warm and moist, green as the sea.

"But I have evidence," he whispered back. "I have irrefutable evidence." He looked away again, out at the cactus shivering in the hot wind, just beyond the motel parking lot.

He left the next morning, before dawn, with one blue Samsonite carry-on and a hotel face cloth shielding his balding head from the hot Nevada sun. Alice feigned sleep throughout this long departure. As he folded his three dress shirts and zipped up his utility bag, as he combed the last few strands of hair over the crown of his head and trimmed his beard, Alice watched. Through half-closed eyes she saw him place a single envelope on the bedside table, cross to the motel door, unbolt the lock and slip away into the rising heat. After he left, she opened the envelope. There was no note, no instructions, no forwarding address, nothing, but a single photograph of a man standing in a field of snow.

That afternoon, Alice dyed her hair. She slipped into the motel laundry facility and quietly removed a pair of jeans and a new T-shirt from one of the dryers. Alice had never stolen anything before and the thrill of it, the getting-away-with-it feeling flooded her veins. Flushing with pleasure, she shimmied into the jeans. She sold her one good suit and bought a bus ticket back to California where she found work at a bakery on a strip right near the boardwalk. From her station behind the kneading tables, she could smell the ocean.

Back at the studio the Host was shocked by their disappearance. "How could you let this happen?" he asked his staff. "Right out from under my nose." But the two were gone. Not a single trace of them remained. A search party was formed, the Host leading the effort. "In the name of science," he blustered. "In the name of justice!" The camera recorded it all.

Following an anonymous tip, they headed north. They hired dogsleds and glided through the Yukon. They assumed that Alice and the Specialist, partners in this absurd crime, would always be together. The Fourth Man's wife came along. She rode just behind the dogs, a fur-lined parka framing her face. She called his name. Her voice echoed across the frozen landscape.

And for a while, that was all Alice saw. Every night before she fell asleep in her little apartment above the bakery, Alice turned on the evening news and there she was, the fourth man's wife. Chilblains had swollen her fingers. Her nose and cheeks were rubbed raw from exposure. She blinked into the camera. "Wherever you are, if you can hear me, call this number," the wife pleaded. "We don't want to hurt you. I just want my husband back."

The heat from the large ovens burned the hair off Alice's arms. It opened her pores and sweat ran down her back, formed half moons under her shirtsleeves. She reveled in the sloppy warmth of the bakery, in the easy camaraderie with her coworkers. Evenings, after the baking was done, her coworkers unfolded lawn chairs on the boardwalk and watched the red ball of the sun slide lower in the sky till it sat on the edge of the ocean. When it broke open and began to sink, the colors bled across the water. Alice often joined them. She liked the feel of the ocean breeze on her arms and neck. The wind lifted her hair and fluttered across her cheeks. She closed her eyes, leaned back and listened to the bakery girls talk about their boyfriends.

In the mornings, when the other bakers wandered outside for a smoke break, Alice would slip into the back room. Nestled into the tiered rising racks, lay warm mounds of dough, resting like sleeping bodies, between the sheets of metal shelving. She gazed at the pastries. The raw, white buns, dusted in a soft layer of flour, slowly expanded as the yeast pulled in the surrounding air and the soft bdoes of dough rose. One morning, when the owner was late and the other girls lingered over their cigarettes, taking one last pull, wandering further away from the back door out toward the beach, Alice slipped her hand in between the rising racks and caressed the new, white flesh.

All the while, miles away, deep in the north country, a search party combed Alaska and the Northern Territory. They found nothing. No sign of Alice. No trace of the fourth man. For eleven months they rode up and down over the snow-packed ground, the dogs barking in the cold, the fourth man's wife crying into the wilderness.

Then, a year later, the Host got a new tip and this one was solid. It led them right to the Specialist. He had taken refuge in a tiny Inuit community, trading his gold watch for the price of a safe haven for twelve months. But, at the end of the year, when he started conducting research, running experiments on the local girls, looking for another Alice, the villagers turned him in.

The morning the authorities went out and found him, Alice was in the middle of cutting dough for hot-crossed buns. The girl who ran the cash register rushed in, calling, "They caught him!"

"Who?" asked Alice, sliding a baker's knife through the dough.

"The Specialist! They caught the Specialist."

Alice let her hands fall to her sides. The girl turned on the TV. Once again Alice found herself gazing into the frozen tundra. The dogs barked outside the igloo. The snow was so cold it had turned icy and blue. They had the igloo surrounded and still, The Specialist would not give himself up. In the end, they smoked him out. Alice watched as the Specialist ran, half-naked across the fields of snow. They shot him with a stun gun and he fell like a wild deer, his body sliding across the ice.

Alice stepped out onto the beach. The sign above the bakery switched on. Neon flooded the glass tubes, hovering and jumping to life in the crystalline air, calling to her, calling out OPEN. She remembered the poppies, bright and red on the wall in the examination room, and the Specialist's shallow-water eyes. She remembered the hotel in the desert, the stillness of the morning air, the cactus shuddering outside her window and the moment—before he left her, before he was gone—when she held his hands, still and cold, in her own. It had been years of waiting and holding herself, of trying to find the answer, the end, the other side of the mysterious pain, and how it had changed her, carved out her insides.

Alice walked toward the shore, stepping closer to the ocean than she had allowed herself to go in a long time. At the edge, she bent down and placed her fingers in the water. Her hands and arms were coated with pastry flour, rendering her whiter than usual, white as a ghost. The flour dissolved off her skin. It shimmered and flickered, falling away from her, toward the sand below. She let her wrists slip into the water, then her forearms, and her elbows. Waves crawled up her skin, licking the clouds of flour until the whiteness shifted. It moved off of Alice and into the water. The air around her grew solid and soft, as if it were made of pillows. And the ocean, which for hundreds of thousands of years had been whining outside the door, falling over and over itself, reaching for the shore, the ocean stopped. The white foaming crests of the waves stilled. The green water, shallow and undulating below her, grew viscous; it grew hard as fine crystal. Slowly, what lived inside Alice—the bright, soft, swelling snow, the cold hard breeze, all of it—slipped out, and the ocean became a field, and the field became a tundra and it rolled out, like a door opening up, swinging loose on its hinges.

As Alice gazed out on the tundra she noticed beyond the last snowy hill, something bright and shining, something calling to her, crying, "Alice, Alice, I'm here." She stepped forward, away from the huddle of shops by the boardwalk and the flickering light of the neon sign and onto the white glaciers. She walked toward the tiny speck and as she walked the speck divided into a shock of red hair and a white lab coat and there before her in the distance stood the fourth man. His hand floated above his head as he waved and he called to her, his voice bugling out, a reveille, calling her name, calling out across the frozen fields of snow.

FINDING & PONDERING
THE GREATEST SQUID
EVER KNOWN TO MAN

 * ✠

An interview with

DR. STEVE O'SHEA, *Senior Research Fellow*
at Auckland University of Technology,
& his research associate KAT BOLSTAD

INCLUSIVE OF, FAIRLY EARLY ON, THIS QUOTE, REGARDING WHAT WOULD HAPPEN
IF A HUMAN WERE TO BE EATEN BY THE NEW AND FAMED COLOSSAL SQUID:

"YOU'D BE LOOKING AT BEING RESTRAINED BY THOSE
EIGHT HOOKED ARMS AS LONG AS IT TOOK THE SQUID
TO SLICE YOU INTO BITE-SIZED PIECES WITH ITS BEAK,
THEN RASP THE PIECES SMALL ENOUGH TO FIT DOWN
THE ESOPHAGUS, USING THE RADULA, A CARTILAGINOUS
TOOTHED TONGUE BEHIND THE BEAK.
YOU'D PROBABLY RATHER DROWN."

---

by BRENT HOFF

THE GIANT SQUID: A TIMELINE

1755: Norwegian bishop Erik Pontoppidan documents reports from fishermen of a huge, many-armed sea monster dubbed "the Kraken."

1800s: Ocean scientist Edward Forbes presents the Azoic Theory, which argues that life does not and could not exist below 300 fathoms (1,800 feet).

1870: Jules Verne writes *20,000 Leagues Under the Sea*, which culminates with a giant twenty-five-foot squid attacking the submarine *Nautilus*.

---

* *Squid not to scale.*
✠ *Also, this is not a picture of a Colossal squid.*

1946: A thirty-foot giant squid washes up on the coast of Norway.

1950s: Underwater topographical mapping makes it clear that not only is the Earth 77 percent ocean, but that 84 percent of that water is more than 2000 meters deep.

1960: U.S. Navy Lt. Don Walsh and Swiss scientist Jacques Piccard climb inside what is basically a steel ball attached to a cable, called the "bathyscaphe Trieste," and lower themselves 35,800 feet down to the bottom of the Marianas Trench, the deepest spot on Earth. Right before they hit bottom, at crushing pressures of many tons per square inch, they see a creature pass their small window.

1965: Sailors on a Soviet whaling ship witness a fight between a sperm whale and a giant squid. After some ferocious thrashing on the surface, the sperm whale disappears into the deep with the squid wrapped around its head. When it finally surfaces again, the whale is dead. The squid's huge head is later discovered inside the whale's body.

1966: Two lighthouse keepers at Danger Point South Africa witness a giant squid repeatedly pulling a baby southern right whale underwater until it drowns.

1977: The producers of *Jaws* ask Arthur C. Clarke to write the screenplay for *Jaws 2*; instead Clark responds with an outline titled *Architeuthis*, which is the scientific name for the giant squid and means "first squid."

1988: Dr. Frederick Aldrich, chairman of Ocean Studies Task Force, posts wanted posters for anyone who can bring him a giant squid, "Dead or Alive." A reward is offered. None is claimed.

1997: A group of giant-squid-seeking scientists attach cameras to sperm whales in hopes they will act as deep-diving videographers and snag footage of the never-before-seen-alive *Architeuthis*. Unfortunately, as the sperm whales descend into deep ocean trenches to hunt, the cameras implode under the intense water pressure.

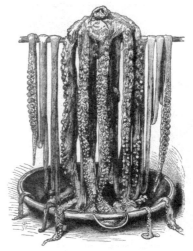

1999-2000: Several more expensive attempts to find living proof of an *Architeuthis* fail. Scientists think the squid is either just to wary of their submersibles, or they've just been unlucky.

2001: An unmanned submersible conducting geological research half a mile down in the Gulf of Mexico captures video footage of a ghostly white creature with huge wing-like fins. This new species, a 25-foot long squid, is observed drifting above the ocean floor using its sticky tentacles like spider web netting to snag passing prey. National Oceanic and Atmospheric Administration biologist Michael Vecchione tentatively classifies the creature in the genus *Magnapinnidae*, which means "big fins."

January 2003: "I saw a tentacle through a porthole," Olivier de Kersauson says. "It was thicker than my leg and it was really pulling the boat hard." Oliver and his fellow French sailors were accosted off the Portuguese island of Madeira by a giant twenty-two to twenty-seven-foot squid while taking part in the round-the-world Jules Verne Trophy race. When they stopped the boat, the squid untangled its giant tentacle from the boat's rudder and disappeared. They felt lucky.

November 2002: A thirty-nine-foot-long mystery washes up on the southern coast of New Zealand. It is a male sperm whale, its head and body covered with deep and unusual injuries. Along with the usual circular scar patterns left by giant squid tentacles are severe lacerations that look as if two-inch steel claws had been raked across the whale's skull.

March 2003: A New Zealand fishing trawler discovers the likely answer to this mystery. When they first see it, it is on the surface attacking a 6-foot-long Patagonian toothfish. Larger than the giant *Architeuthis** and far more aggressive, it is a squid like no one had ever seen before. Down its arms, along with the usual squid suckers, were two rows of nasty, 2-inch-long hooks. And not just stationary hooks—these hooks swiveled 360 degrees and were capable of ripping large animals to shreds in seconds. The fishermen manage to hook the beast with their long fisherman hooks and bring its body back to port.

There, Dr. Steve O'Shea, Senior Research Fellow at Auckland University of Technology, and his research associate Kat Bolstad were the first scientists to examine it. By comparing the animal's beak against beaks found previously in sperm whale stomachs, they were able to identify the squid's genus: *Mesonychoteuthis hamiltoni*, a distant relative of the Giant Squid *Architeuthis*. And once Dr. O'Shea was face to face with his specimen, he was inspired to give it an equally impressive stage name. He dubbed this Kraken the Colossal Squid.

Recently, Dr. Steve and Kat graciously granted an interview to *McSweeney's*.

Architeuthis are known to grow to around eight feet (body length, not including tentacles). Based on this specimen, *Mesonychoteuthis hamiltoni* can grow to around fourteen feet.

INTERVIEWER

How long would it take a Colossal to eat me?

KAT

Well, if the Antarctic waters didn't kill you pretty much straight off the bat, you'd be looking at being restrained by those eight hooked arms as long as it took the squid to slice you into bite-sized pieces with its beak, then rasp the pieces small enough to fit down the esophagus, using the radula, a cartilaginous toothed tongue behind the beak. It would take a while. You'd probably rather drown.

INTERVIEWER

Could you explain why you believe the Colossal is much more vicious than the giant *Architeuthis*?

KAT

We now believe *Architeuthis* to be a rather passive predator. Its tissues contain sodium and ammonium ion gradients, suggesting that the mantle is more buoyant than the arms and tentacles, allowing the animal to remain at about a forty-five-degree angle, tentacles suspended vertically, clasped together, until something swims below, at which point we believe the distal-most extremities of the tentacles—the tentacle clubs—clasp the prey. The struggling prey, restrained by the large, serrated sucker rings of the tentacle clubs, is then quickly dispatched by the animal's beaks, after the squid lunges forwards to restrain the prey with the arms. Its small fins and fairly flimsy tissues indicate that it cannot swim at sustained high velocity over any distance—it would self-destruct. But of course its behavior is as theoretical as *Mesonychoteuthis'*, because no one has ever seen a live adult *Architeuthis* either. Just looking at basic body construction, *Mesonychoteuthis* could be a fast-moving squid—it has relatively enormous and very muscular fins. The fact that it was actively attacking fish does suggest it to be an active predator, and—speculation only—the presence of hooks enables it to restrain large and otherwise aggressive prey.

INTERVIEWER

Do their suckers contain toxin?

KAT

No idea yet—haven't done any chemical testing. Given this species's serious

Size comparison of the Giant and Colossal Squids

Note: The standard measurement is mantle length (the portion above the head); tentacle length varies greatly depending on whether the specimen is dead or alive and whether the tentacle is stretched or relaxed.

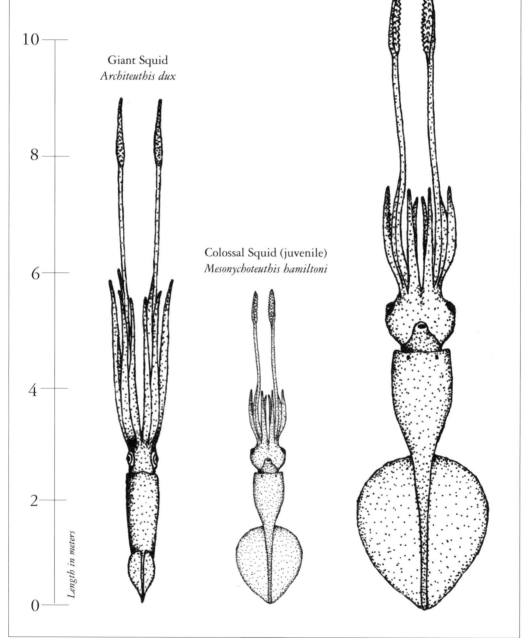

Giant Squid
Architeuthis dux

Colossal Squid (juvenile)
Mesonychoteuthis hamiltoni

Colossal Squid (estimated adult size)
Mesonychoteuthis hamiltoni

Length in meters

arsenal, it is unlikely that it would need any secondary toxin.

INTERVIEWER

Tell me about ink. Do they eject ink? Is it black ink or phosphorescent? [Some squid ink contains phosphorescent bacteria.]

KAT

Black. The juveniles do ink under stress, but again, no one knows about the adult. This specimen did have a considerable amount of ink in its ink sac.

INTERVIEWER

Do they sleep?

KAT

Nobody knows anything about behavior in deep-sea squid yet—this is one of the questions we would like to address in subsequent research.

INTERVIEWER

How many Colossal squids would it take to down a full-grown sperm whale?

KAT

Given the equipment this squid has, the large beaks and hooks, hunting large prey like the Patagonian toothfish is the most energy-efficient way of feeding; it catches and kills one large item and feeds at its leisure, as opposed to chasing many smaller prey items. But the maximum prey size is limited by what the squid can actually swallow behind its impressive beak. All food must pass through an esophagus of maximum diameter 1.5 centimeters—just big enough to stick your thumb in. It's very unlikely that a *Mesonychoteuthis* would initiate an aggressive encounter with a sperm whale.

INTERVIEWER

Were you surprised by this find?

KAT

We were most surprised that the specimen was taken at the surface of the water column, very much alive and in fact attacking fish. *Mesonychoteuthis* has an astonishing depth range, if we are to believe that it regularly occurs anywhere from 2200 meters [about 7000 feet] to the surface in the adult stages—very few other squid species are found so widely distributed throughout the water column. Most occur in the upper 100 meters or so during the larval stages, then drop to very deep waters as they reach sub-maturity, in search of prey.

INTERVIEWER

Have you ever encountered the dreaded Humboldt squid? The ones who are only around 6-10 feet long but hunt in packs, like wolves? The ones Latin divers call "El Diablo Rojo" [The Red Devil] because they are so vicious and prone to swarm-attacks? The ones who are known to send one of their pack out like a lure to distract a diver—which they can do by making their bodies flash different colors like a strobe light—and then, when the diver's not looking, the others fly out of the darkness and attack him/her from behind?

KAT

That would have to be no.

INTERVIEWER

Have you ever encountered the Humboldt squid, Steve? Is it not, as they say, the most dangerous squid known to man?

KAT

No, I've not encountered *Dosidicus* [Humboldt], but it most certainly is not the most dangerous squid known to man, though it might be the largest squid that man is most likely to encounter in coastal waters.

INTERVIEWER

If the Humboldt isn't the most dangerous, which species is?

STEVE

Mesonychoteuthis, because of its sheer size and arsenal. It is, however, one of the squids that the layperson is least likely to encounter, simply because it lives in the Antarctic.

INTERVIEWER

What happens if we discover a larger squid than the Colossal? What will you name it? What comes after Colossal?

KAT

If we find one, you'll hear about it. We know there is at least one other very large squid in the Antarctic, known exclusively from large beaks and small individuals, and it's also possible there are squid down there so big and mean that not even a sperm whale will go near them. Ginormous Squid?

INTERVIEWER

And speaking of size, besides having the largest eye of any animal on Earth [about the size of a large dinner plate], the Colossal also has a colossal penis, no? Unlike other squid who use a specialized arm to stab spermatophores [packets of sperm] in the female's side or back during massive squid orgies, the Colossal lacks that arm. And since squid species who lack that specialized arm generally have large penises...? Shall we alert *Guinness Book of World Records*?

KAT

Well... the mature male of the species is unknown. It's definitely something we'd like to look into.

INTERVIEWER

On the cephalopod web site TONMO, where you and Kat are the resident gurus, there was a funny thread about how the media has been twisting your answers and occasionally flat-out lying in their reporting on this story. I'm specifically talking about the possibility of Colossal squid eating penguins bit where you said you answered with an adamant "no" but they published it anyway. It seems like the same thing happened with *Architeuthis*, no?

KAT

The figures we have given the press since last week have consistently been that this specimen is five to six meters long (very difficult to measure a stretchy squid), and last night we heard on TV that it had forty-foot tentacles. The *Architeuthis* from Tasmania last year was about fifteen feet in total length and in pieces; by the end of the week it was found, figures of sixty feet and one ton in weight were everywhere. We give the press as much information as we are able to state conclusively, and sometimes a little speculation on behavior. With an animal like this, there seems to be little need for exaggeration... but somehow it always creeps in. The largest *Architeuthis* ever found and reliably measured using an actual measuring device—i.e. not paced off, and measured relaxed rather than forcibly stretched—was thirty-

seven feet in total length, with a mantle length of 2.25 meters. This is pretty much the uppermost acceptable measure for the species, given the 105 specimens we've seen.

INTERVIEWER

Cephalopod brains [cephalopods include all squid, octopi, cuttlefish and Nautilus] are quite small. Yet some, like the Giant Octopus, are incredibly bright. [Octopi are said to possess the intellect of a human three year-old.] How intelligent are Colossal?

KAT

A 150-kilogram *Architeuthis* has a twenty-gram brain, and about three quarters of that is made up of two large optic lobes that control the highly developed eyes. We haven't examined *Mesonychoteuthis'* brain yet, but expect similar proportions.

INTERVIEWER

I have read research that suggests some baby octopus are born knowing lessons previously learned by the mother—such as what feeding areas to avoid, and certain individual hunting tricks. Given that octopi never actually meet their mothers, and possess such intelligence in such a short life span, this suggests that perhaps some sort of genetic memory is at work. Are you familiar with this research? What is happening?

STEVE

I am not comfortable commenting here, sorry.

KAT

Sorry, haven't studied octopi enough to help here.

INTERVIEWER

May I ask why? You are self-proclaimed octopi people, after all. I can't remember where I saw this paper and really just want to understand how or why a creature that lives only two years or so possesses such intelligence.

STEVE

I am a taxonomist/systematist—someone who identifies/describes species, not someone who deals with their behavior. This is an entirely different area of science.

INTERVIEWER

Fine, then, I'll answer my own question. It is because, as recent research shows, an octopus's neural network extends throughout its entire body —effectively making them one giant free-swimming brain. And like many animals—including human babies—that are born with physical instincts (suckling for instance),the octopus's unique decentralized brain makes possible what amounts to a much more developed version of "instinct" which one could call genetic memory if one wanted—and that is incredible. Although I have no idea if it is true.

What's your favorite terrifying giant squid attack story of lore?

STEVE

I never have been one to follow squid lore; sorry. I'm a crusty old sort interested in the facts rather than the legends.

KAT

20,000 Leagues is pretty good, and props to them for a fairly accurate *Architeuthis* model, excluding size.

INTERVIEWER

Do you guys eat calamari?

KAT

Occasionally, though I am pretty much phasing out seafood. No octopus!

INTERVIEWER

In all seriousness, what does it say about us that we will travel millions of miles to explore a little moon rock but have yet to thoroughly investigate the life on our own planet?

STEVE

Both are necessary. That we achieved one before the other doesn't really matter; just imagine if they did find life beneath some ice sheet on another planet, and it proved to be prehistoric (or maybe even squid like)—I would be the first to holler and cry for joy. If it proved to be quite advanced, wow! There's no race here, Earthly or extraterrestrial—all it means is that there will be plenty left to explore on our own planet for future generations of scientists.

INTERVIEWER

Sci-fi conspiracy web sites routinely post photos of "globsters"—these mysterious masses of flesh that are found floating on the surface. What do you think they are?

KAT

Usually pieces of whale carcass. You can tell by their distinctive mammalian aroma.

INTERVIEWER

Personal question for Kat: Is science still a man's club? Do you get proper respect from peers?

KAT

Once I prove I know what I'm talking about, and not counting those who make the automatic assumption I'm his assistant, yes. Steve certainly treats me as an equal, and I anticipate the same from other teuthologists.

INTERVIEWER

What's your dream discovery?

KAT

Finding a live ammonite. Ammonites are fossil cephalopods, superficially similar to modern chambered nautilus—basically a squid in a spiral shell. They are thought to have been extinct for millions of years, but since no one has any idea what lives in the deepest darkest trenches, it is possible there may still be some, somewhere.

STEVE

A universal cure for cancer.

INTERVIEWER

What do you find amazing about your research that no one ever asks you about?

STEVE

The "why I do it?" I had never intended to work on giant squid, or giants of any animal variety in general, but it seems to be what I am best known for. I've scratched my thinning head of hair over this many a time—it seems to be thinning faster than it is going gray, but both seem to be accelerating in pace these days. In fact, my research specialty is octopus, not squid, so I'm a little confused myself as to why I get so much press attention on an animal that I've spent comparatively little time on.

INTERVIEWER

Because giant squid are the bomb. Kat?

KAT

I do find it terribly interesting that an animal of the Colossal squid's size still has to pass all its food through that teeny-tiny esophagus.

INTERVIEWER

We know whales eat *Mesonychoteuthis* Colossal squid ranging two to four meters from the beaks found in their bellies, but how do we know that these aren't all beaks of juvenile squid? How do we know there's not a Godzilla squid out there? Since no mature *Mesonychoteuthis* is known, how do we know there aren't packs of fifty-foot Godzilla squid down under the ice cap routinely hunting adult sperm whales like deer?

STEVE

True, we have no way of knowing whether *Mesonychoteuthis* hunts in packs. That would be a sensational sight. These are the sort of dream images we live for, but I think it would be misleading to suggest it occurs. From what we know about squid growth, and particularly what happens to a squid's beaks as the animal matures, I think we can safely say that the beaks recovered from sperm whale stomach contents are those of mature to sub-mature (as opposed to juvenile) individuals.

INTERVIEWER

What do you make of these reports? In 1965, sailors on a Soviet whaling ship witnessed a fight between a sperm whale and a giant squid. Neither animal survived the encounter. 1966: Two lighthouse keepers at Danger Point, South Africa witnessed a giant squid repeatedly pull a baby southern right whale underwater until it drowned.

STEVE

Both can never be discounted, but I do find them hard to believe.

INTERVIEWER

How do we know the Colossal is aggressive? And if it is aggressive, how do we know it's not the very same beast from the legends?

STEVE

There are no reports of *Mesonychoteuthis* being aggressive; that's our theory—and it is common sense, having looked at the arsenal of hooks and general body construction. This is one animal that does not sit down over a cuppa plankton exchanging idle chitchat. However, there is a tremendous amount of nonsense out there, and I am inclined to believe most if not all of these historical reports are mere fables. Nothing like this has been reported for many a year, and when it has there's no way of disproving it—i.e., no evidence.

INTERVIEWER

Kat said: "We know there is at least one other very large squid in the Antarctic, known exclusively from large beaks and small individuals, and it's also possible there are squid down there so big and mean that not even a sperm whale will go near them." Does this squid have a name? Is it bigger than the Colossal?

STEVE

It is something we are keeping under wraps at present. I personally do not believe it to be larger than the Colossal squid, but it is certainly a large squid, and probably more aggressive than *Architeuthis*. It is always possible that there's an animal so mean or large that even the sperm whale will not go near it, or an animal living so deep that the sperm whale cannot reach it. The whale probably dives to a depth of 2500 meters [about 8000 feet], but water depths around New Zealand extend to 9000-plus meters [about 25000 feet]. Sure, there's not so much food down there, so the likelihood of finding large beasts is reduced, but that doesn't mean that nothing exists there. There's plenty down there to explore and discover yet, including some things that will be rather frightening or formidable.

INTERVIEWER

What's your favorite thing about cephalopods? [Cephalopods include squid, octopi and cuttlefish.]

KAT

Their alienness and mystery, and the intelligence of octopi. That an invertebrate has developed the capacity for problem-solving, learning, curiosity and apparent enjoyment of "play" behaviors.

INTERVIEWER

Steve?

STEVE

This might sound a tad peculiar, but what fascinates me most about them are their bizarre sexual strategies. How some of these animals do the business is quite fascinating—the stuff of nightmares. There's also the fascination with their life cycles, but this requires us to view them in captivity and monitor their development. This is why we have spent so much time trying to keep them alive.

INTERVIEWER

Wait, are there giant or Colossal squid alive in captivity?

STEVE

No. This is the next step. We are fully funded by Discovery Channel; one never knows what happens tomorrow.

WHAT KEELER DID TO HIS FOOT IN THE NAVY

by SEAN WARREN

THIS IS ABOUT Keeler, not me, so I don't want you thinking anywhere down the line that I ever did anything to my foot like what he did to his, even though we were both boot squids on board the USS *Constellation*.

Actually, I was just going to turn over a year in the Navy when Keeler showed up and no one was really calling me a boot anymore since I'd been on the Connie for eight months, and when I first saw him in the berthing, sitting in this busted bottom rack that didn't have a privacy curtain and with his stuffed sea bag lying on the deck in the middle of the aisle so that I couldn't get to my rack, I tried to kick it and told him to get it out of the way—like he was a real peon, because that's how it had been for me when I'd first come on board. But really, deep down, I was feeling like a bastard because a dog wouldn't have to put up with half the shit a boot squid puts up with at sea, and what made me feel like an even bigger bastard was that Keeler didn't come back at me with any attitude or snarling at all. He'd been reading a book, a fat paperback, and after I got on him he just sat there with it still open in his hand and sighed, looking down at this sea bag like it was a dead body someone had chained to his ankle. Then he stood up and bent down and started tugging on the strap, but it was stuffed with his whole damn life and hardly budged, and finally I got tired of him not getting it out of my way and I just stepped on the damn thing to let him know I could be just as big an a-hole as anyone else if he didn't do what I said. When I put my foot down something inside the bag snapped real loud like I'd just broken its back. That made me feel the worst of all, but I didn't want to make an idiot of myself apologizing all over the place to a new squid, so I just went right straight back to my rack without saying a word and climbed in and commenced to try to take my nooner.

It was during lunch and the berthing lights were bright enough that I could see his fuzzy shape standing there through the blue cloth of my privacy curtain, not coming after me or working the sea bag or moving at all, and finally I had to look out to see what he was doing because of how quiet he was, and I thought for some reason he might be about to cry, but he was back reading again. I figured the book was one of those Tom Clancy or Stephen King bricks that floated around the ship on cruise, but it was about philosophy. *The History of Western Philosophy* by Bertrand Russell. I didn't know what to make of that, to tell you the truth, but after a while of me looking at him reading real steady like I wasn't there, like he was in a world that was way above mine where nobody could touch him, I told him to move that fucking bag out the way before it got moved for him. He was a skinny tall guy, taller than me, but when I saw the word "Philosophy" on that book and how his eyes wouldn't come off the page at all when I was staring at him, it just set me off. No way could you get out of doing boot squid hard time on the Connie by reading a philosophy book.

It took a little while for me to cool off after sticking it to him hard, and when I finally started slipping off to sleepyland I was asking myself why anyone who read philosophy books would volunteer to have their ass kicked by the Navy. Keeler was gone when I woke up, but he hadn't unpacked the sea bag at all, he'd just pushed it back up onto his busted rack. I could see why he wouldn't want to live there. The Connie was an aircraft carrier, not a cruise ship, and even though it looked humungous tied up to the pier and had all these planes stacked up on the flight deck like dinosaur warhawks when we were out steaming, there were 5,000 squids squirming around below decks and we each had maybe two square feet of living space including the lockers under our mattresses, and no fucking privacy at all except for that little curtain pulled across your rack.

Like I said, Keeler's rack was broken, the metal shelf that the piss- and splooge-stained mattress laid across was out of its grooves and bent down toward the floor, and he didn't have any curtain at all. I was lucky in one way when I first came on board—I damn sure wasn't lucky any other way, being sent to the Connie—because the ship had been working up to deploy over in Westpac and there'd been some extra money to buy new mattresses and sheets and even stand-up lockers for the first class lifers. But Keeler's rack had been vacant the whole time I'd been on board and nobody'd done a damn thing with it, and we all looked at it like it was this busted out crack house in our neighborhood that nobody would be crazy-desperate enough to live in.

Too bad they had to fly Keeler out to the ship right then, because we were all in a lousy mood and sick like hell of looking at each other after floating around together in the Arabian Sea for over three months. What chance did a new guy, especially a boot squid, have of us taking him in and showing him the score?

The Joint Chiefs had sent us out there from the Philippines after Saddam Hussein had popped a couple of shots at our aircraft, or maybe he'd overflown the no-fly zone, or he could have just farted and our satellites had picked it up as him detonating a nuclear bomb. And I know you're probably thinking I must be some kind of unpatriotic bastard, after 9/11 and all, but this all happened before that, and anyway there's just no way I can fake it and tell you how great it is to be out to sea on a man-o-war for over three months, when it's really the most tedious fucking thing ever invented. It melts a man down, turns him into one of the living dead. We worked twelve on, twelve off, but there was really only enough work in most spaces below decks to keep us busy for the first four or five hours, and anywhere else that's what you lived for, to finish your work early so you could maybe get off and... But where were we going to go, what were we going to do? We were used to beer and women in the PI, so you think we're going to be all revved up over playing video games or poker or looking for skin shots in R-rated movies with a few thousand of our squidly shipmates? That was the kind of shitty attitude Keeler was up against. It was like, We been out here for three months while you been Stateside all that time living the high life, so we ain't doing a goddamn thing for you, and if you whine about it we'll just make it colder for you or ride you harder, piss on your mattress, whatever. It kind of gives me the creeps to think back about it, because I wasn't ever a bully type or the sort that got off on being cruel to people.

I didn't see him again for maybe a couple of days and his sea bag sat in his rack the whole time and it made me wonder if they'd given him a rack somewhere else, but if they had why hadn't he come back for the sea bag? Putfark (the guy's real name, I swear), one of the compartment cleaners, asked me if I knew where he was like the rack was a prime location or something, and I guess it was for him because he used to take naps in there when the Berthing Petty Officer wasn't around, and after I told him I didn't know where Keeler was, he started dragging the sea bag out. I told him to just leave it and he looked at me like he wanted to fight, this scrawny little pea-head from some part of Louisiana or Mississippi where the kids eat possum taters and wear raccoon-claw necklaces, but then he threw down the sea bag strap and mumblefucked me and walked away.

Next thing I heard, Keeler was working for Adolfson in the ID Card Shack and that started me feeling bad for him all over again. Adolfson was only a third class, but he hadn't joined the Nav until he was like thirty-five—they must have given him the biggest age waiver of all time—and I used to think he must have been pissed about being that old and having to go through boot camp and being such a junior weenie, because he made damn sure that anyone who worked for him was more miserable than he was.

The ID Card Shack was this little dungeon off by itself, and it had to be the worst job on the whole ship, the ID card thing, because all you did was take pictures and do a little typing and print out ID cards all day, the same thing over and over, a hundred ID cards a day, and when you weren't doing the cards they had all the Ship's Company service records over there, more than 3,000 of them, and they expected you to be filing stuff and you never got caught up because of the ID cards, and squids were bitching all the time about their records not being up to date.

And Adolfson never filed stuff or did ID cards, he just sat at his desk that took up half the little office and had this nasty mini-mart plastic coffee mug as big as an oil drum on it and had himself a good ol' time grinding on whichever seaman was working for him about why the fuck all the filing hadn't gotten done and kissing the asses of any officer or chief who came around for an ID card (but never, ever doing one for them himself). My big moment with Adolfson came this time when four or five of us were watching this R-rated Jennifer Lopez movie down in the berthing lounge and we all knew she'd take her clothes off eventually, otherwise why would it be R-rated, and we were sitting there watching and thinking Goody-Goody, here it comes, and she pulled off her halter and we started getting stiffies and leaning away from each other and maybe thinking of going back to our racks for a little log-flogging, when Adolfson lost it, got up holding his crotch through his dungarees and started yelling, "I got to get me some of that! Suck my dick, bitch!" A couple of the squids told him to cool it, but he kept on holding his biscuit and hollering and ruining it for the rest of us until I just blew up and told him to sit the fuck down and shut up. Well, he's a third class and I'm a seaman and he went off on me like a little old bitch about how he was going to write me up for insubordination, and he actually did, but when the Legal Officer heard the whole story he threw it out. Adolfson acted like a dick every time he saw me after that, told me he'd get me humping stores for him down the line on a working party.

So Keeler had it bad. He was catching it every which way—he was jammed in the ID card craphole twelve hours a day with Adolfson, and when he got off everyone could see him reading his philosophy book or log-flogging or picking his nose, because he didn't have a privacy curtain. Except that, like I said, he didn't come back to his rack for the first couple of days he was working with Adolf Hitlerson. To be honest with you, I was-n't really thinking much about Keeler at all then except for when I went down to the berthing and saw that sea bag stuffed in his rack like it hadn't been touched, and then it was like, he's got to be pulling stuff out of the sea bag, skivvies and stuff to take a shower and brush his teeth, otherwise he's stinking bad. Or he jumped over the side. A couple of times after that, when I was making my rounds dropping off paper from the Old Man with the Legal Officer or the XO, I went by the ID card window and looked in to make sure Keeler hadn't jumped, and he'd be in there bent over a filing cab-inet drawer with a service record open and looking up at Adolfson standing over him making a lot of noise like he was the Main Man, the head Mother-fucker, when all he was really was this a-hole they'd shitcanned to ID cards because nobody could work with him. I probably would have jumped over the side if I'd had to spend as much time as Keeler did with that jackass.

But I didn't know how much everything was working on him until one night when I went to the head to take a shower. There was a movie playing on TV and most everyone was still watching it except me, because I thought it was junk and with everyone glued to the TV I wouldn't have to stand in line for a shower stall and I could get away with maybe taking a Hollywood shower, just let the water come down on me for a whole five or ten minutes. If there were other squids in the head, you could never tell if they were timing how long you'd been in there, scarfing up all the fresh water, and getting ready to report you to the Master-at-Arms. At sea you're supposed to take a Navy shower to conserve fresh water: turn it on, then off, lather up, then on again to rinse, then get out. Some hardcore lifers said you were gay if you took a Hollywood, like you were taking a pink bubblebath, but that's just BS. Any American should be able to take a shower for as long as he wants, anytime, anywhere. But anyway, there I was in the head think-ing I was all by myself and with all four shower stalls wide open for me, not just the one that had the busted head that dribbled water, and then I heard this grunting in one of the shitters behind me, like a squid was working hard to pass that assham the cooks had fed us for dinner. I wasn't going to listen to anyone taking a dump, so I jumped in the shower and turned on the water and it took a couple of minutes to really warm up and then I was cooking, man. When you're at sea a long time and they're always beating it into you about conserving water, though, it's hard to just let the water run without thinking the water police are just about to lower the boom, yank you out bare-assed and drag you straight up to the Man for your dose of Military Justice, so I opened the plastic curtain a crack to make sure there weren't any finks around timing my shower, and what I saw were these two big feet under a stall curtain—the shitters were right across from the show-ers in our head—and one foot was bleeding on top from these fingers rub-bing something, some kind of razor blade across the top of it.

There's a lot of nutty stuff that goes on at sea when you're out there floating around with 5,000 guys, but seeing the fingers working this blade and jerking back like it hurt like hell and then this blood oozing out was without a doubt the craziest thing I ever saw. And then what was crazier was when the fingers took this little smoky brown bottle and dribbled some-thing into the cuts that made whoever it was hiss off a GODDAMN! real loud and started him jumping around inside the stall like his foot was burn-ing. I could almost hear his toes squealing like little animals by how they were flexing, and then Keeler crashed out of the stall hopping around with his mouth clutched open and all his teeth out. He saw me peeking around the curtain and then it was like the whole Navy had found out what he'd been doing. He hopped out of there looking scared shitless and mad at me at the same time, and then he slammed the hatch behind him so that the squids out in the lounge must have wondered what the hell was going on. I made sure I stayed in the head with the shower going as long as I could after that so the only thing they might ask about was if I was taking a Holly-wood, and that would be okay, as long as they didn't ask me about Keeler.

I didn't have nightmares about it, but I sure did spend too much time thinking about Keeler and the way the toes on his burned-up pup had been squealing at me. The only answer I could come up with for him doing it was that Adolfson was driving him crazy and him not having a privacy cur-tain was making it worse. When you're at sea, that privacy curtain is like the front door to your hous. I know I've probably talked about it way too much, bored the crap out of you, but that's the way it is. I couldn't do any-thing about Adolfson, but maybe I could get Keeler a curtain. Putfark and the other compartment cleaners wouldn't do shit when I asked them about it—they were miserable, so why should they help anyone not to be miserable, that was their attitude—so I decided to go on a mission to find Keeler a curtain.

It wasn't as easy as it sounded. I was on board the Connie a couple of weeks before I got *my* curtain, and that was only because I had pestered the hell out of everybody, asked about twenty people including dropping a hint on the Old Man himself (I worked for him), and then it was just there on my mattress one day, and this was just after I'd asked Styles, the Berthing Petty Officer, for about the tenth time and he'd told me they weren't even in the supply system.

The only way I could think of to get a curtain without asking every swinging D on board again was to snag one off another rack. No way was I going to lift one out of my own berthing, so I'd have to go around to other berthing compartments until I came across a vacant rack that had a curtain. I was thinking when I first started out that it couldn't be that hard, there had to be at least one empty rack with a curtain, but I was big-time wrong about that. And another thing I learned was that when you're trolling through a berthing compartment other than your own, it's like landing a plane in Afghanistan and not speaking the language. I got looked at funny a lot, but the worst part was seeing a rack that didn't have a sheet and might be empty and lifting the curtain and then finding this big, hairy body lying there asleep or with the squid actually waking up and staring at me like I'd just busted into his house and raped his girlfriend. That happened to me twice, and the only way I got out of it was to say I was looking for someone who had to stand a watch.

Where I finally found some empty racks with curtains was in the back of the mess crank berthing. A mess crank was what everyone on board called a mess cook, which is just a brand new boot squid who gets sent down from his department, Weapons, Deck, Air, wherever, for ninety days to the Mess Decks to bus tables or wash dishes in the scullery or clean out the galley kettles or do whatever shit job the lifer cooks don't want to do. The crank berthing was no doubt the worst on the ship because they were moving in and out all the time like in one of those crappy neighborhoods where nobody owns the homes and they're pissed off at the landlords (lifer cooks) and about not owning anything, and that pissed-off way of looking at everything just builds up with each crank coming and going until all the smells and darkness and squids not having enough room to live made it just about fucking unbearable.

I'll admit it, I was scared like hell poking around down there. They had busted out most of the little bulkhead nitelights because cranks worked all shifts, so I was walking between the racks in the dark without seeing a damn thing, stepping on piles of clothes, never once hitting down on a clean piece of deck tile, and breathing in all this BO and misery and old food and angry cig smoke, and then suddenly a light yawned on and it was this black dude coming out of the head with a towel around him and looking at me and saying "Fuck you going?" like my white ass was soon to be hamburger. But I kept going, got tangled up in this huge pile of clothes, then I saw another light and went for it and stepped into the cleanest, shiniest, brightest berthing I'd ever seen. It was pretty small, only one cubicle with six racks, but there was this big lounge area with a couple of old couches and a nice card table set-up, and the racks all had curtains and these fat mattresses like the kind the officers have in their staterooms. I couldn't believe I was standing there by myself—it was like whoever controlled that little piece of heaven should have had a crank with an M-16 on watch keeping an eye on it. None of the racks had sheets and I thought they were empty and started working to pull off one of the curtains, but then I saw this old Filipino face sleeping in a bottom rack through a crack down from where I was working and at that point I just thought Hell with it and clipped the curtain cord with my Leatherman instead of fumble-farting around anymore to untie it, and got out of there, stumbling and bumbling back through the dark and getting tangled up with more piles of stinky-ripe clothes and almost falling on my ass about ten times.

But I had the damn thing at last, that curtain, and when I came up I had it stuffed into my shirt like it was a sackful of money. I went back to my berthing and was going to just tuck it under Keeler's sea bag or his rack, but I couldn't just do that. I was thinking someone might lift it, and also I wanted Keeler to know that you didn't have to be a lifer to get things done, you could get along okay if you were smart and not willing to swallow every piece of garbage they tried to jam down your throat.

Then I had this crazy idea about how I wanted to give the curtain to Keeler and I walked around the ship for a while with it tucked in my shirt, but kind of nervous about delivering it, and then I just walked down to the ID card shack. Adolfson was leaning out of his little window on his elbows smiling like he was running for mayor or maybe had just let some officer sodomize him and then he saw me and I never saw the look on anyone's face change so fast, he just wanted to spit out a roofer's nail at me right between the eyes. I went up to him and he pulled back because his style was to bullwhip you from six feet away, he didn't like anyone getting up on him. Keeler was back behind him in the office with his head down, filing service record papers like a dog. Seeing him working that way gave me the little extra push I needed to lean through the window enough to clear Adolfson out and get his attention and pull the curtain out of my shirt. I didn't expect him to act super grateful or anything like that, especially after he knew I'd seen him working his foot in the shower, but it was real low-key how Keeler slid his chair over without getting up and just took it like it was no big deal, and that kind of disappointed me. I didn't need him to be my friend, but if he'd known what the hell I'd gone through... Adolfson knew. He'd probably been counting on Keeler not getting a curtain and that that was somehow going to keep him under his thumb. But then Keeler went from not having any kind of reaction at all to folding and unfolding the curtain on his lap a couple of times like a little old lady and then he looked up at me and said "Thanks," and his eyes were real moist, not like he was going to start blubbing, but just that it had finally hit him how important having a curtain was for anyone on that goddamn birdfarm, and we connected real strong just then, like there were two of us fighting all the BS instead of just one.

It was weird, but I didn't want to see Keeler again at all after that, not ever, so I stayed away from the berthing until it was past midnight and I was too tired to give a shit about anything anymore. Then I walked back to my rack and noticed that Keeler had hung his curtain and this thousand-volt charge of pride shot through me that kept me lying awake for a long time after I'd hit my rack, like someone had just made me the goddamn CNO and I could do anything I wanted. I didn't sleep hardly at all, but I still felt good after I took half a Hollywood in the morning and went up to my office on the third deck. This corpsman named Hernandez dropped off the daily Sick Bay muster for the Captain later on and I just looked it over to see if I knew anyone who'd been admitted or if there were any crazy diseases, and I went down the list and right at the bottom was Keeler, admitted for cellulitis.

We'd done a lot of marching in boot camp and a bunch of squids in my company had come up lame with blisters and some of them had gotten infected, and that's how I knew what cellulitis was. Could you get it from cutting open the top of your foot and pouring poison into the cut? I sat there thinking about it for a while, about Keeler cutting himself open to get away from Adolfson. I would have just blown a hose on him, told him to fuck the hell off, but that was probably because I'd already gotten away with it, when we were watching that movie down in the berthing. Maybe I needed to tell Keeler not to sweat Hitlerson, that it was a damn shame to be hurting himself on account of him being such an a-hole. But what kept me from going straight down to Sick Bay and talking to him was remembering him rubbing that razor blade on his foot, and the toes barking when he poured the poison into the cut. I know I'm not the friendliest guy in the world, but I didn't want Keeler latching onto me if he was this hardcore nutcase.

Right in the middle of all this blowing around inside my head I got a call from down below from another corpsman who said that Captain Crawford, the Senior Medical Officer, wanted to see me. I knew it had to be about Keeler and I was really nervous because even if Crawford just wanted to talk about the weather, it's impossible for a seaman to get a call from a full bird like that and not think he's in the shitsoup, especially since I knew Crawford was good buddies with the Old Man and anything we talked about would go straight back to him.

I could only take being all nervous and trembly for so long, and then I went down and Crawford's door was open a crack and this little tinkle of classical music was coming out, and that made me feel easier because even though I didn't know jack about classical music, I liked it from hearing it on all the old Warner Bros. cartoons I used to watch when I was a kid. Crawford must have seen me through the crack because he told me to come in before I'd even knocked on the door. The office was good-sized, about what you'd expect for a captain on ship, and there were some framed museum posters up on the bulkhead and his rack was behind him, so I guess it was also his stateroom. He stood up and shook my hand man-to-man and said "Welcome, Tom Powers, I've heard good things about you," and that about knocked me over, not him saying he'd heard good things about me, but just saying my first name. There he was, one of the big guys on that monster ship, he could have sent me straight down to bread and water if he'd wanted to, and he was the first man in my almost one year of being in the Canoe Club to use my first name.

It probably sounds stupid to say it, I know, but I would have done anything for him after that, even though he had funny eyes with these really heavy lids that never seemed to blink and gave me this feeling that he could look right down to the bottom of what I was thinking and see all kinds of little white mice running around crazy and confused. He was tall and his hair was going gray, but he didn't have any gut or love handles at all, and he had to tuck his khaki shirt in all the way around to the back so that it didn't bunch up in front.

"You getting Keeler that curtain for his rack really meant a lot to him," he said after we sat down. "He's having a rough time with some things, being on ship for the first time… You know what I'm talking about. You're doing all right—he could probably learn from you. The Skipper says you're doing a great job running his office by yourself."

I just sat there listening, but I could almost feel my feet and ass lift off like I was about to start floating around.

He stretched out a little bit and said, "You know Keeler's on the Ward now down here. I think he just got overwhelmed with everything, but I know he's got what it takes to be a good sailor. I don't want to see him Med Boarded out. That'd be a shame. What he needs is a young guy his age who's making it to tell him that there's more to the Navy than this, just this floating around. You've been in the PI and I bet that keeps you and a lot of the other sailors going around here. I'd like you to talk to him about that. You don't have to get raunchy about it, just tell him this isn't going to last forever."

I wondered if he went around in the PI. He could probably buy a whole damn island on his Captain's pay. But, no way, he probably had a gorgeous wife and huge house back in San Dog with golden retrievers in the back-yard. It was embarrassing to think about him, a Navy doctor and a full bird, catting around Olongapo or Subic with some bar slut. I wanted to talk more, give him some regular guy chatter to pay him back for how he'd stroked me, but then he kind of cut me off by standing up all of a sudden, like he thought I was going to say something not nice about Keeler, and said, "Why don't you go over to the Ward and visit him? I'm sure he'd like to see you."

He walked me across the p-way to the Ward like he was afraid I might run off. It was real small and nothing compared to a regular hospital, with only six racks, but next to any berthing compartment it looked as super-clean and bright and big as a suite at the Hilton. The racks weren't even stacked three-deep like they were in the berthing. They were single-tier and spread out and painted blue and had fat mattresses and all six of them had a laid-out squid who didn't look real sick at all.

It took me a while to get over seeing everyone looking so comfy and tucked in and notice Keeler lying there behind a book with his foot sticking out of the blanket and wrapped in about sixty layers of bandages that made it look like this big invisible-man head was growing on the end of his leg.

He was reading the same *History of Western Philosophy* book that I'd seen him reading that time in the berthing, and he was so into it that his eyes didn't come off the page until Captain Crawford moved up closer and started checking over the bandaged foot. Keeler got this happy shine when he saw Crawford, like he was his sea daddy, but when he saw me behind the Doc his eyes went panicky-mad the same as when I'd seen him in the stall, like he thought I'd told the whole ship the real story about his foot. No way would I ever rat someone out like that, and him thinking I did just made me want to get out of there and not do another damn thing for him ever.

But Crawford brought me around like I was Keeler's friend. We both knew, Keeler and me, that it was BS, and then he left us alone and that just embarrassed me more than anything else, because we hadn't ever really talked at all and I'm sure he still thought I'd ratted him out for being a malingerer, which was the word for him I'd found when I was looking through the Uniform Code of Military Justice to see if there was an Article in there that covered someone hurting themselves to get out.

Him thinking I'd ratted kept working on me pretty strong, so I just said, "You're nuts if you think I told Crawford anything."

He acted kind of like he didn't know what I was talking about, but then he shrugged like it didn't matter anyway, and he tried to go back to his book and I was just going to leave it at that, but something kept us from breaking all the way off.

"Why would you want to come in the Navy if you read books like that?"

"I'm a pantheist."

"Is that some kind of religion where you cut your feet open?" Don't try to make me look stupid when you're the one can't hang being at sea a week.

His eyes flashed around. Then he eased up, shrugged again, and said, "It's not that I want to act snooty, but that's how people are around here when they see you reading. Like they hate you or something. I don't know what the fuck's up with them."

"Probably hard to work for Adolfson and not think everybody hates you. But he's just a jackass. Keep your head down—they don't make anyone stay with him for long, least not if they got anything going for them."

"I ain't never going back there," he said. His eyes were starting to steam. "You live like an animal, they treat you like a fucking animal. I must have been crazy, dropping out of school to join."

"Why did you?"

"Because everyone there dumped on the military. It's a college thing, that the only people who join, the enlisted people, are poor white trash or minorities. But then the fucking professors would go on about how we had to do more for the poor and people of color, and some kids'd do a protest... but if they joined the military it was the worst thing in the world. Slavery and—and fascism. Why'd you join?"

"I guess I got tired of living at home and not making enough with shit jobs to get my own place. Plus, I was sick of school. Sitting in a classroom was just useless to me. Now I wouldn't mind, put me in a classroom. But I still got three years left on contract."

"I'm gonna get out, but after that... I don't know if I'm going back to school right away."

"It's the pits floating around out here, no doubt about it, but maybe you ought to wait til we get back to the PI and you can see what that's about. The PI's crazy, man, women and beer up the yazoo. Not like San Dog at all."

"What's the PI?"

"Philippine Islands, man. Did you get any time there on your way out?"

"They flew me through Guam and Diego Garcia."

"There you go. Hang on til the PI, I'm telling you. Get you a girl..."

Keeler shook his head. "I'm finished, man. This ain't no way to live. Treat you like an animal, spit on you because you read. Those college fuckers may be soft, but this is crazy, it's just about hate and mindless control. How the fuck does democracy work, with the college fools and the assholes around here hating each other? You ever wonder about that?"

Too bad he didn't want to hear about the PI. But he was pretty hardcore against the Canoe Club at that point, didn't know anything except Adolfson and floating around, so nothing I could tell him was going to work.

Believe it or not, that same day I talked to Keeler in Sick Bay, the Joint Chiefs came out with a message ordering us out of the Arabian Sea and back to the Philippines for upkeep. Nobody went to sleep that night after the Old Man announced it. We all played poker or video games or watched the movies that the station ran all night in honor of us heading back, and I sat out on the catwalk that was outside my office and under the island and watched the sun cracking up through the dark ocean in the morning like this blazing huge bubble and thought so hard about my girlfriend Linzi back in the PI that I might have flogged my log right out there if flight ops hadn't started all of a sudden with Hornets screaming off the deck over my head.

We kind of sleepwalked through the next six days, but it was a good kind of sleepwalking, with a little cushion of air under us, not like when we'd been out forever and didn't know when we were going home. I'd be walking around or standing in the chow line with everything kind of blank, and then Zap! this little jolt would hit me out of nowhere to remind me that PI was only five, four, three or however many days away. Even though there were flight ops, nobody did much work because, goddamn, we'd been working twelve on, twelve off for over a hundred days out there, defending democracy and all that happy shit, and there just wasn't much left that we wanted to do except get our asses back to Subic. But I'll tell you one bunch that was working hard on the way back: the squids down in Sick Bay. They were working to make sure they weren't locked up on the Ward when we pulled in. The Sick Bay muster moved up to being the first thing I looked at in the morning after Keeler went in for his foot. There were five squids down on the list with him on his first day, and after we turned around and started back East, one guy would drop off the muster every day. First the suicidal squid, then the squid with appendicitis, then the squid with a kidney stone. Then there was a day when nobody got out, but the next day the Docs discharged two squids with hernias.

Then there was only Keeler left on the list with this squid named Hagan who had hemorrhoids. It was starting to look like Captain Crawford might not let Keeler out in time for the PI, and I had mixed feelings about that because I didn't want him to lose a foot trying to get out, or even be separated with a wacko discharge, and I really thought that if he made it to PI and found a woman that he'd have something to look forward to besides working for Adolfson. But I also felt like he'd kind of gypped the system, only been out to sea a week and then wimped out when all the rest of us non-book-reading slobs had put up with the worst of it for a lot longer. The last part was what kept me from going down to see him until he called me up.

I figured Keeler was probably getting desperate about missing the PI, and I was right. He wasn't reading when I walked in, he was staring up into the overhead with his arm across his forehead like he'd been blinded by all the crazy PI stories that were flying around the ship. He jackknifed straight off the bed when he saw me and threw his bandaged foot down on the deck like he was going to walk right out of there.

"Powers, maaaaaaan." He shook my hand and looked at me like one of those squids who was pulling duty our first night in Subic and was paying one-two hundred bucks to anyone willing to stand by for them. "You gotta do something for me. Captain Crawford says he'll let me off the first day we pull in, as long as someone comes with me on the buddy system, in case, you know, because of my foot."

That was worse to me than a squid asking me to take his duty, because I was a free ranger in the PI, I never buddied up with anybody over there. Nobody'd ever shown me around, and now that I'd been out a little and figured to have a girl waiting for me, I didn't want any clubfoot boot squid slowing me down. This bad picture of me and Keeler popped into my head, me and him going down the afterbrow.

"Dude, I can't be pushing you around in a wheelchair when I got a woman to hook up with."

"You crazy? I won't be in a fucking wheelchair. Look." He tried walking around on the bandaged foot like it was good as new, but he was really hobbling pretty bad. I couldn't see him making it ten feet off the gangway without me going back for help.

But, shit, in the end he talked me into it. It was probably just me feeling sorry for him again, but also he asked me a couple of questions about the PI, where I went, were there really as many girls out there as everyone said, that sort of thing, and when I told him I went up to Subic City instead of Olongapo like most of the other swinging Ds on board, his eyes went buggy like I was some kind of PI God, like he'd give up all his books and college to have one night of what I'd had up in Subic City. When you're a peon like I was, you can't believe how far you'll go for somebody who suddenly treats you like you're a big man.

I left and went over to Doc Crawford's office to tell him I'd take Keeler out, but he wasn't there and that was huge relief, and I took off like I was off the hook, a free man. But Keeler called me up later in the office and said he'd told Crawford I'd buddy up with him, and even though I didn't say anything, I was smoking mad. It was like I was all of a sudden expected to be this nurse, a fucking nurse when all the Navy'd done up to that point was treat me like I was seven years old. And that was how I talked myself into ditching Keeler when the Connie finally made it back to Subic. If Keeler had just asked me himself, I would have gone along with it. But with Crawford acting like it was my job to keep Keeler in the Canoe Club... I'd just given the Navy a hundred and ten days at sea, and now I was going to let them bust up my liberty?

I brought my civvies up to my office the night before we pulled in so there wouldn't be any chance of Keeler finding me in the berthing in the morning. Then he called me a couple of times to try and get me to set up where we were going to meet, and I told him I had to do some work for the Old Man and didn't know right off, and after the second time he called and

I didn't commit I could hear this panicky little tremble in his voice that suddenly went bitter because he knew, even though he didn't say it, that I was dodging him. After that he kept calling like he was desperate, like I was his only hope of getting off that damn ship in the morning, and when I couldn't take talking to him anymore, after Taps, I let the phone ring-ring-ring until finally I just got out of there and pretty much wandered around the ship for the rest of the night.

We moored in the morning and everybody went nuts. It sounded like a cowboy had just opened a gate and fired off a round and a million cattle were stampeding out, and I jumped through a hatch and ran across the Hangar Bay not even thinking about Keeler and pushed through the crowd and saluted the Ensign at the top of the brow and then piled down and whooped like a goddamn hyena when I hit the pier, and took off running. I couldn't believe how fast I was moving, like the speed of freedom was faster than a hornet screaming up into the blue sky after clearing the flight deck when you've been cooped up in a birdfarm forever. It didn't matter if I was riding in a taxi or changing my Andy Jacksons into pesos or walking out the Naval Station main gate and over the Shit River bridge, it felt like I was just blazing along. Then I caught the very first jeepney up to Subic City, and the driver didn't even wait the way drivers usually did, until there were so many squids jammed in you could see the wax in the ear of the joker next to you, he just took off down the road and up around the steep hill that had this blue view of Subic Bay right near the top that made you want to get out and dive off the hillside down into the water just to see if it felt as good as it looked, like it could turn you into a dolphin, and then through this jungle where I'd seen these kids once with sticks chasing a monkey with arms twice as long as its legs, and then, then, Subic City, just this dirt road running between some crappy saloons under a hot blue sky, no neon at all, just wood and maybe stucco and no sidewalks except for two by fours or sometimes these sheets of plywood laid out between the bars, and muddy as a swamp when it rained, and with girls in bikinis or little terry robes standing outside yelling at us, outnumbering us ten to one probably, when we rumbled into town.

Caligula's was my place because my girlfriend Linzi was the bookkeeper there, and even though we'd only been together a few days after the first time I'd gone up to Subic City, we'd been through a lot. Not anyone dying or anything, but she was down on Americans when I'd first met her because she'd had a couple of kids with a Marine who'd wound up marrying an Americana back in the States, and I wasn't real big on her either in the beginning, there were other girls better looking or with bigger scoobs ready to jump in my lap and I'd thought I might want to shop around, but I found out that I liked being with Linzi after we'd banged the first time and then she came around and we did some bar-hopping together, and then I was telling her I wanted to get a place for us out in town so she wouldn't have to live in her piece-of-shit room over the bar that only had this grungy mattress on the floor for a bed. We got up one morning, not knowing it would be our last time together, and she rode back down to the base with me and there were hot rumors flying around that the Connie was getting under-way and I felt desperate, told Linzi I wanted to marry her, like that was going to get her on ship with me, and we hugged and she ran away back over the bridge like me leaving was as tough for her as it was for me, and...

I don't know if I figured Linzi would wait for me, but after I'd been at sea so long I started thinking everyone, Linzi most of all, was just going to be so happy and grateful to see me when the ship got back because of what I'd been through. I never, ever thought she wouldn't be waiting for me at Caligula's when I walked in, but of course she wasn't. There were four girls sitting around the bar drinking Coke and playing pool on the two tables and waiting for the squids to come in, and they came up on me all interest-ed until I started asking questions about Linzi, and one of them playing pool said she'd gone back to Baguio because her boyfriend on the Connie had been gone so long she knew he butterfly on her. The girl playing pool kept watching me and then she knew I was the boyfriend and I thought that might make her mad, like Linzi was her friend, but she came over and handed me a cue and ran her hand through my hair like she was definitely interested. But I couldn't shake this feeling that Linzi would walk in any second and I had to be a straight arrow for her after leaving her behind for so long, and that's how I acted up to when other squids started coming into the bar and the girl knew I was a lost cause by then and took her cue back and moved on. I just started downing beers after that and playing pool and losing a few bucks to the girls and some of the squids because I didn't want to be sober and by myself with this huge sucking chest wound from know-ing Linzi wasn't coming back.

The last thing I remembered was being in a jeepney and talking and there was just this squid and his girlfriend on board with me and I didn't know what they were thinking but they were acting scared, like I was some kind of public menace, and I stood up trying to show them what a nice wor-thy guy I was and then something, the driver I guess, hit me right between the shoulder blades and knocked me flying out the back of the jeepney into this dark dirt road. I crawled around for a while, not knowing where I was, and then I just didn't care anymore and I laid down and felt my cheek press down against all these sharp little pebbles in the dirt... And then I was back on the Connie in my muddy civvies with a headache like a throbbing light bulb stuck behind my eyes and some squid eyeballing me through a crack in my curtain and yakking in my ear.

It was Keeler and he would not shut up and finally I told him to get the fuck out like I wanted him to leave, but he thought I'd said it because I didn't believe what he was saying and so he kept on going, wanting to convince me. Captain Crawford had let him off after all and he'd met some girl out in town, and with Linzi gone I damn sure didn't want to hear about that, I didn't want to hear about some other squid getting laid, but he was talking like, underneath what he was saying, he was trying to thank me for telling him about the PI, like I was his PI godfather or something. Then he started pinging on me to go in town with him and meet his girlfriend, and shit, I didn't even know what day it was, and finally I told him I'd go after I slept a little bit longer. He left and I fell asleep, but then he came back and I could only see this one blue eye staring at me through the crack like I wasn't going to get rid of him again, and I must have slept for a while because the light bulb behind my eyes was turned off and not throbbing as bad.

I said okay but figured I could get rid of him if I took my time, so I showered and put on some fresh civvies and changed the sheets on my rack and then I went down to the Mess Decks to get some chow, but Keeler hung on and kept talking the whole time and never took the hint that me not talking might mean that I wouldn't have minded us just being fucking quiet, and it was all about his girlfriend, on and on, and finally I just turned on my jamming frequency, hardly heard a word of it, until we were off the boat and walking down Magsaysay, out in Olongapo.

It was late afternoon and the sidewalks were full of squids trolling around with beers in their hands and that was the last situation I wanted to be in, walking around town with a million other squids, but it actually wasn't that bad because there were just as many women out. I don't mean bar girls, just regular women who had places to go, and a lot of the young ones wearing these plaid Catholic school dresses were holding hands for protection but at the same time slipping us these sly little looks on the side like they were trying to figure out who the good guys were, who they could trust, even though they'd probably have run like hell if any of us had actually stopped to talk to them. I must have made eye-contact with fifty women out there that way, and that's what finally woke me up and made me aware of things, especially that I still hadn't gotten laid since we'd pulled in, and I looked at Keeler walking next to me and thought Shit, he's still around, and started listening to him, hoping we were heading to the bar where he'd found his girlfriend. He was walking without much of a limp and wearing this big basketball shoe with the laces pulled out on his bandaged foot, and he was also toting a carton of Marlboro Reds. When we were way down Magsaysay and had passed most of the big bars and there weren't many squids left around us, I asked him where the bar was where his girlfriend worked.

"I told you she doesn't work in a bar," he said, like I was a pain in the ass for not listening.

"Where does she work?"

"Man, she doesn't work, I just told you."

That made me mad, made me feel like a dumbass, but the guy was just rattling on. Anyone who'd even listened to ten percent of what he'd been saying would have wanted to stuff a sock in his mouth by then.

Finally we cut off Magsaysay and hiked up this steep road and I was thinking he was going to get us rolled or killed. There was hardly anyone else around and it was getting dark, and when we made it to the top we were standing across from these dark gray concrete shells without roofs that looked like little houses in the middle of being built. But they were deserted and there wasn't any lumber or building materials around, so I guess they could have also been just abandoned. And then in a couple of the shells I saw some blankets laid out and a lot of beer bottles lying around like it was some kind of skid row, PI style. I told Keeler, "You got women all over the place back in the bars, so what the hell is up here? There's no women, just a bunch of stew bums."

We walked around the edge of the site, under this big sign that said "KEEP OUT" in English and a bunch of stuff in Tagalog, and it was almost dark and I could see the glow from fires and smell the burning, and Keeler turned into one shell and we came up against this tall Filipino standing in a doorway with a mop of hair and a big ugly sore on his cheek and a cig blazing and a mean look that only relaxed when Keeler slipped the carton of cigs into his hand. He stepped aside and I followed Keeler and for some reason it looked like the guy was only half there and I stared at him and saw the right sleeve of his shirt lying flat, like he was missing an arm. He didn't like me looking so hard and turned right out the door hiding his armless side and smoking and with his meanness looking pathetic now that we both knew he only had one arm.

I don't know exactly what I expected to find in the shell behind the one-armed guy, but I know it wasn't a gorgeous woman breast-feeding a baby and an old granny sucking a cig in her caved-in mouth and staring flat ahead with these shiny little black button eyes like she was blind. They were sitting around this fat candle and there was some food spread out on a blanket on the floor, bread and gallon water jugs and Oscar Meyer sandwich meat and ketchup and a veggie tray and four boxes of Pop Tarts that Keeler must have picked up for them from the commissary on base, and they hadn't made but a couple of sandwiches by the look of how much there was left of the bread and meat, but the Pop Tarts were almost all gone. I was thinking it was some kind of crazy college Peace Corps thing that Keeler was doing, taking food to a needy family, and how they were living was awful, but all I wanted to do was get laid and the gorgeous woman breastfeeding the kid was turning me on and making me feel like a perv, and I just told Keeler I didn't have time for this Peace Corps crap, that's exactly what I told him, even though I know I should have just choked back the words, even if they'd poisoned me.

Keeler flashed back at me as angry as I ever saw him. "This is my family, man. Bonnie's my woman and this is my family."

He bent over and kissed Bonnie and they looked at each other and she gave him this tiny, surprised, kind of embarrassed smile that was still like someone turning a light on, and then she gently pulled the baby from around her nipple and Granny reached to take him and Bonnie stood up with this dignity and smoothing her blue dress and wanting to ignore me but not being able to completely do it, and enjoying how amazed and knocked-out I was that you could find that kind of beauty in such a shithole. Then she went with him around the corner to another room and they lit a candle and I looked at Granny, who had given the baby a Pop Tart to gnaw on, and I wanted to get the hell out of there to avoid Keeler throwing any more guilt on me, but I figured that one Americano trying to get back to the main drag by himself might be tough with all the stew bums around.

I could hear them banging away in that other room, both of them moaning and groaning, but most of all that beautiful thuk-thuk-thuk sound of the mamba filling the joyhole, and just thinking of a woman like Bonnie getting the snot banged out of her was enough to give me a stiffy right there in front of old blind granny and the baby. Fucking Keeler! I'd ditched him and look what he'd come up with while I was getting stupid drunk over Linzi. I wanted to go around there with him banging her and say Fuck you, pal, I'm out of here, and have fun taking care of the whole family—

Granny, the kid, One Arm, whoever he is. But I couldn't do it, I didn't know what I'd do if I saw him getting his with me so hard up. I might have beat his ass and taken her away from him. Bonnie was that gorgeous.

That all finally made me mad enough to get out of there, fight every bum in Shit City on the way back down to Magsaysay if I had to. I charged out through the doorway and bumped against something that fell real easy and just flopped down on the ground and had a hard time getting up. It was the one-armed guy. I was like Fuck you at first, but then I heard him crying like he was hurt and that took all the juice out of me and I had to go back, and I did and I helped him up with his one arm and then out of nowhere these lights blazed on all over Shit City, big flood lights, and Filipinos in military or cop blue uniforms and clutching machine guns were hustling around talking in low, hard voices like it was a drug raid.

I was scared shitless, I thought it really was a drug raid, that Keeler, the college puke druggie, went up there to buy his stash from the bums and had hooked up with Bonnie along the way. It flashed on me how the cops were probably going to throw me into a little bamboo cage for twenty years and feed me fish heads and rice through the bars, and they were on my left so I turned right to run, but then they got hold of One Arm and pulled him with plastic gloves on their hands and he fell down and they all dog-piled on top of him with their machine guns in his face or ribs like he was really dangerous, and I just stopped dead without jumping in because I thought they were going to start blazing on the poor guy, and I yelled, "Holy shit, don't shoot him! Don't shoot!"

Two cops came up and shoved me back, clutching their guns sideways and up around their chins so that all I could see was their eyes. I tried to hold my ground and watch between them to make sure the other bastards didn't kill One Arm, and one of my cops brought the butt of his gun up on my temple and tried to turn my head away and I grabbed the butt and pushed it down on him so that the barrel must have hit him in the face. It was really stupid, I have to admit, but who the fuck did they think they were, doing that to an American who was just trying to make sure they didn't kill this pathetic one-armed guy? Anyway, the cop didn't like me shoving the gun down on him, and his partner brought his gun down and stuck it so hard in my side that he cracked one of my ribs, and then the other guy came back at me swinging his butt in my face, and he missed, but I lost my balance dodging it and feeling the stab of that rib and went down.

Then I heard Keeler roaring. I was on my ass holding my side and trying to breath through wherever the rib was stuck and I looked up and a bunch of cops were locked on his arms and dragging him out of the shell in his skivvies. Him putting up a fight that way with me on the ground made me feel useless, and then they must have smacked him hard, knocked him out or something, because he just stopped in the middle of yelling and they threw him down next to me and he hit the dirt and slithered around. Then I heard people whimpering behind me and I turned around and saw Bonnie moving in the middle of all these cops, holding her baby and kind of crouched down to protect it and with her beautiful face all seized up and crying at how her whole world, that shitty, awful world, had been turned upside down.

I couldn't do squat to help her. I was just trying to figure out how to breathe with that broken sword sliding around inside me, and I kept figuring that the cops would drag us away next, take us to those bamboo cages and tell the Navy we'd been busted for drugs. But they all left, and when it finally felt like they'd really gone I started talking to Keeler to see how he was, telling him we had to get out of there. He was laid out flat on his stomach and didn't answer me, and I was hoping he wasn't hurt bad. The cops had left on a couple of flood lights and dust was still floating around so thick that I wondered how I could breathe without choking, and I crawled over to where I could see Keeler's face. His eyes were wide open and at first I thought he was dead, and that made me stand up because I'd never been around a dead person, not even at a funeral, but then he blinked and I'd never felt so relieved in my whole life, it was like maybe I'd been dead myself. The cracked rib pain didn't bother me for a while after that.

But it was hell trying to get Keeler up on his feet and going. He acted like he wanted to be dead, with Bonnie gone. He kept saying her name whenever I told him how our asses were going to be grass even if the cops didn't come back, because I could still see some bums sliding around the shells out of the light with these hungry looks on their faces, like they were trying to see if we were hurt enough for them to take us. Why the fuck hadn't the cops dragged them away?

I got so mad at Keeler for not wanting to get out of there that I acted like I was leaving and told him, "I'm not getting killed up here for you being mixed up in some drug deal."

That brought him all the way up like a rocket and he grabbed me around the collar with both hands and I hurt too bad to fight much besides squirm and that felt lame, so all I could do in the end was stare at him real hot from four inches away like he'd have to kill me if he didn't want me coming after him when my rib healed. But he wasn't a killer and he knew pretty quick that I was hurt, but he started yelling at me with wet eyes and his hot breath and spit all over my damn face like this dog slobbery fog, and then I went blank when I put together what he was saying.

"The cops said they were lepers, man! That's why they took them away with those gloves on their hands. They told me they're taking them to this fucking island where the lepers go."

"Shit. Shit. How'd you... hook up with them?"

"They needed me." His eyes wandered off over my shoulder. "Bonnie was standing in front of this dusty little food shop down in town looking at stuff in the window. Everything else... everybody else was moving fast, they were walking along past her or going in or out of the shop. But she was just stopped in the middle of them. I stopped to talk to her and she didn't want to for a while, like she was embarrassed, but then she said she wanted to buy some of the canned milk that was in the window. She didn't say she didn't have the money, but I knew, man, I knew. I bought some cans for her and followed her back up. Here."

Keeler let go of me and I slid down to my knees and that rib must have speared my heart, it hurt so bad. I don't know how long I was on the ground, but after the pain had laid down a bit I told him that he'd done the right thing for Bonnie, even though I couldn't help thinking about how his damn mamba was probably going to fall off from her having leprosy.

He didn't answer, he just went back into the shell and walked around. He was limping when he came out, like the foot was really bothering him again. "She should have told me," he said. "I wouldn't have cared." He stared at me. "I wouldn't have fucking cared!"

Long story short, we finally made it out of there. We started out with me in the worst shape, walking real slow, but after a while Keeler was complaining like hell about his foot and by the time we were close to the main drag, he could hardly walk and we had to put his arm around my neck to keep him up until a jeepney picked us up out on Magsaysay.

Captain Crawford put Keeler back in Sick Bay the next day. Even though he told me he was going to get out and find Bonnie, wherever she was, he never made it off the Connie again. Then he started reading Bertrand Russell again down on the Ward and one day out of the blue, when we were still in the PI, I asked him if they were going to let him out. He just called me an ignorant fuck and put his book up in front of his face, and that was pretty much the end of us, and about a week later they flew him back to the States for a medical discharge.

19.

20.

21.

22.

23.

24.

19) 11th Street, New York
20) 96th Street, New York
21) Berwick Street, London
22) Sussex Gardens, London
23) Bleeker Street, New York
24) Astor Place, New York

I'LL CHANGE COMPLETELY
THREE LINKED STORIES

by STEPHEN ELLIOTT

I.

OTHER DESIRES

Just promise me your devotion.

Sometimes when my phone rings I try to hide in my own apartment. I close the blinds. The phone rings in the front of the studio near the window and I crawl toward the end of my mattress, where the walls meet. While the phone rings I push into the corner and the sheets slide beneath my feet and then the mattress and I'm lying on the wood floor staring into the ceiling which is a web of thick steel beams and spotted white plaster. And when the phone stops ringing I go to check who it is. It's always her.

Early in the morning before I leave for work, I press the play button on the answering machine. Ambellina's thick, steady voice wakes me.

Understand that this decision was hastened by the feeling I get that you need someone to offer protection, love and discipline. I know that you're afraid. But I will keep you safe. Honesty is so important in this relationship. I don't do things in halves. You can call me when you feel jealous, uncertain, or insecure. Please arrange to meet me on Saturday. You can lay your head in my lap then.

"Any letters from your girlfriend?" Valeria asks. It's 6:45 in the morning. I have a headache. I hate myself. We're on the two Internet kiosks in the front of the store. The small round tables have all been wiped down and the blue rags thrown in the sink. The newspapers are stacked beneath the advertisements taped to the wall next to the coffee lids. The bagels are sitting in baskets on three slanted shelves behind the glass.

"Shut up," I say. "Put on the coffee." Valerie has pink hair and she likes to get high. We've worked together in this bagel shop for three years now, since I came here from Chicago. This is the question she always asks and this the answer I always give her, to get up, to change the cauldrons, to unbolt the front door and invite in another working day.

Valerie bounces to Sly and the Family Stone as our first customers arrive, spinning around the large square cutting block. "Do you think it's better to play bass or drums?" she asks. "Because if you play bass then you're in front and everybody sees you. But if you play drums you stay in shape and let out all that anger."

"Bass," I tell her.

The first orders are to-go orders, toasted rolls, egg bagels with dill cream cheese, tall coffees and lattes for people scrambling to trains. Later, people start to sit down. We puts the tubs back in the refrigerator. Valerie switches the music to Eighties new wave. "Such a wonderful person," she sings, raising her fists over her head, swinging them forward from her elbows. "But you've got problems." There are two rooms and a thin hallway between them. The workers, students, and professionals sit in front near the windows. The junkies and the criminals sit in the back. We let them. They hang out by the fire exit and the restroom with the hookers from Folsom Street who break into the bins in front of the chocolate factory at night. The prison bus stops only two blocks away. The dealers hang out on 16th Street and two doors down in the shooting gallery. I stare at them while pouring the beans into the grinder. The click of the phone. The cauldrons lean forward. The whir of the machine crushing the beans. The tap of the espresso filter. The junkies nod toward the Formica. Valerie's boyfriend, Philc, hangs back there with them, juggling ketchup packets, mini-hypodermics hanging from his ears, wearing a thick spiked collar around his neck. He's always dirty. He likes to brag about his skills with a knife. He says he was a knife thrower with the circus. He sleeps in the shopping cart encampment under the overpass. He steals from the junkies when they sleep.

Bell comes to my apartment at 8 P.M. I've washed the smell of coffee and lox from my hair, cleaned beneath my nails. I've changed clothes. There's a bowl of caramel popcorn on the table because that is what she likes. "My husband knows," she says. She walks deliberately, one boot in front of the other. "Yeah, I told him." She sits on the couch, leans forward first with her fists on her knees and then leans back as I assume my position. She's eating the popcorn. She's drinking white wine from my only glass. Between the small couch and the table I am on the floor on my knees with my head in her lap. "You don't mind, do you? That he knows?" I shake my head, rub my cheek on the fabric of her skirt, feel her fingers moving on my head, deciding what they are going to do. There is only the way she wants the question to be answered. She wants me to be jealous and yanks my head by my hair. I breathe heavily when her grip tightens and she twists her knuckles, sending small pins of pain along my skull. My mouth opens. "What?" she asks. She slaps me. "What do you want to say?" She lets go of my hair and reclines. I stare into her chest, the lines on the country of her body. "My husband doesn't want you to see these." She pushes her breasts together with her forearms. "That's what he asked. These are his favorite." She puckers her lips. She's wearing a thin black negligee. When she's not holding them her breasts slide toward her elbows. They are big, but not firm. More importantly, I don't care about her husband. "Look at me," she says. "Look at me." Bell has a broad face and a wide, flat nose. "You're pouting." I nod. "Didn't I tell you I would protect you? What are you so worried about?" Her hands are large. Everything about her is large. I close my eyes then the slaps come, back and forth, until I cry and still more. "Shut up," she hisses. "Shut up. Don't cry. Don't cry. You're mine. Don't cry." And when she stops and her hand slides away from my face I lower my head. I duck carefully toward her. I try to burrow into her, under her skirt, to be inside of her. It's still early. There will be hours more of this. And I will pretend to be jealous of her husband, who may or may not exist. Because it's important to her that I be jealous, so I am, because she likes it.

I met Bell on an online personals board for people with *other desires*. Places filled with leather-clad professionals who charge more for an hour together than I make in a week, and lonely housewives who say they want to *try something new*. The boards use black backgrounds and are suggestive of something wild. A whip hangs in the left corner of the screen. They give you a form to fill out when you join. They ask you what you're into: Eurologia (piss play), Collar and Lead, Smothering, Vibrators, Pain, Asphyxiaphilia (breath play), Amputees, Electrotorture, Fisting, Tongues, Ears, Feet, Cross Dressing, Humiliation, 24/7, Cling Film, Erotic Email Exchange, Cock and Ball Torture. The list goes on and on. They ask your role: dominant, submissive, switch. They ask how often you think about the lifestyle. Twice a week they send you Love Dog Reports. It's all angles, women next to punching bags, free pornographic sites that aren't free. Everybody wants to know your real email so they can put you on their list. It's mostly men using the site. There are discussion boards and the men's names are blue and the women's pink and couples are green, but even the women are most likely men. And then Bell who posted no picture and whose ad read *East Bay Woman looking for a toy to abuse. Must be full-time. No equivocating.* And I responded by saying I would be her toy, full-time. I sent her a picture. I said that she would be my only commitment and I didn't think she would respond but she did. And the bookstores with all of their trade paperbacks and Eric Stanton artwork saying that it's OK to be weird, to accept who we are. It's fun, they say, to play during sex. To tie each other up and take control. It's just sex. It's just a game. Trade places, let off some steam. I was raped the first time by a middle-aged caseworker in a small green room in the Chicago Juvenile Detention Facility. The windows were closed and the room was dusty and hot and filled with stacks of yellowing, creased paper forced into wide brown envelopes. He didn't ask me if it was OK and he didn't apologize afterward. When I masturbate at night I think of him, not of his image, or his sour smell, just the darkness and the fear and the pain. I've never stopped fantasizing about it, replaying it in my mind. And that's what I think about when Bell buckles into her strap-on and pushes me over the table, her thick hand around my neck closing my windpipe, the weight of her wide hips pressing against me. It hurts. "Poor Theo," she says to me, her nails biting into my back. "My little Tolstoy. You just want to hide here." And I nod because when I don't nod the beatings will start again.

The fog is pouring over Twin Peaks into the Mission. It tumbles down the hillside blanketing the small white houses. In Chicago the buildings are mountains but here the hills are real. The wind cuts down the streets. In a few hours the city will be gray. They're running elections for District Super-visor and the streets are peppered in slogans. Daly for Tenants Rights. Cheng for Change. Men are selling paperbacks next to Macondo and Kilo-watt. The cardboard placards fly down the street. I'm standing at a pay-phone next to the movie theater, across from the Copy King where I pick up my mail. It's five o'clock. People are stepping off and onto trains, getting home from work.

I hold my collar tight around my neck. "I can't meet you," Bell says. It was so warm the other day. When the fog pushes in the valley gets cold. She does this. She cancels on me a lot. She wants to know what I'm wearing. She wants to talk sexy. "Get me off," she says. "Imagine me hitting you. Imag-ine the phone between my legs. I'm sitting on your face. I'm smothering you. You can't breathe."

"I'm on a payphone," I say. "People can see me."

"Are you ashamed?" she asks.

"Yes," I respond.

"That's your problem. Have Friday open for me."

"Bell, I can't."

"You what?"

"I have to work."

A bus has stopped in front of me and the driver is out in the street pulling frantically on the cables, his passengers staring through the win-dows.

"Do you know how many submissives answered my ad?" She waits for my answer. "Do you know how many men there are like you, who want a strong woman to keep them in place? Do you think you're the only one I could have? There's thousands of men like you. I get letters every day."

"I'm sorry."

"Do you think I care about that?" she asks. There's a long pause, like she's considering what to say next. "Listen. You will see me when I want to see you. You will make time for me when I tell you to. You will," she says. "You will." Then she hangs up on me. I place my fingers against my fore-head and try to block out the sounds of the city, the shoes on the pavement and the sewers. I lean against the Currency Exchange and sit down for a sec-ond on the sidewalk.

Valerie is running from the cauldrons to the toaster, a bright, pink flash of light. I take over the espresso machine and she shoves a square tub of peanut butter forward and I grab it before it smacks the side of the machine. "Back so soon?" she asks. One click, one shot. Two clicks. Bagels at the toaster. Jam. Cream cheese.

"I'm taking a cigarette break," Valerie says. She stands in the fire exit with a cigarette looking back at the counter to make sure a line doesn't form. There's never been a fire here. She's thirty-five and twice married. She dresses like a schoolgirl with her pink pigtails but the creases around her mouth and her eyes give it away. She wears turquoise pantyhose intentionally torn at the calf. I slice three sections of onion and stick my hand into the caper bin. We used to go to concerts together before Philc started coming around. Now she has one arm crossed over her chest holding her elbow. Philc has a small BMX bike as high as my knees and he is standing on the front wheel of it now, bouncing near the muffin boxes. "Check this out," he says to Valerie, swinging the little bicycle under his leg.

"That's so good, Philc."

I think I expressly said I was looking for a sub in my ad. If you are now my sub, then by definition I am your mistress. Please address me accordingly. Forget about Friday if it is such a hassle. I shall see you in a few weeks.

Pat owns a string of bagel shops but this one was his first. They used to make the bagels next door, but now that's a photo studio and the bagels are baked in a warehouse near Portrero Hill. The store was opened in the Sixties, a gathering spot for protestors. We have a news article framed on the wall above the ATM and it's a picture of a young Pat on a stage speaking to an enormous crowd on a grass lawn with university buildings in the background. The headline reads, *Students say, Not Our War!* He comes in while we're closing. He likes to tell us stories of San Francisco's past. "You used to get a lid of grass for twenty dollars. You could have sex with a thirteen-year-old girl and when her mom asked about it you did her too."

"I doubt it," Valerie says.

I lock the door for the night and Pat sparks a joint. I take a hit and hand it to Valerie. We're tired. We've been on our feet all day.

"Yeah, well. I exaggerate sometimes. Keeps life interesting." Pat folds his hands across his large stomach and lets out a sigh. Valerie's laugh is like a birdsong. "Fucking Reagan. Here's your war on drugs." Pat takes a long smoke and leans his head back, smoke gurgling out between his lips and dribbling up his face. A fifty-year-old hippie in a tie-die shirt and blue jeans. He's probably worth a million bucks.

Report in immediately. I'm waiting.

At the Dress-for-Less I tell the saleslady I'm buying underwear for my girlfriend and she asks me what size my girlfriend is and I say, "Oh, she's about my size."

The apartment's never clean enough for Bell. I don't own very much but what I have lacks character. Just white space. I live on the third floor and dust seems to collect from the windows. I have new dust every day. She told me to prepare her something to eat so I bought chicken breasts and spinach at the Bi-Rite and they're ready for her but she doesn't seem hungry. "Did you get any wine?" I pour her a glass of wine. Hand it to her. Kneel down in front of her. She smells thick, like milk and brown sugar. "Amuse me," she says. I look around my own apartment. It's a foreign place. There is nothing here. I have a small television on a short, dark stand. No computer. I have a Monopoly game, a table, a mattress, a small couch, a phone, an answering machine with blue buttons. I don't even know how I amuse myself. "Are you trying to manipulate me?" Bell asks. "Is this what I want or what you want?"

I flinch when Ambellina raises her hand. I close my eyes and wait. They said I had a twitch as a child. Out in the woods by the border of Wisconsin, miles from the nearest hitchhiking road, surrounded by big brown trees, trunks as thick as truck tires, is a home called Prairie View. All the doors are locked and you have to ask permission just to use the bathroom. They run it on a point system. In CYS they pull a paper bag with a smiley face over your head if they think you're getting angry. Henry Horner Children's Adolescent Center on the grounds of Reed Mental Hospital uses time-out rooms, drugged Kool-Aid, and straps you to a bed when things get out of hand. Thorazine was big for kids in the Eighties. They never let you speak in court. They keep log books full of your flaws. Pass notes about you back and forth, from social worker to caseworker to therapist to hospital intern. They never let you read what they've written.

I want to tell Ambellina something, but I don't trust her. She squeezes the handcuffs closed on my wrists. She also has a blindfold, which she places over my eyes. She runs tape over my mouth and I start to shake my head no and scream but it's just muffled and she's telling me to shut up again but I can't. I knock into the wall. Bang my head against the wall. Everything inside of me is rushing forward and stopping in front of that big wad of tape. She pins me with her leg while she chains my ankles. I'm telling myself not to scream but as I struggle the handcuffs get tighter cutting the circulation to my wrists. I keep screaming these strange, muffled sounds into this tape. I can't control myself. My mouth fills with glue. And she's slapping me and then punching me. "Stop it," she says, reaching between my legs, squeezing hard, her fist landing against my eye. "Stop it." It's like glass, like a car crash, like being held underwater and drowning.

I'm on the floor and Bell is on the mattress. My face is between her legs when she rips the tape off my mouth. I feel the skin of her thighs. It feels warm and it feels like it is everywhere around me and I'm floating and breathing somehow in this dark pool. "Do you want me to take the blindfold off?" she asks and I whisper, no. But it hardly comes out so I shake my head no and she touches my hair. I'm damp. I feel her body moving around me and the dark room. I feel safe. She says something about her child. A girl. She sounds sad but I can't make out what she's saying. Something about her husband and her child. She's very sad about something.

In the morning Valerie has a black eye and I do too. She's stacking plates. I heft a forty-pound sack of beans from beneath the counter. Somebody knocks on the door and then runs away. We're still closed. My body hurts and I feel like I will never get better.

"I don't want to talk about it," Valerie says. Valerie's black eye spreads down her cheekbones where it becomes yellow. She shakes her head.

We're done setting up. It's seven o'clock. Neither of us makes a move to open the door. A lady in black pants, a white shirt, and a blazer is knocking. Valerie stares at her but doesn't do anything. Valerie shouldn't worry. This is our cafe. I pull out a rag and rub down the display case. The lady knocks harder and pulls on the handle, *cack cack cack*, as the deadbolt rattles through the plate glass. "She doesn't need any coffee," I say. "She's already awake."

But Valerie goes to the door and lets the woman in. The woman has a tight face that pulls forward to the tip of her nose, her skin stretched over the hollows of her cheeks, her mouth small and circular. She looks from Valerie to me, sees our black eyes, and decides not to say anything more than "One large coffee please." She looks at her thin, gold watch. "I'm late," she says helplessly.

The lady leaves but more people follow and Valerie and I run back and forth, turning the crank that keeps the shop operating. The junkies fill up the back room. We pour old espresso into the ice coffee jug, stack orange juice and mini-containers full of lox spread and whitefish salad. Philc comes in at some point. He pushes the girl with the tattooed face who is on the nod at the table near the dishbin. "Get up," he says. "You owe me a soup packet." She doesn't answer and he says, "I'll cut you." He's rummaging through her bags, a black garbage bag and a Barbie Doll lunchbox.

"Theo."

A line of customers is forming in the front of the store. But I'm watching Philc and when he realizes I'm watching him and that Valerie is watching him he jumps up and spreads his arms in the middle of the floor.

"Ta-da!" he says. He does a dance step where he walks a perfect square. Then he tries to walk behind the counter but I stop him with the broom.

"You can't come back here. You don't work here."

"What are you doing?" he asks me, his face turning red, throwing his hand slightly forward and spreading his fingers, like he is letting go of something or stretching his hand and that I should be wary.

"What are you doing?" Valerie asks.

"He doesn't belong behind the counter," I say to Valerie and her black eye and back to Philc who is looking at the floor now and rummaging in his jacket pocket for the handle to something.

I poke Philc in the sternum with the broom. A small man with sand colored dreadlocks behind him says, "Say man. Could you buzz me into the bathroom?"

"You think you could take me, bro?" Philc asks, turning his head ninety degrees into his shoulder, crunching his ear against his collar bone, then walking away from me, slapping a fist into his palm. He walks straight back to the emergency exit muttering, "You think you could take me?"

Philc kicks open the emergency exit. It opens to a small yard filled with garbage and recycling.

"C'mon," Philc says, standing next to the bathroom door, biting at his lips.

"Get out of here."

"You're not part of this," he tells me. He raises his boot and lowers it as hard as he can onto the foot of the girl with the tattooed face and she wakes up with a loud scream and falls to the floor holding her foot. Philc pulls a rock out, whips it past my shoulder and a bottle of syrup breaks. He runs up and puts a foot into the glass display case.

"You don't belong here."

"You don't belong here," he answers me back as the front door closes behind him. The girl in the back has curled into a ball and is making small, high pitched noises. Glass and syrup are everywhere. And it's just glass and syrup but I don't know what to do about it.

I look over at Valerie and she's crying so hard she's choking. She looks like a mermaid, her pink hair, all those tears.

We've closed up. Pat is coming to look at the damage. Pat knows, with all of his talk of revolution, this is junkie central. The cost of doing business. I'm cleaning up the glass and mopping the syrup. There's glass in the bagels, so I throw all of them away. Valerie straightens the countertop, dumps out the coffee that's getting old and starting to burn, fastens the cap on the purple onions sliced from this morning. Picks up the pastries and throws them away.

"That's where you get that black eye," Valerie says. "You like to fight. You like to pick fights. You like to pick fights with people's boyfriends." She's still puffy-faced and red. I make an espresso because I suddenly feel tired.

"No," I say. "That's not how I got this."

"Fuck you, Theo," she says. "Fuck you and your problems."

I'm wearing women's underwear and leather pants at the 16th Street BART station, worried that someone will see me when Bell gets off the train. We walk back three blocks to my apartment, past the liquor stores and the transient hotels. Men with blankets on their shoulders huddle between doorways next to the Quick Mart. "You should have gotten me a cab," she says. There's been a fire in the red building on Van Ness. It was a single resident occupancy and spraypainted on the brick is Death To Landlords. "I'm in marriage counseling. You didn't know that." Bell pulls out a cigarette. She never smoked before. She shakes her head. I almost tell her that I was married once to a girl I met in college. How I got thrown out of the abortion clinic downtown. But I think better of it. Because she'd want to know why, or she wouldn't want to know at all. And anyway years have passed. And this is today. "I have a daughter." She hands me her lighter and I light her cigarette for her. She blows the smoke in my face. "Yesterday, in front of our counselor, I told my husband I was leaving him." She stops and I stop with her. She doesn't even seem to care that I almost kept walking. "What do you think will happen to my little girl? Answer," she says. We're in front of my building.

"We should go inside," I suggest.

"You can do better than that."

"Bell, I don't know anything about children."

"Open this damn door," she says.

I make her a cup of coffee. She stands by the window peering cautiously through the blinds to the street. I crawl to her on my knees. She looks down at me skeptically. "You couldn't give me what I want in a million years," she says. She places her leg on a chair and guides my face to her and tells me where to lick and where to suck. "That's where my husband fucks me," she says. I am stretching my neck as she lifts beneath my chin, surrounded by her legs. "Stop," she says, pushing me away. Stripping her top and skirt. She's getting fat. "Do you think I'm the most beautiful woman?"

"I do," I say. We're going through the motions. The next forty minutes is spent with me trying to please her with my tongue until my mouth is sore.

She slaps me a few times over by the couch and for a moment I think this is going to work. She hits me particularly hard once and I feel my eye starting to swell again and she stops. "Lie down on the bed," she says. "My husband doesn't want me to do this." She slides over me. Of course I'm not wearing protection. Nothing is safe. She rides up over me. Like an oven. She says, "Theo, darling." She grabs my hands and places them on her thighs. She lies on top of me, biting me lightly. I grip her legs and stay quiet. Her chest against my chest. This is sex. There's no real threat. If I yell loud enough she'll stop, which leaves us with nothing. And when I say I exist only to please her I don't mean it. And when she tells me how beautiful she is it's because she doesn't believe it. Or when she says she has to punish me and asks me if I'm scared, she doesn't mean it. We don't mean it.

Bell is wrapping a belt around her skirt. I turn away from her and watch the door. "My husband would like to see me with you. He wants to see me with a submissive. Then he'll realize it's not a threat to him. Because, of course, you are not. Then, when I'm done with you, he'll make love to me like a real man. The three of us will discuss it first. I want you to come to the East Bay."

I walk her down the stairs, past the bicycles locked to the stairwell and onto the Mission streets. Bell gets in the cab and I give the driver my money. "Take her to Oakland," I tell him. "She has to meet her husband."

"I'll see you on Tuesday," Bell says.

"I love you," I tell her back.

* * *

Pat and I meet at the Uptown on 17th Street. A holdover from the revolution. The walls are covered with slogans for left wing political movements. The tables are carved and stickered. There are two red couches in the back, a jukebox and a pool table. A view of the hookers who walk by at street level. Pat orders us two Speakeasys and two shots of whiskey and he pays for them. He always pays for the drinks and we never talk about it. He starts like he always does. "In the Sixties," he says, drinking his beer. "We were trying to change society."

"So much for that idea," I tell him.

"You'd be amazed how much fun you can have if you get out of your own head. The problem is that now people are only interested in themselves. What we have is a non-voting generation. That's what they should call you guys, the non-voting generation. You think you can't fix anything until you fix yourselves. Well, let me be the first to tell you, you will never fix yourself."

Somebody throws some money into the jukebox at the same time a rack of pool balls slam into the gully. The Pixies, *I will grow, up to be, a debaser.*

"My wife," I tell Pat. "I didn't always sell bagels."

"What about your wife?"

"Oh man. She was a sweetheart. Long legs, black hair. When people met her they said she had breeding. Because she walked so straight. But you know, she didn't. I mean, we didn't always get along. Like, we didn't agree on a lot of things. We hated each other. She wanted things from me. I felt like I could never give them to her."

Pat's looking in his whiskey glass with one eye waiting for me to finish. I know all about Pat's marriage. His childhood sweetheart. And how her head isn't right anymore. "So what's wrong with selling bagels?"

"Nothing wrong with it." I drink my beer. Pat's good for at least one more round. Maybe two. A perk of the job, I suppose, but still I'm the one that has to be up at six in the morning. I only live two blocks away from this bar. I come here often. When the phone is ringing. When the fog is falling over the hills. I sit here at night with a beer, not trying to get drunk. Just trying to make it last. Staring into the wall and the liquor bottles, the mirror. The mirror is rounded with a dark wood edge barreled around it. I like to watch the young couples that come in here and sit next to each other on the couch. I love it when they lean into one another even though the couch is long, cutting off their own space.

"Listen," Pat says. "There's a whole world out there. How old are you?"

"Thirty-six, if you have to know."

"Keep going, man. You'll be full manager. What would you do if you were the manager right now? If I said, Theo, you are now the manager of Hoff Bagels. I'm talking profit sharing. The whole business. What would you do?"

I look at Pat slyly. "I'd change the world," I tell him, putting down my beer. "If I was manager, there'd be no more war."

Pat looks at me for a second like he's going to laugh, but then he gets the joke and a queer expression passes over his face. It's like somebody's taken the air out of him. He sips on the bottom of his whiskey shot and then chases it with his beer. I give him a blank stare. "Yeah, well," he says, and I feel guilty already. "No need to worry about that. Have another one, all right?"

"All right," I say.

I send Bell a note that I won't be able to see her any more, then sign off the kiosk and go to help Valerie behind the counter. I don't know why I do it. Because nothing in my life has ever worked out quite the way I planned. Because I'm selfish. I do it because I'm lonely and when I don't see her it's worse and because after three years in San Francisco I don't know anybody. Because I don't want to be seen. I don't know anybody and I don't want anybody to know. Because she was so human the last time I saw her. Just a real person, not sure what her next move is. And I don't have room for that. I can't take care of her. No, no, no. And for reasons I'm unsure of. My small apartment. This city and all of the cities. No. And the jungles with their animals. People with their problems. The windows. I woke last night and grabbed at the end of my mattress. The windows. No. It's hard enough.

Valerie doesn't want to talk to me. One time Valerie asked me to walk her to the campsite. She said she was afraid to go alone. All of the homeless were there, below the highway, at the base of Bernal Heights. Shopping carts were everywhere and they had strung tarp among them. A large fire was burning from a steel drum and we saw the men and women huddled around it from across Ceasar Chavez. I asked Valerie why she wanted to go there though I knew it was to see Philc. But I didn't understand that she had to go down beneath the highway and the thick traffic of Army Street, a six-lane-deep river to be crossed. It looked like hell to me, that place she was going, all the people and stray dogs. Valerie looked at me like she didn't know what I meant. "I'm not going there," I told her. Valerie crossed her arms. "You don't have to go there," I said. She thought about it but then she stepped into the street, wading through the traffic and I watched for a minute and then followed. We climbed out the other side and nobody seemed to care who we were. We found Philc's tent near the back, where everybody threw away their trash. Paper and soiled, torn clothing was everywhere, piles strung against the steel mesh fence before the brickyard. He was standing, throwing a knife into the dirt. There were a couple of men sitting nearby sipping on the last of a glass bottle and wiping their beards. One of the men had a bag of peeled carrots on his lap.

"Is that your bodyguard?" Philc sneered. Valerie left me and went over to him. "I've been doing speed. Watch this." He pushed Valerie over to a big tree. She seemed to know what to do. She leaned back against it with her arms straight at her sides and closed her eyes. She looked happy. "Are you guys watching?" he asked the two men. One of them nodded and the other grabbed a carrot stub from his bag. Philc picked up his knife, a truck rumbled over the steel girders sending a shiver through the small plot. Philc threw the knife, striking the tree right next to Valerie's head. But it didn't stick. It fell to the ground and landed bent at her feet.

"That's dangerous," I said.

"Fuck," Philc said gathering his knife. Valerie had opened her eyes.

"Let's go," I told her.

"She's not going anywhere," Philc said looking down at his knife, running his fingers along the blade like he was going to clean it.

"You go," Valerie said. "I'll be okay."

"She's safe with me." Philc's dirty face was full of challenge. "There's room for her in my tent." He emptied a bottle of water onto a rag. There didn't seem to be anything for me to do but to go. I wasn't wanted and it was immediately obvious that Valerie wasn't going to leave unless I carried her out, and I wasn't going to do that. I didn't want to watch Philc throw knives at her head. I worked my way down the path and lowered myself back into the street.

It's game night. Our strangest night. I feel short of breath. The tables are filled with people playing board games. Twenty people, maybe. This group comes here once a week. I don't know who they are. They show up here. They order some coffee. We stay open later than usual. They setup Monopoly, Checkers, Parcheesi. Push the pieces. They play for hours.

"This is our strangest night," I say to Valerie. But she's still upset so she doesn't even answer. "Valerie, look at them," I say over her shoulder. She's wearing a Naked Raygun shirt. Last Tour Ever. She's cutting a bagel for a customer. She ignores me. "I don't even know what I want. If somebody asked me what I wanted I couldn't even begin to answer them."

"But nobody's asking, are they?"

"No," I say. She's facing me with the knife. Somebody shouts *Yahtzee!* Valerie's lips, at the corners, point down. "Nobody is."

I clean up my apartment. It doesn't take long, it's such a small place. I knock on my neighbor's door and ask if I can borrow his broom and I sweep my floors. I fill a bucket with soap and water and wash the walls. I leave my hands in the dark, soapy water for a minute. I stand by the window and watch the action on the street below, the hookers and the police cruisers. If I was in Chicago now we'd watch television. We'd avoid the obvious questions. We'd make excuses for nothing until we were done and we could finally sleep. Then the phone starts ringing.

I buy Valerie a five-dollar bar of soap that smells like cucumber. I take out the trash. Lunchtime, Philc is standing across Valencia street. He has scabs on his cheek and a new tattoo around his neck. I pass him on my way to pick up pizza slices for Valerie and myself. We look at each other but I just keep walking. It's three in the afternoon and the shop is empty except for the girl with the tattooed face who's in the nod at the last table in the back. I remember when that girl started coming around the neighborhood, with her Barbie Doll lunchbox, looking to get high. People would say she was pretty, except for the tattoos. It's like she only had that one thing wrong with her. But that was enough. The blue ink obscures her face entirely. It runs from her ears and eyes and curls under her chin like a beard. She gets in cars and turns tricks down by Folsom Street.

Valerie has finished her slice and is throwing away the paper plate. She pours herself a soda and dumps three ounces of peach syrup into it. She wipes her mouth with her forearm and then puckers her lips.

The light is blinking on my machine and all of my windows are open. The workers from the factory and huddled around the white lunch truck.

You fucking punk bitch. You think you can send me an email saying you don't want to see me anymore and that's it? I don't know what kind of game you are playing. Be as close to a man as you can be and pick up the motherfucking phone or do something that makes me less inclined to rip your fucking thinning hair out by the pale roots.

I really don't have time for your shit. You belong on your back with me suffocating you. Why do you think there is room for you? Don't you think I have my own problems?

I will ambush you somewhere. I will leave permanent marks. I warn you, don't fuck with me. You can't run away. I will be there tomorrow and if you are not available your whole neighborhood will know what a sissy punk bitch who likes to be raped you are. Don't underestimate my cruelty.

At work I stand near the counter. "C'mon," Valerie says. I take a breath before wrapping the last bagel of the morning in paper and handing it to the customer, who walks out the door. Outside they're routing traffic around Valencia and the cars, each pointing in a slightly different direction, seem to be trying to climb over one another but none of them are moving. The cars need to get through. There is no way around Valencia. It's starting to rain. People run past the windows with papers over their hats. Philc and Valerie are in the back with the recycling and the trash, having a cigarette under the porchhang. I open the newspaper; there's been an invasion. I look up and Philc is standing at the counter in front of me. "Hey," he says quietly. "We need to come to an understanding, bro." I fold the newspaper, slide it over by the cookies. "Valerie loves you. Do you know that, man? You're family. You are. I think we can make this work." He pulls a toothpick from his pocket and plays with it between his front teeth. "Maybe we can all get a place together. You know what I mean? The three of us. No more bad times." He speaks calmly and I wonder what kind of pills he's been taking and if they would do me any good and how long they would last for. "Friends for life?" He stretches his hand across the counter. I take his hand because every small bit of peace is worth having.

I put the bagels away and wrap the day old pastries. Valerie comes back to help me. The rain is beating down on the sidewalk and Philc is sitting quietly in the back making origami from napkins.

That time you were tied up before. You looked so innocent. I wanted to draw blood.

But I didn't. Do you know why? You like to think you're smart so you think other people can't understand you. You are so funny! Did you ever think I was reasonable? I mean, I can be a reasonable person but I don't like being played with. You cannot spend time with me and then send some pathetic excuse to disappear. Is that how you handle things? By running away? It doesn't work like that buddy boy. Answer your phone next time I call.

I tell Ambellina I'm sorry and ask if I can take her to see *Casablanca* at the Paramount in Oakland. It's been raining every day and I head to the East Bay. The Paramount is an Art Deco theater from the Depression that plays classic movies. The theater opens early for cocktails and the Wurlitzer. I'm there first, above the 19th Street station, and after fifteen minutes I start to worry that she isn't going to show up and then she is standing in front of me. I try to take her hand but she won't let me. "What do you think you were trying to pull?" she asks. We're moving with the crowd of people down the street.

"I..."

"You what? Do you belong to me or not?" Men are watching her. She's wearing thigh-high latex yellow boots, fishnets, a leather skirt. Her tight curls are cut close to her scalp and dyed fire engine red. She seems to be looking around, smiling to all of them at once. She also seems to be focused on only me.

"Yes," I say quietly.

"What?"

"Yes. I belong to you, Mistress." The guy walking next to me snickers.

We move through the large doors of the old theater, the velvet floors, columns and statues reaching to a roof that ends in a midnight sky. The theater was built to hold thousands. Ambellina sends me for Coke and popcorn and when I come back the seats around us are filled up and the man in the coat and tails at the Wurlitzer is being lowered beneath the ground.

Bogart's face fills the screen and out of the corner of my eye Ambellina is rummaging through her purse. I grew up with Humphrey Bogart. We had a television and my father loved the old Bogart films and would make me watch them whenever they were on. *Casablanca, Maltese Falcon, Key Largo.* "You're not big enough to take me down, see." In his better moods my father would quote Bogart. "Sure, on the one hand maybe I love you and maybe you love me. But you'll have something on me you can use whenever you want. And since I'll have something on you who's to say you're not going to knock me over like you did the rest of them?" My father was a big man with a loud laugh, four inches taller than I am now. He was a violent man who wouldn't stand for being looked at crossways by women or children. He pushed my kindergarten teacher down a small flight of stairs. He was like a hurricane continually destroying our small house. He terrorized everyone within twenty feet. He was lazy and his laziness made him a criminal. He shot himself with a shotgun just before my eleventh birthday, which is when my hard time began, though it might have already been too late.

Bogart seems friendly to me among the roulette wheels and the card tables. His confidence. His big sad eyes. The white linen suits moving casually across the screen while the world is at war all around them. Rick's, a little Free French outpost on the sand. He does what he has to. He betrays poor Peter Lorrie to the Nazis. But the world won't let him alone. The world is bigger than the castle he has built for himself. This is the lesson of Casablanca.

Ambellina forces the gag into my mouth and I catch my breath. I let out a tiny moan while the big, round puck forces open my jaw and cheeks sending a throbbing up the sides of my face.

"Shhh."

The theater is so quiet except for the actors and Ambellina slowly rubbing her thumb and index finger together. There's a hole in the puck to breathe through and I feel her pulling the straps around the back of my neck and fastening it tight to hold the gag in. I grip onto the seats. The strap catches and pulls my hair. I want to move out of this. To squirm. To wriggle down to the floor. I jerk my head one way, and then back. One quick breath. I push back in my seat, my feet pressing the floor. I try to hold the middle and when I can't I lean cautiously into Ambellina's shoulder, and she lets me stay there. Before the plane flies away I've grown used to the pressure against the roof of my mouth. When the lights come on I'm resting; I can hardly feel my hair caught in the buckle.

II.

FOREFATHERS

THERE'S A LARGE WOMAN in front of me in a white dress with dark flowers. She smells like baby powder and she's holding the hand of a small girl whose red hair is scattered across her shoulders to make her look like a doll. The two of them are not related. It's early in the morning and it's a thick, slow line and nobody in it is in a hurry. The girl tries to say something and the lady reaches down and brushes her lips with her index finger.

At the edge of the table I empty my pockets into a Tupperware dish, step through the metal detector with my hands out of my pockets and my palms open. The police officer nods, hands me my belongings, a set of keys and a wallet with a chain that attaches to my belt loop. I'm too young to be a parent, too old to be in trouble. I pour my things from the dish into my hand.

I walk past the courtrooms where the children are tried for crimes committed across the city. Things like robbing parking meters or throwing other children from rooftops. The yellow benches outside the courtrooms are filled today with juveniles waiting for their verdicts. The kids are not allowed in the actual courtroom unless the judge summons them with a question. The violent offenders and the run risks are cuffed to a chair in one-person rooms known as hotboxes.

In the basement there's a cafeteria with eight gray tables, wire chairs, and a vending machine that sells hot chocolate, coffee, and chicken soup from the same spout. I buy a coffee and sit down where someone has left a newspaper. I read about the heat wave and what the newly elected mayor of Chicago plans to do about it. It's the hottest summer on record and people are dying everywhere. Across from me three officers are taking a break. They sit in front of three empty cups. They think I'm on their side. I place my hand over the mayor's face. I run through the plan in my head.

They've placed art along the walls of the lower floors in the years since I've been here last. Cityscapes and still lifes, all of them dirty-looking in cheap metal frames. There's an escalator, and then wider, black, polished stairs leading to the second floor. The top three floors of Western house the jail, a brutal place, always overcrowded and understaffed. Children are supposed to be shipped from here to St. Charles within three months. It doesn't always work that way. Paperwork gets lost. If the parent doesn't show up to collect the child there are proceedings for the child to be made a ward of the court. The state takes custody. A placement has to be found. The placements are run by private agencies like the Jewish Children's Bureau or the Catholic Charities or the Children's Home and Aid Society, who may or may not want the kid the state is offering. The state allocates the same funds, thirty-one dollars per day per child, whether the child is in a group home, a shelter, or a mental hospital. There are children that spend years in here.

I come to a large door and adjust my tie against my reflection. Inside there's another door, and then another, and the intake for the jail and the administrative offices, where the secretary sits in front to greet and vet visitors. The secretary, years ago, was a beautiful Spanish woman named Camilla who took everyone's name as they were admitted into a green binder on her desk. I never spoke to Camilla but I remember her, I'm sure everybody does. She was removed for having an affair with one of the inmates. Someone's dream come true. He was seventeen years old, being tried as an adult. It was his last good time. I was twelve then and knew only what I heard in the lunch hall. They were caught in a broom closet with her skirt up around her waist. But there are other places to have sex in Western, unused offices, of course the showers. The doors don't have windows and are locked from the outside and it's two to four boys for every room, so opportunity exists there as well. Camilla is a nice memory for me, though I didn't know her at all. I just remember her red skirt, and the short pointy heels on her shoes, and where her skirt stopped and her legs began. I thought about her every day I was inside and by the time I got out she was gone.

"I'm here to see George Washington." I almost want to laugh. I'm asking about a young black house-robber named for the founder of our country. *It's no wonder you like to steal*, I'll tell him, *you're on every quarter.*

"What's your relation?" the lady asks. She's not pretty, like Camilla, this one. She has wiry black and white hair, piled on her head like a dead nest. She looks dead. She's old and salty. A safe bet, I suppose, a dead woman.

"Caseworker," I tell her. She looks at me skeptically. I'm dressed in black pants and a button-down shirt, my clothes stuck to my skin from the heat outside. "DCFS," I say, to show I know the lingo. I speak the language. State not charity. DCFS as opposed to Board of Ed, or HHS or federal, which would be ridiculous but you never know. As opposed to Guardian Ad Litem, for which I would have to be a lawyer. And I'm obviously not family. DCFS is easy enough. Department of Children and Family Services and the family-first policy. Caseworkers change all the time. I went through twelve caseworkers before I was eighteen. I didn't know who was looking after me. Most of them I never met. None of whom I met more than once.

"They're in the yard now," she says. She must be retired, I think. She must have taken this job to pass the time after retiring, because she was bored, and she didn't want to give to charity. She wanted to spend her final years in a penal institution helping to punish bad children. I wait in front of her, behind the long brown partition. I don't want her to think I'm going to leave and I don't want her to think I have all day. I've been thinking about this, so I'm ready. I've thought all my actions through. And I've thought that I could fail. If they found me out, came to me from the sides and behind with a net, pulled a mask over my head, zipping it from the back, taping my hands to my skull, cinching the net around me, and dragging me along the linoleum floors back into the ward, a locked white room with a view of the freeway, and leaving me there. Forgetting me again, this time forever. So I wait, tapping my finger lightly on the countertop.

She buzzes the glass door next to her and I grip onto the handle and click inside. The air is like a television tuned to the channel of static. I follow her past cubicles divided each with six feet high walls of fabric. Some of the cubicles are empty and others contain people sitting at computers entering data or talking into the phone. This is the administrative heart of the detention center but it isn't necessary. All you need in a jail is inmates and guards. You barely need guards.

I'm left in a fluorescent room with a table and two chairs, a large ashtray, and a stand with magazines piled across the top of it. I place my notebook on the table and a pencil next to it. Caseworkers always do this. There's always a notebook. I place my hands behind my head and try to relax.

The first time my girlfriend was robbed was three months ago. We had only just started dating. I met her at the restaurant where we work. I have a hard time sleeping and she doesn't like to sleep until morning. She's in law school at Loyola and she waits tables. I had picked up the second job cashiering at the restaurant to keep me busy at night and because of some trouble I was having. That's where I met Zahava.

When she was robbed that time we were in her bed with the covers off and we heard a sound from outside and she wondered what it was and I said I was sure it was just the cat. But it wasn't the cat. When we came out of the room, a few hours later, we were still naked and the bicycle was missing and Zahava's Guatemalan backpack was in the middle of the floor, the front pocket open, her tip money gone. She shook her head and pulled a Lenny Kravitz album from its sleeve. She would have to get another bicycle. She zipped her bag and placed it on the couch. She turned to me and smiled. Easy come easy go.

I pick up one of the *Men's Journal*s. There's a picture of a man on the cover wearing sky blue shorts and no shirt and he appears to be running up a mountain. He looks healthy, and content. His skin is smooth, his chin and cheeks perfect.

I read through the magazine while I'm waiting. It could be a while. There's a whole system of doors and elevators to be negotiated with keys in bringing a child down to the second floor. I read what foods I should eat if I'm going to have a pretty stomach that will attract women. I learn how to improve my biceps by doing exercises with weights and tucking my elbows tightly beneath my ribs. And I learn that it drives women crazy if you pull on their clitoris gently with your thumb and your forefinger and then blow on it.

When I'm done with the magazine George Washington is in front of me with a guard. The guard doesn't introduce himself. The guard says he's going to lock the door and that I have to ring a bell next to the table to be let out. When I ring the bell someone will come and take George Washington back to the third floor, but it might take a few minutes.

"You're not my caseworker," George Washington says to me as the guard is leaving.

"I am now. Sit down," I tell George. "Let's get to know each other."

He's a small kid, and tough looking. Scrappy. He has a muscular face but skin like a baby. They've given him the haircut, his scalp covered in short, black fuzz. The door clicks and latches and George is looking at me, considering his options. Maybe there is something he could use as a weapon: a piece of metal to be quickly sharpened, a dull, heavy object. He could take me hostage, tell the police that he will kill me if they don't let him out. They wouldn't deal with him, and when the standoff was over we would both be headed back to jail.

"Cigarette?" I ask, taking the pack from my pocket. He takes the cigarette from me and tucks it behind his ear. He sits down across from me on the other side of the table. I light my cigarette and toss the lighter to him. "You might as well smoke it. They're not going to let you take it back to the floor." He must know this already. How could he not know that? Of course he knows. He's been here weeks already. He considers the lighter but doesn't take it. He leaves the cigarette behind his ear. Was I like this? No. I was scared and obedient. I would have smoked that cigarette down, hands folded into my lap, staring at the floor. And I would have said thank you. That's the kind of child I was. People did whatever they wanted with me. George is strong and defiant. Fuck you, he's saying, the way he crosses his arms across his small chest and stares at the locked door as if it was a personal insult, but he is stronger than the door and through his will he's going to tear the door right from the hinges. There's only one problem with his theory.

"I have a whole pack," I say and push them across the table to him. He picks the pack up, stuffs the lighter inside, and shoves the pack inside the waistband of his pants. Now he's smiling, kind of like the child he is, curious to see what I'll do. I'm not going to do anything. I can go a few hours without a smoke. I'll buy a pack at the convenience store where the shuttle stops. It's no big deal. They'll search him before taking him back. They'll take his cigarettes from him and divide them amongst themselves. What the fuck, they'll think. What kind of a caseworker would give a juvenile offender a pack of cigarettes?

"So how are they treating you?" I ask. This is the repeat. I learned this over seven years. Every time I met a new caseworker they would ask me how I was being treated and I'd say, "Fine" instead of saying, "I'm being raped." I'd say, "Good" instead of saying the other boys jumped me and forced a bar of soap into my mouth. I'd say, "OK," instead of saying, "I hate it here, they won't let me go outside." And they always ask the same question. They don't change a single word. The administrators, guardians, caseworkers, volunteers, hospital staff. Always, So how are they treating you? Which is what I say now, on the other side, but not really. I have a good idea how he is being treated. He's not giving any back mouth to the guards and the guards are ignoring him. In the yard he stands near the pole. He's getting in fights sometimes to prove himself to his gang. At school he's in one of the classes for the kids that can't sit still. I can see it all.

"Listen, you know, I put a lot of effort into getting here today. How old are you?"

"How old are you?" he blurts back. He's gotten tired of the quiet game.

"I'm twenty-three."

"I'm thirteen," he says. "What about it." Of course he is. It's just the age.

"When's your court date set for?"

"Don't you know?" he asks. He's suspicious. Children in this place are always suspicious.

"I didn't bring my papers with me, so I don't know." He shrugs his shoulders. OK. Fine. I lean back, he leans back. The light hanging over us is dim and fat. I've never been good with kids, not even when I was one. "Give me a cigarette," I say. He looks like he doesn't know what I'm talking about. I don't even know why I'm here. I remember very distinctly standing on Petey's bed two floors up, sometimes stepping on his legs, and looking out the window in our room through a patchwork of wire and saying to myself that if they ever let me out of this place that I would never come back. But here I am. For what? To walk the red lines painted onto the floor outside the classrooms. For this child who's already stolen my cigarettes, who looks like all of the kids that used to spit on me and beat me up, a smaller version of Larry, the most fiercesome kid in Western when I was here. The kid who eventually broke my leg, just days before they let me out. That's what he looks like, this little bastard. He looks like Larry. I shake my head. Consider threatening him. It wouldn't work. It's what he wants. I went through all of this for George Washington. I bought these clothes, dark pants, button-up shirt. Cut my hair, bought this notebook. Took a day off of work, just so I could come here and give this thirteen-year-old asshole some information and now he won't even give me one of my own cigarettes. "If you don't give me a cigarette," I say, finally, staring into the fixture and black marks on the ceiling above it. "I'm going to leave, and you're never ever going to find out why I came here or what I intended to tell you. And that's just fine with me, anyway."

I can see him thinking about it. Curiosity is a weapon with children. Fear and longing for the unknown. What a horrible little room this is. Smells just like this place, too. Rooms smell different when you can't get out. George relents. He takes the cigarette from behind his ear and rolls it across the table to me. I raise my eyebrow. He pulls the packet out from inside his pants, removing the lighter and placing it on the table then flicking it to me with his index finger. It slides across the table and lands in my palm and I light my cigarette with it and I slide the lighter back to him and he tucks it back in the pack and the pack back inside the waistband of his pants.

"What you want to talk about?" he asks now, lightly drumming on his thighs. "Why you messin' with me?"

"The police," I tell him. "I want to talk to you about the police."

Zahava was robbed a second time, just a couple of weeks later. But we weren't there then. After work we had gone with some of the other restaurant employees over to Sunny's house. There were drugs, as usual. Heroin and cocaine in little white paper packets. Everyone pitched in. Zahava went up and I went down and I was sitting against the wall and everything was in slow motion. Heroin is the only thing that makes me relax. Zahava likes cocaine. She likes to have a good time. It's hurting her grades, she says. But she always wants to go out. She was chatting rapidly with Scales, the bartender. Once, when we were at a bar near Belmont, I saw Zahava tuck her hand into Scale's back pocket. She has better posture than the rest of us and I thought to myself, wrapped in my drug-induced blanket, staring at her thin frame and beak-like nose, that Zahava is a door. She is a bridge, a phone booth. The only open space in an enormous maze that I have been trapped in my entire life. She's the only chance I've ever had.

When we came home in the morning my body felt like cake batter and Zahava was complaining of canker sores inside her mouth. Her gums were patterned with pink lined white squares and there was blood around her teeth. I hadn't been able to pee so I went to the bathroom. I stood in front of the bowl and waited. When I came out Zahava was staring at the wall with her hands on her hips, lightly biting at the inside of her mouth. Her stereo was gone along with her music. "I hope they fry," she said this time. "Why not just kill all of them?"

"What do you mean?"

She looked at me like I knew what she was talking about and I shouldn't act stupid. She poked her chin forward and reconsidered. "I don't mean that. Really. I was just upset for a moment."

"I don't care about police," George says. He's getting anxious. I can't hold his attention. I would think the ward would be unbearable for him, the small locked rooms, his eyes darting all over the walls.

"If you don't care about the police why do you tell them so much?" I ask.

He shrugs his shoulders and knits his brow. He has a low hairline that starts almost immediately above his eyebrows. "I don't know," he says, angrily, because he doesn't like that he's been tricked and he doesn't like that I'm telling him he's been tricked. It may be too late. He doesn't know his court date. Maybe it's already passed. They tried him, found him guilty, decided his fate, and he's sitting here waiting for it, waiting for it to come down on his neck like a mousetrap. And it will. They'll split him wide open. But even still. There's other mistakes to be made. No matter how much they pull you apart there's always room for another mistake, there's always something left.

"You think the police are your friends?" I ask him. "Is that why you tell them so much?" His eyes are really darting now and his legs are shaking and his thumb is beating the table. Sure, what's so hard about getting a confession from this kid? Leave him in a small room and wait for him to lose his mind. I stub my cigarette out. I feel almost dizzy, slightly nauseous.

My tongue sticks and the roof of my mouth is thick and wet. There's a sharp pain in the back of my head wrapping itself around my ears like a steel belt and I press my palm against my forehead to relieve the pressure, try to make it stop.

"No. I hate the police," he says.

The third time Zahava was robbed the robbers were caught. The landlady had drilled a wooden plank into the living room floor to keep the patio doors from opening. So they broke the window. It was daytime. The police were waiting for them or the neighbors had been put on alert and were watching. The robbers were ambushed, or caught walking away. The police were called and they responded. "They always return," the police officer told us, standing in a pile of glass in the front room. "Creatures of habit. They catch themselves."

There were two robbers. An older man past forty, a career criminal, just out of the can for the third time. And with him a young, first-time offender named for a general who led his country against the English. And the child will have a gun in his belt.

The burglars were taken to the 24th District police headquarters on Clark Street, a single floor black metal building responsible for all of Rogers Park, then separated. I could trace their steps from the backseat of the car, a sun-filled parking lot shining with blue and white stripes, through the thick steel doors. I know what the room looked like where they sat the younger one and handcuffed his wrist to the loop in the wall. If they felt mean, like they usually do, then they squeezed the cuffs tight on his wrist so that soon his hand would be turning purple. He was sitting on the bench between two desks, his hand raised like he was giving an oath. At one of the desks would be a plainclothes juvenile officer and a typewriter, and at the other a snarling blue jacket with horrendous skin and a tightly clipped brown beard. The officer's skin would be so horrible that it would be as if his face was melting, like someone had poured acid on his face. The bench would have been painted white for no discernible reason and bolted to the wall by two long chains. Next to the plainclothes would be the cell. The door to the cell would be open, offering a view of a clean steel cot and a toilet. And this is where young George Washington would spend the first night of his journey into the whirlwind.

First there would be questions. Legal counsel was not going to be an option. There was no right to remain silent. But maybe he wouldn't talk for awhile. Not until the blue jacket punched his face a couple of times. Or maybe he would talk right away, while the juvenile officer typed. Because he doesn't care, because he's sure he's stronger than them and they can't do him any harm anyway so what does it matter. He's wrong about that. So they ask him if he was there all three times the apartment was robbed and he candidly responds yes. And they ask him if he had a gun on him then too. And he says yes. The police officers are nodding encouragement. He's getting excited. He's surging with his own invincibility. And then they tell him there were two people sleeping that first time they robbed the apartment. How did he feel about that? He shrugs his shoulders. He doesn't feel anything about that. What if one of them had gotten up? What if they had been discovered robbing the apartment? What then? What would he have done if one of the occupants had come out of the bedroom to see what all of the racket was or to use the bathroom? What then? And George Washington pondered his answer for a moment, growing stronger and nodding his head. The air was rushing into his lungs. He was going to peel the roof from the police station and pull the rest of it to the ground. "I would have shot them dead," he replied.

"I'll go take a look."

"Don't bother. Stay here," she says, holding my hand.

"Well?"

"Well what?" I think about asking for another cigarette but don't bother.

"The police," I say. I'm sweating but it's not hot in this room. "Why did you tell them that?"

"Tell them what?"

"That you were going to shoot us. That you were going to shoot the occupants of the bedroom if they walked out of the room? You threw it all away. Why did you say that?"

"Doesn't matter."

"It does matter." I wish there was a window in this room or less light but there isn't. "It matters," I say. "They're going to use that against you. They put it in your report. They told the people that live there you said that. They met them right outside of their building and they said they had caught the robbers and that the youth had a gun and he had intended to use it had they caught him. That means for sure it's in your paperwork. And the prosecutor is going to present that to the judge. And you are never going to get out. You are never going to go home again. You will be here until you're eighteen and possibly longer if they can figure a way. Because it's a different crime now. You've elevated the crime. You are no longer eligible for placement. Who can even imagine what they're going to call that, the places you are going to be. They're going to hold you until you are eighteen."

George's hair and eyebrows come together. He blows air into his cheeks. "Fuck you," he says.

"Fuck me? Fine. Fuck me. Don't talk to any more cops. You understand?" I realize that I'm shaking the table so I grip the table harder and shake it as hard as I can. "I don't care if they smack you with spoons, stick a hook in your penis, or what they threaten you with. You wait. Don't trust any of them. Not the teachers, not your guardian, or the guards or the lawyers. Definitely not the social workers or anyone who presents themselves to you as your therapist. That's a setup. They're out to get you. They fucking hate you." He's crying now. I'm making him cry. "They are out for you. They don't give a shit about you. You're just food to them. They're going to eat you alive. And if a judge asks you, if you even get that chance, which you probably won't. But if you ever do, if the judge brings you into the courtroom. If a judge asks you if you were really there that first time and if you had a gun then you say no. You hear me? You say no. You say it wasn't even your gun. You were just carrying it for the other man. The older man. You were carrying it for him. It was his gun. Do you get that now?"

He's sitting upright. Tears are streaming from his hard eyes. The tears keep running, pouring over his cheeks, snot hanging from his nose, water dribbling over his chin, soaking the collar of his shirt, forming small puddles on the table. I sit and I wait. I can't let the guard see this. I have to be careful. I have to wait and then I have to go. I'll never make it out again. No one will protect me. I'm going to stand up and ring the bell and leave, and that's the last I'm going to see of this place.

The stairs are long and empty. They never search you when you leave. I keep my hands just outside of my pockets. I walk the stairs and pass the guard and his metal detector. A funny thought occurs to me of putting a bomb together while inside and walking right out with it into the hot air and blowing up the rest of the world.

Western is 2300 west and 1100 south. Where I live is far north, east of the train tracks, near the lake and the suburbs, but not quite at either. I'll have to take three buses to get home. The heat attacks me as it has the city for weeks, like a vice. The sidewalk is a pan, the exhaust sticks in thick gray streaks to the sides of white delivery trucks. And as I'm walking away from the building my pace is quickening. I'm so goddamn afraid. I keep imagining that I was caught, even though I wasn't, it's like falling from a window. I'm walking faster, unbuttoning my shirt. Taking my shirt off, popping a button, wiping my face with my shirt. I'm running stripped to the waist. My stomach is turning over. I'm running as fast as I can past the people waiting for a bus and the Payless Shoe Store. I'll yell. I'll get somewhere alone and I'll yell. I'm moving around the pedestrians, jumping into the gutter and then back onto the pavement. The hottest summer on record, they said. "Ain't nobody chasing you," a man leaning next to a newspaper box yells after me. I stop and turn to look at him. He's a large man and his sweat has made his striped shirt transparent over his dark belly. He's laughing, turning a toothpick in his teeth, jingling some keys in his pocket. There's a wire garbage can nearby. A woman standing in the shade of a thin tree is turned slightly away from me, a smile playing beneath the dew of sweat on her lips.

III.
THE YARD

AT NIGHT, WHEN our door is locked, we aren't supposed to be talking. We're supposed to be sleeping. I stand over Petey, naked except for my underwear, trying to see out the window. The springs creak and I hold my breath before placing my hands on the sill. We can never tell if they can hear us or not. Through the window I make out the dark outline of the Henry Horner housing projects, the sharp corners facing Western, and some of the dull gray towers of the University campus and its cement bridges crossing between the building's top floors. I think about University sometimes but I would never go to a school near here. If I ever get out I'll go somewhere far away, another city on the edge of the country.

"See any birds?" Petey asks in a low whisper. He turned sixteen yesterday, three years older than me, but we don't celebrate birthdays here. "Anything?" Petey lies under his blanket, his legs inches from my feet. I think about stepping on his ankles for some height.

"I can see the Circle Campus. And the highway. Same stuff that's always there. That's the Roosevelt entrance," I tell him, nodding toward something he can't see. "Goes straight to Wisconsin."

Petey shifts below me and I catch his sour odor escaping from under his blanket. "Be careful," Petey says. Things have been tense recently, more tense than usual. There's been rumors. Not that anyone talks to us. But you can't help but hear in the school, or in food line, people whispering threats to each another. We listen for footsteps, for a trustee or a guard to swing the door open and pull one of us out of the room. I think about the door open-ing all the time, even when I'm on the other side of it. Petey does too. That's why he wets his bed.

Petey stares at me with his huge misshapen head as I try to see further. I love the streets. I can name every fourth street in Chicago. I wasn't looking out of this window until recently, when we began to talk. Now I climb on his bed every night to look outside and when I'm looking outside I want to jump up and down on the bunk, but I don't.

Before, I didn't want to talk to Petey because of the way he looks, and the way he smiles a lot. I knew the minute I saw him he was a victim. The first time he came into this room I folded my arms over my head and ducked between my knees. It was like a hole had opened in the floor. After that, if he would say something I would look away like I hadn't heard. I stayed close to the wall, on my side of the room. I spent months not com-municating with him. And one day, not so long ago, they beat him up in the bathroom—they always get him there—but maybe this time was worse. I was under the last shower and still covered in soap. He was lying on the tiled floor wheezing, his teeth broken in pieces, a pink halo around his head sliding toward the drainpipe. I tried to look ahead and get the soap off my legs but I couldn't stop staring at him. He was this strange deformed white animal. And he said, "I wonder what they wanted." Then he tried to laugh but started to choke and had to stop. But he made it clear, he wasn't going to hold it against me. He didn't expect me to help.

Now we talk about cars, or about television. Or bands, not that there's ever any music in here. But mostly cars. We both like big cars a lot. I tell him my father drove a 1970 Cougar Convertible with a white leather interior, the original hubcaps, and a 351 Quickstart Engine. And everything is fine, except when Petey asks me personal questions like about Tuesday nights. "Don't ask about that," I tell him. But not too long ago I wouldn't have answered him at all.

I crawl under the sheet and the blue knit blanket. I always try to keep the sheet between my body and the blanket. They don't wash the blankets. We sleep in our underwear, our clothes in the hallway next to our shoes. I close my eyes and think of nice things to dream about. I think about dri-ving in my father's convertible, sitting on his lap while he shows me how to drive around the lot at Warren State Park, the courts in front of us, and the hill where I would sled in the winter. I try not to think about the burned-out shell of the car sitting in the alley, a piece of cinder and ash and twisted carriage, waiting for my father's friend with the truck to come and tow it away.

"People and Folk," Nico whispers to me and Petey at breakfast. The breakfast hall is rows of brown tables, one after another, thirty tables in two columns. Three long Plexiglas windows with steel wire running through them. Open seating divides itself by basic distinctions, People or Folk, the two largest Chicago gangs, and within those subgroups, Deuces, Black Gangster Disciples, Assyrian Eagles, Vice Lords, Gay Lords, Latin Kings, Simon City Royals. Five points and six points, pitchforks and crowns. A separate table for the unaffiliated Knights of Kaba, a Muslim gang from Hyde Park. And within those groups color lines, ethnicities, neighborhoods, age. Central Park and Wilson, Farwell and Clark, 63rd and Cottage Grove. The intersections of Chicago meet here in the boys Juvenile Hall, the tables named after street corners. Toward the back of the room the boys get thinner and smaller and younger. Finally outcasts, victims, fodder. Where we sit. There's two tables of us, the ugliest and the weakest, and we don't even like each other.

Petey smiles and shakes his head, which I take to mean he doesn't understand. Petey doesn't understand anything. He's just big and dumb and ugly. But I understand what Nico is saying. Nico has short blond stubble and nods rapidly as he eats. Things are coming to a head. There's a new inmate somewhere and it's someone from the upper ranks. The soldiers are going to be expected to perform. It's going to go off, and that's why there's the tension and the quiet. The two largest organizations. The worst possible news. Nico forces his entire strip of bacon into his mouth. I take a spoonful of oatmeal. Nico squints his mean eyes together and looks at me as he chews.

Ms. Jolet has wide hips and long black hair. She runs basic math problems on the board and I copy them into my book. I like her, even when she's turned away, with chalk in her hand. She's always upbeat. "You have to start each day happy," she says. She wears bright lipstick, and her ears are full of jewelry. People are always trying to get her attention and she has a way of sharing it, which I hate. I watch her move and how the fabric of her dress hangs on her waist and then outlines her legs, where she is most fat, and fantasize about what she would do to me if she could keep me after school. Come here, Theo. Closer. I fantasize about being only six inches tall and Ms. Jolet taping me to the inside of her thighs, her giant legs crossing back and forth over me, and walking out of the building with me inside her skirt. Behind me the boys pass notes back and forth. Something hits the back of my head. I grab the wet paper with two fingers and let it drop to the floor. This is the good class, for kids that don't get in trouble, kids who don't need as much supervision. I copy the multiplication tables. I understand them now. I'm learning. I think I'm on track for my age, but I'd have to see the other tracks to know. Before noon I raise my hand and ask if I can use the bathroom. Ms. Jolet says yes.

The halls are marked with red dashes that run five feet off the wall. The floor is bone colored. When we're in line we have to walk along the dashes only turning when one group of dashes meets another group of dashes. When walking alone we have to stay between the dashes and the wall. I wear a necklace with a plastic hall pass. Because of my status I can go to the bathroom unescorted. I pass a boy walking in handcuffs flanked by two guards. They're talking about something that has nothing to do with the boy between them and one of the guards takes a long slow look at me as we pass.

I wash my hands before moving to the urinals. As I'm peeing Larry walks into the bathroom and steps to the urinal next to me. Larry is a Vice Lord, one of the heads. Slated to join the El Rukns when he turns eighteen. He sits at the front table in the mess hall. Larry looks like he's made out of bowling balls but he's not much older than me. Maybe a year. His mouth is a thin line, like the cartoon Iron Man. "You're not very big there," Larry says looking down at my penis. I feel my cheeks go red and my breathing get heavy. My peeing slows down. "What's wrong?" Larry asks. "I make you scared?"

"No," I answer. When I first came into Western I had sat at the wrong table and Larry reached across the table and pulled my face into his plate of mashed potatoes and meat loaf. Larry held me there, my hands gripping the ends of the table but I couldn't pull away because it felt like I'd rip my hair out if I tried to move. "What are you doing at this table?" Larry asked, lifting my head up and ramming me down into the plate a few times, smearing the potatoes on my cheeks, the other boys laughing, their plates shivering on the wood, the guards ignoring the obvious. Finally he let go and I stood up, my legs weak, my face a mess of food and gravy. I slowly carried my plate to the back of the room and sat down, then wiped the food from my face with a napkin, then stared straight ahead to the wall until the period was over. That was a year ago.

Larry beat me up a lot when I first came here. He came up to me on the
school yard and hit me with both his fists, in my back and my front, my
wind left me. "Look," he said to his friends. "He doesn't even fight back."
Then one day Mr. Gracie asked me where I had got a black eye from. I was
seated naked on the desk in front of him and he held my chin in his hand. It
was cold. I shook my head and Mr. Gracie let go of me then smacked me
across the face and I said, "No." I kept my arms at my sides. But then Mr.
Gracie hit me again and I cried and I said it was Larry and Larry never
touched me after that.

"You know what's going to happen tonight?" Larry asks, pulling his
pants up, rolling them over his penis deliberately. "Gonna be a big fight.
Whose side you on?"

"I'm not on anybody's side," I tell him and move with an affected calm
to the sink and run the water, turning over my hands. I have long, thin scars
on my left arm from my elbow to my wrist. Each time I look they seem
faded and farther away.

"In all that commotion I could probably stab you. Nobody would
notice. That's messed up, right?"

I dry my hands on the towel, turn to walk out of the bathroom. Larry is
there, in front of me, blocking the way. I try to go around him and he moves
with me, so that I would have to bump him if I'm going to get by.

"Where you going?"

"Back to class."

"Back to class," Larry mimics. I feel my stomach snap closed and a wave
of nausea pass through me. "That's messed up, right? That I might stab
you." I look at my shoes, the yellow laces running through my sneakers.
Larry hits me beneath my chin and my teeth clatter together. "You afraid of
me?" I shake my head. "Why you looking away then? Something in your
eye." I look straight ahead into his face. Larry smiles at me. "I'm only playing with you. You know that. You gonna tell your bodyguard?"

"No."

"You gonna tell your boyfriend?"

Larry moves aside and I step into the halls which are empty and past the
dorm rooms. I try to catch my breath but my neck is tightening on me.
I stick my tongue out of my mouth, stretch my lips as far as they will go.
I pull on the corners of my mouth with my fingers. The floor shifts. I turn
the corner toward class and stop and place my hands on my thighs. I let the
fear run out of me, drain from my nose and my eyeballs. Wait for my breath
to come back.

* * *

They don't give us knives. It's hamburger night. Hamburger and french fries, so even the fork is unnecessary, but there it is. "You gonna eat that?" Nico asks and I shake my head. Nico pushes the hamburger into his face, filling his white spotty cheeks with the meat patty and the dry bread.

"You know what we should do," Petey says. "We'll start our own basketball team. If we practice every day we can probably play for the Chicago Bulls. It's just practice. Why not?"

Nico snorts but the food in his mouth stops him from saying anything.

"You can play basketball, right?" Petey says to me. There's basketball in the yard after dinner but Petey and I never get to play. We hang out with Nico by the back, hoping not to be noticed.

"I'm too short," I tell him.

"You'll grow. I bet you're seven feet before you're twenty. How tall are you now?"

"Five-six."

"Seven feet for sure."

"How tall are you, Nico?"

"Fuck you, Petey."

I turn away. Sometimes the optimism in Petey's voice is disturbing. I turn back to my fork and its dull points. Not much of a weapon. I wouldn't use it anyway. And I don't have pockets, nowhere to put it. And it would probably be noticed, and that would be worse. Mr. Gracie can protect me from the other kids but not from the other guards. The guards can do anything. They make you hold out your hand and they hit you as hard as they can on your palm with a spoon. The pain rumbles through your whole body. They restrained one kid by tying him to a table. Then they forgot about him. They left him in a room tied to a table for three days, then he was taken to the hospital ward and treated for dehydration. Another guard choked a kid to death. Everybody knows about it. Nobody says anything. That guard stands at the front of the room by the food line, a big man with a sloping forehead and an enormous hard round gut hanging over his belt. There were talks of investigations but nothing came of it.

Things seem normal enough. A still air and the sound of chewing. The meat smell. It's not going to happen here. It's not going to happen during dinner. I turn to Nico, who, done with his food, also looks around nervously. We're unaffiliated. Traffic will not stop for us.

"It's going to happen in the yard," Nico says.

"I know. I know." I touch the fork prongs. Hold it with one hand and gently push my other hand onto it.

"If you were seven feet tall," Petey says, "You'd get every rebound."

"If I was seven feet tall I'd put on a cape and fly away."

"We need a plan." Nico wipes his mouth with the napkin. Of the three of us Nico is the only one who is actually a fighter. He's held his own in most fights so far but he knows he is marked because of the swastika tattoo on his left forearm. Nico came into Western a month ago. He told me it was for setting fire to a synagogue but I doubted it. I haven't told Nico that I'm half Jewish. It isn't the kind of thing that's worth telling anybody in here. Nico got an early reputation for biting people during fights in the bathroom, trying to gouge eyes out with his thumb. "So what is it?" he asks.

"What's the plan?" I say.

"What are we going to do?" Nico says, shaking his head. The fork is about to break the skin on my palm and I hold it for a moment to feel the pain. The sound and the smell goes away. The room is a TV set on mute. I pull my hand off and the pain stops and the sound comes back. In front of us hundreds of other boys eat. Some with shaved heads, the newer boys still with the hair they came in with, all of the heads bobbing over the sea of plates. The guards standing along the walls like sleeping bulls. Florescent bulbs swinging on chains above us. All of us in for different reasons. All of us waiting to go to the yard.

At 6:30 two hundred boys line up outside the TV room in a single file. A guard takes attendance, occasionally pulling someone out of the lineup to be escorted somewhere. We stand in order of age, with the youngest, the twelve-year-olds, at the very back, even though one of the twelve-year-olds, Anthony, threw another child off the roof of a building and is being tried as an adult.

We march with six guards. We wear our assigned clothes, brown pants with elastic waistbands that read Property of DOC on the front as if someone was going to try to steal them, or us. T-shirts color-coded by group, green for owls, blue for bears. Nobody seems sure what the animal designations are supposed to mean. Everything is a system but none of it works. I was ordered released three months ago by a judge on the first floor of this very building but nothing came of it. I wasn't even handcuffed. I didn't even know I had a court date. I was pulled out of the line before breakfast. They walked me out the heavy, main door, past the office workers, down two flights of stairs, through the metal detectors and the windows and the security gates to the court rooms. They told me to sit down on a bench and they left me alone for an hour while I watched parents bring their children in and out of the room in front of me. Finally a man in a thin shirt with a small, sharp beard introduced himself as my Guardian Ad Litem. I'd never seen him before. He was eating an orange, which he peeled with his thumbs, and he had a plastic Jewel Foods bag full of papers. He said I'd be heading to placement, maybe a specialized foster home. Would I like that? He seemed nervous. He wanted to know how they were treating me upstairs. Any problems? He put his hand covered in orange juice on my shoulder. I couldn't figure out who he worked for or what he was trying to tell me or what he wanted me to tell him. What if I said, "Every Tuesday he takes me to the last room by the fire exit and I take my clothes off and bend over the table there. Sometimes I feel bad because I never put up a fight. The other boys are waiting to kill me, but Mr. Gracie protects me." What if I said that? Probably Mr. Gracie would be gone and Larry and the other boys would cut me into tiny pieces and that would be the end of it. The judge ordered me fit for placement, which means I should be in a group home. Before leaving, my Guardian said it was just a matter of processing some paperwork. They took me back upstairs and I waited. I waited on my mat, I waited in the lunchroom and the classroom and the TV room. I stopped sleeping. I almost told Mr. Gracie, who had told me never to say anything when we were together unless I was asked a question. I almost told Mr. Gracie one Tuesday night after Mr. Gracie had closed the door and pointed with his right hand toward the corner of the room. "I'm going to get out of here." But I didn't. I've never disobeyed Mr. Gracie and occasionally Mr. Gracie says, his hand over my face covering my mouth, pinching my nose shut, "You're a good kid. Well-behaved. You're going to turn out okay."

We pour slowly, one at a time, through the double steel doors onto the yard. The stronger kids walk casually toward the lone basketball hoop, Larry dribbling the basketball. The rest of us just mill around. It's a cold, damp day. The sky is the same color as the walls. There's a tetherball stand where a leather bag hangs from a long rope. Usually there's a game of tag and there's card games, spades, hearts, and bid whiz. And usually the basketball game is so intense that others wait to play, watching the guys in the game lunging at the hoop, sweat pouring into the collars of their shirts. But today just a handful of boys throw the ball toward the basket, then let it bounce away on the cement. Nobody lays any cards out. No one goes near the hit ball. Other groups walk slowly into corners or lean against the walls.

Nico catches up with me. His face is red as a beet. "Did you see that?"

"See what?" Nobody has a jacket and usually when it is cold like this they'll take us to the gym or just leave us in the TV room.

"They know, you fucking jerk," Nico spits at me. Petey joins us as we walk toward our spot against the wall, near the back but not in the corners. The corners are taken.

"Hey," Petey says.

"The guards," Nico continues. "The guards know. Look at how they were acting. And where are they now? They're gone. They are gone. Oh man. Motherfuckers. Motherfuckers."

I turn around and see it's true, and that groups of boys are congealing together like oil cooling in a pan. Across the top I see Larry whispering in someone's ear then turning in my direction. A smile spills across Larry's face when he notices me looking at him. Larry lifts his shirt slightly and I see the flat slab of metal then the shirt lowering back over the blade like a curtain. My view is obstructed by bodies swelling the yard.

"I'm Jewish," I say to Nico, sticking my thumbs in the elastic of my pants. The sky spinning above us.

"What?"

"On my father's side," I tell him. "I'm half Jewish."

"Why would I give a shit about that?"

"You'd care on the outside," I tell him.

"We're not on the outside, are we, peckerwood? Does this look outside to you?"

Groups are moving together, forcing toward the center of the yard. We try to push through but find ourselves stuck in the coming waves. I lean back and realize that Nico is there behind me and Petey's big shoulder is in my arm. We have formed a triangle. I look through the crowd for Larry's knife. There's a scream through my ear. He's been waiting to do it to me. He has. Waiting. He's been waiting since Mr. Gracie smacked him in the teeth with his club and pointed to me and told Larry, anything else happens to me Larry was going to take a long fall. The kind of fall you don't get up from. Mr. Gracie sealed my fate then. He must have known he couldn't always be there for me. Now I'm doomed. I wait for the blade in my stomach, peeling my ribs. I close my eyes for a second.

The sound of a jaw breaking echoes through the noise. Fists and faces. There are teeth biting near my nose and Petey's shoulder covering my face then jerking away. The boys rush together. The air burns. The arms swing in windmills. Blood flies against the blacktop. All over is smashing and punching. A fist hits my cheek, the ground flies toward me. The asphalt beneath my fingers is full of pebbles and I'm surrounded by knees bumping my ears. I am lifted by my collar from the crowding feet. I turn around and see Nico has gone down and is sitting in a position that resembles a prayer. But then Nico is standing again, his arms bent into his chest, feet planted, chin forward. The triangle between us grows larger. I stretch my arms in front of me sucking air through my wide-open mouth. Guards are rushing into the yard, swinging billy clubs. A gunshot. They're herding us toward the walls. Voices come from the loudspeakers shouting unintelligible directions but repeating them over and over again until they make sense.

"Line up against the wall, single file. Line up against the wall, single file. Line up against the wall, single file."

We're against the wall, our backs facing out, our legs spread, our hands pressing into the stone. Petey is on the other side of me, his head down. Nico turns his head slightly and we look at each other and I think Nico is going to start laughing. A smile grows across my face. He is going to laugh, his face is contorting and his eyes squeezing shut involuntarily, and tears are running over his cheek pooling into his mouth. He's mewing, his tongue licking at the puddles. Behind us, someone is dead. But it isn't us. A doctor is examining a boy that is lying in the middle of the yard with a pitchfork carved into his chest. It isn't us. We're fine.

I grab the bed rail and place my foot against the base and swing around it wrapping my other leg around the pole. This is life. I spin three times this way before I sit down on the bed across from Petey. I'm dizzy and Petey deals me seven cards. I look at my cards and like what I've been dealt. "So how'd you get here?" I ask. I might be feeling more talkative than I've ever felt. I organize first by color, and then by rank. The lights are on in the room. Western is on lockdown. There won't be school tomorrow, and they'll feed us in our room. And maybe the day after that, but then Mr. Gracie will come for me, late at night.

"Stealing," Petey says as an answer, laying a card down, drawing from the deck. "Driving around. I would steal cars."

"Where would you go?"

"The suburbs."

What's done is done. It won't happen again for a while. I'll be gone before the next riot. I've got my walking papers. They can't hold me in here forever. They'll find a placement for me soon. I'll be transferred. Things will be okay and I'll start over, like I always do. When I get out I'm going to learn how to fight. I'm going to stop being scared. I'll change completely. "And you?" Petey asks.

I sit back on his bunk, back against the wall, the window above my head. I grab Petey's foot. "Ha," I say, and shake his foot. I lay down three hearts, the king, the queen, and the jack. That's ten points each but there's still an ace that goes on the end and the ace is worth fifteen. I discard a low spade and Petey finishes my run on both sides, with the ace and the ten.

"Generous of you," he says. We'll never be this close again.

"I couldn't stay put," I tell him, picking one up. I measure my options. One of Petey's eyes is higher than the other. I should be able to win this. My grandfather was a card player. My father told me once that his dad had bet their house and lost. He used to tell me I looked like my grandfather. I try to answer Petey but I don't really know the answer. I pull on my nose. "I was in CYS, emergency placement. There were thirty of us in each room and there were four rooms. There was only two staff members and they stayed in the office with the door locked. I tried to ask them when I was getting out but they wouldn't tell me. Then one of the ladies opened the door and said to me, If you don't like it here, why don't you walk away? It's not like you're in jail. She had hair on her chin. She was the bearded lady. And it was true, the door was open. So I did it. I just left. And she yelled after me where was I going. I said I was going home. I went back to my old neighborhood, but everyone had left. And when they caught me they put me here."

25.

26.

27.

28.

29.

30.

25) Cat Hill, London

26) Nassau Avenue, New York

27) Brinker Road, New York

28) Metropolitan Avenue, New York

29) Conway Road, London

30) 23rd Street, New York

THE CANDIDATE IN BLOOM

by DOUG DORST

THE CANDIDATE IS so tense he cannot walk without crutches. Renata grimaces as she walks behind him through the hotel lobby. Her job is to make him glimmer, and she has been in the election business long enough to know that when the legs fail, the heart soon follows.

He enters the warm whoosh of the revolving door and fumbles his crutches. The tip of one catches in the door behind him, and the door jars to a stop, trapping him inside. Renata watches through the glass that separates them as he tugs and tugs on the crutch, watches his face darken and puff with toddler frustration. She sighs, then pushes backward on the door, using all her weight to create an inch of space that frees both crutch and man.

He galumphs out through a receiving line of three disinterested bellhops in brass-buttoned red uniforms and incongruous fezzes, and he makes his way to the rented yellow bus. The door of the bus squeaks open, cranked by the driver, who doubles as the campaign's district coordinator of yard signs. There are few yards in the district, which is relentlessly urban, but the candidate does not seem bothered. His logic, she knows, can be idiosyncratic.

They have a long night ahead, a night of riding in the yellow bus beneath the arc lights of the city. Renata disapproves of the bus. It is, she argued, pale and bloodless populism—a desperate, flailing stab at aw-shucks bonhomie—and it is doomed to fail, message-wise. The bus is also a fat, slow-moving target for scorn and bullets, and, as she gently reminded the candidate, the campaign had already endured much of both. (Sixty-two bullets, by her count. The scorn is unquantifiable.) But he insisted. "Everyone loves school buses," he said. "We all rode them and sang the same bus songs." Such dreamy evocations of youth are part of his voter appeal, which is limited but passionate. He plays well among registered voters who self-identify as seeking that which cannot be reclaimed.

So, this bus. Idling in a blue diesel haze, it looks as ragged as the baggy-eyed, sag-cheeked candidate himself. Inside, dried gum polkadots the floor, duct tape has been peeled away from green vinyl seat backs to reveal filler that looks disturbingly like hair, seat cushions are minefields of sprung coils. She smells an exhaust leak, imagines her lungs turning cold and blue.

She and the candidate share a seat, and they lurch forward together as the driver clutch-pops in his nervousness. He stammers out an apology to them and jerks the bus into traffic. Angry horns honk alongside them. (Seven horns, she counts, each a lost vote or a vote they've never had.) They rattleclank and rumblebump through the city, potholing with great frequency. The district coordinator of yard signs is a terrible driver.

West of Main and south of Jefferson, they stop for a photo-op at a day-care center. The bus unloads them in a weedy, cracked-concrete playground where a dozen small children run in circles in the failing light, all shrieks and pounding feet and corduroy squeaks. One boy, freckled and lean and exuding the mirthless aggression of a bully, runs past the candidate and kicks out one of the crutches, sending it scuttering across the macadam. The candidate wobbles but does not fall, thank god, and as he clings to his remaining support, Renata looks daggers at the boy. The boy stops in his tracks, chastened and submissive. He retrieves the crutch and hands it back to the candidate, who tousles the boy's hair and calls him scamp.

The press, unfortunately, is nowhere to be seen. She hands disposable cameras to the staff: two spent-looking women who reluctantly stub out their cigarettes to accept the gifts. "For posterity," she tells them.

"Who's Posterity?" one woman says.

"This man," Renata says.

The women snap pictures as the candidate hands out green lollipops to the children. One little girl bursts into tears, and the candidate looks to Renata with the expression of a drowning man. Renata kneels next to the girl, asks her what's wrong. The girl says she doesn't like green. The candidate looks hurt. Green is his favorite.

Renata tells her that her green lollipop isn't green at all, it's a special new kind of lollipop that looks green and tastes green but is really red. *Really?* the girl asks, and Renata says, *Really,* and the girl skips away, happy again. Renata looks to the candidate, expecting to find gratitude. Instead, he looks at her with hangdog credulity: a special new kind of lollipop? Why didn't she tell him they had one? And why on earth did she give it away?

Back on the bus. Renata watches as the candidate smiles and waves to the people outside. The sky darkens to purple-black and he waves. Traffic thins and he waves. The law-abiding return to the fragile safety of their apartments and he waves. Crotch-stained drunks teeter in front of liquor stores and he waves. Floppyjean homeboys flip him the bird and he waves. He waves and waves even when no one is in sight, waves to the televised ghosts flickering behind slatted blinds and iron bars, to the lampposts and their bright sodium moons, to traffic signals winking amber, to retracted awnings and squat blue mailboxes and bags of trash left out for morning pickup.

The bus stops at a red light. On the sidewalk is a street singer, a bone-thin white kid whose face has been picked raw by speed-freak nails. He is offering rapid-fire rhymes in a jagged tenor, punctuated by harmonica lines that punch and squawk and accuse and cry. His shoulders twitch and jerk. At his feet is a cigar box with its lid open; a few coins gleam like miracles in the streetlight. Renata wants to stay and listen, wants to fill his box with coins and tell him that he is beautiful—or someday may be, at least—and that his music, though dissonant and violent and frantic, is in a way beautiful and he has made the world more beautiful than it seemed moments ago (which is to say, wholly unbeautiful, beautiless, beautiempty, beautibereft), but the traffic light turns green, and the bus lurches forward and belches a diesel cloud, and the kid and his music are lost in the engine rumble and the whine of wheels.

She looks at the candidate. His eyes are closed and his head bobs up and down, and she sees he is lost in a different rhythm, in a song that, from first note to final echo, exists only in his own head. He soon falls asleep, his forehead resting against a window scratched with childish obscenities: I DID HEIDI G and FAT LARRY FUCKS ASS and assorted stick figures sporting inflated cocks that remind Renata of birthday-clown balloons. She covers him with the powder-blue blanket she carries everywhere in a canvas tote bag. These days, he seems to doze off before finishing anything.

There is a snap and a crack and a pop as a bullet passes through the bus, in one shatterproof window and out another. Renata pulls the candidate into her lap, shields him with her own body. He stirs. "Thank you," he says into her skirt.

At the hotel is a phone message from her sister, a woman who has a gated estate and four gifted-and-talented children and a husband in perfect prostate health and yet still clutches to the sisterly rivalry of their teenaged years. *Looks like you hitched your wagon to the wrong horse this time*, the message says, the sneer in the words amplified by the desk clerk's meticulous script. What her sister does not understand is that there are no wrong horses. Renata does not lose. Never has. Which is why she is sought after, consulted, handsomely compensated, kowtowed to at pancake-and-prayer breakfasts.

With the candidate safely in bed, Renata reads his draft of the speech he will give at tomorrow's fund-raiser with the riverboat-casino kingpins. She is shocked; his mind has slipped even farther than she thought. In strong black ink he has written at the top of the first page: *America. It is indescribable. It is so vast that even if we could grasp It by the lower jaw and wrench Its head free, we still could not fathom It.* Then thirty minutes' worth of delusions and outrage and paranoia. The conclusion, double underlined: *America is in trouble today not because Her people have failed, but because She is a voluptuary, screwing everything in sight. Because Her shot of nostalgia was administered with a tainted needle. Because tomorrow it will rain and we will die.*

She shakes her head and opens a fresh notebook. Words spill from her as soon as pen touches paper. It is effortless; she is just the medium, the translator, the messenger's messenger. Seventeen cigarettes, six cups of coffee, and two bowls of frosted cereal later, she is finished. She reads over her work with pride. She has assembled all the right words in their ordained ritual fashion: compressed nuggets of ideas and opinions and stances, crunchy and wholesome, glazed with a honey-sweet slurry of metaphor suited to the crowd—"chance" and "fate" and "the inside straight," "split the aces" and "double down," "loosest slots" and "five percent vig," "boxcars" and "baccarat" and "a hard ten on the hop." It's a winner. She'd bet her life on it.

The next day, it rains.

A red tarp has been stretched over the deck of the riverboat. Hundreds of chairs are filled with the polyestered bottoms of men and women who fix the odds on slot machines and break the thumbs of card-counters. A brass band plays a Sousa march. The tarp billows in the breeze.

Renata takes her place in a chair beside the dais. She is sleep-deprived and feels cotton-headed from seasick pills—she is not one for the water. She watches the small group of supporters gathered on the pier behind crowd-control barricades. Some hold umbrellas. Others hold home-painted signs, most of which—though her tired eyes can't read clearly at this distance—appear to lack both verbs and sense. *God Country Pie*, one seems to say. Others: *We People Order Form*; *Leadship Tomorrow*; *Valley Shadow Oil Rod*; and, curiously, *CANIDATE*. She listens as raindrops paradiddle on the red plastic above her head, barely notices as the candidate crutches past her and takes his place at the lectern. The band stops, but the tuba player misses the cue and blats out an unaccompanied B-flat.

The candidate comes across as a new man. Invigorated by the words she has fed him, he delivers the lines impeccably—some incantatory, some gruffly barked, some lilting along with the bob of the riverboat itself. Renata, seduced by her own words, has to stop herself from mouthing along. His skin shines with the fervent sweat of a revivalist. Someone says hallelujah; someone answers with amen.

After a final fist in the air, he casts away his crutches and hops down from the dais to the deck, as if he has been healed by his own spirit. There are handshakes and thumbs-up, ties beating frantic semaphores in the wind, applause like cannon fire. The sun comes out, as if on cue, and casts a blush of red light over everyone.

Renata checks her watch. Five minutes to absorb the glow, then the moorings will be untied, and the paddle wheel will turn, and they will power down the river while lunching below decks. She hopes he does not overeat; at three-thirty he must Charleston at the senior center. She relaxes, lets her head swim all it wants to.

She does not notice the youth lurking in the gangway. He jumps into the candidate's path, brandishing a sword as rusty as the ideology he will later profess to the TV cameras. As the sword cuts its arc through the air, the candidate's legs freeze; his head turns, looking for Renata, begging for directions. But what can she say? Run? Get away?

The hack is a savage one. The candidate slumps to the whitewashed deck. His mouth opens and closes without a sound. The horror—or the revelation, she can't tell which—in what she is witnessing is this: the motion looks purely mechanical, a clockwork of mandible and maxilla winding down, coming to rest at half-past-gape.

    ·Renata weaves past the writhing pile of men who are pinning the assassin to the deck. She pushes numbly through the people who, crying and shouting, surround the candidate. As she kneels in the pooling blood, she sees something rise from the corpse, something curling like smoke in the red light. It plumes straight up to the tarp, then winds outward and escapes into sky, tracing the shape of a calla lily blossom. She does not feel herself being jostled, does not hear the keening of grief and the roar of panic; still kneeling, she watches as the candidate blooms into mystery, into romance and tragedy, into something she can make holy.

31.

32.

33.

34.

35.

36.

31) Kings Road, London

32) Queens Boulevard, New York

33) Kincraig Street, Cardiff

34) 44th Avenue, New York

35) Bairo Court, London

36) Green Lanes, London

CONVERGENCES

by LAWRENCE WESCHLER

COMPOUNDING UNSCIENTIFIC POSTSCRIPT

[TOWARD A UNIFIED FIELD THEORY
OF MASTER-PATTERN METAPHORS]

OF COURSE, ONCE you see them, you start seeing them everywhere: that's the crazy thing with these pattern convergences. Uh-oh, my by-now resigned daughter regularly finds herself sighing, Daddy's having another one of his loose-synapse moments. It's only natural, I suppose, that my speculations on synapses themselves a few issues back should have proved especially compounding: but some of the rhymes in this instance have been feeling particularly uncanny.

Some readers will perhaps recall the capillary mesh of associations from that issue (*McSwys No. 5*): cameras obscura; eyes, pupils, and the hourglass converging of lines of sight: trees, leaves, branchings, and the hourglass convergings of roots and crowns; dendrites, brains, branching templates (family trees, decision trees, etc.) on out into the capillary mesh of the Internet itself {figures 1-4}. For, of course, I concluded, invoking a recently produced map of cyberspace, what else does the Internet, latest product of human consciousness, end up most resembling, other than a mammoth human brain?

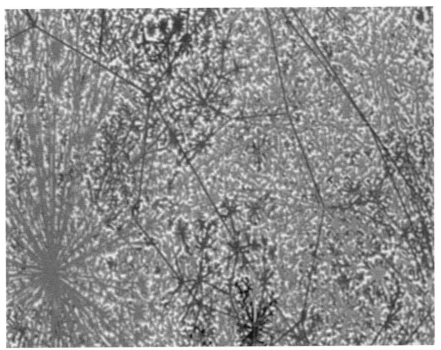

Fig. 1: *Map of Cyberspace (detail), from* National Geographic, *January 2000.*

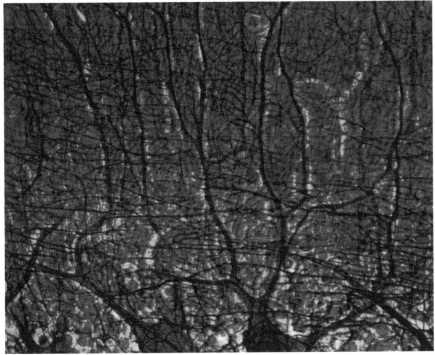

Fig. 2: *Neurons in cerebellum, from Richard Restak's* The Brain.

But, I ended up wondering, is that, once more, just some sort of conceptual illusion, an outward projection onto the world of our own cerebral wiring? Or, quite the opposite, is the human brain in fact now starting to write itself large, as it were, as big as the whole wide virtual world?

No sooner had I sent those lines off to the printers than I came upon the following piece of speculation near the conclusion of neurologist Elkhonen Goldberg's magisterial new volume, *The Executive Brain: Frontal Lobes and the Civilized Mind* (p. 224):

Fig. 3: From the Dioptrique.

> ...With this demonstration in place, the following intriguing questions arise: Do the invariant laws of evolution, shared by the brain, society, and digital computing devices reflect the only intrinsically possible or optimal path of development? Or do human beings recapitulate, consciously or unconsciously, their own internal organization in man-made devices and social structures? Each possibility is intriguing in its own right. In the first case, our analysis will point to some general rules of development of complex systems. In the second case, we encounter a puzzling process of unconscious recapitulation, since neither the evolution of society nor the evolution of the digital world has been explicitly guided by the knowledge of neuroscience.

Likewise, a few weeks later, this passage from Deborah Treisman's marvelously moving contribution to a symposium on art and science in the *Threepenny Review* (Summer 2000):

> The term "naturalist" could apply equally to Galileo or Augustine, Rembrandt or Wordsworth. Some thinkers have combined the facets of naturalism: William Carlos Williams, for example, a doctor who could as easily diagnose illness as write,
>
> > On a wet pavement the white sky recedes
> > mottled black by the inverted
> > pillars of the red elms,
> > in perspective, that lift the tangled
> > net of their desires hard into
> > the falling rain.

Fig. 4: From Eyewitness Explorer's Trees, *Doris Kindersley. (Courtesy Doris Kindersley).*

{....}What are we observing when we observe nature? What are the priests, poets, and scientists drawn to with such force and conviction? ...Nature is a world of patterns-from the symmetrical almost yin-yang of a tadpole embryo to the geometric fan of veins on a leaf once described by William Carlos Williams:

> Upon each leaf it is
> a pattern more
> of logic than a purpose
> links each part to the rest,
> an abstraction
> playfully following
> centripetal
> devices, as of pure thought—
> the edge tying by
> convergent, crazy rays
> with the center

Nature is the bonding of cells into unexpected shapes, the layering of pupil upon pupil in a fly's eye, the splay of brain cells or of branches against a winter sky that combine in another poem, by August Kleinzahler:

> A section of cortex
> stained dark and frozen on a field
> of gray
>   axons, dendrites
> probe and reticulate
>   layered
> as the frigid river's gray no
> one sings of
>   mighty
> almighty oak
> & maple

Nor were the resonances confined to the written word. For had not a brain much like the one anatomized over a century ago in the cerebellum diagram from *Gray's Anatomy* I'd included in the Issue No. 5 piece—indeed perhaps that very brain!—conceived of the amazing graphic I subsequently came upon in Edward Tufte's *Envisioning Information* (p. 77), Joshua Hutchings Colton's 1864 comparative line-up of the drainages of the world's great rivers {fig. 5}? One afternoon, out on the streets of the city, I came upon a more contemporary tree genealogy emblazoned across the front of the tee-shirt of an especially hip passerby {fig. 6}. And then someone else alerted me to the current heroic-absurd efforts of a benightedly inspired artist named Beth Campbell, who's taken to covering over entire gallery spaces with ever more detailed decision-trees, painstakingly anatomizing the possible implications of her almost every choice {fig. 7}: talk about Compounding!

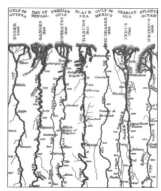

Somewhere in there, *Science* magazine offered up an astonishing supplement to their Vol. 291, No. 5507 issue: J.C. Venter et al.'s

Fig. 5: Colton's river line-up (detail), from Tufte's Envisioning Information.

postersize "Annotation of the Human Genome Assembly"—the whole infernal celestial shebang! {see detail, fig. 8}—and damn if that in turn did-n't end up reminding me of a 1980 poster affording a precise grammatical splay of "The Longest Sentence: 958 Words from Marcel Proust's *Cities of the Plain*", which I'd taken to keeping above my desk (as some sort of caution-ary warning, I suppose) {see detail, fig. 9}.

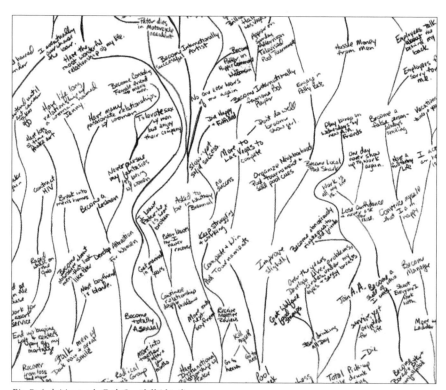

Fig. 7: A decision tree by Beth Campbell (detail).

Fig. 6: The Family Tree of British Rock T-shirt (slightly faded).

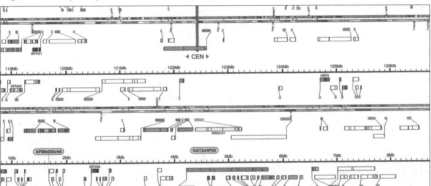

Fig. 8: "Annotation of the Human Genome Assembly" (detail), from Science.

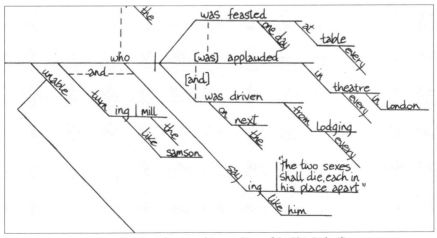

Fig. 9: "The Longest Sentence: 958 Words from Marcel Proust's Cities of the Plain" *(detail).*

But the thing is, it wasn't just trees and branchings. In my original piece I'd noted how one could just as easily have envisioned an alternative metaphorical motif for processes unfurling across time: geological layering, for example, or the way circular waves well out from a pebble dropped into a pond. Why, I'd wondered, was it always trees and branchings? (Because, I—like Elkhonen Goldberg—had speculated, of the tree-and-branching make-up of the brain?) Only, now, I indeed did begin noticing all sorts of other motifs.

The first page of the January 2, 2001, Science section of *The New York Times*, for example, featured an awe-inspiring color photo of Mexico's Popocatepetl volcano in full-throttle eruption {fig. 10}. Page three of the same issue featured an ad for an upcoming lecture series at the 92nd Street Y—"Cracking the Code of Life: The Impact of the Human Genome Project"—whose backdrop 3-D model of the structure of spiraling DNA molecule {fig. 11} made it seem the spewing volcano's diminuitive twin. And two weeks later, reversing scale, the same Science section featured on its front page "A New View of a Nursery of Stars," with photos of entire nebulae in turbulent eruption {fig. 12}.

This serendipitous progression of images in turn reminded me of a (admittedly somewhat overblown) passage from *Clea*, the final volume (1960) of Lawrence Durrell's Alexandria Quartet (p. 89):

Figs. 10-12: Unfurling scenes from The New York Times.

I thought of some words of Arnauti, written about another woman, in another context. "You tell yourself that it is a woman you hold in your arms, but watching the sleeper you see all her growth in time, the unerring unfolding of cells which group and dispose themselves into the beloved face which remains always and for ever mysterious-repeating to infinity the soft boss of the human nose, an ear borrowed from a sea-shell's helix, an eyebrow thought-patterned from ferns, or lips invented by bivalves in their dreaming union. All this process is human, bears a name which pierces your heart, and offers the mad dream of an eternity which time disproves in every drawn breath. And if human personality is an illusion? And if, as biology tells us, every single cell in our bodies is replaced every seven years by another? At the most I hold in my arms something like a fountain of flesh, continuously playing, and in my mind a rainbow of dust.

And then, a few days later, at a bookstore I happened upon a book which just may be the ur-text for this particular sort of metaphorical speculation, Sidney Perkowitz's *Universal Foam: From Cappuccino to the Cosmos.*

Meanwhile, in a different, or maybe not all that different, vein entirely, an email pal of mine, Michael Benson, a passionate stargazer based in Ljubiana, Slovenia of all places, took off on my throwaway pebbles-in-a-pond reference. It was clear he'd already been obsessing on the implications of that sort of metaphor for some time. To wit:

> That comment of yours about waves rippling out from a pebble dropped in a pond resonated with me, because, well, maybe it's just my ongoing space obsession, where one enters a field in which all things larger than a certain size are molded into a sphere or flat disc due to gravity, but I've been concentrating a bit on spheres and discs, as well as the "inside" and "outside" of things. (Again, a tree's fascinating to me partly because it's suspended equidistant between those two). This is from a journal entry from last March:
>
>> There must be some ineffable circular connection between the infinitely large and macrocosmic and the infinitely small and microscopic, as best represented in the perfect circles/spheres of outwardly directed energy (rain-drops on a lake, lunar craters, the sun blazing away in space) and the perfect circles/spheres created by inwardly directed energy (i.e., gravity pulling blobs of matter into spheres, black holes pulling entire galaxies into razor-thin spinning discs). Inwards, outwards: note also that "artificial" gravity can be "made" by spinning a wheel—a direction out and away from a center—and "real" gravity is

directed towards the center of a massive spherical object. But is there really a difference between them, or are they the same? Even if the forces would seem to be directed in opposite directions? Maybe there's a time component, or time-mirror, in there somewhere: and instead of forward/backward, we have in/out?

I ask those who have peeled a mandarin orange, and looked down in amazement to see an exact 3-D scale model replica of a solar observatory picture of the sun in vivid diagrammatic detail: how do you explain the linked inner-outer directions of nature? {Fig. 13} The uncanny linkages, vividly detailed, right under our very noses? What *is* that? The peeled mandarin sits, right now, beside my keyboard, radiating the energy it got from the sun. It's palpable. And it looks exactly like the sun. Could this be how energy zaps between the dimensions? Maybe our ability to perceive it in this way is already evidence of energy transfers. And then you take a bite, and something "blooms" in your sensorium. Why? Where's it from? It blooms, and expands outwards, like rays of light and energy.

Fig. 13: Orange, sun. Sun, orange.

Or, as I say, like the waves welling out from a pebble dropped in a pond. Obviously, neither Benson nor I had been the first to have thought along these lines. Viz, the following, from Leonardo da Vinci's *Codex Atlanticus*, fol. 9 v, which I happened upon not long after I received Benson's email:

> Just as a stone thrown into water becomes the center and cause of various circles, sound spreads circles in the air. Thus every body placed in the luminous air spreads out in circles and fills the surrounding space with infinite likenesses of itself and appears all in all and all in every part.

* * *

And I just find myself wondering, might there be some sort of Grand Unified Field Metaphor that unites all of these metaphors, such that eruptions, for example, simultaneously evince a branching and a pebble-welling characteristic? And indeed, don't they already? Think of the branching tubes and ducts of rising magma in those cross-section diagrams of the interiors of imminently explosive volcanoes, and then of the maps of concentric zones of fallout and damage following any given event {figs. 14 & 15}. No doubt at some sub-submicroscopic level, the furthermost neural dendrites in the brain are in fact exuding spasms of chemical foam, whose electrical consequences well out in concentric waves across the synaptic gap and toward the furthermost extensions of neighboring neurons. And—genes to genius, cereal to cerebellums, concepts to conception—what else, what other, is procreation itself?

Exhausted, spent, I pick up W.G. Sebald's recent historico-metaphysical walkabout volume *The Rings of Saturn*, my newest favorite book, and come upon the following passage (pp. 19-20), in which Sebald in turn evokes Sir Thomas Browne, that seventeenth-century Father of Us All:

Fig. 14: Cross-section.

Fig. 15: Danger zones.

The greater the distance, the clearer the view: one sees the tiniest of details with the utmost clarity. It is as if one were looking through a reversed opera glass and through a microscope at the same time. And yet, says Browne, all knowledge is enveloped in darkness. What we perceive are no more than isolated lights in the abyss of ignorance, in the shadow-filled edifice of the world. We study the order of things, says Browne, but we cannot grasp their innermost essence. And because it is so, it befits our philosophy to be writ small, using the shorthand and contracted forms of transient Nature, which alone are a reflection of eternity. True to his own prescription, Browne records the patterns which recur in the seemingly infinite diversity of forms; in *The Garden of Cyrus*, for instance, he draws the quincunx, which is composed by using the corners of a regular quadrilateral and the point at which its diagonals intersect.{fig. 16}. Browne identified this structure everywhere, in animate and inanimate matter: in certain crystalline forms, in starfish and sea urchins; in the vertebrae of mammals and the backbones of birds and fish; in the skins of various species of snake; in the crosswise prints left by quadrupeds, in the physical shapes of caterpillars, butterflies, silkworms and moths, in the root of the water fern, in the seed tusks of the sunflower and the Caledonian pine, within young oak shoots or the stem of the horsetail; and in the creations of mankind, in the pyramids of Egypt and the mausoleum of Augustus as in the garden of King Solomon, which was planted with mathematical precision with pomegranate trees and white lilies. Examples might be multiplied with-

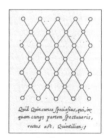
Fig. 16: The quincunx.

out end, says Browne, and one might demonstrate ad infinitum the elegant geometrical designs of Nature; however—thus, with a fine turn of phrase and image, he concludes his treatise—the constellation of the Hyades, the Quincunx of Heaven, is already sinking beneath the horizon, and so 'tis time to close the five ports of knowledge. We are unwilling to spin out our waking thoughts into the phantasmes of sleep; making cables of cobwebs and wildernesses of handsome groves....

And so, indeed, to bed.

Fig. 17: The Hyades, w/ cacti.

WEENA

by BENJAMIN LYTAL

POST-APOCALYPTIC STORY in five acts, dedicated to an imaginary friend of mine named Weena, a very odd and forthright girl who died accidentally, run over by a motorcycle on the streets of Tulsa.

There have to be a lot of transitions. It cannot get boring. There must be production values.

Actually, it will not be with Weena that I make love in the ditch at the end of Act 3. It will be a Weena mannequin that I construct, mounted on wheels. I will roll it and push it, over rubble, and naturally we end up in a ditch, like rain. It will be one of those things I do half from boredom, half from making up a better story about myself. And it will have a letdown like masturbation.

At this point maybe it should become hard to read. There will be a gun-slinging scene with play pistols. Country-western with white butts. We will be using vehicle wreckage for battlements. Somehow the pistols work, shoot bullets.

Opening the first act I am driving a group of us pals down the road, very slowly, letting the tires enjoy the road. Eventually I just stop, I love the road so much. Weena understands, and she opens her door and rolls out onto the street. We all crane our necks and rearrange ourselves in the car so we can see her from better angles. Then it looks like she hiccups but we can't hear it because of a loud motorcycle coming down the road.

Detail of coming war (i.e. foreshadowing, i.e. locusts) should be in from the beginning, so that the atmospheric tension is not lost. The motorcycle should roar like Aries or something, so then when the flying saucer bombs come, they will be like the return of the drunken motorcycle.

This time, at the beginning of Act 4 we'll be BORED, and Jimmy will say, "I just want to go around and inflate everything." The lithe and competent world of Act 1 is snapped in half by Weena's crippling, so the wax flower she keeps by her deathbed is like the remission of nostalgia.

I used to dance like a figure in a pop-up book, doing the splits, clapping, or doing my hips and elbows in twitches and oscillations. Weena would unfurl and billow, or bob like a raft in midstream. Be vague, but give them the details they want. There will be a war in the middle of the story. It will come out of nowhere and be a very unexpected recapitulation with intensifications. Jeeps with mounted laser guns will leap over ditches. Buildings will explode like clockwork.

We make love in a ditch, with these jeeps flying over us. There is a lot of hesitation and distraction. It is all described. Everything takes place in Tulsa.

The place where we're getting dressed before the opening is, obviously, a costume shop. Or no, it is someone's house with a lot of clothes. It must definitely be a safe place. No parents, you can smoke there.

So it is there, in this very faux-wood, fluorescent atmosphere that it starts. But mustn't seem too anti-cool, or too grungy. Just happy kids, the way cool kids really are. My character gets very excited that we are all dressing up on purpose. I volunteer to go and run errands for certain items. For example, someone's like "Saber!" and I go buy a saber.

We try to dress outlandishly in introverted ways, like bold saplings. So this is how we dress. Then when we all get in the car the amazing thing is that it's so chill. It's that rare mix of being both chill and sapling. Like the saplings are rolling their shoulders but not their eyes.

So the drive to the hospital will be very important. First, first, it must make the reader feel the mood is threatened, and that this means more than the end of one night's fun. It's bad that eras never have finales. Second, the city must kind of catch on fire. I might even use some simile like "the sky like a paused explosion," and later in the story it will resonate. There should be neon, we should turn off of the avenue, and I should make Tulsa look like a mournful spaceship.

ELYRIA MAN

by DAVID MEANS

1

THOMPSON SCRAPES OFF the residual mud, the encrustment of years, with
the blade of the shovel, with the edge of a crowbar from his truck, working
carefully around my head, avoiding eyes and orifices until ultimately a face
is revealed. He gives a low murmur. He's reluctant to uncover my eyes. He
fears sockets. But he does it. The uncovering of eyes is a one-shot trick, not
to be repeated. And in any case he has already quickly adapted to the ugli-
ness of my features. He appreciates my originality, the leathery incarnation
of a primal self, as he pauses, leaning on his implement, his hoe or pitchfork
(preferably the three-pronged variety). In the late-morning light I appear
forsaken in my clench-jawed agony, my pale crumpled eyesockets, and my
positioning in the earth: one arm tossed back in a relaxed sleeping position.
(Think of those time-lapse films of couples sleeping together, making
unconscious bodily adjustments, both working in what seems to be a con-
gruence, eerily responding in turn to the other on the white cloudy wrinkles
of fresh starched sheets.)

In the lonely silence of an Ohio field—the irrigation pipes dripping
softly behind him—I look fetal, protean, like a newborn foal just before he
ungathers his legs to stand for the first time. In the contours of my face is

the ungainly intelligence of the greasy womb-wet newborn. Thompson stares down at the form rising up out of the earth and absently chews his tobacco, spits sideways, sniffs, coughs, unfolds the squares of his handkerchief and deposits phlegm and then refolds it and carefully puts it into his coat pocket. The forsaken are nothing new to him. He's seen the look a hundred times at cattle auctions. In his wife's eyes. In the eyes of his kids.

2

Thompson was taking a soil sample when the blade of his shovel touched something firm. Often a digger unknowingly amputates an arm with the shovel blade, decapitates, disembowels the dusty nothingness from a puckered gut. Happens most of the time. The haphazard surgery of the blind digger: the blade driven under the force of a boot, applied pressure condensed to the edge, as slick and quick as a blade on ice. But Thompson was a careful man. When he felt something in the ground he paused to think about it, to consider his options.

3

In town that afternoon the Amish man named John, hitching his buggie to a post, is receptive to hearing about me. He has always wondered about bog folk. Ohio bog folk especially, he adds, looking down at the hardbaked street. Bouquets of Queen Anne's Lace sprout from the cracks. The road is absurdly wide, as if speaking to some long-ago hope for greater commerce.

Me own father claimed to have found one once down to Wooster, John the Amish says, and this one had a small noose-like apparatus around his neck and was gripping a sacred heathen ornament. Them bog people were idolater of the most basic sort. Certainly they weren't God-fearing folk. No sir. They mocked the Lord. But nonetheless, I'd be interested to see your bog man.

Yes, do come down to the farm, Thompson says, cutting him short. He has a limited tolerance for the seriousness of these men; they seemed consumed with the dubious chore of faith. He shakes John's meaty hand. The horse—a beautiful brown and white marbled roan—clomps nervous steel on the pavement. The Amish men shuffle into the tobacco shop (and Thompson with them), peruse the racks of girlie magazines, sneak them into the safe confines of pastoral titles: *Farmlife. Horticultural Digest. Organic Farmer. Model Railroader.* There is comfort in eyeing the gaping lipped pinkness that I suppose somehow reminds them of farm work. Thompson carries the story of me with him into the sweet tobacco smell, orders a pouch of Captain Black

Gold, watches as the girl named Irene moves about behind the counter. A high school dropout in bib overalls, firm breasts behind the right angles of taut denim. He loves the way the straps, secure in the metal hook/button contraption, hold forth an illusion of restraint and looseness at the same time. In those overalls, her body never fails to remind him of the horse/harness physics that governs John's buggy parked just up the street. The strange conspiratorial relationship between the horse—blinded on both sides by small rectangles of black—and the owners whip. Taking the tobacco pouch into his hands, he squeezes to test its moisture; a soft spongy feel indicates a good seal, soft sugary strands ready to be lodge into his pipe. He loves the sensation of his thumb entering the bowl—creosoted and sticky—and packing it soft, lovingly, intuitively not too firm or too loose—the same way he had stuck his fingers into Irene. She smiles uncomfortably and tries to conjure me up. Never heard of bog people, she says. He mentions others—Scotland, the peat there. The best she can do is imagine a decomposed corpse, something from a horror movie, arms and legs akimbo, skin peeling in raglike sheets from his body. If I had my way (and I do, sometimes) she'd visualize one of Matisses bronze sculptures, of the Jeanette series, a fine abstraction indicating both my primal elements—the stately elegance of my form—with the modern thrown-back motion of my arms, the movement into space, a tight-suited diver launching cleanly into a universe of blue and white.

4

I'll come to be known as the Elyria Man, uncovered several miles to the south of that city, just as the Grauballe man was named after that town, although he was found in the Nebelgard Fen. Insofar as one has to be named for a geographic region, this one is fine as any, boring and nondescript in what most agree is the most mundane and utilitarian of states, a state that openheartedly belabors blandness. (On hearing this, Ohioans gather themselves into a defensive haunch.) Thompson embraced Ohio. He embraced John Glenn as the state hero. What more starkly boring symbol than a man circumnavigating the earth ensconced in a capsule equipped with outmoded gear, spinning in the silence of space only to plunge back and capitalize upon that act for a lifetime? Thompson and I agree that it would be better to remain up there, to be slung by gravity's twirl out into the void until radio contact sizzled out. Better to return to earth, heat-shield failing, in a blooming orchid of raw flame and burning metal, striking the Atlantic landing zone in a geyser of steam.

5

Ramrod straight, my Great Uncle Stan is still a bog man—the Minnesota variety buried just north of Red Lake in that wondrous result of paludification. Ramrod Man was grim-faced and stoic in the single photo we had of him standing, still a man, in front of his cabin with his family. The cabin was blown away in one of those great brushfire/sandstorms that predated the Dust Bowl by several years. The Ravishing Winds, as they were known. After the Ravishing Winds, he took the family to Alberta, worked that soil for several years, and then returned alone to Minnesota where he scouted desperately for a homestead he could afford; he was most certainly suffering dementia and starvation when he fell in the bog hole. It is said that he was uncovered, years later, by the blade of the motorized peat-gathering machine (that's another story, one of big-hearted failure, a certain Al Wildberg's desires to compete with the soft coal industry by gathering the finest peat the U.S. had to offer). Wildberg decided it would cut into his gathering schedule too much to call anyone to see a bog man. He gave Uncle Stan a firm kick with his boot, watched his arm crumble, kicked him a few more times and then got into his machine, cranked it up, gave it a bit of choke, and buried Uncle Stan.

6

I'm unconvincing as a bog man. A small twist in my smile betrays me to Thompson. My body is facing northeast along its vertical axis in order to throw the Ohio State archeology team a loop if they come, so that they'll conjure up some sacrificial rite to the spring rain gods. We bog folk often attempt the best we can to make some pretense of history (thus my arm thrown dramatically back and the Hamlet-like thoughtfulness of my browline); my whole demeanor must be that of the hardbitten down-on-his-luck soul handpicked for sacrifice. An easy role for me, I admit.

Thompson proceeds to clear my entire ear, around the bottom of my jaw, while twilight smears the western flank of his farm, lights up the thick crowns of his windbreak. He's talking softly to me, his voice modulating with the breeze. It takes me a moment, but then I realize that he's making a confession, and it's about Irene in the tobacco shop.

Sure she's young, sure, a kid, really. But lovely to behold. So lovely. And along with her girl-smells, perfume and the like, she always smells like a fresh pouch of rough cut.

Before that he said: I did, do love Alice. She's a fine woman and mother to my children—yet it's something in her, well, I guess a demeanor is the

word. We don't mix. Oil and vinegar. We worked this land side-to-side during the great '67 hardships, the the drought of '88, the Dry Spell of '89, the
Cricket Plague of '90, and all the little plagues in between, but that's not
enough, to have toiled through some rough times is not enough at all.
Those irrigation pipes were her idea. I'd have to admit that much.

Then: smelled like pipe tobacco, she even admitted it and we laughed
and then took a turn out in her car—one of those little compact Japanese
deals—to the lake where I must admit we kissed a long, long time, first
one, first time, a kiss lasting a good twenty minutes tops.

He leans down to whisper this fact into my ear, tapping it softly with
the tip of his trowel.

Slipped me the tongue, he whispers, his voice gaunt and tight. She was
up here at the house—snuck up one night—and we were on the sleeping
porch and the house was quiet behind us and we were on the hammock I
have back there and that's when it happened, my dear bog friend, when I
went over onto the other side of sin and salvation and found myself in the
darkness… but here his confession waned. He had reached that point we all
reach when the desire to speak the truth meets up with the pain it produces.

Silently he dug out around the northern side of my head, working gently in the descending darkness. Night swallows dipped through the sky.
The first stars emerged. I saw Asia Minor for the first time in years. The Big
Dipper. The Little Dipper. Polaris nailed the whole spinning arrangement
down and gave me the appropriate sense of firm orderly circular motion.

7

Arriving from Ohio State and points east (Harvard had a fine bog team),
pulling up in station wagons (with the OSU logo), professional types in
horn-rims and chinos speaking in absurdly baroque accents, they would
examine me reverently, find the tuberculous infection in my spine that
caused my hunchback (yes, I suffer certain deformities), brushing my face
with boar bristles, taking their sweet time. Eventually they'd send in a
crane, box me with sheets of steel on all four sides, and heft me skyward.
They'd look up at me in their absurd orange hardhats. The chief bog guy
Schunk would stop and assure Thompson that he'd have full visitation
rights. You'll be given full credit for the find, he'll say. You found Elyria
Man. Who? Elyria Man, he'd point up at me. In the annals of history,
Schunk would get full credit for the name coinage. He'd get all the glory.

If the Ohio State people came, I'd tell them to get off my farm, Thompson says eagerly. His voice is firm and resolute but also soft and wispy and

clearly not directed at me or even at some imaginary Schunk but for the most part at himself.

That's what I'd end up saying to them, he quickly adds. He's tapping a finger firmly against the leather of my cheeks the way you'd play a bongo drum. On my eyelid his thumb resides. His index finger rests in what was once my nose.

8

Tollund Man lay still a good two thousand years. Tollund Man—contrary to opinion—had a sad, forlorn look, and didn't much like being dug up, either. He was resting nicely—after some sheep counting and some concentration exercises, after stretching out a charley horse in his right leg, working it out, rubbing the blood down the leg. Sound sleep. Deep sleep. When the peat diggers came upon him he felt the way you'd feel waking up on a hot, humid morning after bathing in dream-sweat all night. You wake up in a fen, in the dead heart of a summer mid-morning after a good two thousand years rest with a small noose of rope around your neck and see how you feel. Tollund never got over it. He'd be quick to point out that he had to deal with the Danish police, too, who accused him of being a murder victim.

In Thompson's field, I could relate to the Tollund Man.

9

I used to be pretty good acquaintances with this bog girl resting silently up in the scrub pines overlooking Lake Michigan from St. Ignace. She's up there waiting as is the wont of all of us to be exhumed, revealed, her wrists tied with yellow nylon tow rope. She's the milky albino white of subterranean cave dwellers. Pine needles tend to pickle the bodies to an angelic whiteness. The wings unfolding from her spine are the petrified remains of her rucksack. She had one of those neat army issue sacks that matched her fatigue pants and her commando jacket—the same one she said her brother brought back from the war. Her fine blond hair is twirled up into what seems to be an ancient Swabian knot, held secure by a little leather hook and a wooden needle. The placid serene rapture of her face reminds one of Joan Baez when she was singing one of her protest songs. The position of her body in relation to the north/south axis, facing the lake, indicates that a drug rite might have transpired. A cheap nickel Zodiac symbol (Libra) adorns her neck.

10

Coincidentally, Thompson grew up near the bog girl in Michigan, not far down the road, just above the bridge past the rinky dink tourist traps meant to look like authentic Indian lodges. Just another trippy barefoot tourist girl up from Chicago with rich parents hiking the spur line that cupped Little Traverse Bay, smoking doobies with the townies. She had the worldly, assured bounce to her walk and was the first girl he met who made fringe out of her bell bottoms and smoked hash, not pot.

11

My old man would take a hat box down from the closet and remove this skull and hold it out to me and say he was going to do the same thing to my head if I didn't shape up, Thompson's saying. He stops for a moment to light his pipe, drawing the big flame down into the bowl. Thompson is versed in the art of maintained pipe smoking, packing the bowl just right and drawing exactly the correct amount of air to keep it lit for an hour. Old man hit the Jap with his bayonet, thrust and twist as he liked to say. He'd go around the house saying it over and over. Thrust and twist. Thrust and twist. Hand-to-hand on Iwo. Chopped it clean off for trophies. Lots of the men did that. Bleached it, dragged it behind the ship to let the fish pick it clean, packed it up and shipped it home to wife back in the states. Even showed me this photo of a woman and her skull in *Life* magazine.

For a moment, I worry. I imagine Thompson decapitating my bog head and carrying it around in a bowling bag like Perseus, seizing my protective powers.

12

With the sky overhead I conjure a bog dream: my intact genetic material will provide a full history: tooth formation (gnarly); propensity for gall stones; slight anal retentiveness; rectal fissures; cancerous propensities—skin, liver. They'll take the stored genetic material and clone me. Elyria Man, thin, wan, hankering for stimulants, narcotics, and with a propensity for finding solitude, for thriving on solitude, for hunkering down in haylofts, for hiding from the police, for underground activities, for cheap gratuitous stunts, for prayer to the one God instead of the new, multiGod(desses). Gaunt and deprived-looking no matter how much food is brought to me. A smoker, too, taking long solemn drags on the cigarettes, pipes, cigars, bongs. I'll be known as the E. man, yet another clone product escaped from the lab living down to the Cleveland Flats, what used to be industrial decay now post-industrial decay, old post-mod coffee shops gutted by post-millennial riot fires. A clone castoff, one of the many who congregate on the flats. Cleveland, tucked along the lake, the great Clone City, capital for a few decades of genetic tech, the post-Mill boom and bust. Tragic Cleveland—always in the shadow of Chicago—with its lost bid to become the great port city of renown, the hub of the growing hinterlands.

13

In what seems a knee-jerk bout of necrophelia, Thompson sheds his work-pants—in the semi-dark—thinking, as he does so, of Irene's lithe body swinging softly beneath her overalls. She's coming over later. He gave the secret sign at the tobacco store. He broke the vapor seal of the packet of Captain Black. If I break the vapor seal then it's a sign, okay, we'll agree on that, it means you've got to come out to the farm and see me, as soon as you finish up work. In his crotch he feels the imminent twang of her arrival. But he's also thinking of Isaiah, of those words imparted by the great profit, enter into the rock, hide thee in the dust, from before the terror of the Lord, from the splendor of his majesty. He's down in the hole with his palm cupped gently against the underside of my jaw, feeling the stretched glossy drum head skin beneath my chin.

14

We killed her, Thompson's admitting to me. Years back, back when I was just a kid and Jason and I were messing around it got out of hand, I guess that's the best way to put it, and one thing led to another; that's how it felt at least, but I don't remember much, just the rope, the rope bright yellow, I mean fantastic yellow, we were tripping and it was like, wow, check out that yellow rope. We stole it off her father's boat, the whole line and the water skis too. A fine pair of wooden skis. He had a hell of a boat, an old Chris Craft with that deep dark wooden sideboards that used to tear up and down Waloon Lake like mad; and Jason was wild on the skies, kicking one off, leaping the wake. Then she went out, I remember, stoned with her eyes glossy but still seeming able to ski. We opened it up full throttle and watched while the sunlight dappled her wet skin. Then she went down and Jason swung back around to find her and tore right over her. A messed up, drug-induced error, was all it was, the kind of thing that happened back then all the time. We didn't know that. We didn't know a thing. And she was a rich girl with a Chicago lawyer father. All the tow ropes were bright yellow back then. Later, in the Seventies they were blue, then orange in the Eighties.

His breath touches my ears. The drums tingle, the words of his confession swing against the Tympanic membrane—we bog folk have well-perserved Tympanic membranes—all the way round the Semicircular canal, that glorious seashell formation.

15

Thompson comes out into the field with a large, blunt-ended shovel, looking around in all four directions, and then begins covering me up, starting first with my legs and then working up to my gut and eventually, somewhat reluctantly, covering my neck and, finally, after smoking a bowl of Captain Back, my eyes. He stops to pack the dirt down over my sockets, tamping gently with the flat end of the blade. Then he continues. The rush I felt in being buried again and relieved of my own earthly burdens is somewhat, but not exactly, sexual in nature. In an oversexed climate one might describe the sensation as orgasmic, an all consuming sense of skin. That would be a failure of my descriptive powers. But they fail me now.

Back in the barn Thompson hitches the plow to the tractor and roars out. Up and down he goes, matching the furrows. Whenever he plows or combines or tills or fertilizes he, visualizes his field as if from space, far up, overhead, from John Glenn's view, the neat furrows spelling out some geometric arrangement.

16

Irene shows up around ten, hitching her thumbs into the front of her overalls and swaying her hips as she steps through the field. The wind has died and left behind a soft residue of manure smell in the air, as rich and fragrant as anything in the world. He takes his Maglite out and slaps it against his palm to get it to burn steady and swings the orb around as if searching for me and then, finally, after looking a while, holds her hand and says, Oh shit I must've plowed the guy under, I can't believe it, I decided to neaten up the furrows and I was listening to Bach, I mean you know how I am when I'm tuning into some fine music behind the wheel. It was somewhere around here, for Christ's sake, he says, kicking the dirt a couple of times for good measure.

17

She doesn't really believe his story about the bog man, not exactly, and hears some small tremor of untruth in when he claims that he accidentally buried him by mistake, plowed him under. He was talking about this bog guy, she'll tell her best friend June. He kept going on and on about it. Said it was this guy maybe a million years old, maybe a thousand. I just sat there and listened to him, at the store, and then he wanted me to come out and see it and it wasn't there. Said he buried it, but I'm sure he was fibbing. He scratches his ear when he lies.

But that night in the field she did what she had done before and made an inventory of those things she found attractive: the hair on his chest had that middle-age thickness, speckled gray. The simple unassuming way he moves through his house; upstairs, making little two-step dance movements naked in the center of the room, raising his hands up and spinning around. The husky nature of his laugh, coming easy out of her feeble jokes. Standing before him she felt polished down, smoothed against his roughness. He seemed to deeply appreciate the youth of her own body. He held her gently a bit away from him so that her nipples just touched his chest and the rest of her felt suspended midair. She liked the boyish rounded edges he presented, the flesh around his ass flat and glossy; above his rear a small fine patch of hair downy and soft. Good for nuzzling. For hugging. For holding her softly. And his fingers seemed even now after several times making love to still be finding and negotiating their way around her thighs and legs, not just out of shyness but some deeper, innate respect for the topologies of her flesh. He was a good fuck, she'll tell June. Simple as that. The guy knew what he was doing. He was king. He made me come and come again. It's a no-brainer, she'll add. Yeah, he's old enough to be my dad and he says it just about every time we get together but so what, I need a dad, didn't have one, and well that's what I need and that's what he has to offer. She adds to her list: his fatherly tone, not patronizing but kind of a soft shuffle as he offers up suggestions on how to approach this fucked-up world. Ask that manager of yours for a raise, he said. You practically run that show. Without you, Kennell would be lost; he doesn't know his Symphony from his Borkem Riff. Tell him you'll buy a percent of his store. Don't ask him. Offer it up like you're doing him a favor. Assume you're buying in. If he says no then give him a nice little threat. Tell him you've got your eye on that vacant storefront on Maple that would make a hell of a great smoke stand. He'll say we don't have room for another smoke store. Tell him we got room for one with a walk-in humidor and a cute girl behind the counter. That's my advice to you young lady. Take the world by the horns and swing it around is what I always say.

18

The aquifers have dropped to all-time lows; the irrigation pumps have run dry and fried out. On the television weather map, a big fat sun stays pasted to the Midwest. A few weeks later, Thompson mentions me again in passing, trying to point some blame for the drought, to John, his Amish friend.

Started right after I dug up and then accidentally buried that bog man, he says in the street one afternoon. Softly and discreetly John chews his tobacco plug with a rotation of his jaw, a bit of juice on his teeth, and then spits sidelong into the gutter.

Could've figured that out myself, he says, adjusting the brim of his hat with two fingers. The Lord don't have a need of us to go digging the dead out of the soil anymore than the living should be climbing down into the dirt, he speaks slowly with a deliberation that seems weighted by the illogic of his thoughts. His thoughts, Thompson thinks, are heavy with faith. The leadenness of believing so fully in something like a God, something you can't see or taste or touch.

Yeah, right, Thompson says, cutting him off. Well, I guess it's pretty obvious what's causing the dry spell. He gives John a nod so-long, touches the bill of his cap, and walks down to the tobacco shop. Inside the sweet aroma of tobacco and magazine paper mingles with the cool of the air conditioning. Irene is behind the counter popping cigarette packs into a plastic rack, pushing them back against the spring-loaded device so that, later, when she removes them for customers she'll feel the next pack move urgently forward. Along the magazines the men, mostly dressed in loose black trousers, white shirts and suspenders, are digging into their reading materials, covers folded over covers.

Thompson stands for a moment and lets the scene envelope him fully and imagines what he might do to shake things up, to send a small tremor over the peaceful, almost pastoral nature of their longing. You know, bog folk would fit neatly into your longings, he might argue with them. The wet smooth skin resembling that which was once alive but isn't anymore succumbing to the grotesqueries of skin and orifices and the splaying of legs. You'd stare deep into the wild grimaces of Tollard Man, the supplicate almost matronly lips of Roum Woman, the tiny haunches of the Falster Boy, throat slit from ear to ear. You'd gaze long at Windeby Girl in her tight blindfold. At Bocksten Man snuffed and staked to the ground like a pup tent, you'd gape. He imagines they'd listen to him, then, as he spoke. They'd nod and chew their tobacco (softly) and say, yeah, you're Elyria Man for certain, and by virtue of being found around here, we'd have to say you're one of us.

But instead Thompson goes to the counter—white from coin scratches—and watches his own hands lie there while Irene, dressed today in a white blouse and tweed skirt outfit that seems matronly and formal, reaches back without looking and intuitively rests her hand on the golden pouch of tobacco.

THE POOR THING

[THREE WEEKS WITH NEPALI PROSTITUTES IN BOMBAY]

by DAPHNE BEAL

ON A HOT SEPTEMBER afternoon, on the front stoop of her home in central Bombay, a young Nepali woman named Priya pushed up her sleeve to show me a strip of mottled scars and black ink on her inner arm, explaining, "I burnt off my old name, Sonam, with cigarettes."

"Didn't that hurt?" I asked.

"No. A little maybe. But it's not my name anymore—" She glanced at the street and disappeared behind the dingy, pink-flowered curtain hanging in the doorway, leaving me outside to watch a mad scurrying indoors along the length of Falkland Road—Bombay's oldest and most famous red-light district—while a conspicuous, beat-up black van trundled down the avenue.

A few minutes later Priya reemerged, as others did, resuming her perch on a high stool in front of the peeling pale-yellow façade.

"Police?" I asked.

"Police," she said.

"They're gone?"

"They're gone."

That a single police van could send hundreds of sex workers into a frenzy of hiding was remarkable considering Falkland Road, like all of Bombay's red-light areas, led such an overt existence. According to Indian law, exchanging sex for money is legal, but soliciting and pimping are not. This is true even though an estimated 100,000-200,000 sex workers in Bombay spend every evening and many afternoons soliciting, usually for brothels run by madams. By snapping curtains shut for a couple minutes, the women avoided technically being caught. If the police had stopped, their visit almost certainly would have resulted in a bribe, additional to the one each house already paid daily.

Despite her recent retreat, Priya sat relaxed and upright, giving the effect of unflappable poise in the dripping heat. She wore fitted blue jeans, crisp purple button-down shirt, and little black ankle boots, a stylish outfit on this street of well-worn saris and the occasional knee-length skirt. I had met her just a little while before. I was walking up the crumbling sidewalk, past clusters of listless girls and transvestites in the open doorways, when I heard a short, high-pitched whistle. I turned to see pretty young woman sitting jauntily on a high stool about thirty feet away, her eyes fixed on me and a mischievous set to her mouth.

"*Namaste*," I said, raising my hands prayer-style as I approached.

She bobbed her head slightly to one side, swinging her feathered bangs and waist-length, silky black hair.

"Are you Nepali?" I asked her in Nepali.

"No," she answered—in Nepali—a slight smile on her face, just enough to reveal a gold-capped incisor.

"I don't believe you. Where're you from?"

"Here," she said, giving me a full grin. Her gold tooth matched a gold necklace, a flower nose ring, a delicate wristwatch, and little hoop earrings. She was slightly better off than many in the area.

"And before here? Where's your family's home?"

"Nepal, maybe."

"Kathmandu?"

"From a town north of Kathmandu."

"How many days from the city?"

"Two days walking."

She said she was Tamang, which, out of all of Nepal's castes, is the most reknowned for sending daughters to work in the sex trade in India, even though girls from every caste, from Brahmin to untouchable, can be found in Indian brothels, as can girls from all over South Asia. Anywhere there's serious poverty or political strife there is fertile ground for traffickers, who show up with promises of marriage or work in the big city. Many of the women were tricked or kidnapped and sold into prostitution, but just as many, if not more, migrated to the "City of Dreams," as Bombay's called, propelled by hunger or simply lack of opportunities at home.

Now that Priya was resituated she asked me, "Does *hajur*"—sir—"want a soda?" Her formality surprised me.

"No thanks. I'm not thirsty." I had already had two that afternoon. "Please use *didi*," big sister, I told her, "instead of *hajur*."

But she hailed a passing tea boy anyway and asked him to bring a Thum's Up.

"Sit," she said, moving back on the stool to make room for me. She wrapped her arm around my shoulders, so that we were looking out at the heat-drenched street together. Traffic moved at a sluggish pace, with oxen clopping along among the two-tone taxi sedans and dusty red double-deckers. Across the way decaying, pastel-colored buildings, up to five stories tall, seemed to sag under their own weight. I looked at the women in the windows high up, framed by crooked shutters, and thought, *fire trap*. But of course what I could never take my eyes off of for too long were the girls and transvestites, called *hijras*, in every wide, shadowy doorway, leaning forward and making kissing noises to passers-by, or silently swinging both arms, a sign that they were available.

A couple of young men bounded up the steps to talk to Priya, and I wondered if they were *goondah*s, thugs, hired to protect the brothel, and if I would soon be in trouble. But then one pulled out a broken cap-gun and they started doing scenes from a Hindi film, striking action-hero poses. Priya rolled her eyes and ignored them.

"How long have you been here?" I asked her.

"A year and a half."

"How old were you when you came?"

"Nineteen," she said, as the boys knocked into us. She gave them a tongue lashing in Hindi, which they seemed to enjoy, and they backed off to play in front of the closed-up house next door.

The tea boy delivered the Thum's Up with a winsome smile and dashed off through the crowd with his slotted wire basket of teas. His name was Mohammad when he arrived from Calcutta, she said, but now he was calling himself Raju—a savvy move in this sometimes dangerously anti-Muslim town.

"Split it with me," I said, holding out the soda. "I can't drink it all." She went inside, and when she returned with a glass, a couple of girls poked their heads out to look at me. The humidity soon gave way to drizzle. "*Hajur* should come inside," she said, calling me Sir again.

"*Didi*," I reminded her. I wondered if the *gharwali*, the brothel keeper, would object to me entering the house. But as I stood inside the door of the long, narrow room and my eyes adjusted to the dim light, I didn't see a *gharwali*, just a group of five or six girls in their twenties crowded onto a high wooden bed that took up most of the width of the room, itself little more than my arm span. Nicked-up and darkly varnished, the bed filled with girls reminded me of a boat riding high on the water. On one side, a slim passageway led toward the back of the house, hidden by another curtain on a string, behind which other beds were likely lined up end-to-end like vessels in a lock.

The aqua-blue, windowless walls were dirty and scratched up from the rub of bodies and pollution. High above us, a ceiling fan turned slowly, and just beyond it was a little wooden sleeping loft. Priya didn't introduce me to the girls on the bed, but directed me to the five-by-five foot area of wall covered with photos of Hindi film stars. Pointing to each, she recounted in detail the different actors' roles and their off-screen romances. The drizzle turned to steady rain, and the boys who had been horsing around outside now stood inside the doorway, adding their commentary to Priya's. When she shut them up, they just grinned sheepishly.

"No Manisha Koirala?" I asked her, referring to the pop-culture pride of Nepal. Manisha was especially popular with Nepali girls in the sex trade, probably because her vampishness was a more viable option than the virtuous-girl ideal. She also held out the promise of film stardom—Bollywood was so close by—even if she was the niece of Nepal's former prime minister.

Priya turned me by my shoulders to the opposite wall where the brooding starlet had a place of honor all to herself next to the little mirror hanging at eye-level. "People say I look like her, is it true?"

Both Priya and Manisha had wide-set eyes, light-brown skin and long black hair, though the resemblance stopped there. "Yes, but prettier," I said, the only possible answer, and she smiled, pleased. She crossed her arms over her chest and asked, "What work do you do?"

"I'm a journalist," I said.

"Do you work at an office?" she asked and watched me carefully to gauge the truthfulness of my response.

"Yes," I said. She tilted her head skeptically. "How many girls live here?"

"Three. Four if you stay with us," she said smiling, still testing me.

"I don't think so," I said, and she chuckled as she took my empty soda bottle.

"Come again," she said—my cue to go—and I stood up.

"When should I come? Tomorrow, the day after?"

"The day after at two o'clock." Then she leaned over and cupped her hands around my ear whispering, "Do you do this work in your country? Stay in a place like this?" I had been asked this a few times already on Falkland Road. It was a natural question for a girl in pants who didn't seem to play the wife, daughter, or mother role. Why would I come here if I wasn't looking for work?

"No, I stay in an apartment and work in an office," I said. She gave a shrug. I asked if I could bring her anything when I returned.

At first she said no, but then she called to me on the steps, "Bring me perfume, a large bottle. They don't sell any good kinds here." She had clearly just decided how I could be useful.

"What type?" I asked.

"Whatever kind *didi* wears," an improvement over *hajur*. "There are too many bad smells here!"

After weeks of searching I'd finally met the girl I was looking for. She wasn't a child, but not quite a woman either, and she was the first person who wasn't afraid to joke around or invite me inside her brothel. She seemed like she was just trying to make the best of her situation, and like she probably knew what she was getting into when she decided to come to Bombay.

I'd been following the issue of Nepali girls working in the Indian sex trade for more eight years at that point, ever since I got back from studying in Nepal in 1990, and saw Mary Ellen Mark's photo essay *Falkland Road* with all the Nepali faces in it. I was shocked. Nobody had mentioned this phenomenon in the ten months I was there. How did these hill girls end up some two thousand miles from their village homes and families?

Then I saw Mira Nair's *Salaam Bombay*, where one of the main characters is a young Nepali girl who's been sold into a brothel and is being "readied" for her first client. By the time I went back to Nepal in 1994, people were talking about girl trafficking a lot, both in the press and in the development community.

A handful of NGOs were committed to preventing trafficking—radio songs with cautionary lyrics, vocational schools for girls in high-risk areas— and to rehabilitating girls who had returned from working the sex trade. AIDS was also a hot topic (a new problem, with a good amount of foreign-aid money attached to it), and girls coming back from India were being blamed for bringing the disease home, even though they were arguably not the only ones. People talked more openly about sex-related issues, because they couldn't afford not to.

In 1995, Human Rights Watch International put out a book-length study called *Rape for Profit: Trafficking of Nepali Girls and Women to Indian Brothels*. In 1997, a documentary on the subject called *The Selling of Innocents* won an Emmy. Articles on the topic appeared with more frequency in the West, always telling the same nightmare story: Naïve, small-town girls were being tricked or kidnapped by persuasive Indian men, who came to their villages, promising marriage or well-paid work in a shop or home in India. These traffickers then sold the girls to brothel keepers in Indian cities where the girls had to work to pay off their own buying prices. By the time the debt was paid off several years later, they were usually too ill or ashamed to go home. But if they did, they were almost always sick or traumatized, or both, and then ostracized by their own community. Even though it had parallels all over the world, it was an especially dramatic story in the context of Nepal, with its Shangri-la reputation of beautiful mountains and spiritual, friendly people.

By 1998, people in Kathmandu seemed almost weary of the issue. There were articles daily in the local papers (many of them luridly told), dozens of NGOs were dedicated to it, and Prince Charles had recently auctioned off his Himalayan watercolors to raise money for a girls' rescue and rehab center. And yet, the numbers of girls going southward continued to grow.

At the same time, the popularized scenario, with its cast of villains and innocents, was beginning to unravel a bit. As it turned out, some of the most infamous traffickers were Nepali women who had worked their way up through the red-light ranks. There were politicians who protected them, and officials at the border were easily bribed. The figure of 6,000-7,000 trafficked girls a year was considered outdated, but whether the amount had grown to 12,000-20,000, no one could say. It was estimated that 100,000-200,000 Nepali women and girls were working in the Indian sex trade at this point, about a third of them children under the age of sixteen, but again, these figures were for a group of people that by necessity existed under the radar.

Personally, I didn't recognize any of the types of characters presented in the usual account. My friends who were hill girls weren't worldly or formally educated, but they were certainly wise to the ways of sex by the age of sixteen or seventeen, frequently bawdy in their humor, and unlikely to simply leave everything they knew to go off with a stranger making vague promises.

Also, Nepal, once relatively isolated, no longer seemed to have a culture conducive to the kind of inexperience described in the story. In 1990, hill girls who lived or worked in Kathmandu almost always wore the traditional garb of ankle-length skirts and velveteen blouses, and they acted deferentially toward the Hindu upper castes. By 1998, with democracy in full swing, gaggles of teenagers laughed loudly in the street, showed up in discos, and wore low-riding blue jeans, tight T-shirts, and platform sandals. When I was a student an exciting night on TV included Pakistani sitcoms. Now nearly a hundred different stations were beamed in by satellite, and there were Internet cafés on every corner. Cows still roamed the streets and the city was on the brink of a cholera epidemic, but even when I was trekking, I met a girl in a remote village who wanted me to help her sister in Kathmandu get a visa to the U.S.

Finally, I began to meet advocates and social workers focused on a less clear-cut trafficking situation. They spoke of the distinction between "hard trafficking," which included girls under sixteen and anyone who had been duped, and "soft trafficking," which had more to do with migrant labor than with the black-heartedness of traffickers. One advocate told me that after nine years of research he believed that a significant number, perhaps as many as ninety percent, of young women going to India knew what they were signing up for, as did their parents, in words anyway, even if they didn't understand the risks of AIDS ("still a death sentence here," he said) or the psychological repercussions.

Driven by financial hardship, these somewhat-knowing young women had few other choices besides carpet-factory work and becoming a servant, both little better than slave labor, literally. In soft-trafficking, the trafficker paid money to the girl's family, and a contract was made so that a portion of her wages, after a period of time, would be sent back to her family. In some cases, the girl was going to stay with a family friend or "auntie" running a brothel.

Nepali girls went with traffickers, as opposed to on their own, because most didn't have the basic literacy skills to read a sign at a train or bus station, which would make the three- to four-day journey to a distant Indian city a dangerous one. It also made sense for a girl to say, when asked, that she was taken unwillingly because of the stigma attached to the work.

In Priya, I felt like I'd finally found someone who could give me some insight as to what free will or choice actually meant in this situation.

Two days after my first visit, I arrived at Priya's house just across from the

Murli Beer Bar, promptly at two, where the sooty, flowered curtain hung closed in the doorway, keeping the intense sunlight out. I hesitated, wondering if they were sleeping or working, when one of the cap-gun boys appeared, grinning and offered to call inside for me. Priya pulled back the curtain from the floor where she was having lunch with the two other girls.

"Come in!" she said and stood up. The other girls just glanced up at me from their tin plates of rice, yellow dahl, and gristly meat.

"You sit here," Priya said, patting the seat of the high stool.

"I can sit on the floor," I said.

"No, sit here," she insisted, and I did, drawing my legs up out of their way as I looked down at them. All three girls were in their twenties, and the oldest wore a long, sleeveless canary yellow housedress that looked like a nightgown. *Gharwalis*—madams—on Falkland Road favored this style of dress, which along with their characteristic physical bulk seemed to give them the heft and the desexualized armor they needed to manage their businesses. But this girl was young and only a little heavier than the others. She seemed on equal terms with the other two as they talked among themselves in low voices.

Priya looked up after a few minutes as if just then remembering I was there, and I opened my satchel. "Here, I brought you this," I said and handed her the bottle I'd bought that morning. She sniffed the nozzle and sprayed some on her neck. A cloying vanilla scent filled the small space.

"It's good," she said, passing it to the others. "How much was it?"

"300 rupees," I said, around eight dollars, which I knew was a lot for them. They studied me for signs of this kind of wealth, puzzled by my plain clothes.

"I'll sit here now," I said as I got off the stool. Finally, the other two told me they were Lila, in the yellow dress, and Mira, who wore a modest, moss-green salwar kameez.

"Do you have a camera?" Priya asked.

"I do," I said, and produced one from my bag. They all looked pleased.

"Take pictures of us," Mira said, the first full sentence she had spoken to me. Lila stacked the dirty plates and tin cups in a cooking pot in the corner while Priya and Mira stood shoulder-to-shoulder against the flowered curtain, at first somber and then playful, imitating the stars' photos. Lila joined in.

"You promise you'll bring us the pictures next time?" she asked.

"I will," I said.

"We should go to Haj Ali mosque at Chowpatty Beach and *sapha hawa kanchow*," literally, "eat clean air," Priya said, proposing a tourist outing, not a religious one. Suddenly we were up and getting ready to go, and I followed her and Mira out into the blazing heat where Priya hailed a taxi. Lila watched us go from the doorway.

"Someone has to stay in the house," Mira explained.

As we made our way down the traffic-clogged artery of Falkland Road and out onto the more swiftly moving avenue toward the beach, I revised my earlier theory that they were prohibited from leaving the red-light area, as so many were, which was why brothels were dubbed "cages." I also wondered if Lila was the brothel keeper or if they all simply looked out for each other, which from everything I'd heard would have been an unconventional arrangement.

When the taxi stopped, I tried to pay but was surprised when Priya insisted she would, since I had suspected I was being pushed into the minor benefactor role. We crossed the street to the pedestrian causeway leading out to the Oz-like white mosque that seemed to waver in the heat. At the end, the girls wanted to go down to the shore first to enjoy the view of the dishwatery expanse of Arabian Sea with the other tourists, and we picked our way over the rocks down to the softly breaking waves as Mira cried out giddily "*Chíplo!*"—slippery.

Now, *this* was a filmic backdrop, as they passed the camera back and forth between them, suggesting different combinations of the three of us. The breeze blew their hair and Mira's long, chiffon neck scarf. It all reminded me of one of the more lighthearted scenes in a Hindi film I had seen recently called *Satya* ("Truth"), set in Bombay, of the hero frolicking with his girlfriend by the sea. Priya pointed out two little boys playing in the shallow water behind us, and the girls cooed over them and took their picture from a distance.

As we made our way up the rocks toward the mosque, young men, in an almost courtly way, offered the girls their hands to cross the tidal pools. I wondered if the girls looked like prostitutes despite their modest dress. Probably yes. Mira, in her salwar kameez and candy-pink lipstick barely covering what looked like a painful cold sore, played the girl-next-door to Priya's bad girl, in her cobalt blue blouse and jeans with a big nickel buckle that said simply "ARMY." They didn't look like students or like brides of navy personnel, which were two other reasons why young Nepali women would be in Bombay. Perhaps most telling was the fact that they were out alone, without husbands, parents, or children, not just on an errand but a real excursion.

Inside the mosque's courtyard of blinkingly bright white marble, we took pictures under a diminutive, pruned tree. And on the way back to the road to get a taxi, Priya and Mira began whispering about the two couples just ahead of us—two nattily dressed young Nepali women holding hands with their Indian dates. One girl wore a gauzy neon-green salwar kameez and the other a sturdier, cotton beigy-pink one. They spoke with an exaggerated vivacity, gesturing, as the boys, in pressed oxfords and cotton dress pants, listened raptly. The boys were both noticeably darker-skinned, which shouldn't mean anything, but did here where caste and ethnicity still play daily roles.

"Are they *aimai?*" Mira asked, using an informal word for women in Nepali, which I took from the context to mean slang for prostitutes.

"I'm sure they are. Look at their clothes and—" Priya nodded her chin at their interlaced fingers, the kind of public display one rarely saw in married couples, let alone unmarried ones.

"They are," Mira agreed. They studied the girls with a combination of curiosity and envy. Prostitution on Falkland Road existed at a whole level below what these girls were a part of. The women in the worst situation were those who worked outside the train stations and truck stops without the protection of a brothel. Then came Falkland Road and the adjacent district of Kamathipura, where the majority of the clients were low wage migrant laborers, who had left their wives and families in some faraway town for months, if not years at a time. The ranks of prostitution continued upward from there, all the way to the high-class call girls who doubled as aspiring film actresses or fashion models. I wondered if Priya and Mira had ambitions beyond Falkland Road, in which a "date" included a pleasant afternoon outing with conversation, rather than just a few heated minutes in the back room.

At the house, Lila's face was shining as she wiped down the last of the pocked concrete floor and dropped the rag into a bucket of dirty water.

"Did you rest while we were gone?" I asked her.

"Rest?" She looked incredulous. "No, I cleaned the whole time."

"It looks nice," I said. The floor and dishes were gleaming, and there were new sheets and a clean if graying blue-and-white coverlet on the first bed, already in use by one of the street boys catching up on sleep. Mira told me to sit as she heaved him, undisturbed, down to the far end. The house, barely ventilated, smelled fresher too.

Priya called Raju for a tea before I could refuse and then repaired outside to her stool. Mira climbed onto the bed with me to sort through her jewelry in the locked tin cashbox kept on a single high shelf nearby. After a little while the man got up, drowsily at first, but when he saw my camera, he perked up and quickly departed. He soon returned in a zippy white outfit (*Saturday Night Fever*–style, complete with flared pants and long, pointed collar) and his hair combed back. He insisted on several photos now that he was dressed for it, and wouldn't leave until he had taken one with Mira, who made a grim expression when he wrapped his arm around her. He had brought leaf-wrapped packets of flower garlands as gifts for the house, but Mira was unimpressed. When he left, she explained that unlike the young man who had called inside the house for me earlier in the afternoon and was "a *very* good person" (she rapped her sternum for emphasis), the man who'd just left was "very naughty," and she added, "he eats women's money!"

Lila carefully draped the strings of marigolds and jasmine around over two framed images of Hindu deities that hung low on the wall, near the kerosene burner in the corner. Then she took down the framed photograph of the mosque we had just visited and did the same—a kind of omni-religious offering.

Mira held up a hand mirror to examine the cold sore on her lip. "It hurts!" she exclaimed.

"Have you seen a doctor about it?"

"No, I went to a doctor once before when I had a skin rash, and he sold me expensive medicine that didn't work." The street was filled with dubious storefront clinics.

A scrubbed and glistening baby girl toddled in from next door and gurgled happily when I set her on the bed with us. Mira gave her a couple of candies from a packet of cherry Bonkers, and the girl handed one to me. Soon after, a holy man in pilgrim's clothes came and swung his censer at the doorway, filling the house with smoke, and gave ash blessings. Though Mira looked mildly irritated, as if by a pesty kid brother, she unlocked the tin box with a key kept under a pillow, and gave him a rupee.

Here was a home where things had an order: The house was kept clean; religious offerings were made; a holy man was given alms for the asking; a visiting baby was treated to candy; and in turn the baby welcomed the outsider. This was not the ragtag existence I had first understood it to be, but one marked by a well-developed sense of etiquette, albeit one at odds with the girls' gritty work.

Having completed the *puja* for the house, Lila turned off the light and fan, which made the narrow room especially dark and close. Mira and Priya each stood in turn while Lila passed the *puja* plate of sandalwood paste and flowers and incense up and down the length of their bodies, front and back, in a blessing. Mira then did the same for Lila.

Afterward, Lila pulled back the curtain to reveal the dusky pink glow of late afternoon light. I knew working hours were just ahead, but the girls told me I should stay the night. "Go tomorrow!" they whined playfully in Nepali and Hindi. I could sleep in the little loft in back, near the fan, they said.

"*Bichara!*" The poor thing! Mira said, tsking. "She has to sleep at a hotel."

"*Manché auncha?*" People are coming? I asked to be sure. It still was hard for me to believe that after our mostly ordinary day together, here was where our paths diverged.

"*Auncha, jancha,*" They come, they go, Priya said, a little impatiently.

"This is what we do," Mira added with a quiet matter-of-factness.

When I arrived at this same transforming hour a couple days later, the street felt like morning in other parts of the city, just as the shops were being opened. People splashed buckets of water onto the sidewalk in front of houses, and the street had begun to hum and rumble with the anticipation of business ahead. The flow of pedestrians on the sidewalk was denser and more purposeful than in the afternoon, and illuminated windows and doors showed girls and *hijra*s lounging, leaning, beckoning, crouching in brightly colored if now faded clothes. Their faces decorated by circles of rouge, stripes of blue eye shadow, and spidery eyelashes had the effect of neon signs flashing "Open... Open... Open..."

Next door to the girls' house was a small group of aging and weary-looking Nepali women. One, whom I recognized, was squatting and smoking. With tangled hair and leathery skin, she gazed at the street from watery eyes outlined in black kohl—her disarray probably from hash.

But inside the girls' house, the atmosphere reminded me of Friday night at a college freshman year, with everyone crowding into one small room to get ready. Their staticky boom box on the shelf blasted Bollywood songs as they primped, jostling each other in front of the little mirror between the first bed and doorway. Lila smudged some black herbal toothpaste on the other girls' cheeks and laughed at her handiwork. And with the flimsy curtain closed and the fluorescent light flickering, they danced: Priya pulled up her collar and shook her hips, mock-tough, and Mira threw back her shoulders and did a kind of hula-wiggle. They were brassy and giddy among themselves to a degree that I never would see them with customers.

Their guy friends dropped by to preen, checking collars, hair parts, and skin. They teased and were teased back. One boy put his arm around Mira, saying, "She's my *bouddhi*," my old lady. (Why is this the same phrase the world over?) She shook him off and watched him go, saying with a sigh, "He loves me, but I don't love him."

Just after dark, Lila, Mira, and I went outside. Soon after, a thin, older man in ragged clothes came up a step and asked Mira in a low voice simply, "*Kítna?*" How much?

"Seventy," she said, about a dollar-eighty, but he had already turned on his heel to walk away.

"How much, how much?" she called, hopping off the stool ready to bargain, but he didn't come back. She had a sweetness, even in tonight's somewhat racier outfit of a knee-length black skirt and turquoise T-shirt, and soon enough another customer—a small young man in a faded maroon shirt and loose pants—arrived, and without ceremony they went inside, returning so quickly it was hard to believe anything had happened.

A couple of men stopped to ask me "How much?" but Mira and Lila jumped in to explain I wasn't working. The next time it happened, in my pidgin Hindi I told the men I was too expensive.

"No, really, how much?" one of them insisted.

"A million dollars," I said. They huffed mildly and walked on. Mira held up her hand to slap me five.

Moving in and out of the house at intervals, Mira and Lila were both working. I counted five or six customers for Mira that night and fewer for Lila. Priya seemed to be taking the night off, hanging out on the first bed inside—the ersatz parlor—looking at the photos I brought from our Haj Ali expedition, or taking phone calls across the street at a dry-goods store.

After an hour or so of working, Mira gave a little sigh, and said, "*Ké garné?*" What to do? "We do this kind of work." But when the next customer came, she held back the curtain for him and told me cheerily, "Okay, I'm going into my office."

"I'll stay out here and be your secretary," I said. She laughed and slapped my palm again on her way in. Each time she went in she was gone for about five minutes, sometimes less. The transactions seemed practical more than brusque, and the girls treated the clients not as friends exactly, but as people with needs. After all, these men were also migrant laborers who had left their homes and families to earn a better life.

A few minutes later, as always, the man left first, and Mira emerged tugging her skirt into place and smoothing the front of her t-shirt. And for the briefest of moments, as she arranged her clothes, she pursed her lips, looking down at herself with an expression I had seen her make before just after a customer left. It made me think of the Nepali word for sour, which people often drew out for emphasis: *ameeelo*. But then she shook everything into place, and the smiling, pink-lipsticked girl came forward again.

Priya was gone the next time I visited. She had been with a customer at a hotel for more than a week. Her local boyfriend was sprawled asleep on the girls' first bed.

"*Bichara!*" Poor thing! Mira told me as we leaned on the headboard watching him. "He's been crying because he loves her so much, and because he has no mother and father."

"Are you worried about Priya?" I asked her.

She wobbled her head yes. "I was supposed to go to the hotel but I didn't want to."

"Do you ever go outside the house with men?"

"No. I'm afraid to," she said, adding, "she may be gone for a month." Whatever drawbacks brothel life had, at least there was some built-in protection in hired thugs and paid-off cops. But I also wondered if this was Priya's leap forward to the next level of opportunity.

Lila came out from the back, toweling her wet hair and belching. (A yellow plastic water drum and a hole in the floor in the back served as a bathroom.) She and Priya's boyfriend had been drinking beer, it turned out. He was passed out, not asleep, which I should have gotten from his muddy trouser cuffs on the pillow. Hot words passed between Lila and Mira about him, which resulted in Lila trying to shake the boy awake, then yelling and slapping him. Finally, she poured a pitcher of cold water on his head, and he staggered out into the street.

Another young man came in and wanted money from them. Lila handed him a folded wad of rupees from the strongbox, and he left.

"Who is he?" I asked.

"Our brothel keeper," Lila said.

I'd never seen him before; he didn't live with them or arrange clients. I hadn't read or heard of male brothel keepers, or ones that lived outside the house. "How much do you pay him?"

The two girls looked at each other. "Four-thousand rupees month," about a hundred dollars, Lila said.

"And he doesn't buy us anything, no food or electricity or clothes!" Mira added, indignant.

"How much do those things cost?"

Lila shrugged. "I don't know."

"They're expensive," Mira added and carefully reapplied her lipstick in the mirror over the lingering cold sore, and tugged at the scarf around her neck. Lila busied herself sorting jewelry in the strongbox, uninterested in talking more about money.

Mira and I went outside to sit in the rosy-colored evening, where crowds were sparse because of the Dasera festival, in honor of the Hindu goddess Durga, being celebrated elsewhere in the city. We watched green and white fireworks burst in big silent blooms over the ramshackle rooftops of the saltwater-taffy-colored buildings and leafy trees. She told me a horse that belonged to the big, two-wheeled cart across the street had died that day, and they hauled him off in a truck.

"*Bichara*," Mira said for the second time that evening, and clucked her tongue. The open sewer wafted at us through the car fumes from the puddles of black ooze a few feet away.

"Do you send money home?" I asked her.

She wobbled her head yes, keeping her eyes trained on the street.

"Are your mother and father alive?" I asked.

"My mother is. My father died when I was little—" which would have meant no dowry for her to get married—"my sisters and brothers are in school."

"You help pay for their education?"

She wobbled yes again.

"Did you go to school?"

"Only through second grade."

"Can you read and write?"

"Just my name," she said and gave me a little shrug and sigh: "*Ké garné?*" What to do?

"When did you come to Bombay?"

"I came a year and a half ago with Priya to *gumne janne*," travel around. "Lila is my uncle's daughter. She came a few years ago."

She told me she and Priya had come alone, without a *dalal*, a trafficker, which was extremely difficult, and that she was sick in the hospital, flat on her back with a fever for two months when she arrived. I wondered if it was stress or a physical disease, like malaria, or some combination of the two.

"Can I ask you some questions you don't have to answer?"

"Yes." Business was slow, she had the time.

"Do the three of you use condoms?"

"Yes, always."

"What if he refuses?"

"We tell him to *jao*!" Go! This was heartening talk, even if I didn't think it wasn't entirely true, given Mira's persistent cold sore. AIDS awareness was definitely on the rise in the red-light districts. There were at least two major condom-distribution and education programs in the area, but a 100% condom usage seemed unlikely. A local AIDS specialist estimated that 75,000 clients sleep with HIV-positive prostitutes in Bombay's red-light districts each day.

"Do you ever kiss them?" I asked.

"Never!" She was disgusted. (It's not an especially prevalent Nepali custom to begin with.)

"How much money do you make in a night?"

"Maybe three or four hundred." Eight or ten bucks.

Around 9:30, two men showed up with heftier physiques and nicer clothes than the usual laborer clientele. One was in his late thirties or early forties, with thick black hair, and the other was a tall man in his fifties with a bushy gray beard and round, taut belly.

"*Kosto moto*!" How fat, Mira said mildly, of the bigger man after they went inside. Then she told me the *moto* man came the other day and wanted to sleep with her, but then he went to have dinner with his friend, who was a trafficker. "By the time he came back we were closed up and asleep, *bichara*," she said—her third "poor thing" that evening.

A few minutes later she went inside and I followed her. The *moto* man had agreed to pay four hundred the other day and now he wanted to pay three hundred. After listening to the negotiations for a few minutes, I said, in a mix of English and Nepali, "Three hundred?! You should pay four hundred or a thousand or a *lakh* (100,000) for such a young and pretty girl." And they all looked at me like, What the hell are you doing?

And frankly, what the hell *was* I doing? I excused myself and went outside, a little shaky. The men left, to return later. Mira and Lila came and sat down with me. Four hundred it was, and nobody mentioned my gaffe.

* * *

Not long after, Mira and I were hanging out on the steps when a young man stopped and asked me in English if I knew this was a prostitution area.

"I do. I'm visiting my friends," I said.

He told me he had just moved to Bombay from Calcutta, where he got his bachelor of business administration at Calcutta University. The polite conversation lasted a few minutes, and he left.

Maybe twenty minutes later, he came back, this time with big owl-like glasses on and carrying a heavy, hardback tome under his arm. I wondered where he had gotten the props. He paused to chat again. "Please don't mind," he said, "if I just say that you have a nice face and a nice body and I am very happy to talk to you."

I said thank you and he left.

In a little while a messenger arrived with a note for me: a love letter from the student in carefully printed English on notebook paper. He said he was too ashamed to come talk to me again, but he wanted to know if he could show me around Bombay the next day. "My heart will ache," he wrote, if I couldn't go with him. "Just say yes or no." I translated the note into Nepali for Mira and Lila on either side of me, chuckling as I did, and feeling like I was back in junior high. I told the messenger a simple "no" as the note requested, and began folding up the letter to keep, but Mira gently took it from me and handed it to the messenger. She asked him to explain to the sender that I was leaving India tomorrow, which was true. Her compassion—for the drunken boy, for the horse, for her client, for the hapless student, for me—outshone my own at every turn.

Around 11:40, the other two men arrived with newspaper-wrapped packets of snacks in hand, and Lila and Mira asked me to stay the night, again saying I could sleep in the loft. As I considered it, the *dalal* went out to get beer, and the *moto* man stayed. He had red, betel-stained gums, and with the crinkles around his eyes and intense gaze, he reminded me of a secular *sadhu*, a Hindu mendicant, both repulsive and appealing. But both he and his friend were bigger than I was, unlike most men on Falkland Road, and suddenly I knew I had to go. Being an outsider didn't preclude my being a young woman, and ultimately on Falkland Road there was only one thing young women were for.

"Okay, see you tomorrow," I told them all.

"You're going?" Lila asked. Mira gave me a frowny pout, and I made one back at her. She laughed, and I jumped into one of the trolling cabs.

* * *

When I arrived the next afternoon to say goodbye, the girls were sitting on the steps, looking tired, under the heavy, yellow-bruised sky. Behind them in the open doorway, a prostitute past her working years was cleaning their floor.

Lila had a mouthful of black herbal toothpaste and slurred her words because of it, or because she'd been drinking.

"How late did they stay?" I asked Mira.

"Until two. They were 'all-night' customers," she said. "The big man went to Dubai today." Saudi Arabia was the next stop for men who weren't earning enough working in Bombay.

Inside, I gave Mira a paisley green salwar kameez—her favorite color—which she loved, and Lila a bottle of perfume. I said I'd come back after I'd said goodbye to some women I knew across the street. A little while later, I dashed back to their house through the pouring rain. It was dark now, and when I peeked inside the girls' closed pink curtain Mira was standing barefoot on the bed in the new outfit looking happy, as Lila helped her figure out how to alter it.

"It looks great," I said.

"I know," Mira said turning to show me, when I felt someone grope me, and I whirled around.

"What the hell are you doing?"

A trim, middle-aged man grinned. "It was an accident madam!"

"It was no accident. Would you do that to your mother or sister?" I had picked up this particular rhetoric over the last few weeks. "What if my brother came to Bombay and did that to your sister?"

"Please don't be upset, madam. I am a police officer, look?" He held up an open wallet to show me his I.D., which might or might not have been real. I couldn't tell in the dim light. I didn't know if he was he trying to intimidate me or reassure me, or both somehow.

"Then why are you touching my ass?" I yelled. "Do you know my good friend Deputy Police Commissioner Venketasham? Should I tell him what you're doing?" The man backed off, chuckling, but not nervously enough. In this place that had once seemed like pure mayhem to me, I now expected certain codes—among them that if I was inside or right in front of a brothel, I would be treated with the same small amount of deference as the other girls. If I walked down the sidewalk during working hours, I could expect to be harassed, but at the house, the worst I might get were long stares.

When Raju arrived a few minutes later, I gave him a waterproof Timex to wear in downpours like the one outside, when he had to take off his fake

Rolex. He seemed pleased with the combined status and practicality of it. And then I left the group of them standing in the doorway, without a phone number or address to contact them again. ("We don't have one," Mira had told me apologetically.)

As I rolled down the window of the taxi, they called out, "Remember us, go safely, come back soon."

Last June, I returned to Falkland Road and found the street visibly changed. About a third of the ground-floor brothels had been replaced by restaurants, gaming parlors, and beer bars, and I was told that increased property values in central Bombay had pushed many brothels to the suburbs (a tightly woven, chaotic sprawl that doesn't resemble its Western counterparts). Many women had left for the industrial city of Surat in Gujarat, where factory workers, many of them employed by multinational corporations, would provide a steady clientele.

Mira, Lila, and Priya's house had been combined with three others around it to make a space occupied by a cheap Chinese restaurant, its front entirely open to the street. The trio of young men standing at the front counter had no idea what I was talking about when I asked for the girls by name. A Nepali woman on the sidewalk thought she knew who I meant, and led me and my friend, an Indian social worker, into a narrow, muck-lined alley past a dazed little girl standing in a tattered dress, her shaved head covered with scabs, and her face powdered eerily white. We were taken up a rickety staircase to a hallway of semi-partitioned rooms where bored, angry women stared at us. Arriving at the last alcove, we found there was in fact no one named Lila, Mira, or Priya here. With a warm smile, our guide refused a tip for helping us.

On the street, my friend ran into the boyfriend of a prostitute she knew well, and he led us back through a large, open room where men hammered patterns onto aluminum pots over an open fire. The smoke and clanging followed us up a ladder-style staircase to the woman's room, which she shared with three others and her twelve-year-old son. She told us that there were so few customers these days, because of police harassment, that she frequently went without eating.

When we left, her boyfriend took us on one last search for the girls I knew, though when he realized it had been a while, he laughed and said, "We don't even know what happened ten days ago, let alone a few years ago. Everything here changes overnight!"

37.

38.

39.

40.

41.

42.

37) Bank Street, New York

38) Crawford Gardens, London

39) Westchester Road, New York

40) Bank Street, New York

41) Driggs Avenue, London

42) Kingsland Street, London

BLUE

by SAMANTHA HUNT

YOU DIDN'T GIVE birth to me, did you?" I ask my mother while she is tightening the strap of her bathrobe. She stops, opens her robe a crack and shows me her belly button. It is popped and spread as a manhole. "You did that," she says. "Why? What did your father tell you?"

"He said I was in the water and you found me."

"That certainly would be unusual," she says.

"He said I am a mermaid. He said mermaids don't have legs or a voice or a soul unless they marry a mortal."

My mother listens to my voice. My mother looks at my legs. "I see," she says, but I don't see so well. I thought my trouble seeing might be a characteristic of the depth of the sea that I am from. Maybe it is a region so dark blue that our skin has no pigment and neither do our eyes, if we are lucky enough to have eyes at all.

"There's a word for that region," my grandfather says and turns to his dictionary to find it but can't. "I can almost remember it," he says. "It starts with had- or ha-. I read it in *Scientific American*," he says and tears through the dictionary looking for it. "It was here," he says. "Someone took it," he says and looks at my mother and me with suspicion.

I try not to meet his gaze but he's tough and he can stare a long time so eventually I have to look out the window.

I was thirsty. And anyway it's mine.

The beach where the channel opens into the salt marsh is usually less crowded because the smell of sulfur can be strong in no wind. The mouth of the channel expands so that it is uncrossable and children have drowned trying.

Jude has brought three blankets and at the edge of the dune he uses one and a piece of driftwood to make a shade tent. I fold my pants and sit cross-legged back down on the sand with a deep curve in my shoulders. I am worn out by desire for him, like a girl in a book.

He removes his shirt and sits directly in front of me. He has odd scars on his torso that he tries to keep secret. I put my toes on his back, right where his jeans end and walk my feet up his vertebrae. He is bony like a fish. When I sit up, I sit around him, one leg on either side of Jude's. I touch his back with my stomach. I curl my hip bones towards him as if I were a monkey or a bean. But he doesn't notice and after he exhales three times, he stands to walk down to the water.

All the things Jude's name rhymes with, all the words you could spell with the letters of his name don't measure up to him. "Lost at the bottom of the sea" comes closer. My grandparents both once worked as typesetters before their press closed down. I'd be a sloppy typesetter, using the more economical "Jude" in lieu of "Rocky place down by the water," or "Smooth night with stars for navigation."

I met Jude right before he went to the Persian Gulf on a boat. He was taller than anyone I had ever seen. He told me my skin was so pale that he thought he could see through it. The acetate pages of an anatomy book, he said. One page holds blood with oxygen, one page is blood without. He said he could see what I had eaten for lunch and then he poked me in the stomach, which made me feel awkward because he is fourteen years older than me and fourteen years younger than my mother and sometimes one of them will remind the other of *"And the red bird sings I'll be blue because you don't want my love."* I've never even heard of that song.

When I was younger, before I met Jude, my father disappeared. He was a big drinker and one day he had too much to drink and came down to the ocean. The way I imagine it, he watched the sun set on the horizon line and then decided to walk out to it. Later, police found his footprints in the sand and they found where the footprints disappeared into the ocean but they never found his body.

The day I met Jude I was wading in the ocean. When I looked up, Jude was swimming near the shore. He looked like a horse. A seahorse. There he is, I thought and meant my father, because I had heard that in quantum physics the possibility exists that one day the molecules of a body could arrange themselves just so that a person would be able to pass through a wall that appears solid to the eye. That is how much room we have between our molecules. I thought of that, then I thought, "This is the place where all of my father's molecules went." Then Jude was coming out of the water and I thought in quantum physics there is a possibility that all the molecules of my father would find each other again and would walk out of the water looking at least a little bit like him.

But Jude didn't walk out of the water. He stayed there for a long time and he must have been freezing because the ocean this far north is rarely suited for swimming, though some children do. But this man didn't look like a child. He looked like my father.

"Hello," I yelled to him. He turned towards me, looked a long time, shook his head and waved. "What are you doing?" I asked.

"Looking for something," he said.

Me too. "Me too," I said, but the waves were very loud between us.

Finally Jude walked towards me. His lips were turning blue like a drowned man's. Horrible things happen all the time this far north but I wasn't afraid of him. He seemed bent and so kinder in his bentness.

"You look like you've been in the water forever," I said.

He stood where the waves began to break, where what was blue became white, a sheet of white paper roiling with what was written there. Jude kept walking towards me. "My name is Jude," he said, so I saw he was not my father, but barely. We watched the water. A sheet of white paper from him to me, the whole story on those waves.

When Jude was in the Gulf he had a boy from Galveston, Texas in his platoon. The boy really was just a boy, eighteen and tiny. He had a few, two or three, billy goat hairs growing from his chin, but not enough to start shaving yet. He was quiet like Jude and so they were often lumped together at mess or on watches. The boy had a girlfriend back in Texas who he missed so badly that sometimes he'd howl like he was a wolf, and he said it helped him get all the longing inside him on the outside. So Jude let him howl. He never teased him about it, though some of the other soldiers would. Jude thought the wolf-boy was fine, because lots of people had strange reactions to the war and what they saw and being a wolf didn't seem so bad.

But the wolf-boy, after some time in the desert, started to forget the boy side of his personality. He started to become all wolf and it was a little bit disturbing to the other soldiers. Jude still went on watch with him, but the boy had stopped talking altogether. In fact, the boy had stopped walking on two legs when he didn't have to. He'd carry himself on all fours with his head bent low to the ground as if he were trying to catch a scent of something. And even then Jude still tried to think, "Well, he just misses his girlfriend. He'll be all right." And Jude continued to think that until the day a group of them—wolf-boy, Jude, and twelve other soldiers—were sent on a mission into _____, a town that had been all but destroyed, first by missiles, then by mines, then by the black smoke of oil wells on fire.

The town was tiny and all the soldiers found were twenty-six dead Iraqis and a radio that was picking up music from a station in Adbaly, Kuwait. Jude picked his way through the town alone because he didn't really trust the other soldiers to avoid triggering a mine. Their job was to dig a grave large enough to fit the twenty-six bodies they had found and to cover the bodies up, because the bodies were not the bodies of soldiers but civilians.

After searching the town, the soldiers and Jude began to dig. The digging took far longer than they thought it would, because the heat was too much and they had to wait for the sun to set. They did not have enough shovels and so had to dig in shifts.

After an hour on duty Jude surrendered his shovel to another soldier and walked away into the dark town to get some peace. He walked outside the light of the soldiers' lanterns so that he could see the stars. In the desert the stars were the only thing that reminded him of the ocean. He couldn't see the stars that night. The smoke of burning oil was too thick between him and the sky.

He walked through the paths in town that passed between homes that no longer had roofs or walls. He was touching the warm walls, which were mostly ruined. He was thinking about the land mines. He said he thought about the triggers on the mines and he was so lonely he said the mines' triggers made him think of a woman's clit. He was that lonely. In the dark he thought of all the clitorises and pressed himself up against the wall that was still warm from the day or the fires. He thought of the land mines that were like girls. He shut his eyes and imagined he heard himself fucking the mine. He heard skin against metal skin, a slapping, a slobbering, a huffing. He was fucking a land mine. It was so real that he could hear it. He opened his eyes. The sound was still there. He listened. The sound was real.

Someone was there, slobbering and huffing. Jude crouched. He thought there might be an Iraqi person still alive or a wounded soldier. On his knees he crept along the wall until he saw a light and heard the noise grow louder. Jude slowly, silently peered through the door from where the light came. It was the wolf-boy. It was the wolf-boy huddled over an Iraqi girl who had been dead for two days. Her head had been raised up on a rock as if it were a pillow and in her hand she still held a slip of paper. The wolf-boy was licking her. He was slobbering, huffing on her as if to lick the girl clean and whole again.

"What the fuck are you doing?" Jude said, standing up and crossing the debris of broken bricks quickly, trying to grab the wolf-boy though he didn't know what he was going to do if he caught him. It didn't matter because the wolf-boy reared up. His mouth was sick with blood. The wolf-boy howled and in a move very unlike a wolf, the boy pointed his pistol at Jude and ran. He ran foot, foot, hand with pistol, hand. The wolf-boy ran straight out to a dry field of crops growing beside the town. The field was dry, it was burnt, except for the land mines buried there and the wolf-boy touched one of the mines and saw stars on a night too dark with smoke for stars.

When Jude was in the Gulf I opened up the hole in my chest my father left me. I stored some new things there. There was plenty of room. Things like nail clippers, thread, addresses. Those things easy to lose that drive you mad to find.

When Jude was in the Gulf I liked to imagine how difficult it was to get my letters past the war censors with their big black markers and that something I had written to him would arrive looking like this:

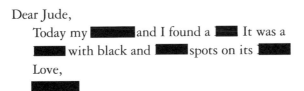

When Jude was in the Gulf I cleaned empty hotel rooms for money. In most of the rooms a man had taken a woman or girl and loved her with her face against the wall so she couldn't see him. When I cleaned at the motel I'd touch the wall with my own face. I couldn't see him. He was in the Gulf. The walls tasted like salt. Imagine how the wall and the women and the girls feel through each winter, playing the one love scene they remember over and over again.

When Jude was in the Gulf I tried to wrap my arms around the dresser in my bedroom. My cheek was doughy from sleeping where I'd been crying and the dresser's corner left a red imprint. "Kiss me," I said and kicked its leg when it didn't. The varnish smelled sticky and old like Worchestshire sauce. I stuck out my tongue to taste it but became scared that the emptiness of the dresser would suck me into its vacuum so I let go.

In our house there are drawers of lead type my grandfather has kept since the printing press where he and his wife had worked shut down. There are cardboard files of pretty pictures that my mother has torn from magazines, the contents of my grandmother's house including a yellow velvet loveseat with lion's paws for feet and almost every toothbrush my family has used since we moved into this house the year before I was born. Underneath the sink there used to be a box where we kept spent lightbulbs until my mother decided to store coffee cans there instead. I don't know what happened to the dead lightbulbs. We have three sewing machines and four computers because my grandfather buys cheap ones from the classified section in the weekly newspaper. All five bedrooms have beds but those that are not in use are covered: one with contour maps of the islands off the coast where we live and the other with records, mostly my mother's opera and European folk song LPs. We aren't trash. I know Venus is the loveliest planet.

We have so many rugs that in the living room we have spread them out on top of each other. We have two pianos even though my mother is the only one who knows how to play. The saddest thing we've held onto is my father's wing chair. It is frightening because the upholstery is still stained from his hand oil and he has been gone for so many years. In the kitchen we keep the china from both my mother's and grandfather's weddings, a set of Spengelware, and an ever-expanding set of daily ware that we acquire one piece at a time when we shop at the A & P Superstore. One dresser is for cloth napkins. The rotation for their usage is such a long cycle that our napkins always smell like the wood of the dresser by the time we use them again.

Despite the evidence of objects surviving the people who once owned them, my mother and grandfather agree that if they hold on to everything, their chances of surviving are better. I don't agree with their thinking, though I can imagine one situation where all the debris in our house could be useful. That is when the ice caps are done melting and my house is underwater—then I could see my grandfather and my mother fashioning a raft out of what they once owned, a couch or a table, and climbing aboard, paddling the raft towards the Rockies.

I myself would be happier to live more Spartan-like and sturdy. Each item of detritus is potent with its past. Because of this, I prefer the house in winter, when the things lose their smell.

My room is mostly empty, except for a few pictures on the wall. One picture is of a polar explorer who, during an earlier war, left Elephant Island on a far smaller boat than the boat he'd arrived on. The picture is tattered but I like it because the explorer was so brave. He left his marooned crew behind where their ship had been frozen in the pack ice. In a small launch he went for a rescue. He sailed into a cove on Georgia Island in the Antarctic where he ate some albatross meat after not having eaten meat in a long time. He crossed severed glaciers with brass screws, taken from his boat, fixed to the soles of his shoes so he'd not slip on the ice. Though he still did slip. In thirty-six hours he covered forty miles. After the first hour or two his brain began to repeat words in the same patterned battering his boat had suffered. Oddly, he felt that the words did not grow out of him but came from some exterior source. They said, "The girl who sold seashells will someday rot in hell." The words repeated and repeated until their stresses were highly over-accentuated and he could not stop and in fact found himself marching across the crevassed tundra in time to the pounding of the words.

I like the picture because it is the same with me, only with me the words are, "He loves me not. He loves me not. He loves me not."

Scientists came to where we live to study us because we have the highest rate of alcoholism in the country. Higher, they said, than even the Indian reservations in the west, higher than Florida or Texas or Louisiana or all the other flat states.

Jude and I are at his house. The people who lived here before Jude, alcoholics, used to pour their bacon fat on the carpet in the kitchen just like it was a dirt floor, and where there is not bacon grease from some ancient and filthy breakfast, there is the aroma of old cat urinations. Despite these odds ,Jude tries to make his house pleasant, or he tried to once and the evidence of this effort is still visible, if barely. For example, he has spread a colorful serape across the back of his couch and tied back the kitchen curtain with a bandanna. He buys a new bathmat whenever the old one gets too dirty. And on the refrigerator he has taped a picture of me from a long time ago, when we first met. You can't tell it's me but it is. You can't tell it's me because I have my back to the camera, bending over the railing of a highway bridge looking down into the water. This is the picture Jude likes though.

We have been drinking for a long time, since his shift at the Iron Works ended. Now it is dark out. He says, "I've been reading about the volcanoes on the Pacific Rim," or "Once I met a man who was a professional card counter in Reno," or "One night I jumped overboard," and those are all stories I like to hear. Though he sits on the far end of the couch from me, I think maybe he will get drunk enough so that he won't notice if I hold his hand.

His telephone rings and he walks into the kitchen to answer it. He walks carefully, with his torso bent more forward than a sober person's. "Jude, you are wasted," I tell him.

He turns slowly. "That's right. That's right," he says and walks into the kitchen to answer the telephone. "Hello?" he says. "Ah you know, nothing," he says. "No. Nobody's here," he says to the phone. I look down at my hands. I am. I am here. "No. No nothing," he says and then, "Okay," and then hangs up. I wait for him to come back to the living room but he doesn't. In a little bit I hear nothing. In a little bit longer I begin to wonder, "Am I here? Maybe I am not here." I have another drink. In a little bit longer I hear something in the kitchen. It is the sound of Jude talking to a woman who has come into the kitchen. She is one of Jude's girlfriends and I can hear her and Jude breathing. Through the doorway I can see the kitchen table trying to move away from them like a wounded animal or a crippled person, like humping. I try to leave but I am so drunk my body is heavy. I stand and stumble. Then she hears me. "I thought you said no one was here," she says. "That's right. That's right," Jude says again. I think I'll be sick. I hear her move away from him. She is straightening herself up when I walk through the kitchen on my way out. He doesn't bother to straighten himself up. I look at Jude. And Jude looks at me. That's what's wrong with my eyes.

Outside the drinking problem scientists are everywhere, collecting data. Leaning against the house, listening through special scientific instruments, jotting notes on clipboards, changing shifts. My eyes are killing me. I have trouble seeing and stumble and scream, "Get your science off me!" but it is just a tree and just its branches. I lean against the tree. I throw up on its roots as if I am a watering can watering the tree, only I'm not using water but throw-up instead. I finish. I rest my head on its bark. I could use something to drink. "I could use something to drink," I scream at the scientists. They don't answer so after some time I really can't say whether I'm here or not.

That's how gross it can get here, living this far north. Week after week there is more of the same. My mother will come into my room and want to know what I am doing since it is Saturday night and I am a young woman. If she makes me go out, I'll still go to Jude's. There is nothing else to do. He has a stethoscope. I'll listen to his heart through his shirt so his scars of gill-cutting don't show. I'll close the bathroom door, though not all the way. I'll lift my shirt. Jude will peek through the half-closed door if he is not asleep on the couch. I will listen to my own heart. Then I'll hold the stethoscope above the mold in the shower and it will say, "We never would have left the ocean had we known what a horrible place this is." And I'll say, "Me too."

Sometimes in the winter I spend the hours from four to six driving around town. It gets dark out so early and I feel the only way I'll get warm is with the car heater blowing directly on me or if I take a hot bath, but if I take too many baths in one day my mother will become nervous. She'll knock on the door, imagining that I am in the tub either jerking off or killing myself.

As I drive through town I talk to Jude even if he is not with me. I pretend he is in love with me. "I'll be cheap, Jude," I tell him when he's not there. He meets women at the Iron Works or he meets girls on the street or in mini-marts or they just get into his car if he looks at them. I suppose he is that handsome that that could actually happen. He doesn't always tell me. Sometimes I find their clothes. Sometimes I find their pictures. Sometimes in the pictures they are smiling at Jude. I look until I think I will be sick.

I drive out to the Iron Works but the men change shifts, get into their own cars and go home. I linger long at stop signs but no one ever gets into my car. All the doors are unlocked. Eventually I have to call a man I know, not very well. Jude knows him too because the man is the same age as Jude. Old. The man and I decide to have dinner together and hear some music. At dinner, when I return from the ladies room the man says, "Pay the tip." So I do and thank him for dinner. "I'm not taking you out," he says. "You still owe me half."

Later that night he says, "I like a lot of talk while we're doing it." I think of all the unleashed dogs on the streets. Their conversations in howl.

Still later, the ceiling in his bedroom.

The hair on his back.

Jude is very mad about the man. He says he won't see me.

I say I am having trouble seeing him too. "I have to go to the eye doctor," I tell him, but he has already hung up the phone.

Instead of the doctor's I walk down to the water. I walk along the shore a long, good distance. There are no people on the beach this far from town. I walk even further so I can be all alone and away from my bad decisions. I even, for a minute, run along the shore feeling light and lifted. After deliberations I decide to leap. Halfway through the leap I see something horrible and immediately long to be back on the sand. I abort my leap. I fall back to the ground. Up ahead I see a creature flapping like a fish without air, only it is far larger than any fish. I run to see this suffering thing and as I approach I can see that it really is not a fish but rather it is King Neptune on the shore. He is hurt. I am scared but I ask him, "Do you want me to throw you back?

"Oh, dear. If you could," he says.

I edge up to him slowly. I don't want to alarm him any further. I am surprised that someone as powerful as King Neptune could be hung up by something as shifting and dirty as a beach. "What happened?" I ask while trying to lift his back.

"It's embarrassing," he says.

"You don't have to say if you don't want to. You are the king of the ocean." He is a tremendous creature, like a whale. So large I could be swallowed or crushed if a wave rolled him onto me. I am getting quite wet in my efforts to assist the King.

"No. It's all right," he says. "Broken heart," he says and uses his arms to push toward the water. "There was a young girl," he says. "Here, on the beach. I wanted her."

A broken heart. If a heart were to break there'd be a lot of blood. But there's no blood.

"Do you know my father?" I ask him.

"What? A sailor?"

"Kind of. Yes."

"Sorry," he says.

"No. He wasn't lost at sea. It's not your fault."

King Neptune smiles, like god. Like 97% of the world's water is in ocean. Like 75% of the world is covered with ocean. Like everything is his fault.

"What about Jude? Do you know him? He's down here a lot," I say.

"Yeah. I think so. He's friends with that girl who has lost her mind? The one who thinks she's a mermaid?"

I stop helping King Neptune get back into the water. "What I can't figure out," he says, "is why she'd want to be a mermaid. All mermaids do is swim around and kill men when they get the chance."

I stop helping him and when I start again I push hard. "I'm going to be a different kind of mermaid," I tell the King.

He turns and looks at me. His eyes are just as pale as mine. "You don't get a choice," he says and then, "because the ocean has everything except mercy."

I shove his back so that he'll awkwardly be forced to bend at the hips. He is an old man and I am certain that he won't have the flexibility in his bones, that it will hurt him. I push so hard the vertebrae in his back cuts me.

"Fuck King Neptune," I think because growing up as a mermaid was a hard way to grow. When I was younger other children would not befriend me; instead they would say, loud enough for me to hear, "That house, that house is rotten in and out. That girl, that girl's got bugs in her hair." I'd fake to pick a bug from my scalp and eat it. Delicious.

When I was younger I'd go down to the water and each wave would ask in a thug accent, "You want I should take care of those kids? You want I should tell your father?"

But I'd let the children live.

I push and push King Neptune and then later, after I have given up, I can see clearly. King Neptune isn't there and underneath my cut hands is a rock shaped like a king, a rock deposited on this beach when the ice age flowed home, beaten, in retreat.

Here I am relieved that we begin drinking very, very young. There is little else to do and it seems to make what is small, us, part of something that is drowned and large, something like the bottom of the sea, something like outer space. That is why we continue living in remote places. There is no one here to tell us just how sick and swallowed we are.

Rather, here, at dawn the birds make too much noise, not a song but ugly shrieks and caws.

At mid-morning I wake up. I wonder what he is doing. I wonder about his wonder before I remember that he is dirty despite the flood.

At noon he says a word.

At mid-afternoon he hates the word because noon is gone.

At evening-time I see him, the sun asleep inside his ribs.

At night I imagine I am giving birth to Jude. Mostly I think this because that's how badly I want his head between my legs. It never occurs to me that I imagine he's my baby because that's what we act like. I never think that. Instead I think, I will have a drink with Jude and sharing that is almost as good as fucking or at least pricking our fingers and touching them together.

I am sure this is not uncommon but I've always required very little prompting to convince myself that this is a scientific experiment. Just my life, specifically. Almost everyone else is in on it. Jude's either innocent or he's the lead scientist.

I've always wanted to be a scientist.

So I've tried to make friends on the other side, people who might pass me a dangerous hint from the resistance, saying, "There are others like you." That hasn't happened yet.

After a few days Jude and I make up. We have to, as neither one of us really has other friends. Jude takes me out for Chinese food. His hair looks Chinese, soft and black like a Chinese crow. I wonder how the two pieces of evidence work together in the experiment.

"Testing," he says. "Testing," because he pays for our lunch and he stares at me silently for extended periods of time. Where I'm from that means, "Take me home with you and kiss me." But Jude drives me to my car. "See you tomorrow," he says and leaves even before I can get my keys out of my pocketbook.

I tell myself, "He's got to get over to the lab and type up a report: Subject delusional—wholly believes in monsters of experimental fabrication, namely,

love

death

ocean

mermaids

mercy

The words fall like drops in some ancient water torture.

When I get home I tell my mother, "I've always wanted to be a scientist." I am hoping that if I tell her this she will let me in on the experiment.

She doesn't. Instead she says, "I've always wanted to be a *Christian* Scientist," then tries to convince me to become a Christian Scientist with her. She knows little of the liturgy—the same bit most of us know about them not going to doctors. She thinks about them because years ago she lost a baby at the hospital. She wishes she had become a Christian Scientist before she went to the hospital. I tell her, "The baby was dead in your stomach before you got there." But she likes to blame the hospital.

"What does their name mean?" I ask her. "Why are they scientists?"

I am thinking that if she says, "Because they conduct secret experiments instead of going to church," I will join up. But she doesn't answer me. She stands holding the hole in her stomach.

At that moment a census enumerator comes to the door because we failed to mail in our response. When I open the door I tell her, "My father walked into the ocean one night and so my mother cannot move away, cannot remarry. She is frozen in this awful place waiting for him to return. That is pretty common. And I am a mermaid. That is less common. Mermaids have salt water where other people have souls. Mermaids have to get a man to fall in love with them if they want a soul. If he won't marry her, the mermaid has to kill the man. So that might be one less person for you to count."

"She's single or married?" the census enumerator asks.

"Still single."

"OK. I'll check single. Soulless."

"And my grandfather lives here too," I say.

That's not really what happens. The enumerator knocks so loudly that my mother and I quickly run upstairs to hide. We don't want to talk to her. Eventually my grandfather opens the front door and lets her in. He answers her questions. Not the same way I would have but the way he sees it. "I live with my daughter-in-law, forty-seven, and her daughter, nineteen. We're all single. We're all white." I yell from upstairs to remind him I'm blue. "I'm blue!" But he doesn't hear and the enumerator leaves with diluted information.

There's an uncertain pool called the ocean. The enumerator knocks on its door. The water opens up and lets her in. If she enters she'll get the information she needs. "I have thousands of husbands and wives," the ocean will say and show the enumerator the bones of the husbands and wives lying on the sea floor. The enumerator will record this data but the enumerator won't be able to file a report because the ocean door will close behind her. The ocean is thirsty and no wire of transmission is possible outside of this: a wave rolls onto the beach leaving a spray of darker sand. Maybe it is the enumerator screaming for help, maybe it is just because they built a seawall thirty miles down the coast in a town with more money than ours. They are using that money to try to steal our sand. Determine what that means. Like the enumerator, use scratch paper as required.

My grandfather has told me he remembers a time before longitude and latitude. That would make him older than I believe physically possible, but he insists that he remembers the headline: *Tiny Lines Circle the Globe! More on page 24.* He explains how these longitude lines can cause problems for printers and typesetters like him. How spreading a round thing to flat distorts the truth of what's between the lines. Mercator Projection makes up solid land that's not actually there so that molehill Greenland makes a mountain.

Jude runs his hand through his hair but this book is flat and the space between each line of text, line of Jude's black hair, stretches out so that what I read, what you read, is more than one width of truth. He runs his hand through his hair and my ground shakes as his action expands and is stretched between the longitude lines in my head so that his molehill, "You're too young," makes my mountain, "Rope, knife, gun."

My grandfather still misses his wife so badly that he spends most of his time typesetting dictionaries, like they once did together. He has to mix and match fonts and sometimes he leaves words out if too many letters are missing. He'll find a way to write lost love without any Ls. "I think I have a drawer of Officina in the attic," he says to me. "Would you, dear?"

"Please no," I say.

"Come on."

"It's scary up there," I tell him.

"Yeah. I know," he says and grunts, which means *Will you do it anyway?*

I take the attic stairs slowly lifting both feet to each stair before advancing to the next in order to give any scary thing fair warning that I'm coming and that it should clear out. There is a row of hanging garment bags and behind them a dark area in the eaves that is blocked by the bags. Anyone or anything could live there.

Along the shore, when I was young, my mother, father, and I use to comb through the debris that storms would deposit on the beach. The sand and seaweed coated everything and made the entire beach look the same, grayed, hiding the valuable things, baseball caps, old photos, canvas bags, or money in with the driftwood and sand. It required a slow and discerning eye to separate the worthwhile from the junk. My father had such an eye. "There's a work glove," he said to me once and eyeballed it up ahead. I ran to grab it and clutched it quite close for a minute until I realized that the strange weight inside the glove was not sand that had accumulated there but was rather the part of the glove's original owner that belonged inside the glove, namely, the person's hand. I screamed and ran back to my parents. "It's not a glove. It's a hand. A *hand*!" So my mother and I turned back to run in the opposite direction, away from the hand. But my father had to see it for himself. He walked up to the hand and grabbed it as though he were shaking it, saying, "Pleased to meet you." He felt around on the fingers and decided to carry the hand back to where we were standing. My mother and I were in the car when he caught up with us. I saw the hand in his hand and I locked all of our car doors. He knocked on my mother's window. She opened the window but only a crack. "What are you doing?" she asked.

"He's got a wedding ring on," my father said. "I think we should take the hand to the police." And then, turning to me, he said, "He might have kids."

"Put the hand in the trunk," my mother said through the window. I leaned forward as far as I could away from the trunk. I thought that hand was the hand of death and I didn't want it to creep through the ventilation system and grab me.

All this to say that our attic has similar properties as sand. It can obscure things, for example, hands of death or drawers of type in gray darkness. The attic is long and wide. It is poorly lit and filled with junk so that when I reach the top of the stairs looking for the fonts there is a moment when my eyes have to adjust to the attic's darkness. That moment opens wide like a door and in that moment I see a man standing in the gray against the back wall of the house. The man looks at me. He stares like water and lets me know that if I'm not going to do my job as a mermaid, somebody else will. The man is familiar to me, very familiar. I stop breathing. I try to make a sound for help, but with no air there is no sound. I am frozen and in that freezing my eyes adjust to the dark and the man dissolves into a lamp with a guitar propped up behind it, an illusion of bad eyesight. I make a mad dash for the drawer of Officina and the closer I get to the drawer, to the back of the attic, I notice something that I wish I hadn't. I grab the drawer and look once very quickly. I shouldn't have looked. There are footprints on the attic floor and they are wet. There are wet footprints where I had seen the man. I run.

I make it to the stairs but because I am running the letters are spilling out of the tray. A B D E F H H H H H H. Some letters spill under my feet while I run. An H is my two legs, my two arms, and the bridge between. At the top of the stairs I trip on the letters. My body contorts into Z, Y, N. I C on my back at the bottom of the stairwell. I hit my head, slamming it straight into unconsciousness. I remember how the King said, "You don't get a choice," and I am scared for Jude.

When I wake up at the bottom of the stairs, my grandfather is there petting my head, saying, "Honey, honey, honey." I try to move. The drawer of type has spilled below me, cutting letters into my skin. The attic stairs creak and the spilled letters cut me.

"Oh," I say, "I'm hurt." He helps me up. He is old and not too strong, but he gets me into my bed. "Grandpa, someone was up there, something wet."

"Probably the rain," he says.

"No," I say but my head hurts so badly that I just want to close my eyes. My grandfather pets my head so I do close my eyes. I fall asleep.

The bruises that form one day later are in the shape of the letters I fell on, though soon they grow into one big black and blue, like an entire essay. These bruises are so odd and I am so scared for Jude that I think I will use the black and blues to write him a note that says

mayday – from the Fr. *m'aidez* a distress call.

I drive over to Jude's house that afternoon once his shift has ended. I want to show him my letter bruises and the odd words that they spell. Even more than that I want Jude to touch the bruises as if they were Braille letters, as if he had to use his fingertips to read the words on my hips and back.

It doesn't work out that way exactly. He lets me in but I become too shy to mention the bruises when I see him. "Let's have some drinks," he says and smiles.

"Yes. Let's," I agree, and though the curtains of his living room are drawn, a sliver of setting sunlight sneaks in and illuminates all the particles floating in the air of Jude's house. I sit down in the light and Jude brings me a drink. He tells me about a type of fish caught in schools and used in the fabrication of ladies make-up. He tells me about an idea he has for an opera where all the gods of all the religions of the world battle it out in song. He tells me about the war again and again as if it won't ever go away. While he talks we continue drinking until we are drunk.

Finally my shyness dissolves. "Look," I say and lift just the back of my T-shirt.

"Fuck," he says. "What the hell happened?"

"I fell," I say.

And then he does touch me just as I had imagined, very lightly with his fingertips. He reads the weird words on my back. He stares and reads and finishes another drink. And when he is done reading he understands that these words are a warning, that something frightening or dangerous is lurking nearby. Maybe it is my father. Maybe it is this dull town, or the U.S. government. Maybe it is the ocean.

"Let's go," he says and stands looking down at me. "We've got to get out of here quickly. This town," he says and curses. He walks away to find the keys to his truck. He staggers a bit. "Come on," he yells from the kitchen with more urgency in his voice then I have ever heard Jude muster. The truck's engine turns over and I run outside. I don't even bother to close the door to his house. I don't look back as I climb into the passenger seat beside him.

It is not difficult to decide where to go. We live so far north that there is only one road south from here. It will be hundreds of miles before we have to decide where we are actually going. For now we are just going south. Jude is weaving a bit but there are not many cars on the highway up here and so I am not too worried about how much he has had to drink. I look in Jude's rearview mirror. I feel easy and ready. I feel buoyant and mostly I feel Jude's fingers on my back and it feels like love.

I look in the rearview mirror and even from here on the road less than an hour south of Jude's house I can see how that town sits in a pit of sadness like a black hole, a wallowing cavity. The town stares at the ocean that it loves even though the ocean thinks the town is small and stupid, even though the ocean beats the town throughout the hardest winter months. I look back at the town and I feel free. Jude gives the truck a little gas, trying to increase the distance between us and back there.

I look in the rearview mirror and quite suddenly there is a beautiful blue. It is bright and light, truly a gorgeous color. This blue is chaotic and changing. I recognize it immediately. "Jude," I say, "Look," and I point into his rearview mirror. "It's the ocean. It's coming up behind us," I say. He looks and I watch as he sees all the blueness that is behind us, all the blueness that is rising up like a tidal wave so quickly that I am certain it will catch up soon. "It is going to pull us back there," I say.

"You think that's the ocean?" he asks and I nod my head yes. He checks his mirror again. "You're right," he says, he slurs. "At first," he says, "I thought it was a bunch of cop cars chasing us with their lights on but now I can see you are right," he says. He accelerates.

"I don't think we can outrun the water," I tell him but he continues to accelerate. He smiles at me. I look again in the rearview. The color blue fills the entire mirror and I think that is how a disgusting, drunken, northern small town works. It enlists one beautiful thing like the blue ocean to keep people stuck and stagnant and staring out to sea. I watch the blue in the mirror. It is so beautiful that I say to Jude, "Fuck the dry land. I'm a mermaid."

"You are?" he asks and is surprised enough that he looks away from the road. He looks at my face for a long bit and then he looks down my body to my legs. But he looks too long. We collide and burst through the guardrail and then we are sailing down into the deep ditch beside the road. Our crash is like a shotgun blast or a broken mast or a filthy past and once the crash is over I can hear the truck sizzle.

"Are you okay, Jude?" I ask.

"Oh," he says. "Oh," and then stops because just then the water rushes in like a bunch of police officers with their blue lights flashing, with their guns drawn. The water rushes in like a bunch of police officers would rush in to surround the smashed-up car of two drunk people who are evading the law. The water rushes in and throws the two of us into the back of a patrol car that returns us to town, that passes close by the ocean on the way so that the ocean has a chance to tell us, "Don't you two ever try that again."

THE PROBABILITY OF GREAT
EVENTS SETS LIFE IN MOTION

by Robert Olmstead

OFTEN I COULD hardly breathe. My heart felt cramped and then I would lose consciousness. I knew my heart was in a bad way. It was suffering an hysterical condition borne of an emotional crisis by the name of my second wife. With her there was trouble from the start. When we got married I was still married to my first wife and even after I divorced, she never forgave me that. What a wound she was for a very long time.

I told this to the counselor at the V.A. when I went looking for help for my heart and he thought stringing beads would be good for my nerves. So I ordered supplies from a mail order company and one thing led to another and before I knew it I had a white canvas tent, folding tables and satin-lined presentation cases with glass lids and I was traveling to craft shows and festivals and county fairs selling my work. I am known for my hematite necklaces and have a patented design on my Lost Angel Hearts.

What I wanted was a product straddling art and design, something that was marketable without compromising my principles. What happened was a Saturday a few years ago in Paris. Lady Di tragically met her demise and that Sunday I was raking in the cash in Cincinnati. Lost Angel Hearts were leaving the table like free pussy at a cop convention.

"You know," I said to a crying woman. "Seventeen seventy-six." But she didn't get me.

"Excuse me?" she said, daubing at her red nostrils.

"Seventeen seventy-six. We fought a revolution so not to grieve over dead kings and queens. Does it ring a bell?" Apparently it did not. The woman bought five and the rest is my small personal history, me and the Lost Angel Hearts. I guess you could say I am now quite a hit and a minor celebrity and have a serious regional reputation. I feel healing and self-growth through my art jewelry. What I am telling you is that I found myself on a real emotional upswing.

But there is more than that. I have a girlfriend named Naomi who has a daughter named Cat and they pay attention to me and this is also quite nice. It is not the most extreme and intimate relationship between me and Naomi but it seems to work for both of us. Naomi says that eventually she wants to know me better but I laugh and suggest that in all actuality she really does not want to know me better. But still, I listen to what she says. Like, she told me I should grow my hair long and so I did and now I have long hair and I look better for that. Naomi feels for me in many ways. She thinks my heart was born in a deep shadow. Comparatively speaking, I am doing swimmingly.

This morning we eat breakfast at the Big Boy. It is the all-you-can-eat buffet for seven dollars. I eat too much. They're making money on Naomi and Cat and probably breaking even on me, but there are some big hogs here who can really pack away the product. There is french toast and clots of scrambled eggs. There are piles of bacon, ham and sausage. There is gravy and biscuits and pancakes. I watch one guy whose mouth is a transfer station to his stomach. He keeps it full the whole time, just working in another forkful for every one he swallows. The big hogs eat like it is love and passion they need and they are helpless for it. You see a man hold up a paw with bacon coming out between his fingers on the way to his pie hole and you know you're seeing someone in the grips of a powerful force. I feel for the big fat whites and big fat blacks, hog men and hog women and their hog children popping sweat from their foreheads and their eyelids quivering in food ecstasy.

Naomi says I am being too critical and I internalize what she says. I think one of my problems is that I approve of myself and very few others. She suggests that I myself am eating too much and should take better care of myself lest I become like one of those hog incubators of heart disease. Lately she's been dropping little hints about cohabiting. I myself am intent on preserving maximum differentiation between cohabiting and not cohabiting.

After breakfast we leave for this Labor Day celebration in a little town in Ohio in the school district where Naomi and Cat live. We set up the tent and unfold the tables and one by one we carry out the presentation cases. I am still bilious from the Big Boy and it is ungodly hot. The sun is a glare in a white sky and we are all set up when I figure out we are across from the karaoke tent. I immediately resign myself to our situation and feel better for that. I sit to the back at a card table and begin making jewelry, my stomach still in all-you-can-eat turmoil, while Naomi works the front tables. Today is busy. Trade picks up early. Where I sit I have a boxy little black and white TV and a radio and I make necklaces, chokers and bracelets. I wear headphones with no music. It keeps people away. They think I am involved, but occasionally snap my picture. Since September 11, I cannot keep up with the demand for Lost Angel Hearts.

Overtop my sunglasses I see Miss Labor Day Festival go by and I feel a lurch in my groin for which I am mildly ashamed. She looks like a white black woman. She wears deep red lips and painted fingernails and a powder-blue satin sash that crosses her bare tanned shoulder. She wears a crown and silver heels. She has a set of teeth that don't fill her mouth and a somewhat predatory nose. Cat says she's fourteen and not a virgin. Says she's a slut. Says she acts just like her mother who is a royal bitch. Cat's fourteen too. At the Big Boy she ate some melon and half a pancake. Seven dollars. Cat gives me a kiss on the top of my head and goes wandering. She's looking for Jesus-boy. I begin to have this nagging feeling that nothing is wrong except nothing is wrong.

A fat guy begins to sing a Paul Anka song. The fat guy has been back to my tables several times. He's here alone when it being a festival most everybody else is with someone else: family, friends, lovers. He wants to buy, but can't make up his mind. Maybe singing a love song will help him decide. Clear to see he's got something bottled up inside that he cannot deal with.

Across from the karaoke tent there's an Elvis impersonator. I think how sometimes it comes over me that I would like to set off a bomb and kill hundreds of people, how I would like to strangle a beautiful little puppy for how utterly innocent and offensive it is.

Now the fat guy is singing Frank. He's really belting it out. He's singing about how he did it his way. He's reaching for the high notes and his voice strangles in his throat. They say Frank got more pussy than you can shake a stick at. I want to take out my revolver and relieve him of his misery. Watch him melt in the street.

On the whole, I decide, I like sitting across from the karaoke tent.

Performing draws the more sensitive people, the kind of people who buy my jewelry. I look up and the fat guy is back again fingering the merchandise. I am sad for how pathetic he is with his trousers dragging off his ass and his big aching breast throbbing with homeless love. He is sweating profusely and I think how easily the salty water on his face could be tears.

I switch the channel to the talk shows. I like television. It is more normal than life, more wholesome and all done in the name of good natured fun. TV can't kill you like some things can. I especially like the shows on TV where two guys square off over current events. It is provocative to me for how I agree with the one guy and then I agree with the other guy and go back and forth like that between the two opinions constantly changing my own mind as to which one of them I would like to shoot in the mouth. But as we know, opinion is transient and work is permanent, hence Labor Day and life isn't about what you say you're going to do, but what you actually do and on and on and on.

But it's good because you can learn a lot by following current events. I will give you an example. During a fleeing from Cuba several years ago, people took to the seas in all manner of rude craft, risking sharks and storms and the Bermuda Triangle and Fidel's machine guns. Having been at Guantanamo when in the service, I followed this closely and learned that many of them used weed whackers for outboard motors. I thought that was extremely clever and something I will remember.

The big guy walks away but he doesn't go far. He is conflicted all through his face. He decides to do it again. I can tell that and then he does. He heads for the notebook that contains the selections. He tells the guy it's a Tokens song. He's rocking on his feet. He wants for the music like a kid who has to pee. He sings, Hush my darling. Don't fear my darling. The lion sleeps tonight.

I get that his name is Bill because they call him Bill. Bill finishes up and they remind him he hasn't paid yet, so he does the reach. He's prancing and sweating like a drunk doing shots or a fool touching electricity. Bill pays for his performance from a fat worn-out wallet and then he heads for the book again.

The Elvis impersonator wanders back. He wants to sing too. He and Bill size each other up. Do enough of these events and you begin to see the same types over and over again, the same scenes played out, and when it's all over, the same sad inconsequence.

Bill paces and Elvis sets that trademark sneer. Bill is first up, "Pretty Woman." I turn my head away because in looking at him, I see his legs begin to shrink and his great barrel begin to grow. Heat pours off him like a furnace. Bill finishes up with his not-even-close Roy Orbison and daubs at his forehead with a handkerchief. He puts a cap on his head and then reaches behind himself to give a little tug to his shirt to make sure it covers his fat ass. It's a long reach with him turning half around himself before it's accomplished. Then Elvis steps up and goes into "Stuck on You." They say Elvis got a lot of pussy too. Bill doesn't look like he's had any in ages. It's apparent he has a lot of love in him, but he's not what you'd call a ladies' man. Elvis starts in on the Poke-salad song. He's talking to two old women sitting in folding chairs, telling them they probably haven't been down South much. The two old women watch him perform in that respectful and retarded way that is the style of old people. Lord have mercy, he sings. Mamma was a workin' on a chain gang.

Bill can't take it. He heads out for a sausage sandwich with onions and peppers, or maybe a beef cow. I think how he wouldn't eat so much, wouldn't hurt and yearn so much if I were to shoot him. I point at his broad departing back, site, and jerk my hand up. I blow across the tip of my finger as I imagine his skinny legs liquefying and melting him onto the grass in a heap. Life is merely a choice between chaos and conspiracy.

Naomi makes another sale. She catches my eye and moves her mouth— get busy. Naomi says she loves me. She says she loves me so much she wants to have my baby. I told her if I had a baby I'd eat it. She thought I was joking. I told her for what a baby costs we could buy a Harley. It makes her want a baby all the more. Some women can be real chumps for guys like me.

A woman comes by I have seen before. She's a good customer, but painfully thin. Offensive in her thinness because she thinks she is so beautiful. Her arm bones and leg bones are thin as a slice of air. Her joints protrude as is common in the regular pictures of starving children. She buys a bracelet and I want to shoot her after the sale because she is so fucked up, but then she picks up another bracelet so I can't complain.

Down the way four little girls are engaged in a dance contest. Dance is by far the least of the arts. It is physical and emotional and vain. Except ballet. When I was overseas I saw dancers who could shed themselves, shed their beings and become like swans or butterflies.

A guy who looks like Fred Goldman comes by, stands next to the thin woman. She appeals to him. The Fred Goldman look is a pretty common look for a man. I think Fred is on the radio now, fomenting the state of justice in America as he is enmeshed in the snare of his own grieving-self-righteous-victim-death-cult. Radio must be a tough gig for a guy who is apparently as vain as Fred with his waxed handle bar moustache. Death has got to be even uglier for a guy like him.

The thin woman makes another purchase and as she walks away Fred checks out her stick legs and bony ass. She has a gesture I hate. It is to walk with her forearm extended and parallel to the ground, letting her hand dangle like something useless. Three of my bracelets now hang from that bony wrist. I have the feeling I do not want my jewelry next to her skin. Her skin is so close to her bones there would be no flesh wound if I shot her. To hit her would shatter bone and break her to pieces and the sound she would make would be squeaky and pathetic. The four little girls from the dance contest step up to the microphone and they sing a song that frames the age-old question: Whose bed have your boots been under?

Cat wanders in. She's as tall as Naomi, but manages to get her arms around her neck and her bottom on Naomi's lap and then her feet come up and she curls her legs and Naomi is holding her like she's a little girl. Cat's in eighth grade. Her state-wide proficiency test scores arrived just before school started and told us that she is below average. I hate school and often wonder why more boys don't pick up guns and kill school people. When it happened in Colorado I wasn't surprised. America is like living inside a vise. They set the jaws the first day you step inside a school and then they start turning the screw. The educational-industrial-complex.

Six or eight kids in yellow T-shirts stand up and sing a song about God's love. I ask Cat who they are and she says they are from Camp Comfort, a place where abused and neglected kids go for a week in the summer. She says the people there are really nice.

"That little boy was locked in a closet," she says. She wraps a strand of hair around her finger until her finger turns blue. She's talking baby talk to her mother. She's saying, "Jesus-boy has really cool eyes. He wanted a love gift of five dollars and said for that my cares would be taken care of forever."

"You don't have to give anybody five dollars to be taken care of," Naomi says.

"Then who will take care of us?"

"You have to take your cares to the real little baby Jesus."

"Will he take care of us?"

"God watches over us," Naomi says and Cat snuggles more closely to her mother's neck.

"God loves me," she says, her voice muffled in her mother's neck and T-shirt and gives me a big wink.

"God loves everybody," Naomi says and I think sometimes this world is more than I can suffer. Cat reaches for my water cup.

"Don't drink that," I say.

"Why not?"

"There's a sweat bee dead in the ice," I tell her. She makes the ick sound and crinkles her nose. Kids.

I take some blame for Cat being below average in school. One day she was at my house doing make-up school work because Naomi works days at the Kroger and Cat had the strep throat. She had to write three separate paragraphs about who she would love to meet and who she would want to be if she could be anyone and what time in history would she love to live in. She asked me my opinion and so I told her if I could meet anybody I would want to meet God because he is responsible for us existing and I would want to ask him why did he made it so fucked up and if I could be anyone, I'd want to be someone who is in extreme pain so I could understand what that is really like and if I could have lived in another time it would be in the beginning so I could have prevented this all from happening in the first place.

A little girl gets up and sings a song about another little girl named Fancy who is pimped by her mother. Before the song is over she curtsies and her family and the two old women in the lawn chairs applaud. You'd think she just cured cancer the way they go on and on and on.

So anyway, Cat must have jotted down similar sentiments—who to meet, who to be and when to live—and the next thing we know Naomi is sitting down with a guidance counselor and being asked if Cat is hooked on the Internet, if Cat is a loner, if Cat tortures little animals, shit like that, and then Cat's psychology is being tested. I know I can be impatient with people who are stupid. It is one of my faults, but I wanted to just kill somebody I was so mad.

But not today. People are enjoying this day. They are celebrating how hard they have to work. Makes you wonder who invented Labor Day. Real bright working people. I stand and stretch. I feel my bones.

Down from us is a religious booth and the older guy waves when he sees me. Their table is piled with stacks of tracts. There's an older guy and a young guy, never very busy. Cat has a crush on the young guy. She calls him Jesus-boy. We run into them a lot. They are both vets. The young guy has a shaved head and a scar that burls from behind his ear and hooks around to his temple in the shape of a big skin question mark. Earring holes in both his ears. Blue tats painted into his arm skin. An eye that wanders in the socket. He was in an accident and almost died and found God when near to death. He's in religious training and the older guy is his spirit guide. When people take it in the head like he did there is usually damage in the brain's region of common sense.

I like the young guy. He's an innocent Jesus-boy, but the older guy has a way about him that makes me want to shoot him. We run into each other a lot and he ought to know enough by now to stay clear of me, but he doesn't. He claims he likes me but what he doesn't realize is that I hate him more than he could ever like me. He sees me and comes my way and when he's this close I think how easy it would be.

"Hello," he says, "how empty the suburbs." Like I know what he means. He keeps up in a soft sonorous voice, the voice of cartoon evil. He has been irritating me all summer. He's a warrior for Jesus. He wants to give me a place where I will be understood when discussing my problems. His name is Nial.

I say, "Why are you guys hitting up little kids for money? Why don't you ask the old people? They have all the money." I indicate the old women in the lawn chairs. I think they hear me because they give me a hurt stupid look.

"We all contribute however we can. It's what Jesus wants."

"Shut up to me," I say, but he goes on about fellowship, worship and service to God and humankind.

When he gets finished I ask, "Why did he say that at the end?"

"Who say what?"

"Him. At the end. Why hast thou forsaken me? He should have gone down like a man."

"He wasn't a man. He was a God."

I say, "I hate crybabies."

He tells me, "Nothing goes unless something has gone before it."

I say, "Fuck you."

He says, "Come to service."

I say, "What for?" So far a typical conversation for us.

"Religion teaches you your place in the world. It teaches you the right way to live. It teaches you how to pray. There is natural human need to give thanks. It helps us in death. Even though your body dies your soul goes on and that love continues."

"I go down there, I go with a machine gun."

"You just say that stuff."

"Religion is part of the inadequacy campaign," I tell him.

"I am your personal link with Jesus Christ our savior." When he says the word *personal* he makes these little air quotes around it. These guys are like rust. They scare me more than the communists. You can never get rid of them. They thrive on abuse.

"He's coming," he says.

"Inadequacy campaign," I say.

"You need help with the spiritual conflicts you now experience as a result of combat. You, son, are in post-trauma. You have moral, ethical and spiritual dimensions that need to be addressed."

"What makes you so holy?"

"Vietnam caught up with me."

"Take it somewhere else. I ain't buying."

"Killing in war violates your nature as God gave it to you."

"I'm all right," I say. "It isn't like that."

"Killing seems all right at the time, but it can come back and haunt you."

"What I'm telling you is I was a clerk and I got run over by a jeep at Fort Drum twenty years ago."

"I still care for you. Allow me to demonstrate that I care about you."

"Suck the pipe," I say.

"We are in the pre-rapture time," he whispers. "The Lord is coming."

"When?" I say.

"Soon," he says. "It will be very soon. Get right," he says. "The right world view is the Christian world view."

Then he sees someone else he's working and goes after them and I can feel the sweat on my back and I am shaking a little.

"Honey," Naomi says. She has dragged down her sunglasses and she is looking at me like she really cares for me. "Maybe you should listen to him."

"What are you talking about?"

"It can't hurt."

"It can't hurt," Cat says.

"No," I say. "I suppose it can't." But when she says what she says I know that we are through because I have already talked to someone at the V.A. and that's enough. My mind can't work fast enough to keep up with what I am feeling. Naomi, I think. Oh, Naomi.

"Talking to someone," she says, "can be a good thing once in a while."

"Talking to someone can be a good thing," Cat says. But I don't say anything more because right then I know that I will be moving on soon. I know that I will not look for someone else, but someone else, another woman, will surely find me. She'll think I am not perfect, and she will be convinced that with time she can help me and she will become emotionally attached and we will become romantically involved. I am sad and I want to cry for the loss I have just experienced and then I am not.

The young guy is watching us and I wave him over. I know his story. He doesn't get on well with the modern world either. It's how I grew up. New Canaan, CT. Father has an affair. Mother has an affair in revenge. Sister tries to kill herself. Best friend electrocuted in a snow storm. Join the military. Smash it up on a night jump at Fort Bragg.

He comes to me, drawn by proximity to Cat. We shake hands like brothers. He grins and his naked head goes like a jack-o-lantern. His blue tats are like thin beautiful serpents. We light cigarettes and I extinguish the match between my thumb and forefinger. I close the heat slow and don't feel a thing. My fingers are that calloused from all the hematite. The young guy licks his lips, smiles and nods. Naomi smiles too and Cat makes the ick sound. Then the young guy reaches up to his face and takes out his eye and holds it in his hand. It is blue glass and it looks up at me from the nest of his palm. This time Naomi and Cat are silent as the dead and what Jesus-boy just did makes me want to take off my leg or a finger. It makes me want tear open my chest and give him my heart. I look up into the black empty socket that held his glass eye. His grin is a slash across his face. I nod my approval and reach up to pull back my hair and we compare the scars that loop our skulls like braided ropes. I think how nothing is wrong. I think how one day soon I will reach down and with a great tearing sound strip away the shotgun taped underneath this table. I will rack the forearm to make that beautiful singular sound and I will sweep a craft's fair street. Violence is not banal. It is beautiful. It is coherent, articulate, ineffable, illuminating, edifying, forever everlasting. My heart climaxes with these thoughts and flutters and the chemicals change in my brain and I sigh as my mind relaxes. I wonder how many of us are a pill away? How many of us don't have it okay and is there a better place on earth and will we find it someday? I let down my hair and raise my hand and point my finger at Elvis. He's coming soon, I whisper. Soon.

THE GATHERING SQUALL

by JOYCE CAROL OATES

SHE KNEW: her mother was terribly upset. Because her mother was asking, "Are you going to tell us who it was?" and there was no *us* in the Uhlmanns' household any longer.

"Momma, I said. I didn't see."

"Of course you saw. You're not blind."

"I didn't. I did not."

"But you know. You know who did this to you."

She said nothing. She was lying where she'd crawled the night before, so tired. On her bed atop the rumpled rust-colored corduroy spread her mother had sewn for her when she'd been in seventh grade. How long ago, her brain was too fatigued to calculate. Oh, her sunburnt arms, shoulders! Her face burning as if someone had tossed acid onto it. This was punishment enough for the night before.

Her mother leaned over her, so close Lisellen could feel her warm ragged breath, yet Mrs. Uhlmann was hesitant to touch her, just yet. In another minute she would, Lisellen knew. Lisellen was lying in a tight little pretzel knot, knees drawn up to her chest. Face turned to the wall like they say dying people do. Was it shame, you wanted to hide your face? Or, dying, did you feel you'd had enough of the world, its busyness, its annoying attentions? Needing to hide her bruised and swollen face from Mrs. Uhlmann's eyes. Her older sister Tracy used to say their mother could tell by looking at Tracy's mouth how much she'd been kissed by her boyfriend, that kissing left an unmistakable look if you knew how to identify it. But Lisellen had not been kissed. Duncan Baitz had not even tried to kiss her. Not one of those guys had tried to kiss her.

"God damn, girl, I'm losing my patience."

"Momma, I said I don't know."

The night before, staggering into the bathroom to stare at herself in the mirror, Lisellen had been more astonished than shocked. What a freak she'd looked! Her upper lip was swollen to three times its normal size, there was a crust of red (blood? had her nose been bleeding?) around both her nostrils, her hair looked as if an animal had gotten into it. Now, hours later, her lip throbbed, the delicate skin pulled tight to bursting. The sunburn would cause her fair, freckled skin to peel, maybe to blister. And there were the hot dark eyes she'd had to acknowledge in the mirror, brimming with hurt and disbelief.

She was of an age, oh God it had seemed to be going on forever, this age when all things were in reference to others. The opinions of others. When she could not have a private thought, except somehow it was directed toward staring witnesses whose judgment of her was ceaseless and harsh, but might be amended by an appeal of hers, a helpless smile, a childish disarming gesture.

She must have been whimpering in her sleep. A feverish half-sleep in which she couldn't find a comfortable position. She hadn't removed her clothes, only just kicked off her sandals. She hadn't had the energy. Like a sudden summer squall out of a cloud there'd come Lisellen's mother into her room slamming the door with the flat of her hand—"Lisellen! Good Christ, what is it?" For just that moment, Mrs. Uhlmann had been more frightened than angry. The hour was very early: just after 6 A.M. Already a hot splotch of sunshine was moving across the plaster wall above Lisellen's head. Mrs. Uhlmann woke early, nerved-up and ready to begin the day, needing to fill the house, emptier since the departure of two of its inhabitants with purposeful activity, a smell of brewing coffee and the cheering noise of the kitchen radio. And so, waking, she'd heard the whimpering from Lisellen's bedroom; unless it had been the whimpering that had wakened her. And the shock of seeing her daughter lying in that contorted posture, face almost touching the wall, not in bed but on top of it, still in her clothes from the previous day—this had caused Lisellen's mother to cry out, and go in stumbling haste to fetch ice cubes, thinking at first the problem was just sunburn.

Well, sunburn. Fair freckled thin skin like Lisellen's, if you had sense you kept out of the sun. It was Mrs. Uhlmann's side of the family, not Mr. Uhlmann's. Lisellen knew better than to risk sunburn. Sunstroke. On the wide glaring-sandy beach at Olcott. Where sunshine broke and rippled in the choppy lake in an infinity of rays. Where there was always wind, so you were deceived the sun wasn't so hot as it was. And the partly clouded, veiled sky so you might think the sun's rays would be diluted. Though Lisellen knew better of course. Only she'd had to take a chance. *Didn't want to miss out. Any of it.* She wasn't of a legal age to drink but there were ways of beating that, if you had older friends. If you hung out in the parking lot, not inside the tavern.

At the Summit, above the dunes. Swarms of young people were everywhere inside the mustard-colored stucco building, on the outdoor terrace where there was dancing, in the asphalt parking lot and on the beach and amid the dunes. Deafening music was played by a local band that called itself Big Bang, six or seven sedated-looking guys of whom Lisellen could claim she knew the straggly-haired drummer, sort of, the older brother of a girl in Lisellen's tenth-grade social studies class last year. And there was Duncan Baitz, the misunderstanding between them...

In her upset Mrs. Uhlmann hadn't been able to locate the rubber ice bag. So she'd wrapped ice cubes in a kitchen towel for Lisellen to press against her swollen face. But the ice cubes soon melted from the heat of Lisellen's throbbing skin, dripped and ran and wetted her, making her recall the sticky mucus-moisture rubbed and smeared on her legs. On even her belly where her white cotton panties had been yanked down, torn but (at least, she had this to be grateful for, she clung to this small vestige of dignity as one might cling to a barnacle–encrusted rock in terror of drowning in the surf) not torn off.

She knew: word would spread all through Olcott of what had been done to her. But what had not been done to her was more crucial.

She was making a sick-puppy sound. She was shivering. Wanting to evoke her mother's sympathy, but not her mother's alarm. Wanting her mother to know *Yes I've been hurt, your daughter has been hurt. Mommy take care of me.* But not wanting her mother to drive her to a doctor. Not wanting her mother to dial 911, to summon police.

Lisellen made an effort to sit up. Pretending to be weaker than she really was except as she tried to raise her head a wave of dizziness weakened her.

Like an energy outage, the TV screen suddenly wavering on the brink of collapse.

Honors student, they'd teased. She had believed there was affection in their teasing.

That she was smart, that she did well in school, performing easily on tests the others struggled with, disfigured her like acne. She knew, and she knew that the resentment and even the dislike of her classmates was warranted. At Olcott High she had a certain aura, outside school very little. Not-pretty, and not-sexy. There were many other girls like Lisellen, most of the girls in her class in fact, but Lisellen wasn't patient with her lot. She yearned to be one of the summer girls blossoming like hills of dandelion and tiger's lilies, overnight bobbing bright colors in the wind. So fast. It could happen so fast. With some girls, as young as thirteen. Lisellen was sixteen but looked like fourteen. Other girls were sixteen looking like eighteen. She didn't disdain them, nor even yearned to be one of them; she yearned only not to be left behind by them.

She'd crept into the house the night before praying her mother would be asleep and would not hear her. It was nearly 1 A.M.; she'd promised to be home by 11 P.M. Calculating that probably her mother wouldn't wait up for her. Mrs. Uhlmann trusted her younger, honors-student daughter, as she had not trusted Tracy. Tracy who'd been a little wild. Tracy who was nineteen now, a nursing student in Rochester, working this summer as a nurse's aide in the hospital. Tracy had moved out in the season their parents' marriage had finally broken up. Twenty-six years!—Lisellen had thought, with the heartlessness of youth, that the elder Uhlmanns' love had only just worn out. Like a roller-towel in a public restroom, eventually the contraption breaks and the towel becomes filthy, hanging in tatters.

She'd hated her sister. *Good timing, Trace. Thanks for leaving me behind.*

Tracy said, *Every daughter for herself, man.*

Tracy had meant to be funny. She hadn't been.

At the Summit Tavern, in the asphalt parking lot and on the beach, in the slovenly dunes there was an atmosphere of high-decibel festivity. On the terrace the music made thinking more trouble than it was worth, like trying to run in loose sand. Like wading in rough surf. For a brief tormented while Lisellen had believed she'd been left behind by the people who had brought her: the hike back home was three miles, unless she dared telephone her mother to come get her (she wouldn't have dared). She was hurt to have been left behind by Duncan Baitz in whose car she'd been brought to Olcott but determined to have a good time anyway. In fact, Lisellen's friends (she wanted to think they were more than just stray people she knew from school) hadn't left the Summit just yet. The crowd was so large, she'd lost them. Baitz was a vivid presence in Lisellen's life though she had to suppose she wasn't much of a presence in his. He was older, a year ahead at school. But he looked and behaved as if he were older still. Once, he'd asked Lisellen out. She'd stammered yes, yes she'd like that, but somehow, it was never clear to her how and why and had become the subject of obsessive hours of pondering, Baitz had never called her, he'd been politely indifferent to her ever since. Why?

He must have interpreted her remarks as negative, somehow. Oh, but why?

True, Baitz had stopped at her house to pick Lisellen up to take her to Olcott, but someone else had make the arrangements. Lisellen had crammed herself into the back seat of Baitz's car, one of several passengers shrieking with laughter, sitting on one another's laps, while in front beside Baitz was a male friend of his, a stranger to Lisellen. She was conscious, in Baitz's presence, of a certain degree of tension that remained mysterious, heartrending. Not that Lisellen was one to brood, *Why don't you like me anymore, Duncan, what happened?* She didn't think that Baitz was even attractive, with his odd blunt head like a bucket and his prematurely creased forehead; the Baitzes lived in a ramshackle house on the weedy edge of Strykersville, Mr. Baitz an auto mechanic. Lisellen had a vague idea that their fathers knew and disliked each other but not why. Lisellen's father was a man of smoldering hurts and grievances that sometimes flared into alarming emotions; you didn't try to comprehend their source, only how to extinguish them. Lisellen guessed that Mr. Baitz might be of the same type, being of the same generation. Her father had done better than Mr. Baitz, though—he'd been a trucker as a young man, bought his own truck, bought several trucks, was now in business for himself, as he liked to define it. Since he'd moved out of the house, leaving just Lisellen and her mother behind, Lisellen had begun to think of her father as she thought uneasily of Duncan Baitz. *You can't make them like you. You can't even make them see you.* When Baitz glanced at Lisellen, if only by accident, and unsmiling, a sensation like a machete lashed through her body leaving her weak, stunned.

Sixteen, Lisellen was too young to be served what's quaintly called *alcoholic beverages* at the Summit. Still she was drinking. As Big Bang hammered at her head from all directions, Lisellen discovered that, despite its repellent taste, she could swallow mouthfuls of beer. Though sometimes coughing, choking, causing the stinging liquid to drip from her nose in a way some observers found funny: as if Lisellen were doing it on purpose to amuse. (Oh, God! She would recall this with mortification. At the time, it had seemed hilarious to her, too.) The Summit on a Saturday night in midsummer was jammed with people, most of them young. Mrs. Uhlmann had only grudgingly allowed Lisellen to go to the beach; she had not known about the Summit, which had a certain reputation. Mrs. Uhlmann, grimly predicting that Lisellen might get caught up in a wrong crowd, would have seen her worst suspicions confirmed. For here were loud men in T-shirts that exposed their corded, oily muscles, their lurid tattoos. (Some of these were bikers from Niagara Falls.) There were "older" men in their thirties and perhaps beyond—some as old as Lisellen's father, though far more youthful in dress, hair style, behavior. And girls and young women: not behaving very soberly. Where couples were dancing on the terrace, almost you could see minuscule haloes of perspiration in the air like dust motes. Strobe lighting from a long-ago era. Lisellen was impressed that certain of her friends were stoned, even as a part of her stood aside in disdain, thinking *Not me! Not me like you, not ever.*

Yet somehow there was Lisellen in a loud group in the dunes. Running and stumbling along the pebbly beach. By this time her skin was beginning to burn in alarming patches on her face, her shoulders and arms. The tender exposed skin of her upper chest. It was fully night now, the slow-sinking sun had finally disappeared, yet still the air was warm and muggy with gnats. Lisellen understood that things were swerving out of control. Her sandals were sinking into the sand as she ran, and the sand itself appeared to be sinking, tilting at a drunken angle. On the immense lake waves slopped and sloshed. There was a sound of laughter mixed with the relentless downbeat of the Big Bang. Mixed too with a faint stink of dead things: rotting fish strewn on the beach, clam shells, vegetation in long snaky clumps. By day, flies buzzed; by night, gnats got into your hair, eyes, mouth. Lisellen realized she was the only girl in the dunes. There had been one or two others, they must have turned back. The guys were teasing Lisellen by chanting her name—*Lis-el-len Uhl-mann*—in a way that was meant to make her laugh, the name sounded so pretentious, so somehow complicated and silly. *Honors student honors student!*—a loud boisterous singsong chant, Lisellen wanted to interpret it as affectionate, not malicious. And the hands grabbing at her, affectionate and not malicious. A rough kind of flirting. More like grade school than high school. And some of these guys were older, and not known to Lisellen. She was being pulled laughing into the water. A lukewarm sudsy surf it was, like water in a washing machine. Someone was splashing water onto her, Lisellen sputtering with laughter. Her bare shoulders, breasts. Wetting the dress her mother had sewed for her, gorgeous orange poppies on a white background, flaring skirt, a beautiful dress, a dress to make you smile, a dress Lisellen had wanted her father to see but he had not, a dress to flatter her pale freckled skin and boyish body. She'd been disappointed, most of the girls at the Summit were wearing just tank tops, cut-offs, jeans that fitted tight as if they'd been poured into them, the more glamorous wore clingy mini-skirts that bared their gleaming thighs. These were girls with boyfriends. These were girls who were dancing on the terrace, or sitting with their men inside, in booths. Not girls racing along the beach shrieking with laughter as if being tickled to death.

The boys were so much taller than Lisellen, and bigger. Panting like dogs they formed a circle around her. They were only playing, she knew. She slapped at their bold hands, their quick-darting hands, the pinching fingers, she saw their grinning mouths and eager eyes, the sweat gleaming on their faces. And some yards away there was Duncan Baitz, staring at her. He wasn't in the circle of guys, he was standing on one of the dunes, as if he'd been approaching them but had paused, and stood now irresolute and frowning, his expression unreadable. Was he smiling? Grinning? Or was it a look of alarm—*See? See what you've brought on yourself?*

"Was it that Baitz boy?" Mrs. Uhlmann's guess was sudden, as if she'd been reading Lisellen's mind.

Lisellen stammered no. No it was not. No she didn't remember who it had been, she hadn't seen his face.

Always Lisellen had had a sense of something in her mother gathering, tightening with tension. The sensation was almost unbearable and yet thrilling. *The Gathering Squall* was the title of a nineteenth-century watercolor Lisellen had seen in a Port Oriskany art gallery, and the feeling she had about her mother was like the feeling generated by that watercolor in which the sky was dense with clouds, near-black, though riddled with rays of sunshine like rents in fabric, and a lone fisherman stood at the edge of a lake, a lake reflecting black, so intent upon the fishing line he'd cast into the eerily glassy water that he was oblivious of the gathering squall. *Run! Run for your life!* you wanted to shout at this fool. For in another minute lightning would erupt. The squall would hit in wind and biting rain drops and a smell of sulphur.

In Mrs. Uhlmann, Lisellen had a sense of a coming storm. Fierce, explosive, pitiless. Yet thrilling. You were frightened of the squall, yet you want-ed it. You craved it. There was raw emotion here, needing no story to explain it. *You married beneath yourself* was a remark that might actually have been made to Lisellen's mother by one or another of her female relatives. *You made your bed now lie in it.* These were not subtle women. These were good Christian women with a genuine sympathy for one another, including Mrs. Uhlmann, whose name among them was Florrie, and who'd married Lisellen's father instead of staying in school to graduate with her class. (And she hadn't even been pregnant with Tracy, Lisellen had calculated the dates.) Today you could no more believe in a stone speaking than you could believe in Florrie Uhlmann behaving recklessly in love but, presumably, that was what it had been: reckless behavior, love.

Lisellen loved her father, too. Still, she was afraid of him. His moods. His sarcasm. His air of reproach, obscure hurt. The way he spoke over the phone, to someone who owed him money or who had crossed him somehow. The way sometimes he looked at his youngest daughter, as if he hadn't any idea who the hell she was, except something to do with him, a responsibility of his, a blame of his, yes but he could be proud of her too, he could be affectionate and teasing in the right mood, and it was this mood you hoped for, like switching on the radio in the hope of hearing music you liked, though knowing probably you would not. When Uhlmann Trucking wasn't going well, you could be sure that Clarence Uhlmann's mood would follow, but when things went well, as sometimes they did, you couldn't be sure that Clarence Uhlmann's mood would follow, because—you just couldn't. Uhlmann was a man to drive a hard bargain, it was said. Lisellen smiled, thinking of her father *driving a hard bargain* as he drove one of his trucks.

In April, Lisellen had returned home from school late one afternoon, and there was Mrs. Uhlmann, vacuuming the living room, her face glowing as if she'd polished it with steel wool. In a state of euphoria she shouted at Lisellen over the noise of the cleaner, which she didn't trouble to switch off, "He's gone." Lisellen shouted back, "Who?" Mrs. Uhlmann shouted, "Your father." Lisellen was stunned. She'd known there was trouble, that ever-tightening tension, but they'd lived with it for so long, why now? "*Gone—* where?" she'd asked. But Mrs. Uhlmann ignored her, hauling the vacuum cleaner into another room.

Now Mrs. Uhlmann's attention was fierce upon Lisellen. She was handling Lisellen, using her hands on her, as you might handle a small child. Not wanting to hurt the child, but not indulging the child, either. Firmly turning Lisellen from the wall she'd practically crawled into, turning Lisellen onto her back. Lisellen didn't resist. No point in resisting. Thinking *I was not raped, she won't find evidence.* With a familiarity that startled Lisellen, for mother and daughter were naturally reticent with each other, inclined to physical shyness, Mrs. Uhlmann lifted the badly rumpled skirt of Lisellen's orange-poppy dress, that was stained with beer and a dried snot-substance. Mrs. Uhlmann saw the torn panties. The panties stained like the dress. These she pulled down, more hesitantly now, as Lisellen shut her eyes. The lower part of her body had been insulted but had not been injured. The boys had hardly touched her there. The most they'd done was rub themselves against her, like boys wrestling together. They'd careened and crashed against her as in a game of bumper cars at the Olcott Amusement Park. Lisellen's pale fuzzy pubic hair, that seemed to her so comical, and sad. Her flat girl's stomach. Hips narrow as a boy's. And her legs too thin, though hard with muscle. *Lis-el-len! Uhl-mann!*

"Was it that Baitz boy, that bastard, was it him? It was, wasn't it?"

"Nobody did anything, Momma..."

"Somebody did something! I can see it, and I can smell it. He hit you, your face. Look at you! And your clothes ripped, and—*disgusting.*"

Mrs. Uhlmann gave a choked little cry, yanking down Lisellen's skirt. Lisellen said, pleading, "I wasn't hurt, Momma, really. It wasn't Duncan. Not what you think..."

"You're lying. You want to protect him."

Lisellen lay with her eyes tightly shut, seeing him there at the edge of the jeering circle. He'd said something to them. She hadn't heard his words but she'd heard his voice. They paid no attention. They were pinching her nipples through her dress, snatching between her legs, one of them dared to jam his thumb into the crack of her ass. The more Lisellen pleaded for them to stop, the more excited they were becoming. Like dogs she'd once seen cavorting crazily over the part-decayed corpse of a groundhog. Who was the first to unzip his pants, Lisellen wouldn't know, and would not want to know. And where Baitz was at this time, she wouldn't know. The ordeal ended when someone shouted at them from one of the dunes. A stranger, thank God no one who knew her. A young man, with one of the glamorous mini-skirted girls. Both were shouting at Lisellen's assailants, and so the guys broke and ran along the beach laughing and stumbling as they zipped themselves up. Lisellen was crying by now, thoroughly ashamed. The girl in the mini-skirt comforted her and led her back through the dunes to the parking lot and the couple drove Lisellen home insisting it was no trouble, it wasn't out of their way. "If it was me," the girl said, incensed, "I'd call the police. Somebody'd be arrested." Her companion said, "Well, it isn't you. So let it go."

She would not accuse him, she had no need. All that had ever passed between them of significance had not required speech. And so this morning, driving to her estranged husband's new living quarters, a rented duplex in Strykersville near the trucking yard, Mrs. Uhlmann rehearsed only the words she would greet him with: "Something has happened to your daughter."

They had not communicated in ten days.

It was not yet 7 A.M. Uhlmann would be awake and up, but still in the duplex. Mrs. Uhlmann struck the door with her fist as if bitterly resenting that the door was locked against her. Though she was the one to have banished Uhlmann from her life, she still thought *If he has a woman with him, I will spit in both their faces.*

There appeared to be no woman. Uhlmann was startled to see her, blinking as if she'd wakened him from sleep. Yet he'd shaven, he was nearly dressed. He had no need to ask her if something was wrong, only to listen to what she would say and, once she'd said it, to ask, as she knew he would, "Who?"

"She won't say."

"Won't *say?* She *won't say?*"

Florrie felt now the injustice of it, too. That their younger daughter who had always been the good daughter, the obedient and docile-seeming daughter, the one used as a rebuke to the headstrong elder, should behave now so mutinously.

"Won't say who it was—did what to her?"

Uhlmann was a man not hard of hearing but requiring words to be repeated so that they might not be misunderstood. For words, speech, speaking with others was not a strength of his; if asked, he might have disdained such strength, as over-fastidious, effeminate. But he wanted now to know. He was taller than Florrie by several inches, and heavier by fifty pounds, yet he moved with the wary alacrity of an ex-high school athlete. Even in sleep his body was restless, his muscles twitched and clenched. When upset, or confused, he had a way of smiling savagely with half his mouth, the effect like a razor slash. He was smiling now, waiting for Florrie to reply.

"Abused. Did things to." Florrie gestured vaguely, very much embarrassed, in the direction of her lower body. "Not—not the worst. But her face has been struck by him, it's swollen and bruised and she's just lying there in her bed, crying." Florrie paused. For perhaps this wasn't true, exactly. What had happened to her daughter, beyond the range of Florrie's knowledge, was beginning already to fade. "She has been shamed."

Again Uhlmann asked, staring at her, "Who?"

Meaning: who has done this, who is to blame.

This moment Florrie would long recall as, in the moment preceding an accident, even as the wheels of your vehicle begin their helpless skid, belatedly you think it has not happened yet, you can prevent it.

"She's protecting him but it's that Baitz boy. The one who's always hanging around."

"Is he? Is he hanging around?"

Seeing, but not wishing to fully see, the sick dazed look in her husband's face as she told him, "He drove her to Olcott last night. He came by to pick her up, just sat out in the car and she ran to him. There's been something between them... She refuses to say what."

Uhlmann nodded as if what Florrie was telling him was a fact he knew, a fact he'd always known, or, as the father of the shamed girl, should have known. A father knows such things. He had failed his family by not knowing. In that instant Florrie understood: lifting her eyes to the face of her repudiated, disdained and humiliated husband of twenty-six years. His face had become haggard. A clay mask, it seemed suddenly to Florrie, about to shatter.

She was in his arms suddenly, sobbing. She was not a woman to weep easily, or with pleasure. Uhlmann's reponse was immediate, instinctive: he held her, had no choice but to hold her. In his clumsy arms she shut her eyes smelling the rank tobacco odor, the smell of the previous night's whiskey, all that she had come to loathe in him. Florrie had married for love and made a terrible mistake, maybe.

But there was Tracey, and there was Lisellen. She had her daughters, no one could take them from her. In her husband's arms she was weak as she had not been in a long time. A sick, sliding-down sensation that shocked her, it came so powerfully. As in the first acquiescence to physical love. That moment at which you pass from the merely emotional to the physical, knowing there will be no return.

Would it begin again, her love for this man? She could not bear it.

She was too old, she could not bear it. These emotions she had passed through, and had come to detest.

"I don't want you to—"she paused, trying to think: didn't want him to do what, exactly?—"hurt anyone. No."

Uhlmann made a sound of assent. It was hardly more than a grunt, or might have been muffled laughter.

"No. Promise me, you must not."

Yet Florrie foresaw: she would defend this man, she would support him. She would not lie for him if she was questioned by police, for she was not a woman to lie, her soul abhorred any kind of moral weakness, but she would say, choosing her words with care, that her husband had acted as a father must act, in such circumstances; that was Uhlmann's way, that was his nature, and so she would support him through whatever would come of this moment.

The arrest, the trial.

The aftermath of the trial.

It was still early when Uhlmann arrived at the Baitz house: approximately 8:20 A.M.

The Baitzes lived on the scrubby outskirts of Strykersville, about two miles from the place Uhlmann was renting. An old woodframe house it was, once painted eggshell blue and long since weatherworn and faded, Baitz Gas & Auto Service close by. The garage may have been open for business, a single dim light within. No one was visible behind the front door, the gas pumps were unattended. Uhlmann parked his truck in the driveway of the house. His twelve-gauge double-barreled shotgun he hadn't fired in years, since the duck-hunting with his cousins in the Adirondacks, lay on the seat beside him. It would not be clear afterward whether Uhlmann had intended to use the gun. His intention might have been simply to protect himself. Possibly he'd meant to talk with Ed Baitz, the boy's father. More and more it would come to seem to him, afterward, that that was what he'd intended: just to talk. He and Baitz were of the same age, and of the same background, Baitz would understand his agitation, Baitz would know what had to be done. Except it was the boy who appeared in the driveway. Not Ed but the boy, Duncan: unmistakably this was the son, Uhlmann recognized him at once, though Duncan Baitz was looking older than Uhlmann would have believed him, hardly a kid any longer but someone out of high school, too old to be hanging out with high school kids; and unshaven; in jeans, a soiled T-shirt, some kind of asshole flip-flops on his bare feet.

The bare bony white feet, the flip-flops: the way Duncan Baitz was staring at him, that sick scared look: that did it.

The kid saw UHLMANN in white letters on the side of the truck, at once he began to back off. Here was his mistake: even as Uhlmann was getting out of the truck and speaking to him, he turned and began to run. When Uhlmann shouted after him, he began to run faster. It was the kid's mistake and not Uhlmann's. This was not the behavior of an innocent person. It was panicked behavior, and very stupid. For Duncan Baitz had at least thirty yards before he would have reached the barn he meant to hide inside, when Uhlmann lifted the shotgun and aimed for the moving target of the T-shirt, not a moving target shrewd enough to zigzag but simply to run in a single direction, away from the line of fire, and pulled the first of the triggers.

So tired! Lisellen felt as if she had not slept for days.

Drifting to sleep in the bathtub. Warm sudsy soothing water. Her mother had rubbed Noxema into her sunburnt face, on her smarting shoulders and arms, and these she kept clear of the water. She understood how lucky she was: that worse hadn't happened to her, and was known throughout Strykersville to have happened to her. She was grateful that her mother hadn't insisted upon taking her to the doctor, or called the police. Above all grateful to be alone.

The sticky residue of whatever had happened to her was washed away. She seemed to know that her mother would throw away the orange-poppy dress, neither of them need see it again.

Neither of them need speak of it again.

This bathroom, upstairs beneath the sloping roof. The hook-latch on the door. This was one of Lisellen's safe places. Her father had torn out the old stained tiles and replaced them with shiny buttercup-yellow tiles from Sears, the floor was a smart rust-red linoleum. Through her life Lisellen would recall this bathroom, the sloping ceiling above the tub, the myriad cracks in the plaster that resembled a mad scribbling in a foreign language, and most of all the big old stained-white tub that fitted so cozily into the small space.

Shutting her eyes she saw the rapt grinning faces as they moved upon her. At the edge of their hilarity, the boy she had wanted so badly to care for her, backing away.

He had left her to them, had he? For that, he must be punished.

Again she felt the quick-snatching hands that seemed to her

disembodied, as her assailed and demeaned body would come to seem depersonalized to her, a female body lacking an identity, the body of any adolescent girl and not her own. They would not have wished to hurt *her*. She would come to interpret the episode as embarrassing, awkward, bad luck. Bad judgment on everyone's part. Too much beer, excitement. They had not meant to hurt her, had they? In a way it had been flattering. A kind of flirtation gone wild. Almost a kind of love. Maybe. Duncan Baitz would have to consider her in a new way, now.

Lisellen rubbed her fingers over her pear-sized little breasts, feeling the nipples harden.

SOUL OF A WHORE
A PLAY IN THREE ACTS

by DENIS JOHNSON

ACT II

[Act One, which appeared in Issue No. 9, took place in a bus station in Huntsville, Texas, where two convicts fresh from the Huntsville prison—Bill Jenks, former TV preacher, and John Cassandra, a reformed hellraiser—encountered Masha, a demon-possessed stripper. At John's urging, Bill Jenks reluctantly accomplished an exorcism, during which Masha's demon delivered three mystifying predictions concerning the future of Bill Jenks: "You will meet your mirror; you will raise the dead; and when you die, on that occasion an innocent will be killed." Act Two begins a year later.

Soul of a Whore premiered in February 2003 at Campo Santo/Intersection for the Arts in San Francisco. It will be remounted there in January 2004 in repertory with Johnson's next play, Psychos Never Dream.*]*

Split scene: Left, hospital waiting room. Right, hospital room.

LIGHTS UP STAGE RIGHT

Hospital room. Early summer morning. Dark but for the light of the monitors, and a bit of dawn.

SIMON *lies in bed, a silhouette.*

SIMON: I have kissed your prayers kissed your prayers
    Roller coaster rollin' through the rain
    The oceanic shoulders of the throng
    Undulating slowly breakfastward
    Mobile tit!

NURSE has entered.

NURSE: A lovely one is coming!
    Lovely! I'll just crack the jamb before
    The hot of the day, so's you can breathe the morning.
    ...Oh, Lordy God, it smells so sweet and green
    It almost nearly stinks.

SIMON: Soft fuck-me music
    Plays the little baby radio
    Bare room shaken by a passing train

NURSE: The little baby radio. That's cute.

She turns on radio. While she fluffs his pillows, records his vitals, etc:

JIMMY BOGGS [*sings on radio*]:
                All your promises
                The things you said

NURSE: That Jimmy Boggs is just untalented.

JIMMY BOGGS [*sings on radio*]:
                Using grand words
                Like eternity and love

NURSE: A singing voice like garbage-cans turned over.

She cuts the radio.

SIMON: Your holy pussy your precious cunt

There's never been a sweeter ride to Hell

NURSE: How quiet and—*delicious*—is the air.
    Like anything can happen in the world.
    What an atmosphere… Ah, God. Ah, God…
    They mow the lawns, it drags me back to Dallas…
    I wish they had the ice cream trucks again…

Meanwhile, WILL BLAINE has entered in medical smock.

WILL: You wish they had the ice cream trucks again.

SIMON: The generous wide feet of pachyderms

NURSE: We're almost done here, Doc.

WILL: I'm not a doctor.
        Just a tech.

NURSE: Blood?

WILL: In a sense.

NURSE: Let's see—

SIMON: Geezing bugspray in the slimy night

NURSE: —Do you have orders? I don't seem to have—

Will: Uh—no. I'm not your colleague. Actually,
    Simon is my brother.

NURSE: Simon's brother!
    But it's a little early, don't you think?
    Official hours—

Will: I drove down from work.
    Been floating on that road since midnight, after
    The post-injection wrap-up drinks at Mursky's

Bar and Grill but definitely mostly Bar,
Drifting through the general emptiness
From Huntsville: Seven hours in the rain
And more than slightly drunk, and I saw never
A single car. Or house. Or tree. Or star.

NURSE: Oh well, that's Texas! It's a long old ways
Between and not a whole lot when you get there...
My niece got married to a Huntsville man.

WILL: I'm over at the Unit. At the Walls.

NURSE: The Walls?

WILL: The prison?

NURSE: Oh. The prison? Oh!
They executed someone there last night!—
Some crazy feller killed his wife and all
His little children... Well, my niece's husband
Thomas Hill works at the Walls. I guess
He goes around confusing people, too,
Looking like the uniform of something else.
...Well now, since you're a tech, you're probably...
There's things to do the *fam*ily might not...
We like to avoid unsightly *sights*—

WILL: The bag.

NURSE: I'm gonna change the bag, and such.

WILL: Okay.

NURSE: His little children! God Himself can't tell you
Why that feller killed them. Well, he did,
And now it's eye for eye and tooth for tooth.
They strapped him to the slab and—life for life.

WILL: I'd say that's pretty much it, in a nutshell,

That's what we do.

NURSE: You do? *You* do? Do *you*?

WILL: With his last breath he proclaimed his innocence.

SIMON: A white-tail deer goes walking past in the rain
    A dream of volcanoes rides past on a train
    A spider crouched alive betwixt her lungs

NURSE: I'm sorry; but it stops him—

WILL: When you yank
    His crotch a couple yanks, it shuts him up?

NURSE: Manipulation of the scrotal—*well*—
    I know! The whole world's highly entertained!
    He's quite a favorite hereabouts. A team
    From Dallas, on the first of every month,
    Descends upon us, specialists from Dallas—

WILL: How about that!—lining up to plunk
    The magic twanger of my brother's scrotum!
    My helpless brother's balls! Nurse… Vandermere:
    I'm not here visiting the vegetable.
    This thing they're gonna do—I'm here for that.

NURSE : What—thing?

WILL: Wal now I don' perzackly know.
    I would assume the staff would know.

NURSE: The staff?

WILL: The personnel employed here. Such as you.

NURSE: I don't know *any*thing about a *thing*.

WILL: A medical procedure, I presume,

At which, for reasons they have not explained,
They want the whole damn family to assemble.

NURSE : But… nothing's scheduled…

WILL: Nothing.

NURSE: Not a thing.

WILL: The vegetable's entire day is free.

NURSE: What you don't seem to realize is a coma
    Doesn't make them deaf. They hear us talk,
    They understand, and Simon knows what's what.

WILL : You claim the calabash is cognizant.

NURSE : If *I* was being visited by you,
        And *I* was in a coma—I would die!

WILL: I think—Is that my sister-in-law out there?

NURSE: I'd slip on out to sea and sail away.

WILL: It is. Ah, God!—the other one! *Her* sister!
        What's this all about?

SIMON: Who owns the rain

NURSE: It doesn't take a death-grip!

WILL: Like he cares!
    He didn't even blink. He kinda sorta
    Rolls his eyes around though, doesn't he.
    A six-foot-long Señor Potato-Head…
    And not one blister, huh? Not one hair singed.
    That's what ya git fer smokin'!—might as well
    Be ashes, huh?

NURSE: He got like this from smoking?

WILL: Not exactly smoking—breathing smoke,
    Smoke inhalation. Very bad for you.

SIMON: I would kiss you even if it killed me

Meanwhile, JAN and STACY have entered.

JAN: Let him a*lone!*

WILL: It shuts him up, or so
    I'm told—and as we've just been demonstrating.

SIMON: Even if it killed me I would kiss you

JAN: Simon, hon? … I think he's glad to see me!

STACY*:* Simon? Can he hear? His *voice* is all—

SIMON: Kuala Lumpur Kuala Lumpur Kuala
    Lumpur

JAN: See! He knows Ko-ala Lumpur!

STACY: All those voices, all those different—Jan,
    I never heard those voices before.
    Did you ever hear those voices before?

NURSE: Visiting hours haven't really *started*—

STACY: He's like a boombox on a merry-go-round!

WILL: This is Simon's wife, my sister-in-law—

JAN: Jan.

NURSE: I'm pleased to meet you.

JAN: This is Stacy,
  Simon's sister-in-law, which is because
  I'm Simon's wife, and she's my sister—Calling
  Koala Lumpur! Simon!

STACY: Can he hear?

JAN: Are you receiving, Simon?

WILL: No. He's not.

STACY: He talked right *to* me!—He was buying gold
  In Koala Lumpur when the fire struck
  That shopping mall and pumped it full of smoke
  And choked him till he got like this! Now, Simon,
  Form your thoughts, take all the time you want,
  Visiting hours haven't even started—

WILL: He isn't "forming" any "thoughts." All right:
  You're here; he's here; everybody's here.
  Now how about a little explanation?

JAN: Well! The lights came on!

NURSE: It's eight A.M.
  It's still a half an hour till *official*—

WILL: And not "Koala." K-*U*-A-L-A—

JAN: He was buying *gold*, he was *investing*—
  Tragedy strikes us anytime it wants,
  Even in places like Koala Lumpur—

STACY: *Kua*-la Lumpur, *Kua*-la Lumpur, Jan—

JAN: —No matter what you try to call yourself!
  You can't escape life even by pretending!

Meanwhile, THE DOCTOR has entered.

DOC: So, Simon draws a crowd!

NURSE: They jumped the gun
    A couple minutes, Doc—

DOC: Good morning, all!

SIMON: I have a dog who is a lilac bush

JAN: We *have* a dog who is a lilac bush!

SIMON: Kuala Lumpur Kuala… Kuala… Kuala…

STACY: Lumpur—Lumpur—*Lumpur*, Simon, *Lumpur*!

JAN: But, see, our dog is *buried* by the lilac!
    We always say he's turned in*to* the lilac!
    So, Doctor, when he says I have a *dog*,
    He's talking about our actual *universe*,
    And an actual dog, also an actual *lilac*.
    And even if we don't have a koala bear,
    There actually *are* koala bears in China,
    Or over there where Kuala Lumpur is.

DOC: …Mind is the only actuality.

Breakfast chimes sound.

STACY: Oh, Doctor… Nasum? That is so… pro-*found*.
    Like what if this life isn't really real?

DOC: And what if we're like Simon, in a realm
    We can't imagine, in a spastic coma—

STACY: A hospital in some enchanted dream,
    A magic hospital … A "spastic coma?"

DOC: What life we truly live we'll never know.
    The only hope we have is to assume

That what we see is where we are...

STACY: Doctor,
     Why does Simon jabber like a zoo?

DOC: The human brain, the... May I know your name?

STACY: Forgive me: Stacy Daley Morgan Blaine.
     But I should drop the Blaine, as I'm divorced—
     Again! But then, I didn't drop the Morgan—

DOC: Now, isn't "Blaine"—? Now, Simon, *you're* a Blaine—

STACY: Well, I was married to him first. He gets around.

DOC: In rather a tiny circle!

WILL: He's a sucker:
     Snoring in the kingdom of the vegetables
     He ain't a whole lot dumber than he was.

DOC: I see, and, Stacy, that makes you the patient's—?

STACY: Former wife and current sister-in-law.
     I'm sure you know my sister, Jan—

DOC: Of course.
     A real Penelope!—

STACY: And Will, our brother-in-law—
     Jan's former brother-in-law, but now her current,
     And currently my former brother-in-law.

DOC: Pleased to meet you, Will. And, Stacy: *charmed*
     And *very* pleased.

STACY: The feeling's... *mutual*...

SIMON: I sound like I'm shrinking

STACY: —And! A "spastic coma?"

DOC: The injury to Simon's synapses,
      The anaerobic outrage to his brain,
      The shock of oxygen-starvation on
      A mystery so frail as the electric
      Pilgrimage an impulse undertakes
      Along a route of stimulated nerves
      Has induced in Simon Blaine a wild condition,
      A hyperactive, vegetative state,
      A chronic, spastic, comatose condition
      Marked by baffling random episodes
      Apparently the property of the dark
      And chiefly somnolent prefrontal lobes:
      Pseudo-verbal, faux-autistic, splashed
      With flowery jets and startling and bright
      Ejaculations with aphasic overtones.

STACY: Overtones... and episodes... I see...

DOC: He reads out almost epileptic when
      We hook him to the EEG. And so...

STACY: He has these fits.

DOC: And so he has these fits.
      —A rare and baffling form of coma.

JAN: *Rare?*
      There's never been another coma like it!

STACY: And nothing can be done?

DOC: A case like this,
      We offer consolation. Never hope.

JAN: But you're not *God.*

DOC: And I don't claim to be.

JAN: But he's right there! Right *here*—Simon!
    Wife to Simon! What are you thinking, Simon?—
    I wish I could join him there. I struggle to get there.
    But how do you struggle? I struggle with my heart,
    My soul. I make an effort in my chest.
    With my love, my force of love. It's bullshit!
    He's there and I'm here. What are you thinking…?
    TELL ME! TELL ME! RE-TARD! WRETCH! *TELL ME!*

DOC: Nurse!

NURSE: Ma'am! No!

WILL: Jan, *stop* it!

STACY: Stop it, Jan!
    [*A brief struggle.*]
    Stop it, stop it, stop it, stop it! STOP!
    …There are comas and there are comas, Jan.
    This is one of those. The kind the very
    Wisest doctors cannot comprehend.
    So let's stop beating around the bush, OK?
    Your husband isn't ever coming home.
    This spastic coma person isn't Simon,
    'Cause Simon's off in Coma-Simon-Land
    Married to a Spastic Coma Girl.
    He doesn't hear a single word we say.
    He doesn't, and he didn't, and he won't.
    So no more sex. Just learn to masturbate.
    —Oh, well! I'm sorry! I don't make the rules!

WILL: Will someone give this stupid bitch a shot
    And put us all out of our misery?

STACY: You wish you had your little death machine?

WILL: You bet your plastic boobs.

DOC: Now—now—now—now—

STACY: *You're* the reason I divorced him, Will—
    When we were living in North Houston, Will—
    I don't forget who introduced him to
    Sylvester's Big-as-Texas Topless Lounge—

JAN: I wouldn't be caught dead inside that place!

STACY: You've always been a rotten influence—

JAN: In there it's all black light and fuzzy dice!

DOC: Ah, me!—it's difficult to make a point
    In these surroundings. Why don't we adjourn—

WILL: No. What procedure have you scheduled here?

DOC: Excuse me. Was there something scheduled?

WILL: Yes!
    I drove all night from Huntsville to attend—
    To what were you referring, Jan? You claimed
    Some bold experiment was taking place—

DOC: Have we experiments on the agenda, Nurse?

NURSE: Not from now till three P.M.—No, sir!

JAN: 'Cause all *you* know to do is grab his pecker!
    Experiments won't save him! He needs faith!
    You saw the pictures on TV, *you* watched
    The faces of those red-hot, burning people—
    Like faces in a painting, witnessing
    Their resurrection in a revelation,
    Riding escalators toward the flames
    Like souls ascending toward Atomic Heaven—

STACY: Or Hell! Pockets of Hell! Of Hell!—I mean,
    Subterranean shopping center fires
    Are breaking out all over God's green earth.

It's punishment for something—*you* know what:
Divorce, and dope, and gambling; lesbians,
Teenage sexpot prostitution rings,
Child-molester grandmas, *Mardi Gras*—

WILL: What the hell full name is Stacy short for?

STACY: It's not. I'm only Stacy, *ma cherie*!

WILL: And *now* what? What are *these* fools up to
    Out the window here? Will someone promise me
    My family is not a party to
    This further nonsense in the parking lot?
    Here we have a maniac with a cross,
    I mean it's big, this sucker's big enough
    To mount a dolphin on, he's standing there
    Beside it like he's posing for a photo—
    Looking stupid, I don't have to add—
    And, am I psychic? Why am I so *sure*
    That these two *other* maniacs are coming *here*?

JAN: That's William Jennings Bryant Jenks, the healer.

WILL: A heeler. What is that? A person?

JAN: Yes,
    A healer is a person.

WILL: There are dogs
    Called blue heelers—fact my neighbor has one.
    Had one, I should say. It's dead. It drowned.

MASHA and BILL JENKS enter, both in quite conservative garb, MASHA in
gray, BJ in black. BJ's hair has grown out; he wears it swept back in a shining
pompadour.

BILL JENKS: Where's this drowning victim?
    …This is the man who drowned?

STACY: Nobody drowned him. He was in a fire.

BILL JENKS: Is this a burn unit?

NURSE: Perpetual Care.
     He wasn't burned.

BILL JENKS: The fire didn't burn him?

STACY: More like he suffocated in the smoke,
     Which you could almost say the fire drowned him—

WILL: Coincidence, here—I was telling how
     My neighbor's dog got drowned last Sunday morning.
     Nobody home, he went and jumped right in
     The swimming pool and couldn't clamber out.
     Hung on—hung on—hung on till noon, almost—
     Gave up; went under; drowned.

BILL JENKS: How do they know?

WILL: They don't. I do. I let it drown. I watched,
     Sipping a Bloody Mary on a Sunday morn.
     The rest of God's creation was at church.
     Sunday Morning; drinking alone: I love it.
     I don't like heelers.

WILL and BJ stand, each facing the other, as in a mirror.

BILL JENKS: Are you copying me?

WILL: Are you copying me?

BILL JENKS: Cut it out.

WILL: Cut it out.

BILL JENKS: All I have to do is remain silent.
     …Well, aren't you going to copy that?

WILL: Aren't you going to copy that?

BILL JENKS: You win.

WILL: You lose.

MASHA: Brother, we're in danger.

WILL: Will Blaine...

BILL JENKS: Bill Jenks.

STACY: Well! *Bill* and*Will*! Could be
      You guys are twins! Twins torn apart at birth—

SIMON: Watch me jack off with my solar flare

STACY: Simon Blaine, hush! You've got company!

MASHA: The lesser demons bow to something here.
      Satan's pouring honey down my spine.

BILL JENKS: Satan can't be everywhere at once,
      And right now he's in Hollywood or Vegas.

WILL: Who publishes the diabolical
      Itinerary? There a cable channel?

BILL JENKS: He gravitates toward Soddom and Gommorah.

WILL: Really.

BILL JENKS: Sure. The old boy craves a little
      Action same as everybody else.

WILL: Was it "20/20?" Or "60 Minutes?"
      I thought they made a worldwide fool of you.
      —OK, it's rude of me to say so, sorry—
      What'd you call your outfit there in Dallas,

Church of the Holy Sacred Bank Account?
Ripped of your congregation, shot a guy,
Landed up in Huntsville, where I work:
I bet I've seen you, out there in the fields
Hacking with a hoe (—excuse me, ma'am!),
Slaving away with black-eye susan's winkin'
And stinkin' like a Dallas trollop (—'scuse me!);
Suspected dealer, quantity cocaine—

BILL JENKS: Oh yeah, I shot a man. He didn't die.
    I get the chance again—who knows?

WILL: You'd think a guy would sense his status!—Yeah,
    They had you on with Ron the Levitator
    And that frog-voice freak transvestite with a lisp
    Driving his spangled automatic wheelchair,
    Jimmy—

NURSE: Boggs! "The Singer of the South!"
    You oughta heal his *singing*!

BILL JENKS: There are limits.

WILL: I have to say, he does looks like he's healed.
    Healed by whom, by use of which powers,
    I couldn't guess. Or even healed of what.
    But, anyway, he's acting different now.

BILL JENKS: That's right. He ran a marathon last month.

WILL: That's right. He came in way behind the pack.

BILL JENKS: That's right, and running on two legs. His spangled
    Wheelchair graces our museum now.

WILL: They mentioned that—You have your own museum!

BILL JENKS: Most of one. Construction's underway.

WILL: Construction's stalled, according to "60 Minutes,"
    Stalled while the IRS and FTC
    Shine a light on your money.

BILL JENKS: Let it shine,
    There ain't a lot to see.

WILL: You claim you're clean.

BILL JENKS: Nope. I just claim there isn't any money.

SIMON: THERE'S NEVER BEEN A SWEETER RIDE TO HELL

BILL JENKS: This one's getting agitated now.

STACY: I take it you're a husband and wife team?

BILL JENKS: We are as siblings.

WILL: Ooh, you two are *juicy*.

SIMON: I'll climb back up your cunt and suck your mind
    The way we used to do when we were lovers

JAN: Simon! Shame on you!

STACY: Well, talk about a mouth!

BILL JENKS: You recognize him, don't you? Yes. You do.

MASHA: It's him. It's him.

STACY: Do you *eat* with that mouth?

DOC: Actually, he's nourished through this tube.

MASHA: I'm free of you! You hear? Leave me alone!

WILL: Just grab his scrotum there to shut him up.

Just reach on out—go on—and shake the hand
Of the old banana, with a manly grip.

NURSE: Doctor Nasum, please, this doesn't seem—

WILL: Take hold! There can't be any harm in it,
    Right? Big deal, as far as he's concerned...
    I used to get him down and drool a strand—
    Now this'll git 'im, if he's there a-tall—
    And slurp it back—

NURSE: Now, what on *earth*!—

WILL: Aha!

STACY: You can't spit in a coma-person's face!

WILL: You get a pain response? Huh, buddy? There!

NURSE: For goodness' sakes alive, he's *hurting* him!

They restrain him, DOC and NURSE taking either arm.

WILL: The point is that I'm *not*. He doesn't hurt.
    But everybody else—this family,
    Our parents, this man's wife, his wife's relations—
    Het up by this fireball of faith,
    Yinked and yanked by hope in God like gobs
    Of spit He dangles from his fat, red mouth—
    His doctor shouldn't let them play these games.
    I want this sucker ceremony cancelled!
    Who is actually in attendance here?

NURSE: It's Dr. Cassady. He makes his rounds
    Just after lunch on weekdays, Sir.

WILL: Then page old Hopalong immediately.
      Come on!—He doesn't want to see his patient
      Used like bait to fish for dollars, does he?

SIMON: LET IT THUNDER FARTS AND RAIN DOWN VOMIT

JAN: STACY!

STACY [*grabbing Simon's crotch*]: Hon, it's simple courtesy.

MASHA: He's wild for me. The demon's wild for me.

WILL: Jesus Christ, Morticia—lighten up!

BILL JENKS: I'd like to be alone with Simon now.

WILL: Go right ahead. Remember—manly grip!

DOC and NURSE begin dragging WILL out.

BILL JENKS: No—Let him stay. I want him here. Let go.

DOC: If *I* were Simon's primary physician—

BILL JENKS: Go on, the rest of you. Leave us alone.
    [*To* MASHA:] You especially. We can't have you here.

All exit. BJ alone with WILL and SIMON. WILL collects himself, goes to window.

WILL: What's he saying…? (Jesus. What a morning…)
    Sights… heights… Keep your eyes—the prize—

BILL JENKS: Keep yours sights
    On the heights
    Keep your eyes

WILL: On the prize. The guy's a public nuisance.

BILL JENKS: He's with me.

WILL: He would be, wouldn't he?
    …I'm calmer now.

BILL JENKS: No need to apologize.

WILL: I feel no need. I'm not apologizing.
    My position hasn't altered; I'm just calmer.
    Simon, too.

BILL JENKS: I don't expect you'd welcome this
    Invasion of your realm—

WILL: It ain't my realm.
    I'm not a doctor. I'm just Simon's brother.

BILL JENKS: I thought you were a medical man.

WILL: I am.

BILL JENKS: Then please don't be so hostile. I don't go
    So far as to suggest you look on us
    As colleagues, but I think we share a goal.

WILL: I'm a technician of a very special kind.
    I don't fix people. Quite the opposite.
    I supervise the termination teams.

BILL JENKS: Sounds like you're in the personnel division.

WILL: No.—The tie-down team, the I.V. team…

BILL JENKS: I see.

WILL: Next to me, boys, Lucifer never fell.

BILL JENKS: You execute the folks.

WILL: That's not quite true.
    We execute the sentence, not the person.

BILL JENKS: And who, exactly, executes the person?

WILL: "To execute" means "to carry out."
    Well, I guess in the end we carry them out.
    … So you do the opposite of what I do.

BILL JENKS: I've never raised the dead.

WILL: But—in a sense.

BILL JENKS: I've never raised the dead.

WILL: Why don't you try?
    Go where the dead go. Haunt the mortuaries.
    Give 'em the razzle-dazzle of your gift
    And see if anybody cheats the grave…
    —What's the matter with him now? My God!

BILL JENKS: The demon's agitated. SETTLE DOWN!
    …I wonder where you know my assistant from?

WILL: Morticia? Man, I've seen that honey shake
    Her titties! You a preacher, or a pimp?

BILL JENKS: The line between the two is faint. I think
    It moves. I've found myself on either side.

WILL: You didn't move yourself?

BILL JENKS: Not to my knowledge…
    Maybe… If I moved, I didn't feel it…
    Well, I just had to ask. Not my affair,
    But I was curious. Now you can leave.

WILL: You think you're safe alone? I mean, he's strong—
    He may be out of it, but—

BILL JENKS: I'll be fine.

WILL: The Lord protects you.

BILL JENKS: I believe he does.

WILL: You trust in the Lord.

BILL JENKS: I find him predictable…
    We've got three this week. Uh. Tuesday, Wednesday,
    I think Thursday… Thursday?

WILL: So do we.

BILL JENKS: Yes, three… Three executions in three days?

WILL: Hey, I don't make the reservations, boys.
    I just fly the plane.

BILL JENKS: Here and yonder,
    Even in prison, I've met up with good
    And decent people. But… How do you say this…?
    I've never met one in the mirror.

WILL: …Yeah…
    Oh well, that's life, huh?

BILL JENKS: That's life on Death Row.

WILL: I don't get you. Do you believe, or not?
    Do you really heal? And cleanse these souls
    Of maladies and spirits? Do you care?

BILL JENKS: The gift is real, but I just turn a buck.
    I turn a buck, He executes His vague
    Intentions on a baffled universe:
    Win-win… Of course, He screws with me.
    That's His style—the gift, and then the gag.
    And in return I fail to reverence Him,
    Fail in gratitude. I fail to love Him.

WILL: Wow! You *are* an existentialist.
    It's a little hard to see that message landing

Anywhere. It's no surprise you're bankrupt.

BILL JENKS: Aah, they're just watching television, man.
    I tell it like I see it, but I doubt
    There's anybody listening. Faith is scary.
    Faith affords its consolations, sure—
    By opening the maw to the dark depths
    Where going blind and getting lost and hurt
    Seem understandable and natural,
    And all night long two graces fall like rain:
    A tragic sense of life, and hope of Heaven.

WILL: Are grace and Heaven all you've got to offer?
    Man, I've watched one hundred twenty people
    Die because I killed them with a button.
    I've seen them breathe their last—the air
    Goes out, and out, and then they kind of shiver
    And there's this second where you know it's over
    And it ain't never gonna start again.
    …On summer evenings I sit on my porch
    And listen to this train that comes along.
    I listen to the wheels bang on the tracks,
    I listen to the whistle drag the air
    And fill the world, and fade, and leave it empty,
    And I am gonna tell you: Heaven never
    Dreamt of anything as sweet as that:
    To listen to a train and not be dead.

VOICE ON RADIO: Insects are often the only witnesses
    To a crime.

BILL JENKS [to Simon]: Did you turn that thing on?

WILL: It wasn't me.

BILL JENKS: Well turn the damn thing off.

VOICE ON RADIO: The President's order has been disobeyed

Soft music on radio…

BILL JENKS: All right. It's time you left us, please.

WILL: Don't *heal*, or even *touch*, or even *think*
    About—Don't—don't… Don't hurt him. He's my brother.

BILL JENKS: …No. I wouldn't hurt him, Mr. Blaine.

WILL exits.

BILL JENKS falls and weeps.

*RADIO laughs hysterically—SIMON joins in. BILL JENKS quells them
with a laying on of hands.*

SIMON: HEALER! …HEALER, NOLI MI TANGERE!

BILL JENKS: All right. They're gone. I'm here. Who are you, demon?

SIMON: Etcetera non sequitur mon cher

BILL JENKS: Is it you? Are you the same one?

SIMON: E pluribus non sequitur tyrannis

BILL JENKS: I saw this movie. Everybody saw it.
    Are you the demon who prophecies, or not?

SIMON: Oh. This. Yes. That.
        Jack
        Sprat
        Begat Jehosephat.

BILL JENKS: Cut it out. Get serious. You know
    I coulda had your ass in Huntsville—
    Coulda sent you to the Pit. You owe me.

SIMON: Coulda shoulda woulda hadda oughta.

BILL JENKS: God! There's something *wrong* with me or something.
    There's something wrong with me or something wrong
    With money. Anyhow, we tangle wrong,
    Me and the dollar… What a mess, what… All
    Those people on the money—can't they see me?

SIMON: I love you. Love you with a love that burns.

BILL JENKS: If I'da lived a hundred years ago,
    I'd be riding circuit, I'd be praising God
    And healing hearts and saving souls
    And money'd never touch me long enough
    To suck itself inside me like it has.

SIMON: I love you with a love that burns and smokes.

BILL JENKS: Okay, okay, you're probably aware
    We've got a hearing set for Wednesday next
    To go and file for Chapter—I don't know—
    Eleven, Thirteen, Twenty-one—they make
    The whole thing sound like Vegas, don't they?
    They tap you out as quick as Vegas, too.
    But you know me: I'll bet my shorts and socks
    And get back in the game, or hitchhike home
    As naked as my Mama made me. Anyhow,
    The Institute is broke, but the Foundation
    Holds several thousand shares of Motorola.
    Here's the thing: This Freddie Spendersnap,
    The NASCAR racer, wants to make a swap,
    My Motorola for a razor-thin
    Controlling interest in his hot dog thing,
    His vending franchise thing. It sounds superb,
    It's very liquid, totally set up—
    I mean, you figure hot dogs are forever—
    But Motorola's flirting with Verizon,
    The big fat cell-phone company; oh, yeah,
    Verizon makes my Motorola pretty—
    But if the Feds resolve to yank tobacco
    Sponsorship of NASCAR, man, the brokest

Sucker in the South is gonna be
The guy with fifteen hundred red and white
Striped hats and fifteen hundred hot-dog carts.
But. Cell-phones give you cancer. They could tank.

SIMON: "Spendersnap." I think you made that up.

BILL JENKS: …Why can't I be like simple John and stand
My cross in a melting Texas parking lot?
What did he have to endure to get like that?
Remove from me these bonds of self… Release…
Shit. Am I praying to you? Praying to a demon?

SIMON: Jenks, I reject your terminology.
"Demon" is a term whose definition
Seems to shift its shape as much as we do.
Call me a teenymeanymotherfucker.

BILL JENKS: …So… am I Motorola, or Freddie's Franks?

BLACKOUT

LIGHTS UP STAGE LEFT

Hospital waiting room. MASHA at the window.

WILL enters. Comes up close behind her.

WILL: Look at this guy. Just can't wait to give
His life away. He's chomping at the bit.
He's straining at the traces. Giddyap,
Ole hoss. Drag that contraption into
The third millennium. You get farther and farther
From Calvary all the time. Farther and farther
From the place of skulls. Farther from Golgotha.
…An overpowering scent of blossoms on
The air today. Inebriating.

MASHA: Just about a stench.

WILL: Or is it your perfume?

MASHA: I wear no scent.

WILL: But I can smell you. You smell womanly.
    My my, you give a man an appetite.
    You're womanly. Dazzlingly. Deeply.

MASHA: I don't hear such talk. It strikes me deaf.

WILL: I know you from Sylvester's. I know you
    From head to toe three nights a week stark naked,
    No matter how you cover up in gray.
    I don't forget the times I watched you dance.
    First time, I said to my buddies, Hey now, there's
    The type I crave, a dancing contradiction:
    I crave my women simultaneously
    Loose and tight.

MASHA: You're talking to the walls.
    You're talking to the moon. Nobody hears you.

WILL: You cast one glance and liquefied my bones
    And alla that. Sweet Jesus, what a rack.
    What a set of pins.

MASHA: Would you not swear?

WILL: "A set of pins"?

MASHA: You took the Lord in vain.

WILL: I'll take him anyway that I can get him,
    Honey baby lover fucker-doll.

MASHA:
    ...Who's the ones with everything stripped off?
    Who's the peep show? Is it really me?
    I strut along and toss down feed to you.

You hunch there with your glass of screwtop wine
And all the feelings naked in your face.
You gobble me down with your eyes, but you don't see me.
You see the act, you see your fantasy
And not the person working at a job.
You see me panting for you, but I'm bored,
My ankles hurt, my car got repossessed,
I'd like to move because my rickety
Apartment's on the building's sunny side—
The prancing slut is prancing in your head.
You got me backwards. I'm not under cover.
I never was so hidden as when I was naked.
…And plus fact is I ain't no Norma Jean.
I'm sort of regular, with decent legs.
Dim light, I'm gorgeous.

WILL: Dancing decent legs.
   Decent legs made for indecent dancing.

MASHA: I think I wish to stop this conversation.

WILL: Dim light, spilt liquor, dancing decent legs.
   …Where does he keep you stashed?

MASHA: In Hawk Hills. Outside Fort Worth. Way outside.

WILL: I think you need to get to Houston.

MASHA: No.

WILL: But not downtown. Just out there by the lake.
   I'd put you by the golf course. Weekend nights
   We head downtown, see what the action's like.

MASHA: I don't like the city. I never did.
   It smells. It stinks. I mean it reeks.

WILL: The smells and lights and noise and all the tense
   Faces and the cries of the lunatics.

You've gotta get out of Hawk Hills, swoop down
To Second Street and put the world before you.
Downtown. In the night. That's where you hide.
Do you know what this is?

MASHA: Money, yeah. So what?

WILL: Two dollars.

MASHA: Stick it up your ass!

WILL: Come on.
    You never took a little nap for money?

MASHA: You can go to Hell!

WILL: I'll take you with me!
    ...All I did was watch. Not like the others.
    Everybody knows what goes on there.
    "They dance till two and then they screw." That's right.
    Sylvester pimped you as a nightly thing.
    You sucked and blew and bent and spread and squirmed
    For college jocks and gap-tooth farmer boys
    And fat-ass salesmen in their Cadillacs.
    You gave each other phony names and fucked,
    And they were all your dirty little husbands,
    And Jesus Christ can strike me down and turn
    My guts to pus if I've said one false thing.
    Look me in the face and tell me Jesus
    Jack is gonna cancel who you are.
    ...Baby... You are suckin' my cock with your eyes.

MASHA: Don't. Don't. I'm bad luck. It's just gonna hurt you.

WILL: I would kiss you even if it killed me.
    ...Jesus won't protect you. Hell with him.
    You wanna hide? You wanna leave yourself?
    You need a stack of credit cards, a beauty parlor,
    Stocks and bonds and money in the bank,

A little sports car and a big suburban wagon,
Air-conditioned condo by the golf course,
Fifty inches on your television.
Jesus isn't gonna give you that.
I'm the one who's gonna give you that.
My fingerprints on your velour.

MASHA: Oh, stop.

WILL: I'm gonna lift your skirt.

MASHA: You can lift it a little bit.

WILL: I'm gonna lift it higher.

MASHA: You can lift it a little higher.

WILL: I'm gonna lift it all the way up. Do you want me to?

MASHA: You can. Okay. You can if you want to.

WILL: I'm gonna do whatever I want.

MASHA: I know you are. Okay. I know you are.

BLACKOUT

LIGHTS UP STAGE LEFT

BJ and SIMON as before.

SIMON: I love this guy. You're such a baby loser!
    You shit yer pants while pissing on yer shoes.

BILL JENKS: You owe me, bud. I left you free to wander.
    Didn't I leave you free for fun and travel?
    Haven't you had some share of fun and travel?

SIMON: Of course I have!—This year or so, since Huntsville,

I've circuited the earth a dozen times,
Entering any soul who offered entrance.
From sin to sin I've wafted like a spore.
I've bent the gambler to his knee,
I've dragged the junkie through the grime,
I've parked the harlot on her corner,
I've sent the rapist on his round.
I've given reasons to the traitor,
Glossy varnish to the liar,
Piety to hypocrites—
And left them hobbled and alone,
Waiting like dogs for any scent of me.
And next, who knows? Some other galaxy.
Prepare for take-off! Five, four, three, two, one…
IN WHOSE NAME DO YOU CAST OUT SPIRITS, HEALER?

BILL JENKS: I'm not casting anybody out.
　　　We're talking here. We're making simple average
　　　Conversation as we grope toward
　　　An understanding.

SIMON:　　　　　　　Or you cast me out.

BILL JENKS: I could. I could. So why not demonstrate
　　　A modicum of flexibility—
　　　On both our parts? I let you play with Simon;
　　　You hand me out my standard three predictions.

SIMON: You've had your three. And one just now came true.
　　　Today you met your mirror, as I'm sure
　　　You gather. Sometime soon you'll touch a corpse's
　　　Clay and set it throbbing on the slab,
　　　And when, one day, as all men must, you die,
　　　That day an innocent shall be killed.

BILL JENKS: Unless today's the day, there's bigger fish
　　　To get the griddle under. Bankruptcy
　　　For one.

SIMON: It's coming sooner than you think.

BILL JENKS: What's coming sooner? Bankruptcy? Or death?

SIMON: You get no more prognosticating, Jenks.
    Now, do your worst. I'm all strapped in.
    IN WHOSE NAME DO YOU CAST OUT SPIRITS, HEALER?

BILL JENKS: What do you mean? The usual. J.C.

SIMON: LIAR!

BILL JENKS: I don't name names. I've got the gift.
    I cast out demons in my own damn name.
    —Is that what you wanted to hear? Stand back.
    I've got the gift. It's mine from my conception.
    The powers picked me out, and since the womb
    I stand above humanity and spit.
    I cast out demons in my own damn name.

SIMON: I FLEE!

BILL JENKS: Don't flee! Don't *flee*! Nobody said to flee!
    Come on! Have you got a message for me?
    Prophecy! Gimme a tip on the market!

SIMON: JAN? JAN? DARLIN'?

BILL JENKS: Wait a minute, wait—

SIMON: Where's Jan?

BILL JENKS: Excuse me, I was talking to—

JAN enters; DOC and STACY close behind.

SIMON: Jan? I'm cold. I'm—

JAN: Simon? Simon?

SIMON: I FLEE.

BILL JENKS: NO!

JAN: SIMON!

SIMON: JAN? I LOVE YOU—

BILL JENKS: Simon!
    Come back!

SIMON: Back where?

BILL JENKS: Not yet!

JAN: Oh, Simon!

DOC: *Simon?*

BILL JENKS: I'm talking to the goddamn demon, Jack!
    —Just a general sense of—up or down?
    Buy or sell? Telephones or hot dogs?

SIMON: Jan, I'm tired. I'm thirsty. I love you, Jan.

JAN: I'm here. Simon?

SIMON: Jan. I'm cold. I'm *cold*.

BILL JENKS: I got a conversation going here!

STACY: Doctor? Is it Simon?

DOC: Yes, it's Simon.

BILL JENKS: Just—back *off*—

DOC: It always has *been* Simon—
    But this is Simon after a miracle.

STACY: But cool, but neat, but so *je ne sais quoi*!

SIMON: Stacy? Jan—? Jan—

JAN: Simon… Simon…

BILL JENKS: Everybody: Take a minute here—

JAN: Simon, have you been *cold… all* this time?

BILL JENKS: DEMON, DEMON, GIMME SOMETHING HOT!

BLACKOUT

DAPHNE BEAL is working on her first novel, set in Kathmandu and Bombay. Her work most recently appeared in *The London Review of Books* and *Vogue*.

TOM BISSELL is the author of *Chasing the Sea*, a book about his journey to the Aral Sea in Uzbekistan, the largest ecological disaster in the world. His collection, *Death Defier and Other Stories from Central Asia,* will be published next year. Born and raised in the Upper Peninsula of Michigan, he now lives in New York City.

T. CORAGHESSAN BOYLE, whose name has recently been edited down to T.C. Boyle, with only the "Boyle" awaiting the fatal stroke of an editor's blue pencil, has published many stories and many books and won many prizes and consumed many things. His latest book of stories is *After the Plague* and his new novel is *Drop City*. His new-new novel, now a-writing, is *The Inner Circle*.

DOUG DORST lives in San Francisco, where he is finishing a novel, *Alive in Necropolis*, and a collection of stories, *The Surf Guru*, both of which will be published by Nan A. Talese/Doubleday. His story "A Long Bloodless Cut" appeared in *McSweeney's* No. 9.

STEPHEN ELLIOTT's most recent novel is *What It Means To Love You*. His first novel, *A Life Without Consequences*, was based on his experiences in group homes as a ward of the court in Chicago. He lives in San Francisco, where he writes a weekly poker report for mcsweeneys.net. His next novel, *Other Desires*, will be be co-published by MacAdam-Cage and McSweeney's Books.

BRENT HOFF has proposed several new reality television shows. He is considered by most to be a lucky man.

SAMANTHA HUNT is currently writing a novel about experiments with electricity, and is trying to stage *The Difference Engine*, her play based on the life of inventor Charles Babbage.

DENIS JOHNSON is the Playwright-in-Residence at Campo Santo/Intersection for the Arts in San Francisco. He is the author of seven books of fiction (including *Angels* and *Jesus' Son*), five books of poetry (including the anthology *The Throne of the Third Heaven of the Millenium General Assembly*), and *Seek: Reports from the Edges of America and Beyond*, a collection of his journalism.

BENJAMIN LYTAL is a young Oklahoman who works in New York. This is his first published fiction.

IAN MCDONNELL, an English-born art director, currently resides in Australia. He has photographed hundreds of aerials.

DAVID MEANS's last collection of stories, *Assorted Fire Events*, was a finalist for the National Book Critics Circle Award, and won the Los Angeles Times Book Prize. His new collection, *The Secret Goldfish*, is due next year from Fourth Estate/Harper Collins. He lives in Nyack, New York.

JOYCE CAROL OATES's books include *Blonde, Broke Heart Blues, Black Water*, and *Because It is Bitter, and Because It Is My Heart*. She won a National Book Award in 1970 for her novel *them*. Her next novel, *The Tattooed Girl*, will be published in June.

ROBERT OLMSTEAD's novels are *America by Land, A Trail of Heart's Blood Wherever We Go*, and *Soft Water*. He has written a memoir, *Stay Here With Me*, a textbook, *Elements of the Writing Craft*, and a short story collection, *River Dogs*.

A.G. PASQUELLA was born and raised in Dallas, Texas and then escaped to the frozen shores of Lake Ontario. He currently lives in downtown Toronto.

ALISON SMITH's memoir, *Name All the Animals,* will be published in the spring of 2004.

SEAN WARREN was born and raised in Los Angeles, but now writes from Germany. He has written a novel about Tom Powers in love, titled *American Sailor in the Philippines*, and a Young Adult satire about a tyranny built on homework, *Patrick's Paper Airplane*.

LAWRENCE WESCHLER recently became the director of the New York Institute at NYU, where he is trying to start his own magazine. He is the author of, among other books, *Mr. Wilson's Cabinet of Wonders* and, most recently, *Robert Irwin: Getty Garden.*

MENU AND DIRECTIONS FOR USE OF THE

McSWEENEY'S ISSUE NO. 11 DVD

DELETED SCENES

Get it straight:

1. Tom Bissell reads from "God Lives in St. Petersburg"*
2. T.C. Boyle reads from "Blinded by the Light"**
3. Sean Warren reads from "What Keeler Did to His Foot in the Navy"[U.S.S.]
4. Stephen Elliott reads from "I'll Change Completely" ✚
5. Doug Dorst reads from "The Candidate in Bloom" ✚
6. Samantha Hunt reads from "Blue" ✚
7. David Means reads from "Elyria Man" ✚
8. Daphne Beal reads from "The Poor Thing"***
9. Joyce Carol Oates reads from "The Gathering Squall"[†]

STALACTITE (*a*) AND
STALAGMITE (*b*)

✚ Indicates that this scene features optional camera angle(s). Possible results of using this feature: a) you will see an intern eating a burrito while watching the author read; b) you will see an intern eating a sandwich while watching the author read; c) you will see Karl, a porcupine pufferfish; d) you will see photos of bog people.

EXTRA-DELETED SCENES

1. A Night at the Brava Theater with Denis Johnson
2. A Scene from Denis Johnson's *Soul of a Whore*, Act II, as performed by Campo Santo at Intersection for the Arts, San Francisco
3. Dow Mossman Reads from His Work
4. Lit-Cribs: Jonathan Ames
5. A Short Film by Marcel Dzama and Neil Farber of Canada

BEHIND THE SCENES OF THE DELETED SCENES AND EXTRA-DELETED SCENES

1. The Making of McSweeney's Issue No. 11 DVD
2. The Editing of The Making of McSweeney's Issue #11 DVD
3. The Editing of The Making of McSweeney's Issue #11 DVD (with Audio Commentary by John Hodgman and Sarah Vowell)

OUTTAKES FROM THE DELETED SCENES, EXTRA-DELETED SCENES, AND FROM BEHIND THE SCENES OF THE DELETED SCENES AND EXTRA-DELETED SCENES

1. Bloopers!
2. "Amazing Grace" sung by and with accompanying ukulele by Samantha Hunt
3. "Summertime" sung in Nepali by Daphne Beal
4. "Banjo Song" played on a window sill by Tom Bissell

* Subtitles available; drawn from *The History of the Goths and Visigoths*, in German and Portuguese.
** Subtitles available; drawn from *A Biography of Gerald Ford*, in Portuguese.
[U.S.S.] Indicates that the author is in the Navy, and thus the reading is audio-only.
*** Subtitles available; drawn from Spenser's *The Faerie Queene*, in Spanish.
[†] Subtitles available; drawn from the Book of Genesis.

Approx. running time: 121 minutes

WIDESCREEN
VERSION